THE ARC

THE ARC

Tory Henwood Hoen

ST. MARTIN'S PRESS
New York

First published in the United States by St. Martin's Press, an imprint of St. Martin's Publishing Group

www.stmartins.com

Designed by Donna Sinisgalli Noetzel

Library of Congress Cataloging-in-Publication Data

Names: Henwood Hoen, Tory, author.
Title: The arc / Tory Henwood Hoen.
Description: First edition. | New York : St. Martin's Press, 2022.
Identifiers: LCCN 2021043918 | ISBN 9781250276773 (hardcover) | ISBN 9781250276780 (ebook)
Subjects: LCGFT: Romance fiction.
Classification: LCC PS3608.E627 A89 2022 | DDC 813/.6—dc23
LC record available at https://lccn.loc.gov/2021043918

Our books may be purchased in bulk for promotional, educational, or business use. Please contact your local bookseller or the Macmillan Corporate and Premium Sales Department at 1-800-221-7945, extension 5442, or by email at MacmillanSpecialMarkets@macmillan.com.

First Edition: 2022

10   9   8   7   6   5   4   3   2   1

For my family of origin:

Caroline, Robin, Oliver, and Nick

Don't be satisfied with stories,

how things have gone with others.

Unfold your own myth.

—RUMI

THE ARC

URSULA

Chapter 1

June 2, 2018, 11:26 P.M.

As their taxi slipped down Fifth Avenue past Seventy-ninth Street, Ursula realized she was about to throw up. She closed her eyes and inhaled deeply, the inky green blur of Central Park to her right. Its two-and-a-half-mile border had seemed luxuriously long when she'd strolled it earlier that spring, buzzing with caffeine and cautiously hopeful about the start of a new season. Now, its length felt torturous and unending. James's hand moved under her dress to the inside of her thigh, exactly where she had wanted it moments ago when they began kissing. Now, as nausea overtook her, she wished for a collision and a quick, albeit tragic, death. *So young. Just thirty-five. Clever. Successful. Quite attractive, depending on whom you asked. So much to look forward to. Pity that she had left her young cat behind. Who would take care of her? Any volunteers? She's a very sweet cat . . .*

The taxi swerved hard into the right-hand lane, jolting Ursula out of her morbid reverie. She opened her eyes and tried to focus on the confused galaxy of taillights up ahead. She searched for a soothing mantra, but all that came to mind was her middle-school JV soccer cheer—"Be aggressive! B-E aggressive! B-E-A-G-G-R-E-S-S-I . . ."—and that was no help.

The taillights spun into an evil vortex, a mocking Charybdis that portended imminent humiliation. It was happening. She had to warn him.

"I might throw up," she murmured, staring down at her pale, freshly shaven knees. James opened his mouth as if to ask a question but said nothing. He transferred his hand from her thigh to his own as he leaned back, his prior enthusiasm turning to concern.

After a beat, she confirmed—"Yep, this is happening"—as she lurched over her legs and expelled a stream of Sancerre onto the plastic floor mat of the taxi, some of it splattering against the Mansur Gavriel bucket bag she'd bought to celebrate her recent promotion.

"Damn it," she thought, leaning her head back against the seat. It had been a decent first date until then.

Chapter 2

June 3, 4:07 P.M.

"Wait, you threw up on him?" asked Issa, her eyes wide. "In the taxi?"

"Not *on* him," Ursula said. "But next to him, yes." Using her straw, she created a violent whirlpool in her green juice, which had been listed as Self-Compassion Nectar on the menu. She leaned forward to take a sip, but the foamy liquid got lodged halfway up the straw. She leaned back, then tried sucking once more. Unsuccessful again. "I'm glad they don't have plastic straws here because I don't want sea turtles getting them stuck up their noses, but this thing doesn't work."

The straw was made from avocado husks, which she knew because there was a sign on the counter that read, "Finally! Avocado husks are here!" with a colorful arrow pointing to a ceramic mug of beige straws. For some reason, the mug had breasts.

Issa watched as Ursula struggled with the straw for a few more seconds before plucking it out of her nectar and flinging it to the far side of the round, marble-topped table.

"Always so dramatic," observed Issa.

"I'm not dramatic," grunted Ursula, closing her gray-green eyes. "I'm deathly hungover."

"I noticed that," said Issa gently. Ursula looked like a sapped, feral version of her normally vibrant self, and her hair was even wilder than usual. A voluminous cloud of honey-blond waves that fell around her shoulders, it recalled the look of a particular babysitter that Ursula had worshipped as a child, whose hair took up substantial space and whose bangs appeared to defy gravity. Ursula remembered aspiring to that fluffy volume throughout her childhood, but by the time she entered high school in 1997, straightening had become de rigueur, and she woke early every morning to fastidiously iron her hair. It wasn't until college that she began to re-embrace its natural chaos. Now, her hair distinguished her from the many women intent on taming their natural texture. She enjoyed feeling like a wild-maned lion in a sea of slick seals. Issa once told her she looked like a combination of Kim Basinger from *Batman* and a tumbleweed, and Ursula rather liked this comparison.

"What happened?" asked Issa. "No judgment, but why did you vomit on a first date?"

"I don't know," Ursula wailed, rubbing the bridge of her nose, where a spray of freckles had reemerged now that it was June. "I guess I hadn't eaten enough. Yeah, I hadn't eaten anything since noon. And we went to this wine bar in Harlem, where it turned out his friend was the bartender. So the drinks were just flowing, and James weighs like 250 pounds. He has that former-football-player body, you know? Like he used to be really muscular and rocklike, and now he's softer, but he can still absorb an infinite amount of alcohol."

"Whereas you're a wiry little whippet," said Issa.

"I guess I am. Anyway, it was really fun. I have no idea how much I drank. We were just talking and making out, and then we got in a car to head downtown, which was fine for about fifteen minutes. Totally fine. But then an evil demon overtook me."

"The evil demon known as drinking a gallon of wine on an empty stomach," said Issa.

"That's the one."

"How did James respond?"

"He was really nice about it," said Ursula, feeling a simmer of shame.

"That's a good sign."

"I don't know. I just don't think we're going to build an enduring relationship on a foundation of puke," said Ursula, leaning back in her chair and tugging at the velvet scrunchie she wore around her wrist.

"Maybe not," said Issa, recentering the gold pyramid that hung on a long, thin chain around her neck. Whereas Ursula's outer appearance often mirrored her ever-shifting inner state, there was a consistency about Issa's look, no matter how she felt on any given day. Her straight black hair hung symmetrically; and her short, blunt bangs framed her smooth forehead, giving her face an organized look. Upon meeting her, no one was ever surprised to learn that she was an architect. She looked the part: even her ear piercings—four on each side—provided a sense of balance and intention. Though she often wore bronze-colored eyeliner to bring out the golden flecks in her dark-brown irises, today she was makeup-free.

"What happened with the Lebanese guy?" Issa asked.

"I don't know. Maybe mutual ambivalence," said Ursula, taking a sip directly from the glass that left her with a green-foam mustache. "After our fourth date, neither of us followed up. I think he might have moved back to Beirut."

"Hm," said Issa, using a napkin to brush Ursula's upper lip. "And what about that really sweet guy—the veterinarian?"

"Really bad square-toed shoes," said Ursula, shaking her head and placing her hand over her mouth in horror.

"*Oooof.* That's rough." Issa winced. "But you broke up with him over that?"

Ursula shot her a confrontational gaze and held it until Issa relented. "Fine. We can draw the line at square-toed shoes. That's fair."

"He also had that newly divorced energy, you know?" said Ursula. Issa didn't know, because she'd never dated a divorced man.

"It's like, you know, before the start of the Kentucky Derby, when the horses are all hyped up and they're in their little starting pens? And they're so full of fervor and anticipation? It's like that. These men shoot out of their marriages like horses out of the starting gate. The longer the marriage was, the more aggressively they shoot out. And then they career all over the racetrack, trying to assess where they fit in the pack . . ."

"The racetrack of dating?"

"Yes. They career all over the racetrack of dating, and the next few minutes are anyone's guess. Some crash, some burn out, and a few straighten out and then end up doing well. But when you encounter one of these horses right out of the gate, watch out. They're way too excited and completely unpredictable."

"So a newly divorced man has the fervor of a racehorse?"

"Exactly. It can be overwhelming."

"Maybe this veterinarian racehorse was just excited because he liked you," suggested Issa.

"Ew," said Ursula, suddenly disgusted. She didn't want to think about that particular man ever again. "You know, I'm barely attracted to anyone, even if they're great. Almost everything turns me off these days. I'm pretty much only interested in men who are speaking an indecipherable language that I have no chance of understanding—like Icelandic. It's like I don't even want to engage anymore. I just want to project something onto them and then never find out what they're actually like. Ever. Yes, that's it: I want to date an Icelandic man who promises to never speak a word of English. I think that might work."

"Healthy," said Issa. "Wait, what about Virginia's friend? Didn't she set you up with him?"

"Ugh, the worst. He was one of those guys who starts every other sentence with 'Look . . .'" said Ursula, switching to her bro voice. "'Look, you've gotta think about it like this . . .' 'Look, in my industry . . .' 'Look, I'm a dipshit.'"

Issa laughed. Ursula made a convincing tech bro. Or was she a finance bro?

"Did I tell you about Nicole? The shark?" asked Ursula.

Issa shook her head, her glossy hair sweeping her collarbone. She would have remembered Nicole the shark.

"Well, I saw a documentary last week," said Ursula, "about a great white shark named Nicole. She lived in the waters off Cape Town, but every year, she would disappear for nine months. This isn't normal behavior for a female shark, and the scientists who were observing her had no idea where she went, so they eventually put a tracking device on her. It turns out, she went to Australia—to find love. She didn't like the local South African sharks, so every year, she swam the 12,000-mile roundtrip just to mate with a higher-caliber foreign shark. Then she would come home, relax, and do it all again the next year."

"So, we're going to Australia to find you a mate?" asked Issa.

"We probably should. But that sounds exhausting," said Ursula, massaging her own temples in slow circles. "It's okay. I've slipped into a state of ambivalence. Acceptance. Maybe even peace. I don't need a partner. I'm doing fine. I'm good at my job. I have friends—too many friends, actually. I should get rid of some. And Mallory keeps me weirdly busy."

"A cat can only keep you so busy," said Issa.

"She needs more attention than you'd think." Their eyes met and Ursula laughed, burying her forehead into her crossed forearms. After a moment, she sat up and tapped on the surface of the table. "I like this marble. It's very cooling on the face."

The lounge was outfitted with ten such tables, each accented with a brushed-bronze ring around the edge. White Carrara marble and rose gold dominated the palette at The Stake, the nouveau feminist wellness club where she and Issa convened as often as their schedules allowed—usually once or twice a month. Ursula had joined two and a half years ago at the insistence of her then-boyfriend Sean's sister, Hannah, who was an early investor in the enterprise. "It's a space for modern women to cleanse their psyches and manifest their most audacious goals, unfettered by male influence," Hannah had explained. "But it's more than just a community. It's a *movement.*"

Ursula, whose expertise was in brand strategy, had noticed a lot of young companies describing themselves not as brands, but as *movements*. Movements that sold yoga pants. Movements that sold electric toothbrushes. Movements that sold generic Viagra in discreet unmarked packages so they wouldn't embarrass you in front of your doorman or neighbors. Movements that sold $188 serums that would jolt your aging face back to life. Thoughtlessly buying products was out; joining movements was in. But you joined by buying the products.

"Why is it called The Stake?" Ursula had asked Hannah at the time.

"You know, like Joan of Arc. And like so many witch trials throughout history. The stake was the site of punishment for women who asserted themselves, who dared to speak, to lead, to challenge authority," explained Hannah. "This club is reclaiming the symbol of the stake. Today, it's a place where women gather to summon their strength and pool their power."

"Rather than where they go to be publicly burned?" clarified Ursula.

"Exactly," said Hannah, flicking her pointer finger at Ursula to emphasize how correct she was. "Do you want to hear the tagline?"

Ursula waited.

"Aflame with ambition."

"Clever," said Ursula, pretending to sneeze so that her condescension wouldn't hit Hannah directly in the face.

"We also considered *Be well, bitches*," said Hannah. "But *Aflame with ambition* seemed more positive, more productive, less prescriptive. We don't want to tell women how to live. They're free to be well or *not* to be well, you know? It's okay to not be okay."

"Of course," said Ursula. "That was a good decision."

Once The Stake opened its doors in a Manhattan penthouse near Madison Square Park, Hannah had reminded her to join every few days, dropping intel about high-profile women who were signing on as early members: the politically outspoken host of a major network morning show, a celebrity chef who worked exclusively with ten "life-affirming" ingredients, the right-hand aide to the mayor of New York City, a former Olympic figure skater turned climate-change activist. Ursula resisted for weeks and then joined anyway. In the two and a half years since, she had spent more time at The Stake than she had ever anticipated. She was no longer in touch with Hannah or her brother, whom she had dated for three frustrating years. But The Stake had become a hub in her life, and she had even convinced Issa to join.

Despite their participation, however, they both remained conflicted about the authenticity of the club's mission. Some argued that rather than advancing the feminist cause, The Stake bastardized it.

Still, it had its merits: it offered a café and bar, stylish-serene work-spaces, and exercise classes that focused more on awakening the spirit than on toning the muscles (though they did that, too). Then there was the spa, whose director, a former *Vogue* editor turned wellness guru, had patented a series of therapies called Soul Softeners™, which were designed to relieve specific types of psychic pain.

For those who needed an immediate and high-aggression release, there was the Smash Center, a white-walled room full of porcelain dishware. Before entering, you chose from a selection of vintage cricket bats and protective goggles, and once inside, you could de-stroy things until your anger abated. The next door down was the Scream Den, a soundproof padded chamber that was bookable in fifteen-minute intervals. It was in high demand. (The Stake's founders planned to add two more Scream Dens once they secured their next round of funding.)

Gentler therapies included Hush-Brushing, where you sat in a beanbag chair and a therapist brushed your hair while repeating phrases of your choosing, which ranged from soothing ("Shhhhh, ev-erything will be okay") to classic ("This too shall pass") to colloquial catchphrases by popular heroines like Lizzo ("You are 100 percent that bitch"). The main lounge featured a Swaddle Station, where mem-bers could zip themselves into adult-sized cradles, push a button, and then be mechanically rocked (very, very slowly) to a selection of adult lullabies, custom-composed for The Stake by singer Maggie Rogers. Tucked up a staircase was a row of booths called Sobbing Pods, where you could cry in silence or to a soundtrack of '80s love ballads. A box of tissues was mounted in each pod, and an attendant was available for an optional hug on your way out. Finally, the Womb Room was a sensory deprivation tank where you could float in complete darkness in a bath of warm placenta-infused saltwater, eventually losing your sense of where your own body ended and your "mother's" began. Ur-sula had only tried it once and deemed it "terrifyingly therapeutic." Upon exiting the Womb Room, she had wept for two hours on one of The Stake's rose-hued velvet sofas, which was perfectly normal, and even encouraged—the club was explicitly designated as a no-judgment zone where members were encouraged to "feel their feelings." Neon signs with encouraging statements like "We've Got You, Girl" and "Female as Fuck" hung throughout the club.

Massage therapies ranged from typical Swedish and Deep Tissue to the more inventive. For example, if you opted for the "Animal Instinct" massage, you could choose from a selection of five beasts— deer, fox, blue whale, ocelot, or flamingo—and the masseuse would integrate the ethically extracted musk of that animal into the oil for your massage. Ursula had tried out all five musks in the weeks after her breakup with Sean two years ago. She preferred the ocelot.

"Would you like to try a complimentary Bodhisattva Baby?" A Stake staffer appeared at the table between Issa and Ursula, lowering her tray so they could see the sand-colored blobs on offer. "They're vegan, gluten-free, and brimming with high-strength CBD. They're made of a proprietary bean blend."

"Beans are so hot right now," said Issa, citing a rising dietary trend she had noticed.

"What are those ones?" Ursula asked, pointing to four pink blobs on the far side of the tray.

"Oooh, those are Buddha Babies," said the staffer. "They're a little stronger because they're infused with Xanax. Do you have a prescription on file with us?"

"Yes," said Ursula, supplying her name and membership number. The staffer set down the tray, pulled a tablet from her back pocket, and verified Ursula's prescription. Issa gave her friend a surprised look. Reaching for a Buddha Baby, Ursula insisted, "It's worth doing! If you see the in-house doctor, she'll write you a prescription that they link to your account. Then you can get Xanax added to anything on the menu."

"Noted," said Issa, picking up a Bodhisattva Baby. "Cheers." She smushed it against Ursula's blob.

"And stay tuned," said the staffer, picking up the tray. "Later this year, we're hoping to introduce a version that contains psilocybin. Those are called Enlightenment Bombs."

"Jesus," said Ursula, whose last brush with psilocybin had been during a slightly traumatizing mushroom trip in college.

"Now we're talking. Sign me up," said Issa, pointing to herself. "Issa Takahashi."

"Will do. May the femme be with you." The staffer uttered the club's unofficial salutation, deferentially bowing her head over the tray before moving on to the next table.

"I have to go pretty soon," said Issa, looking at the time on her phone. "I have book club this week and I haven't started the book."

"Such a Basic Book Club Bitch," said Ursula, using the clunky moniker she'd invented and was determined to propel into the zeitgeist.

"Says the biggest Basic Book Club Bitch of them all!" Issa fired back. "Aren't you in four book clubs?"

"Three and a half," admitted Ursula.

"That's obscene. Anyway, I also have to finish some renderings for a client review this week." Issa intended to open her own architecture practice someday, but at present, she led the New York office of her uncle's global firm, which was based in Tokyo. His prominence in the industry was both an advantage and a hindrance to her own professional growth, but she knew she would carve out her own distinct niche in due time. It wasn't a question of if, but when. Issa had an innate confidence that Ursula found comforting. They were both only children, but their outlooks differed. Issa, who had grown up in a Tribeca loft back when the neighborhood was full of actual artists, was grounded by a sense that things would work out as they were meant to. Ursula was perpetually convinced that disaster was imminent.

"Do you want to spend a few minutes in Purple Rain before we go?" Issa asked, referring to The Stake's steam room, where bursts of lavender-scented mist alternated with warm downpours from the ceiling, set to a soundtrack of Prince's greatest hits. Down the hall, a trio of moist-skinned, towel-clad women had just exited.

Issa and Ursula stood up, tightening the sashes of their white waffle-textured robes and sliding their feet into their slippers, whose toes were embroidered with flames. In the hall, they paused to look at a board advertising upcoming club events:

- CPR for the Soul: Resuscitating the Heart Chakra
- Friend or Foe: The Hidden Perils of Cinnamon
- Navigating the Labyrinth of Female Friendship

"I hate the term 'female friendship,'" said Ursula.

"Me too!" said Issa. "But why? I like friendship. I like females."

"I think I hate when 'female' is used as a qualifier. And I hate the idea that there's some fixed notion of female friendship that we all agree on," said Ursula.

"Right, like you get together at your feminist wellness club and drink green juice and complain about dating." Issa smiled.

"Right. Who does that?"

"No one I know," said Issa.

As they stepped into Purple Rain, they could see it was empty, except for a lone, hazy figure in one corner. They shuffled to the far side to sit, shrugging their robes off their shoulders. Steam hissed from under the white-marble benches, thickening the air with heavy lavender vapor.

"So are you really going to take a break from dating?" Issa asked, closing her eyes and leaning her head back against the wall of white subway tiles.

"I think I'm done," said Ursula. "Permanently done. Romantically retired. I made the effort. I've had four long-term boyfriends—no, five." She paused to think. "Well, four and a half. And I did what everyone said: I tried the dating-app thing for six months. I corrected my resting bitch face. I learned how to hold eye contact. I got into bourbon. I'm tired, Issa. I'm so tired."

"I don't blame you," said Issa, who was able to convey empathy without the hint of pity Ursula sensed in the voices of other happily coupled friends. Issa had been with Eric for ten years. They had all met in college in rural Massachusetts. Ursula and Eric lived on the same hallway freshman year, and although Eric was not an artist,

Ursula had invited him to a figure-drawing class one night, just for fun. The nude model—who turned out to be particularly confident fellow freshman Issa—entered the room, slipped out of her robe, and then dramatically threw it to the floor. She lay down on a platform in the middle of the room, the clean, sculptural lines of her body lending themselves perfectly to the exercise. Afterward, the three of them drank cheap canned beer on the lawn outside the art center. They had been hanging out ever since.

Though Eric had undoubtedly taken note of Issa's beauty during that first encounter, their romance didn't ignite until after college, once they had both had sufficiently tumultuous relationships with other people and then felt ready to commit to someone trustworthy and comfortable. When they reached that point, it was on: first date at twenty-five; living together at twenty-seven; engaged at twenty-eight; married at thirty. And though the relationship timeline suggested an adherence to convention, there was nothing conventional about Issa herself. One look at her fashion choices and notably short bangs, not to mention her hyperbrutalist architectural designs, indicated that she made her own rules. She'd been wearing diaphanous Eileen Fisher tunics since before they became subversively cool— usually paired with Givenchy sandals or Balenciaga boots and the odd Issey Miyake piece. She was one of those magicians who had managed to fully retain her own identity within a romantic relationship—a feat Ursula sometimes envied. And Issa had pulled off what appeared to be, so far, an exceptional marriage; but she never judged Ursula for not accomplishing the same.

"Can I just be *your* girlfriend?" said Ursula, leaning her head against Issa's damp shoulder.

"Obviously," said Issa. "You've always been my girlfriend."

Ursula smiled, and then lifted her head.

"I just don't think you should take yourself out of the dating pool," said Issa. "That would be a crime against humanity."

"Fine," conceded Ursula. "But just because I *want* a stable commitment doesn't mean I'm entitled to one. I'm good at certain things, but maybe sustaining a romantic relationship just isn't in my skill set."

"I don't know. Sometimes I think the people who flaunt their healthy relationships are actually the worst at them. Remember Lisa Hutchens?" Issa looked around to make sure Lisa, who was a member of The Stake, wasn't lurking somewhere in the steam. Lowering her voice, she went on, "She dated, like, twenty guys in our first few years in New York after college, and there was so much drama. Then she finally had one seminormal relationship, and now she's a dating coach."

"I believe she's actually a 'whole heart coach' according to her Instagram," said Ursula, matching Issa's hushed tone.

"Exactly!" exclaimed Issa. "She married some private equity guy, and now she's telling everyone else what to do with their hearts."

"Their *whole* hearts," clarified Ursula.

"Yes, their whole hearts. So you don't need to solicit Lisa's whole-heart services, but I don't think you should quit. Maybe you could just be more open-minded about who you date?"

"*Whom* I date," said Ursula.

"Shut up," said Issa, who knew that Ursula was nitpicking about grammar as a way to avoid the topic at hand. "Don't change the subject."

"Lately, the guys I meet in real life end up being even weirder than the ones I meet on the apps. Because sometimes you don't even have baseline information about them," said Ursula. "But the apps are terrifying too. They're fun for a few months, and then they start to make you feel like you're in a weird video game with real-life consequences. Like, choose wrong and you could get an STD! Choose *really* wrong and you could get murdered!"

"Is it really that extreme?" asked Issa skeptically. She had never used a dating app.

"Yes. No. Sometimes. Not really," said Ursula. "But it's absurd how little information you have to go on before you decide whether to meet someone. A few photos, maybe some witticisms they've put in their profile, possibly some banter over text. It's just so hard to screen for sensibility. Honestly, it's hard to screen for *teeth*. Did I tell you I got coffee with a guy who only had four visible teeth?"

"What? Where were the rest of them?"

"I don't know!"

"Why did you meet him?!"

"He only had one photo, and his mouth was closed!" said Ursula. "This is what I'm trying to tell you. If I can't even find a guy with teeth, how am I going to find someone who is smart and handsome and doesn't hate cats—maybe even values cats for the magical creatures they are—and appreciates my neuroses and isn't a chauvinist and can cook and recycles and knows that bowling is overrated and loves Chris Rock and Tilda Swinton, and . . ."

"Whoa, whoa, whoa." Issa held up her hands. They disappeared into the steam in front of her. "You have to open up your mind. You're being too specific."

"Am I?" said Ursula. "Or is love actually about specificity? You know those coffee mugs that say, 'The key to a good relationship is hating the same things'? Maybe that's exactly what it is, but it's also liking the same things and being ambivalent about the same things. And also hating something for a while but then coming around to liking it, together at the same time. Like, you don't care about gardening at all, but then you evolve into it together, so the other person never feels abandoned. One day you just wake up and say, 'Is it time for us to finally buy some mulch?' and your husband nods, as if the exact same urge had been simultaneously building in him."

"That's a tall order," said Issa.

"I want my life partner to be a tall order," said Ursula. "I don't want him to be one of a thousand interchangeable guys who are 'nice.' I want him to accept how annoying I am, and not just accept it, but enjoy it. And I want him to know, deep in his heart, that bowling is fucking boring and overrated. Because it is."

"I will never understand your beef with bowling." Issa shook her head. "Can I ask you a question? This is a serious question, so take it seriously. Do you think you might have some reluctance around commitment?"

"Like I'm deluding myself about wanting a partner, when I'm actually just deeply commitment-phobic?" asked Ursula. "No, it's worse than that. I've had multiple long-term relationships, so this isn't your run-of-the-mill commitment problem. In fact, I'm *completely* capable of committing—but only to noncommittal men. The emotionally available ones just don't do it for me. They have to be emotionally avoidant and fully resistant to personal growth, and then I'm totally on board."

"Sick puppy." Issa smiled. "But you're more self-aware than you used to be. I'll give you that."

"I think the real issue," said Ursula, "is that I'm weird—very, very weird. Not in a cute, quirky, rom-com way, but in a slightly disturbing way. Not like, 'She crinkles her nose when she laughs! Wacky!' But like, 'She walks down the street with her cat in one of those bubble backpacks,' or 'She uses a vibrator as a face massager.'"

"I'm sorry, what?" Issa turned to Ursula.

"Yeah, I got one of those backpacks where the cat can see out of a clear bubble, like a spaceship. I haven't used it yet, but . . ."

"No, the other thing. The vibrator on your face."

"Oh, well you know how everyone is into facial massage lately? To promote circulation, stimulate your muscles, drain your lymphatic system . . ." said Ursula.

Issa nodded.

"Well, I saw this thing that was being sold for $199 as a facial massage tool, and it looked exactly like a vibrator," said Ursula. "So I just got a mini vibrator for $11 and I use that instead."

"Your face does look really good," said Issa. Then, cautiously, "Is that *all* you use it for?"

"Yesssss," said Ursula, rolling her eyes. "This one is explicitly for facial use."

"Hm." Issa cocked her head to the side, wondering if she should get a vibrator for her own face.

"The point is," said Ursula. "I'm not normal, and my weirdness has never properly aligned with someone else's weirdness, and I don't know if it ever will. I just can't imagine it. But I refuse to rein myself in anymore. I'm going to put my cat in the backpack, and that's that."

The lavender steam hissed and then abruptly shut off. A brief silence followed as "Darling Nikki" ended and "When Doves Cry" began. Out of the mist, a woman appeared in front of them. She had short, bleach-blond hair that was slicked back, giving her an aerodynamic look. "I don't mean to eavesdrop," she said in an Australian accent. "But I was sitting over there and I heard you talking. I think you might be interested in this." She pulled a business card out of the pocket of her robe and handed it to Ursula.

In gilded, embossed serif font it read: "Be more particular." Ursula flipped it over. On the back were just two words—The Arc—with a URL listed underneath.

She looked up. "What is this?" she asked.

"It's hard to explain," said the woman. "It's probably better if you just check out the website."

"Okay, thanks," said Ursula, looking at the card, which had an authoritative weight to it.

"Enjoy your steam," the woman said as she headed for the door and left the room.

"That was weird," said Ursula.

"Yeah, who brings business cards into a steam room?" asked Issa.

"The Arc," Ursula said aloud, wondering what it could be.

Suddenly, the ceiling emitted a downpour of lavender rain. Ursula closed her eyes and leaned back, letting the heavy drops hit her face. *Blap, blap, blap.* On her eyelids. Above her lip. *Blap, blap, blap.* From the waterproof speakers, Prince moaned:

> *The sweat of your body covers me.*
> *Can you, my darling? Can you picture this?*

Chapter 3

June 7, 7:42 P.M.

Ursula unlocked the front door of her Brooklyn apartment and anticipated Mallory's ritual greeting: a soft, grateful squawk that Ursula interpreted as "I missed you so much," but which actually meant "Feed me now."

"Yes, my little Bundt cake," she said as Mallory smashed her forehead into Ursula's shins. She kneeled down and took her cat's small gray face into her hands. "You know I always come home."

She threw her keys on the table by the door, missing the ceramic dish she'd bought explicitly to keep things from getting lost, and traversed the living room to the wooden cupboard where Mallory's food lived. Ursula could hear the cat's paw-thumps behind her as her squawks increased in intensity, volume, and cadence. She pulled out the bag of dry pellets and poured them into a plastic food puzzle—an orb that released one pellet at a time when knocked around the floor. Her vet had insisted on feeding Mallory this way to prevent weight gain. "Make her work for her food, just like she would have to in the wild."

Ursula's apartment, on the ground floor of a brownstone in Carroll Gardens, was not exactly wild, but it did have a garden and a fireplace, which was rare at her price point. She had moved in after Superstorm Sandy ravaged low-lying parts of the neighborhood, getting an almost unheard-of deal on rent.

Mallory attacked her food puzzle with a joyous pounce, chasing it around the floor as if it were a desperate, doomed chipmunk.

Ursula opened the fridge and pulled out a half-full bottle of pinot noir, which she preferred to drink cold in the summer, although the solstice was still fourteen days away. She poured a generous glass—a "country club pour," as Issa would say—and then regarded the bottle, wondering if there was such thing as the human equivalent of a food puzzle. A wine puzzle? Like one of those silly straws she'd used as a child, with twists and loop-de-loops that forced you to suck with all your might to extract the liquid. Make you work for your pinot noir.

Mallory maneuvered into the corner of the living room, where she jammed her paw at the puzzle in pursuit of the final pellet. Ursula had adopted the steel-colored cat two years ago as her relationship with Sean crumbled. They had been wildly in love for a while—that's how she remembered it, at least—but when she brought up the question of marriage two years in, the relationship began its swift descent. Emergency landing. Brace for impact.

She had tried to backpedal. Forget marriage. What about just moving in together? Staying in their own apartments but sharing a dog? How about a long vacation to clear the air? Sean wouldn't commit to anything more than a week in advance, ever.

One day, she stumbled upon an animal adoption event in the park a few blocks from her apartment. The delicate cat with wide, moss-green eyes caught her attention immediately. A middle-aged woman wearing a fluorescent-yellow volunteer vest came up beside her and looked at the cat, whose cage was labeled:

> Mallory, ~1 year. Russian blue. This dainty cuddle bug is a deep, empathetic soul who gets along with cats, dogs, children, everyone! Loves a little catnip on a Saturday night, and will be your best friend in no time. Spayed, fully vaccinated, dewormed.

"*Such* a beauty," the volunteer said. "She is—I kid you not—the sweetest cat I've ever met, and I've met a lot of cats. A *lot*."

Ursula had no doubt.

"She was living behind a dumpster on Staten Island," the woman continued. "She had a litter, although she's no more than a baby herself. Maybe one year old, I'd guess. An absolute doll. Her kittens got snapped up last week, but she's still here."

Ursula held her hand up to the bars of Mallory's cage, and the cat tentatively sniffed her fingers. She looked into Ursula's eyes as if evaluating her, and Ursula found herself gently hoping that the cat would approve. Just then, a man approached with his toddler daughter, who was pulling his hand so forcefully that her body formed a 45-degree angle to the ground.

"A kitty cat!" She pointed to Mallory.

"Yes, a kitty cat!" said the dad. The toddler stopped short of the cage, where Mallory had scurried toward the back and scrunched herself down into a headless mound of fur. She sat completely still, her body a perfect bell curve.

"I want her!" squeaked the toddler.

Ursula suddenly felt possessive of the cat. She held her breath as the man explained that this wasn't the right time to get a pet, because Baby Brother would be here soon. The toddler eventually conceded, and they wandered off toward the puppies.

Ursula stared into the cage, and Mallory lifted her head and met her eyes again.

"I'll take her," Ursula said to the volunteer. She'd left her apartment that morning in search of coffee; she returned with Mallory in a borrowed plastic carrier. Once home, she set the carrier on the floor and opened its wire door. Mallory waited a full minute before cautiously stepping out, looking around, and then bolting under the couch. Ursula got down on her stomach and could just make out the dark outline of Mallory's domed back. "It's okay," she said. "You're very safe here." After she'd put out food and water, she called Sean, chirping with excitement about her new acquisition.

"You impulse-bought a cat?" he asked.

"No, I impulse-*adopted* a cat," explained Ursula.

He seemed miffed that she'd made the decision without him. "Well, would you have supported it?" she asked.

"Now we'll never know," he said.

"I guess we won't. By the way, are you coming to Roger's barbecue with me tomorrow?"

"Maybe so, maybe no," Sean said.

Ursula knew that meant "probably" in Sean's personal patois, which was a labyrinth of equivocation and quivering half commitments.

Within three months of Mallory's arrival, Ursula and Sean broke up. The cat never took to him, perhaps because he whistled at her as if she were a dog. His whistle repelled her, yet he persisted.

Her pinot now poured and in hand, Ursula began leafing through her mail, separating it into three piles: Read Right Now, Deal With Later, Toss Immediately. Tonight's Read Right Now pile consisted of the *New Yorker* and an L.L.Bean catalog. She wavered between the two, but then shifted the *New Yorker* into the Deal With Later pile, next to which sat the business card from the woman in the steam room. "Be more particular," it reminded her.

She and Issa had taken guesses about what The Arc might be: An escort service? A cult? A Greco-Roman wrestling society? A fetish-matching startup? A portal into an alternate world where men's fertility expired earlier than women's?

She picked up the card and set it down, along with her wine, on her mid-century coffee table, then flopped onto the couch and began leafing through L.L. Bean. Ursula had lost her taste for women's fashion magazines long ago—too formulaic, too spineless—but she loved perusing catalogs, because she could insert whatever narratives she pleased. Red wine and L.L. Bean was her idea of a nice little Thursday night. She flipped the pages, letting the flannels and fleeces soothe her like a salve. A multiethnic couple in shawl-collared sweaters laughed on the steps of a farmhouse, their heads thrown back, faces tilted toward the sky. A group of glossy-haired, vest-clad young women carried logs, their eyes alight with optimism. An older couple in rubber-soled duck boots navigated a leaf-strewn dirt path, their shepherd mix trailing them with a dog-grin that said, "Now *this* is living." A lumberjacky man carried a tray of grilled corn on the cob, presenting it with chivalrous panache to someone who waited just out of the frame, someone who had obviously tamed his rugged heart. His eyes blazed as if his entire future rested on how this corn was received. Maybe he was offering it to Helen of Troy herself, thought Ursula. The face that launched a thousand corncobs. Perhaps he even had an engagement ring squirreled away in one of his black-and-red-checked pockets, which he planned to unveil once Helen had raked her teeth across two (Or three! They were so good!) perfectly charred and buttered cobs.

Ursula wondered if a flannel-clad man would ever hold out a corncob to her as if she were the only woman that mattered—perhaps had ever truly mattered—to him. She dared not let herself hope for such things.

She took an emboldening sip of wine, pulled her laptop onto her knees, and typed The Arc's URL into her browser.

A black screen appeared, and then the words:

> **Lasting love is in the details.**
> **It's time to be more particular.**
> *Enter your email to learn more.*

The text faded to black and an entry field popped up. Ursula stared at it. "Seems like a scam," she thought. "I'm probably going to be abducted."

But her curiosity trumped her incredulity. She typed in her email address and hit "Submit."

She resumed leafing through the catalog, feeling nostalgic. Not for her own childhood, but for the L.L.Bean childhood that she never had: canvas tote bags artfully strewn about the mudroom, a golden retriever curled up on the couch, families laughing in matching pajamas. Since when had matching pajamas become such a thing?

Her work inbox chirped with a new message: *Urgent—Brand Meeting Tomorrow Morning.*

One of her clients was summoning the "dream team" for an 8:30 A.M. check-in. Ursula growled, startling the cat, who had been lying on her back on the floor like a starfish. Mallory curled upward into a precarious crunch position, held it for four seconds, then slowly relaxed back onto the ground, legs and tail splayed.

"Eight thirty in the morning?" thought Ursula. "That's psychotic."

She replied: *Perfect. See you then!*

Chapter 4

June 8, 8:23 A.M.

"Ursula!" her client Brad yelped too excitedly, rising from his chair as she pushed open the heavy door of the glass-walled conference room. Embossed on the door was the word "Indubitably," underlined by an illustrated roll of toilet paper that was unfurling from the tail of the final "y." The same logo was embroidered on Brad's navy fleece vest, which he wore year-round. He held one hand toward Ursula and one toward the man who sat at the far end of the white table. "This is Mike Rutherford. *The* Mike Rutherford."

Ursula had heard plenty about *The* Mike Rutherford. *The* Mike Rutherford was a billionaire. *The* Mike Rutherford was friendly with multiple former presidents and a few music moguls. *The* Mike Rutherford had garnered attention for purchasing the most expensive apartment in Manhattan real estate history. (The Italian marble bathtub alone cost $1 million.) *The* Mike Rutherford was here this morning because he was the lead investor in Brad's company. Ursula knew that he had also once expressed interest in her friend Stephanie's startup, although the deal fell through when *The* Mike Rutherford's associate tried to seduce Stephanie's assistant by saying, "Hey, you're cute. We should fuck once this whole #MeToo thing blows over." Although this kind of interaction roiled Ursula, it never shocked her. Over the years, she had come to see the New York business world as a grimy spiral of money, ego, and strings-attached sex. Ursula always conducted herself judiciously, but the more she witnessed, the more she felt tainted with a feeling of filth by association. She and her female colleagues often mused about what it would be like "when women were controlling the majority of wealth"—as if that day were inevitable, albeit a long way off. For now, she played the game as well as she could.

"Such a pleasure to finally meet you." Ursula set her latte down on the table and held out her red-manicured hand.

At fifty-seven, Mike was solid and somewhat handsome in an overgroomed, overconsidered kind of way, although she suspected he had an incredibly hairy chest. He had a robust upper body, and she assumed he probably partook in some martial art, as was the trend these days among New York City males intent on self-cultivation. His salt-and-pepper hair had a silver streak in the front, where it swooped across his forehead, and he wore a leather bomber jacket that made him look like Tom Cruise in *Top Gun*. Ursula could tell this was not his normal garb, but rather what he donned when he wanted to impress young startup types. It looked expensive and brand-new—the leather showed no sign of wear.

Mike gave her hand a confident, and borderline painful, shake.

"Whoa," said Ursula, smiling and shaking out her wrist, pretending to be impressed by his uncontrolled power.

"Sorry about that. Just came from jiu-jitsu," said Mike. Then clarified: "Brazilian jiu-jitsu."

"Niiiice." Brad nodded his head, then remembered he had only made half of the introduction. "Mike, this is Ursula Byrne, our secret weapon. She's associate of strategic awesomeness at our branding agency, Anonymous & Co."

"Close," said Ursula, before correcting him. "VP of strategic audacity." She paused briefly to let the self-loathing pass. She often hated her job and herself for having chosen this career, but unfortunately, she was good at it. She was *very* good at it, or so people told her. But her competence didn't make her more confident—she was perpetually convinced that her latest good idea would be her last, and that she would soon be exposed as a fraud. Regardless, she stayed the course, because what else was she going to do? "I don't love the title, but it came with the promotion."

Brad and Mike laughed in a surprised way, as if they weren't used to appreciating jokes made by women.

"I'm here to push Brad's team toward game-changing ideas that have longevity," said Ursula. "Indubitably might be an early-stage startup today, but we want them to build a brand that will see them through the next five years, ten years, and beyond. I always tell them they need to think big if they're going to *be* big."

"Love it," said Mike, nodding. "Love that ambitious thinking. You seem like you've got a great brain."

Ursula wasn't sure how to respond to that. "It does its best," she offered. "For my team at the agency, it's about tapping into the current zeitgeist to create brands that will resonate both today and tomorrow. We anticipate their evolution, and we build that into our strategy."

"Ursula can see around the corner. She did the brand strategy for Coctus," said Brad, citing the highly profitable sex-toy company that Ursula had helped usher into the market. It sold cactus-shaped vibrators, and the tagline was: *Look forward to your next dry spell.*

"A unicorn-maker," said Mike, looking at Ursula with what might have been genuine respect, but it was hard to tell. Ursula suspected that his affect had been cultivated to convince people of his sincerity even when he was completely insincere.

"I don't build the companies," said Ursula. "I just help finesse the story."

"My dog's name is Finesse!" said Mike, now looking awestruck by the coincidence.

Ursula dropped her jaw in enthusiastic disbelief.

"You know," said Mike, shaking his finger at her to indicate that an idea was percolating in his mind. "I'd love to get on your calendar." Ursula assumed this was a phrase Mike deployed to make people who weren't as important as him feel good. He probably had an emotional intelligence coach who had taught him: *Act as if their schedule is busier than yours to convey humility and approachability.*

"Only if your calendar will allow it," said Ursula, respectfully, seeing through his ruse.

By now, the other members of Brad's team had filled in the seats around the conference table. He tapped his pen, which read "Good

Vibes Only," thrice on his legal pad: *thwap, thwap, thwap.* This meant he was ready to start.

"First of all, thanks for being here on such short notice. Mike's flying out to SF later today, and I really wanted him here for this conversation. As you all know, we're about to start fund-raising." Brad paused dramatically for applause and then pumped his arm. "Cha-ching! But before we go out to new investors, Mike raised a good point that I want us to discuss." Brad took an intentionally dramatic pause, allowing the suspense to build. He clasped his palms in front of his pursed lips, closed his eyes, and took a long, thoughtful inhale through his nose. Then, extending his hands outward toward the room, he said matter-of-factly: "We're a toilet paper subscription service. We're called Indubitably. Why are we called Indubitably? Well, frankly, I saw the word in *GQ* and I liked it. I didn't even know what it meant at the time. I just liked it. But now, we all know what it means: *without a doubt.* We also know that I love brands that end in L-Y. I fucking love an adverb."

There was an enthusiastic "whoop!" from an overcaffeinated team member.

"But Mike, as our lead investor, is here to ask the tough questions," Brad continued. "And his tough question this week was, 'Should this company really be named Indubitably?' So let's dialogue."

Brad, who was twenty-seven, had hatched the idea for Indubitably while in business school at Wharton. He had been working on a completely different idea (a special mechanism that allowed you to karate-kick your front door open rather than simply turning the knob when you came home), when it occurred to him that there was an even greater white space in the market. "I'm our customer," he loved to claim, as if this should both impress and reassure the listener. "I'm that guy who never has toilet paper!"

Ursula had urged him to refine this element of his founder story, but he insisted on keeping it authentic and personal. "I know what you're thinking. How hard can it be to buy toilet paper, right?" This is when he typically paused for acknowledgement. "Harder than you'd think. And it's not just me. I talked to tons of guys. *Dozens* of guys.

Every single one agreed that toilet paper acquisition continues to be one of the major pain points in so many men's lives—and I want to provide the solution." Brad was one of a rising class of young male entrepreneurs who, upon leaving school and the protective bubble of their childhood homes, realized they actually needed to do things like dishes, laundry, and basic household management. But instead of just learning how to do these chores, they founded startups so that "no one would have to feel as overwhelmed as I did when I . . ." In Brad's case, figuring out how to keep his apartment stocked with toilet paper had been so traumatizing that he was now dedicating his career to sparing others the same pain. He saw himself as not just an innovator, but a savior.

"I have some thoughts," ventured Ursula. "While *indubitably* is a really exciting word"—she nodded encouragingly at Brad, who had championed this name from the beginning and who paid her agency an $18,000-a-month retainer—"it's also challenging. It's hard to say; most people don't know what it means; it's not SEO-friendly; and it's not actually relevant to or descriptive of your service."

"Well, I wouldn't go that far," said Brad, glancing briefly at Mike, who was leaning back in his chair, his fingers laced behind his head and his elbows jutting out to the side. Casual. Ursula had once taken a body-language course in which she learned that this posture, known as "the Cobra," was a silent signal of authority, superiority, dominance. Brad cleared his throat and continued: "It's relevant because we make sure our clients always have toilet paper—without a doubt. Like you might not have clean laundry, or food in your fridge, or soap, or even electricity, but you will always, *always* have toilet paper. That's our guarantee—indubitably."

A silence settled. Brad took an aggressive gulp from his gallon-sized water bottle, which had line delineations with motivational messages on one side. Near the top, it read: **HYDRATE LIKE YOU MEAN IT.** The halfway mark assured: **YOU GOT THIS.** Then came **DIG DEEP.** And right before the finish line: **H_2O NO YOU DIDN'T!**

He set the water bottle down with a clunk, then asked: "What if we spelled it differently?"

"I-N-D-U-B-I-T-A-B-L-E-E?" offered Simon, the company's social media lead. "Or we could just do one 'E' with an accent."

"Indubitablé?" Brad tried it out. "Indubitablé! In-doo-bit-uh-blay! Indu . . ."

"I think we run into a lot of the same obstacles," pressed Ursula. "Plus some new ones."

It had taken Ursula a good thirteen years to develop the diplomacy and sangfroid she was now able to deploy in professional settings. She thought of her career less as a "path" or a "journey," and more as a "war" that might never cease—an endless series of battles fought, tactics employed, defeats weathered, victories relished, and lessons learned. She was the general of a one-woman army, and survival was its own reward. She had begun the war at twenty-two, two months after graduation, when she landed a job as a junior copywriter at a small marketing agency, where she worked for a ruthless creative director whom she nicknamed "The Despot." The Despot alternated between calling her a genius and telling her she "could easily be replaced"—it depended on the day, his mood, and the relative intensity of what he referred to as the "immense pressure he was under." Despite his volatility, Ursula stuck it out for two and a half years. Some of the work was unbearably bland, such as writing instruction manuals for high-end German vacuum cleaners. But she had one client, a luxury paint company, for which she named colors. This was her first glimpse of the undeniable joy of being paid to do creative work. Initially, she played it safe with her ideas, offering up dreamy-sounding shades like Citrus, Morning Mist, Mahogany, and Amalfi Blue. But by the time she had named at least fifty shades of muddy beige, she began to take artistic liberties: Ambivalent Mushroom, Sinister Sunbeam, Obscene Rose, and Upwardly Mobile Mauve. Her favorite had been Dream Deferred, which she named in homage to her favorite Langston Hughes poem, but The Despot didn't get it and argued that it didn't sound aspirational enough. "That's because it's about the denial of opportunity, the wilting of aspiration," rebutted Ursula. The Despot had dismissed her explanation: "Too

cerebral. This isn't your senior thesis, Ursula. It's a frickin' paint color."
He'd insisted they call it Regal Raisin instead. Soon after, Ursula began
sending her resume out in search of a work environment where she
could unleash her intellect among like-minded collaborators.

Since then, she had successfully hopped from agency to agency,
working her way from copywriter to copy chief to creative director.
Her new role as VP of strategic audacity placed her firmly on an
executive track—she was primed to be a chief creative officer at any
number of brands or agencies if she played her cards right. Though
she had achieved what most would consider unequivocal success, she
still had not found that elusive cadre of kindred spirits: creatives who
were both left-and right-brained, whose imaginations whirred wildly
but whose sensibilities were grounded in real life. The more she ad-
vanced, the more she wondered if she was the only one who straddled
that divide. For her, increased success went hand in hand with an
increased sense of isolation. Would she ever find her people?

"All in favor of sticking with Indubitably?" Brad loved to facilitate an
atmosphere of faux democracy in the conference room. He raised his
hand with conviction and looked around the room until a few more
hands went up. More than 50 percent of the hands remained down,
and not just down, but under the table.

"Gotta go with my gut on this one," Brad said. "Gotta go with
that founder's instinct. I've wanted to run my own company for as
long as I can remember. Well, at least since I went to business school.
Did I know it would be a toilet paper company? No. But I knew it
would be a game-changer. *Indubitably is that game-changer.* And I
think it's clear: We've already got our name. We've had it all along.
Really appreciate your time though. Thanks for always pushing us to
be better, Mike." He squeezed Mike's shoulder. "Ursula, we couldn't
do it without you." He raised his arm to pat her shoulder, but then
retracted it. He was terrified of touching a woman inappropriately in
the workplace, so he refrained from touching them at all. Normally
it wasn't an issue, since his eleven employees were all men.

Chapter 5

When Ursula got home that night, she vowed to have a tech-free evening. She had read that was supposed to be a key component of mental health—reducing screen time, avoiding blue light, reconnecting with simple analog pleasures. Even as she was making the vow, she knew she wouldn't follow through on it, but making it and knowing she would fail was better than not making it at all. She filled Mallory's food puzzle, ate some leftover pasta, and felt bored already. She went into her bathroom and poked around the shelves. She still had a snake venom rejuvenating mask that she'd picked up during a trip to Japan with Issa two years before. The packaging had a photograph of a cobra on it and the text was entirely in Japanese, with no sign of an expiration date. She decided to go for it. Unlike the goopy mud masks of her youth, squeezed from plastic bottles purchased at CVS, the new trend in masks involved a face-shaped bamboo cloth, saturated with gelatinous potions and enclosed in a plastic sheath. She peeled open the top and scooped out the slimy object within, using her fingers like lobster pincers to unfold it. She placed it over her face, aligning the eye and mouth holes as best she could, patting the edges so that the mask submitted to the contours of her skull. She looked in the mirror and shuddered at the haunting face looking back, grabbed her phone from her pocket, took a selfie, remembered she was supposed to be forgoing technology, deleted the selfie, and then wandered into the living room.

Mallory looked up at her with wide eyes and skittered into the bedroom.

Ursula settled onto the couch and pulled a wool blanket around her, its broad red-and-black stripes engulfing her. It was perfectly warm in her apartment, but she liked to self-cocoon after a long week at work. She glanced around her living room, wondering if it was time to redecorate. Built-in bookshelves took up one corner, so those were there to stay. But the rest of her décor was fungible, just as she liked it. Most of the works of art had been made by friends or collected on various travels. She still had the line drawing she'd done of Issa the night they'd met in college. On the wall next to it, Issa had traced Ursula's silhouette in red chalk during a drunken dinner party a few years ago, and Ursula had never bothered to wash it off. There was also an antique set of fire tools she'd lugged home from a flea market in Paris. The space near her street-facing windows had become a jungle of various potted palms and large-leafed ferns, a few of which had bite marks on them. (Mallory had a taste for plants.) And then there was the bronze sculpture—the only piece by her father that she owned. It stood five feet tall and resembled a slender human form that was in the process of melting, its tortured face twisted in distress. The sculpture had always frightened her, but she was deeply attached to it. Or at least, she felt she *should* be attached to it. And according to her mother, it was worth about $20,000, though she had never had it appraised.

Ursula's eclectic taste was her own, but she had inherited her creative instincts and existential struggles from her parents. Both artists, they had provided a confusing blueprint for how to cobble together a livelihood. They had met in 1982 at an artist's residency outside Millbrook, New York. Ursula's mother, Orla Byrne, was a freckled, copper-haired beauty who used her own body as a paintbrush, covering herself in acrylics and then flailing across large canvas surfaces. Ursula's father, Jürgen Kraus, was a somewhat well-known German sculptor who, after debuting to some acclaim in his twenties, later eschewed the notion of art as commerce. Rather than sell his work, he abandoned most of it in open fields or by lonely highways so the sculptures could "chart their own course." Jürgen had arrived at the residency to give a three-day master class. By the second night,

he and Orla, who was just thirty-two to his sixty-nine, were sharing a cabin. Two weeks later, they began cohabitating in a rented
ramshackle farmhouse in the hamlet of Ancramdale, fifty-four miles
south of Albany. And two months after that, Orla missed her period.
Jürgen immediately grew distant, although he bought the farmhouse
for Orla to live in—going so far as to put it in her name, a gesture
meant to counteract his general disinterest in having a child. He came
and went throughout the pregnancy, but in the end, Orla gave birth
on her own to a daughter who bore her last name: Byrne. Jürgen
didn't meet Ursula until she was four months old. He deemed her
a charming child, and for the next three years, he made occasional
visits, during which he worked on a series of sculptures that he never
quite finished. He spent the rest of his time between his other abodes
in Berlin and Tangier. A few weeks after Ursula's third birthday, Orla
received a call from Jürgen's manager, whom she had only met once.
Jürgen had died of a heart attack in Milan's central train station.
While the location was somewhat baffling (it remained a mystery
why he'd been passing through Italy on that particular day), the cause
of death was not—he had smoked incessantly for nearly six decades.

Orla wasn't particularly devastated by this news. At heart, she was
a lone wolf, dependent on no one—especially not a *man*. At least not
anymore. She'd enjoyed a sun-drenched childhood in Pasadena, the
third of four children (and the only daughter) of a wealthy engineer
who ran a company that built water-management systems. She was
expected to marry one of any number of dashing Southern California
bachelors who made their interest in her clear. Her family seemed
eager for her to make her choice, and at the age of twenty-five, she
did. But before her wedding to Chip Davies could take place in the
fall of 1975, her father died, leaving all of his wealth to her three
brothers—and absolutely nothing to her. The expectation was that
her brothers (one of whom was four years her junior) would take care
of Orla and her mother as necessary, just as Orla's father had done.
As was tradition, fiscal decisions would rest firmly in the hands of
the male members of the Byrne clan. Orla's engagement crumbled
in the ensuing weeks once Chip realized that not only would there

be no inheritance, but that Orla also had what he called a "latent feminist temperament" that he found troubling. The injustice of it all roiled Orla so deeply that she fled to the East Coast, vowing to live on her own terms. She landed in New York City's Greenwich Village, where she reconnected with a high school friend who had embraced the counterculture of the late '60s when Orla had not. But she caught up quickly, falling in with a pack of artists—painters, filmmakers, poets—who inspired her to pursue her creative impulses. She began by modeling for the odd photographer friend, but before long, she was taking her own photos, sketching, and painting. She wasn't particularly talented, but she loved the lifestyle. Her friends flitted between the city and a series of upstate homes (a vestige of the time some had spent participating in Timothy Leary and Ram Dass's psychedelic experiments in the '60s), and eventually, Orla began spending the majority of her time in the country, where she had time and space to create her large-scale paintings. Her brothers, who disapproved of her bohemian lifestyle but remained fond of her nonetheless, offered her money from time to time, but she always refused. She saw it as a corruptive gesture, a sinister and manipulative tool used to oil the machinery of the patriarchy. Though she struggled to sell her artwork, she cobbled together a modest living by doing commissioned calligraphy projects and working at a local plant nursery near Rhinebeck. By the time Ursula was born, Orla was making just enough to keep her daughter fed and her art studio supplied. Despite the privilege she had once known, Orla found that the spartan creative life suited her.

In some ways, Orla was relieved by Jürgen's death. Though she had been in love with him at first, she soon became annoyed by his unpredictable comings and goings. Without him, her life felt clean and unencumbered again. She threw herself into her projects, confident that her capable little daughter could manage most of her own upbringing. Orla relished the idea that Ursula would grow to depend on no one—not even her. At four, the child showed signs of self-sufficiency: dressing herself, running her own baths, cutting her own hair when the mood struck, and attending to the various needs of a squirrel (whom she called Soft Shadow) that had taken up residence on the roof outside her bedroom window. Orla believed children's time should be unstructured, and she also hated to be disturbed during daylight hours, when she retreated to her studio in an old sheep shed. As a result, Ursula's days—when she wasn't in school—were long expanses of time in which she woke alone, poured herself cornflakes, and then left their little wooden house to explore the surrounding woods. Some of Ursula's best friends were trees.

During those long days, Ursula burrowed deeply into her own fantasies, which almost always involved managing complex family systems. She often visited her father's workshop—untouched in the years after his death—to select a specific array of screwdrivers, hammers, nails, and screws, taking them into the unmowed yard, where she organized them into elaborate family units. In general, hammers made good fathers. Screwdrivers made selfless wives and mothers; screws and nails were children. She would load them into a toolbox (their school bus) and drag them around the yard, depositing them at various stops—a stump, a flowerbed, the terrace steps—depending on their ages and, therefore, their appropriate places of learning. The game usually consisted of cycle after cycle of the daily routine; it was all quite methodical. Thumbtacks were dogs and cats. The rebellious teenager was usually a wrench named Zack. Once in a while, the families would be visited by a set of pliers (the unhinged aunt), a saw (the world-weary uncle), or a hatchet (the wise old grandfather). Occasionally, if a screw or a nail behaved very badly, it would be given up for adoption and left at the base of the maple tree. By the time Ursula outgrew this game, dozens of nails and screws lay around the tree, rusted after years of lying out as orphans.

There was no greater happiness than playing Tool Families, and for years, Ursula could amuse herself this way from first light until darkness, assuming she was not interrupted. She hated being interrupted. If she saw someone approaching—a neighbor child, for instance—she would quickly gather the tools into a pile and pretend to be shining them.

"What are you doing, Ursula?"

"Cleaning my father's tools."

"Can I play?"

"It's not a game, and anyway, I'm finished." She would toss all of the tools—moms, dads, teenagers, children—into the box and run to deposit it in the shed, making mental notes so that, when she resumed her game in private, she could pick up where she left off.

If she was not interrupted, she would play for hours, sometimes facilitating painful divorces or tragic deaths, followed by unexpected second chances at love. When she grew bored or couldn't figure out how a certain narrative should play out, she'd kill everyone off. Tomorrow would bring a clean slate—a chance to start over and do better, unencumbered by the mistakes and messiness of today.

As a girl, Ursula was content in her little life with her mother, but she longed to be part of a big boisterous family like the ones she sometimes saw on TV. Her favorite sitcoms all involved lovable constellations of siblings overseen by exasperated-but-doting parents. Her preoccupation with family dynamics eventually grew into an explicit expectation: someday, she would seamlessly fall in love with a handsome man and become the adoring mother of her own brood.

But that hadn't happened. Nothing had been seamless. Her matriculation to college served as an awakening, an opportunity to view her upbringing from a distance and to imagine a different kind of life for herself. While her mother railed against the evils of capitalism and had refused her brothers' financial assistance up to that point, she was forced to ask them to pay for her daughter's education. The only other choice would have been insolvency for Orla or debilitating student debt for Ursula. At her school of choice, a New England liberal arts college with a politically incorrect mascot, Ursula quickly realized she was surrounded by the scions of extreme wealth: the daughter of an iconic Hollywood director, the son of an Italian count, the granddaughter of a Saudi oil magnate, a couple of Greek shipping heirs, and a bunch of Turkish kids who carried their books in Louis Vuitton totes. She briefly dated a Park Avenue boy who kept an Alfa Romeo on campus. In short, Ursula had been exposed to money, or rather, to its inheritors. She had seen the promised land in the form of her friends' lifestyles (Cartier watches casually worn to the dining hall, summer "cottages" on Mount Desert Island, winter jaunts to Saint Barths or Telluride, Augusts in Saint-Jean-Cap-Ferrat), but the tail end of her uncles' generosity coincided with her graduation. Which meant that if Ursula wanted to continue to swim in these affluent circles, she would need to make her own money. And lots of it.

Upon arriving at college as an idealistic freshman, she had quickly selected her major: visual art. But unlike her mother, Ursula was not one to fling herself naked onto canvasses. Rather, she took an analytical approach to her work, often employing mixed media to make forceful arguments against issues like child labor or the illegal poaching of rhinoceroses. She counterbalanced these cerebral projects with whimsical drawings of and poems about animals. A talented illustrator and writer, she regularly lost herself in her assignments. Issa would often join her in the drafty art department drawing studio, where they would listen to Talking Heads and let their imaginations crackle late into the night. Ursula would later learn that this experience was called a "flow state," but to her, it was more like flight. The ascent was sometimes effortful, but soon she was swooping and sailing with the natural currents of her inspiration, eventually touching down when she was satisfied with what she had created. But midway through her junior year, the exigencies of the real world intervened, and she became plagued with a rising anxiety that took the form of pragmatism. Convinced that neither her "think pieces" nor her animal portraits could translate to a lucrative career, she abruptly changed her major to international relations and churned out a thesis titled "The Semiotics of Neoliberalism in a Postmodern Global Economy." Yet paradoxically, when her classmates began going to recruitment fairs and attending on-campus interviews, she couldn't muster the enthusiasm to even apply for jobs in foreign policy or global development. Despite feeling intense internal pressure to become more practical in order to survive, she could not fully tear herself away from the creative life. She felt caught between worlds and wholly unemployable. The summer after she graduated, she moved to New York with enough money to survive for three months. In mid-July, she attended a fortuitous cocktail party at the house of a pseudosocialite near Union Square. There, she met a man (The Despot) who offered her a job as a copywriter. The pay was meager, but it was enough to live on, enough to launch her. As her college friends migrated from small luxury apartments in the East Village (subsidized by their parents) to large luxury apartments in the West Village (still subsidized by their parents), she trudged from deep Brooklyn into somewhat-closer Brooklyn, most recently settling in her charming little nest in Carroll Gardens.

Her sitcom-fueled familial fantasy never left her, but she eventually realized she had never observed long-term commitment up close and wasn't sure how it worked. She spent her twenties moving from one relationship to another, like a frog leaping between lily pads, reluctant to plunge into the unknown depths beneath. She figured that eventually, one of these romances would stick and blossom, but only recently, around her thirtieth birthday, did she start to consider that her career, rather than a romantic partnership, might end up being the organizing element in her life. This was convenient, since her thirties coincided with the rise of fourth-wave feminism. Being a career-oriented woman was practically expected in the hyperam-bitious circles in which she traveled. Those who knew her assumed she had remained single on purpose and on principle. As various friends fell into marriages (sometimes effortlessly, sometimes more strategically), Ursula became increasingly emphatic about how much she loved her work, though that was not always true. By thirty-five, she had received various industry accolades and was making enough money to live modestly in Brooklyn and enjoy the occasional indul-gence: an overpriced handbag now and again, the odd Mediterranean vacation, last-minute tickets to a Beyoncé show ("Nothing has ever been more worth it," she and Issa had agreed), and her membership to The Stake, which she justified as necessary "self-care." The money was decent and her work came naturally; but convincing herself that it fulfilled her did not. She couldn't shake what felt like a series of in-born contradictions: a mistrust of wealth but a craving for it; a love of autonomy but a longing for partnership; an impulse toward creative chaos but a need for security and structure; and a desire to both retain and relinquish control of her fate.

Managing these contradictions was exhausting. Ursula vacillated between wanting to work her way into the wealth-dripping set—which she associated with a kind of liberation from mundane stressors, like paying rent—and longing to burn it all down by abandoning capitalist mores entirely. And yes, she wanted to be someone's wife and someone's mother, but she guarded her independence with the ferocity of a wolverine. She wanted to trust that everything would work out, but she was hounded by self-doubt. She wondered if she had morphed into some dysfunctional amalgam of the identity her mother had renounced (the acquiescent wife with a prescribed role and social standing) and the one Orla had ultimately assumed (the relentlessly independent artist with a nearly empty bank account). Burdened by this polarity, Ursula often felt at war with herself. She dreamed of a middle ground: empowered autonomy without loneliness, retention of self within a solid relationship, safety amid the challenges of the unknown. But she had no idea how to achieve that middle ground, or if it was even attainable. Perpetually conflicted about her priorities, she just kept working and turned her energy outward. She could at least make money while she wrestled with the rest of it.

Mallory leapt up onto Ursula's blanketed lap and began kneading with her paws. Ursula reached over her and picked up the *New Yorker* from the coffee table. She examined the cover, whose illustration was, as always, clever in a self-satisfied way. "Don't you want to be smart? Informed? Intellectually smug? Read me," the *New Yorker* taunted her, and she felt a twinge of annoyance.

Her phone chirped. A message from Issa—a GIF of a dog on a skateboard. He was alarmingly skilled.

"I really want to discuss this dog in more depth, but I'm doing a digital detox tonight," Ursula texted back.

She then took a quick look—really, really quick—at her inbox.

There was a new email. A message from The Arc. Her finger pounced at it like a hungry fox to a vole.

> Ursula,
> Thank you so much for your interest in The Arc. It's a rare, self-selecting group that gets this far.
> We believe that lasting love is <u>particular</u>. You should be with someone who loves and appreciates you for your idiosyncrasies, and vice versa.
> Based on our initial research, we think you're ideally suited to take advantage of our service, which is why I'd like to invite you to meet with me to learn more. I've copied my assistant Nadia, who can help schedule a time that suits your doubtless busy schedule.
> Your champion in lasting love,
> Dr. Corinne Vidal
> *Founder and Chief Relationship Architect, The Arc*

Ursula paused. Lasting love? This already made her feel conflicted. On the one hand, there was no way that whatever magic The Arc offered could actually work. On the other, she desperately hoped it might.

"I'm not committing," she reassured herself. "I'm just finding out more. It's basic due diligence."

She replied to Nadia to set up an appointment, then put her phone away and recommitted to her digital detox. She opened the *New Yorker,* but within minutes, she was asleep on the couch, still wearing her face mask, its venom-slick surface glowing in the warm lamplight.

Chapter 6

June 14, 3:23 P.M.

The car pulled up outside The Arc's midtown headquarters. Ursula could easily have taken the subway from her office downtown, but it was the first truly hot day of the summer—83 degrees—and even a few minutes on a subway platform in that heat could turn the most put-together person into a sweaty mess. After thirteen years in New York, she knew how to calibrate these things. She wore black cigarette pants and a loose linen tank top (also black) and not-too-high-heeled sandals (black with tortoise-shell-patterned straps) from her favorite Brooklyn boutique, Bird. Black was her defensive color, a protective combination of armor and an invisibility cloak. She wore it when she wanted to see, but not necessarily be seen. Plus, it provided a blank canvas against which her wild hair could take center stage.

She pulled out a mirror to check that her berry-toned lip stain had not smudged. Lip color was also armor, drawing attention to her mouth but also creating a barrier between her and anyone who might wish to interact with it. In general, Ursula liked to have multiple layers buffering her from the world: lipstick, nail polish, sunglasses, scarves, sunscreen, argan oil, denim, leather, silk, texturizing sea spray. Even though she styled herself to look mostly "natural," it still took a significant number of lacquers, glosses, garments, mists, and serums to make her feel sufficiently shielded from the unyielding sensory assault of life in New York City.

Ursula entered a mirrored foyer and announced herself to the bored-looking man at the desk. After scrutinizing her driver's license, he picked up a phone, waited, and then said, "I have Ursula Byrne."

A voice on the other end chirped a response, and he set the phone down and nodded for Ursula to proceed. "Thirteenth floor." She felt a nervous throat-twinge, as if a small mouse were punching her from the inside of her esophagus. "Why do I feel like I'm about to go on the most fraught first date of my life?" she wondered, hitting the elevator button.

As she rode up to the thirteenth floor, she envisioned what the office would look like: white walls, marble countertops, minimalist chairs in an airy waiting room, touchscreens, the gentle thrum of technology and algorithms vibrating through the filtered air. That seemed to be the agreed-upon aesthetic for "disruptive" companies these days, with the occasional accent color—millennial pink, sun yellow, terra-cotta red—thrown in for differentiation. She rolled her eyes, unable to suppress her cynicism. Why was she even doing this to herself? She had almost made peace with the prospect of being single indefinitely, and yet here she was, entertaining the idea that this mysterious operation might actually conjure up the partner she had yet to manifest on her own.

She was surprised when the doors opened to a sleek wood-paneled hallway, elegant in its Japanese-inspired simplicity and dimly lit by six gas lanterns with actual flames. The air carried the scent of charred cedarwood, suggesting the warmth and comfort of a sauna. Rustic, primal, and soothing to her citified senses, it was the exact opposite of the slick, tech-laden space she had expected. Few things surprised her these days. She was usually a step ahead of those around her—she was paid to be—and she respected anyone or anything that could catch her off guard.

There was no signage and nowhere to go but down the shadowy hallway—more of a tunnel, really. Issa would like this space, Ursula thought, as she walked on, no longer nervous, just intrigued, then content. She felt a flicker of something that resembled hope.

When she got to the end of the hall, she stopped, confused. She was surrounded by solid walls, but no doors—a dead end. As she turned back toward the elevator to see if she'd missed something, a wood panel slid from the wall like a sliding gate, cutting her off from the hallway she'd come down and enclosing her in what was now a perfectly square chamber. Before she could become claustrophobic, the wall to her right slid open, offering an escape. She stepped through into another wood-paneled room with no furniture and no windows. A young woman stood waiting, her long black hair parted in the center and pulled back in a tight, low ponytail.

"Ursula, welcome. I'm Nadia," she said with a warm smile. They shook hands, and Nadia gestured for Ursula to follow her down another wood-paneled hall, turning to ask, "How was your journey here?"

"Very nice." Actually, it had been. There had been almost no traffic from Ursula's office in SoHo to The Arc's headquarters near Bryant Park.

Nadia smiled with satisfaction and pressed her hand gently but firmly against one of the wood panels, which slid open to reveal a room whose entire front wall was an uninterrupted expanse of glass, offering a stellar view of Bryant Park. Ursula realized she hadn't seen natural light since she'd entered the building, and it was both reassuring and jarring. Part of her missed the cocoon of the paneled halls.

"Dr. Vidal will be in shortly," Nadia said. "She's looking forward to meeting you. Can I bring you anything in the meantime? Coffee? A matcha latte? A natural orange wine? Magnesium-fortified water? A cocktail?"

"Oh," said Ursula, disoriented by the breadth of options and the time of day. It was mid-afternoon, far too early to drink hard alcohol, but she panicked and heard herself say, "A Negroni?"

"Of course." Nadia backed out of the room in one swift step.

The panel closed, leaving Ursula alone. She crossed the space and approached the glass wall, her chest tightening as she imagined falling from this height—thirteen stories—onto the sidewalk. But then she remembered that she was supposed to cultivate positive thoughts, per her former therapist. So she imagined herself as a flying squirrel, arms spread wide, floating over the canopy of trees below.

Again, Ursula was surprised by the set-up of the space: It was open, almost empty. The floor was gray concrete covered by a nubby sisal rug. There was no desk or couch. And while she had expected designer chairs that conveyed a sense of sophistication—some Le Corbusier or Mies van der Rohe things—what she found in this room were two huge half-orbs, carved out of a porous black rock and mounted on three legs each. They reminded her of the molcajetes she'd seen in Mexico: volcanic-rock mortars used to grind spices and make salsas and guacamole. These human-sized versions were angled slightly upward and looked like they weighed at least a ton each. They were separated by a table made of a wide slice of tree trunk, its gorgeous rings on display for a mesmerizing effect. Ursula lowered herself cautiously into one of the molcajetes and shifted for a moment before realizing it was the most comfortable chair imaginable. No matter how she contorted herself, she felt wonderfully at ease. She was the guacamole.

The panel slid open again and a striking woman entered holding two ruby-toned Negronis, each containing a single giant ice cube.

"Ursula," she said warmly, as if she were greeting a beloved niece. She had a posh British accent, a deep velvet voice, and an aristocratic air.

She set the drinks on the tree trunk and held out her hand, her thumb at a firm right angle to her pointer finger. "I'm Dr. Vidal. It's such a pleasure to meet you."

Ursula maneuvered out of her chair to shake hands and then re-settled into the cavernous seat.

Statuesque and serene, Dr. Vidal had smooth skin and luxurious-looking thick black hair. Her fingernails were painted a translucent cream, and her full lips were shiny but lipstick-free. Ursula guessed she was in her mid-fifties, although she had an ethereal energy that made her age hard to pin down. (Ursula would later describe her to Issa as having "Cleopatra vibes.") She looked organized, intelligent, and disarmingly confident—like she knew something secret but inarguably true about the art of living. Ursula yearned to know whatever it was.

Settling delicately into her molcajete, Dr. Vidal lifted her Negroni ceremoniously toward Ursula.

"To you. And to the courage and curiosity that brought you here."

Clink.

Synchronized sips.

Swallows.

Silence.

The herby gin sizzled down Ursula's throat. "Well, thank you for having me," she said, suddenly feeling as though she were lucky to be here, to be in the presence of Dr. Vidal, to be invited to do whatever it was people came to The Arc to do.

"I imagine you're wondering what this is all about," said Dr. Vidal, sweeping her arm in a circle, as if she fully understood why someone might be skeptical of both The Arc's cryptic mission and its byzantine headquarters.

Ursula nodded.

"I look forward to answering all of your questions. But first, I'd love to ask *you* a question: How much of your life would you say you've dedicated to romantic pursuits?"

"Like, dating? Or relationships? Or sex? Or thinking about relationships? Or swiping on dating apps? Or talking to my friends about . . ."

"All of the above."

"God, I don't know how to quantify it. Months? Years? I've been preoccupied with relationships for my entire life."

"How much energy would you say you've spent in pursuit of love?"

"Too much."

"And you are thirty . . . ?"

"Five. Thirty-five."

"Tell me, Ursula. Do you really *want* a life partner? Do you want to find someone to navigate the coming decades with?"

"I do," Ursula answered without thinking. "But . . ."

"But?"

"I don't want to settle. And I don't want to abandon myself in the pursuit."

"That's a very healthy attitude. I'm so glad to hear you say that, because there's no need for you to settle or to self-abandon."

"Are you sure? Because I worry that I'm running out of time. I'd rather be single than keep compromising, because it's wearing me out. But I feel depleted."

"That's not uncommon," said Dr. Vidal. "But I can assure you: It *is* unnecessary. From now on, there's no need to worry. You will not have to compromise."

Ursula wanted badly to believe her. She took a long sip of her Negroni.

Dr. Vidal went on, "For too long, there has been this concept of 'the one.' I'm searching for 'the one.' You'll know when you find 'the one.' Unfortunately, it's a fallacy. And many people, especially intelligent young women like you, know that. But it's often countered by an equally misleading belief: that there are dozens—maybe hundreds, maybe thousands—of compatible partners for each of us. I don't know about you, but neither of those theories ever satisfied me. Why should you have to wait for 'the one' to find you—or not? What if he or she or they narrowly miss you? On the other hand, why should you have to settle for one of a hundred compatible partners? Surely they aren't equally compatible. Surely there is a hierarchy. But how do you assess that hierarchy? How do you stay focused while casting a wide net? How do you keep an open mind while also being sufficiently discerning?"

Dr. Vidal's words poked gently but effectively at Ursula's anxieties.

"What if I told you that we can give you an opportunity to meet the person—the *particular* person—with whom you'll have the greatest chance at lifelong happiness? What if I told you that your years of wasting time in pursuit of love were over, and that from here on out, the time you dedicate to the pursuit will directly correlate to the quality of your match? Tell me, have you tried traditional dating apps or services?" Dr. Vidal leaned in, as if fascinated to hear Ursula's answer.

"Yes," said Ursula. "Not until recently, but over the past year or so."

"And?"

"They were interesting at first," said Ursula. "Then kind of frustrating."

"Why frustrating?"

"It's hard to account for all the variables that go into finding a truly compatible match. No—it's more than hard. It's impossible."

Dr. Vidal nodded compassionately. "The mainstream apps screen for superficial qualities—height, profession, location, astrological sign, cat person versus dog person. But you want more."

"Exactly," said Ursula. "How will this guy operate in a crisis? Is he a real feminist or just a self-described 'feminist' who actually wants to teach you how to do things you already know how to do? Does he understand that he can like both cats and dogs—he doesn't have to choose? Does he know not to put metal in the goddamn microwave?" Ursula felt her pulse quicken as she flashed back to a man she'd dated in her mid-twenties who almost set her apartment on fire while attempting to reheat an aluminum-foil-wrapped burrito.

"So you know what you want," said Dr. Vidal. "Or what you think you want. And yet, you haven't found it. Why do you believe that is?"

"I'm flawed," Ursula said. "Deeply flawed. And probably too picky. And full of self-contradiction."

"But your self-contradictions make you who you are. You're not flawed, and you're not picky," said Dr. Vidal. "You're particular."

"Maybe too particular," Ursula admitted. "I don't know. I'm obviously doing something wrong."

"That's not obvious to me," said Dr. Vidal. "What's obvious is that you're experiencing cognitive overload on the apps—too many options, but the wrong ones. What's obvious is that you could benefit from the expertise of a third party that can help you put the puzzle pieces together. A third party that appreciates and knows you—perhaps even better than you know yourself."

Ursula squinted her eyes in dread. "A third party who knows me. Like, my mother?"

"No," said Dr. Vidal, smiling. "Let me be plain: The Arc is a relationship solution for mature, clear-thinking adults whose top priority, at this stage in their lives, is to build a lifelong connection that clicks on every level: the physical, intellectual, spiritual, artistic, emotional, practical, and existential. A connection that illuminates the soul, nourishes the heart, and grounds the psyche. Of course, we take into account superficial preferences—physical type, education level, pet allergies, religious beliefs—but there's so much more to profound compatibility. We accelerate the filtering process so that you, our client, can spend less time searching and more time *thriving* with your ideal mate." She paused. "Have you had prior relationships?"

Ursula nodded.

"How long did they last?"

"Two years. Then three years. One and a half years. Six months. A month. A week. A few hours."

"Well, what took you years to learn and discern in your previous relationships will take our team just a few weeks to sort out."

"But how?" Ursula vacillated between skepticism and wonder.

"It's science. It's also psychology, spirituality, technology, instinct. It's a dynamic combination of left- and right-brain strategies. We call it 'relationship architecture,' and our proprietary approach goes much deeper than your typical algorithm, or even a custom matchmaking service. We use a complex analytical matrix to create a complete emotional and psychological map of every client. We measure you on a number of levels: neural activity, sleep habits, genetics, nervous-system calibration, spiritual connectivity, pain tolerance, dietary sensitivities, Myers-Briggs type, Enneagram number, flexibility, physical strength, fight-or-flight response, hormone levels, to name just a few. We also screen for softer sensibilities. For instance, did you notice last week's full moon? For how long did you look at it? Did you remark on it to anyone else, or did you just appreciate it on your own? We want to know all of that. The way you do—or don't—experience a full moon can give us an incredible amount of information about you. And then we use our findings to pinpoint your ideal partner—and not just the person who is ideal for you today, but the person who will develop into an even more ideal partner for you in ten years, twenty years. The person who can appreciate the full arc of your life. The person who has the potential to lovingly hold your hand as you draw your final breath."

Ursula gasped in spite of herself.

"I know." Dr. Vidal nodded. "It is alarming. This is a serious endeavor. It's not for the frivolous, the noncommittal. It's not for the faint of heart, shall we say. It takes both fortitude and faith. You will need to reveal things about yourself that you may not have told anyone. Perhaps you've never even revealed them to yourself. Confronting these things may be uncomfortable at first. Have you ever done therapy?"

Ursula laughed. Of course she'd done therapy.

"Well, if therapy is a level three or four when it comes to being vulnerable, we'll take you to a ten. Perhaps even an eleven. Of course, the process is completely confidential. Any information you reveal will be used solely for the purpose of finding your ideal partner. But the application process is demanding. It requires a serious investment of both time and money. That is to say, The Arc is not a solution for the masses. Male clients pay $50,000, and female clients pay $40,500. We've calibrated our fees based on the gender wage gap—it's only fair."

Ursula appreciated that, but still, the fee seemed outrageous. "How do you match people with such certainty?"

"Years of research. Years and years. You see, it's not just about matching people who are the same on every axis. Sometimes we match for similarities, of course. But sometimes we pair people at opposite ends of a given spectrum to create complementary polarity. Sometimes we'll pair one person's extreme quality with another's more neutral quality, to create a specific synergy. You see? We formulate a level of compatibility that you, as an individual, would never—not in a thousand years, if you had them, which you don't—be able to achieve for yourself. Even if you dedicated every minute of your day and ounce of your energy to solving this puzzle, you would never come up with the information that we're able to extract and analyze. In short, we've perfected the art and science of relationships so that you no longer have to use yourself as a lab rat in your personal search for love. You are not a lab rat, Ursula. You are a woman who is worthy of and ready for the relationship of her life."

Ursula couldn't speak.

"Think about it: no more disappointment, no more uncertainty," Dr. Vidal continued, sounding increasingly excited. "Rather than wasting your time on unfulfilling dates, invest that time up front with us. If we are able to match you—I say 'if,' because we can't match everyone—your work is done. There is no swiping, no deliberating, no agonizing. You will be immediately introduced to the person who will quickly become the love of your life. Your days of searching and wondering will be over. It's that simple—for you. Our side of the equation is incredibly complex, but for you, it's just a matter of saying, 'Yes. I am ready.'"

Ursula took a breath and tried to collect her thoughts. "So, you can't match everyone?"

Dr. Vidal shook her head. "We don't believe in mediocre connections. If we did, we wouldn't be who we are; we'd be no better than your run-of-the-mill dating app. At The Arc, we are as discerning as our clients, and we won't initiate a match unless we know it's exactly right. Sometimes that means our clients have to consider things they may have never considered. For example, would you be willing to move abroad for the right partner?"

Ursula furrowed her brow. New York felt like an extension of her own body at this point, integral to how she functioned. But perhaps she was being too rigid. "Maybe?"

"That's something we take into account," said Dr. Vidal. "Even though The Arc has only existed for four years in its current form, our pool of clients is vast and global. We'd try to find you a match in New York City, if that was your preference. But many of our clients relish the idea of matching with someone in another part of the world and then building an entirely new life. It's all possible."

"But how do you . . ." Ursula's brain had stalled.

"As we like to say," Dr. Vidal continued, "*Love is particular.* You're an individual—you're not a 'type.' You deserve to be with someone who appreciates you for your idiosyncrasies, and vice versa. When it comes to love, we want you to believe that anything is possible."

Ursula nodded, her body humming with adrenaline, Negroni fire, and something unfamiliar—something warm and peaceful that made her want to surrender control. Something in between hope and trust. She didn't have a name for it.

Chapter 7

"That's the craziest thing I've ever heard," said Issa from her pedicure chair. "But also the coolest. You have to do it."

"Issa, it costs $40,000!" said Ursula. "Well, $40,500 to be exact." They were at The Stake again, watching as two nail artisans affixed pulverized rose quartz granules to their toenails to cultivate loving energy "from the ground up."

"So? People spend that kind of money—or *more*—on all kinds of things: cars, apartments, education. The Arc's fee wouldn't even cover *one year's* tuition at our alma mater! Do you realize that? And don't get me started on the fertility market. Egg freezing costs $15,000 and people are doing that without batting an eyelash. My cousin spent over $40,000 on IVF last year."

"Well, maybe I should save up for *that*," said Ursula. "Skip the partner. Go straight to the kid."

"Well, you can do that, too. But these days, everything is expensive—real estate, reproduction, relationships. It's just the age we're living in."

"Your relationship was free," countered Ursula.

Issa tilted her head, running a quick fiscal analysis, then refocused. "If you want to do it, you can afford it."

"I can't believe this is even a thing," said Ursula, flexing her toes so the quartz would catch the light.

"This toe treatment? Or The Arc?" asked Issa.

"Both. All of it. The state of romance. The state of humanity. Life itself," said Ursula. "I can't believe anything is a thing. What kind of dipshit pays $40,000 for a dating service?"

"This dipshit," said Issa, playfully poking Ursula's knee. "Wait, could you get Anonymous & Co. to pay for it? Like, as part of your benefits package? You've worked your butt off at that agency for eight years."

"You think I should march up to my boss and be like, 'Hi, Roger. I've been a good employee. Could you spare $40K so I don't have to go home every night and cry into my cat?'"

Issa smiled and shook her head. "You're so hard on yourself."

Ursula didn't know any other way to be; her inner self-critic was relentless. And although the thought of trying to get her employer to pay The Arc's fee was absurd, she wondered if there was another way. She supposed she could sell her father's sculpture, but that seemed heartless—and she wasn't sure she trusted her mother's appraisal any-way. Then she thought back to the recent meeting at Indubitably and the fact that she owed Mike Rutherford an email. He had wanted to get on her calendar, after all, and maybe spending an hour with a billionaire could help generate some fiscal momentum.

Issa interrupted her thoughts. "Okay, money conundrum aside, let's just play this out. If you decide to do it, how does it work?"

"I give them $40,500. Then I spend seven days locked in their headquarters . . ."

"Whoa!" Issa blurted. "Seven days? Can you take that much time off work?"

"It's not ideal, but I think I could," said Ursula. "And during that time, they scrutinize me from every angle and ask me questions about my childhood and poke and prod me. They monitor my heart rate and my hormone fluctuations. It sounds like there's also some kind of obstacle course I have to do."

"Like on *Double Dare*?" asked Issa.

"Yeah, stuff like that. And at night, they observe me to see what position I sleep in and how much I move and if I talk in my sleep."

"Sounds intense. And kind of creepy," said Issa. "But also, smart. Like, Eric wants to snuggle *all* night. And when he finally falls asleep and relinquishes his grip, he sleeps like an octopus—limbs everywhere. I, on the other hand, want to snuggle for thirty seconds and then part ways until morning. You know how I sleep in a tight ball?"

Ursula nodded. She'd shared a bed with a balled-up Issa many times since college. Her friend was an abnormally self-contained sleeper.

"So, it would be amazing to have someone match you with a partner whose nocturnal style is compatible with yours," Issa continued. "You could actually sleep comfortably for the rest of your life! I can hardly even imagine that—it sounds amazing." Issa's marriage was so peaceful that her biggest qualms had to do with exactly that type of thing: Eric snuggling her too affectionately and for too long before they both drifted into contented slumber.

"Okay. Whatever. So then," Ursula continued, "they take what they've learned about you and they find your perfect match. But the value proposition is that it's not someone you would choose for yourself. It's someone who they think—no, they *know*—will grow compatibly with you over time."

"So, not a DJ." Issa grinned.

Ursula covered her eyes with her palms in shame. It was true that many of her ex-boyfriends had been aspiring—but ultimately unsuccessful—DJs. Right after college, there had been Adam, the investment-banking analyst who was obsessed with '90s hip-hop; and then, briefly, there had been Jean-Christophe, the French graphic designer who spun electronic dance music in Bushwick every other Tuesday night.

"No more DJs for me," said Ursula. "Hopefully. But I guess that's up to The Arc."

"Don't you have any say in who your match is?" asked Issa. "Do you get to pick from a selection?"

"No," said Ursula. "That's the thing. They assess you, and then a few weeks later, you get your match. That's it. No swiping, so to speak. No choice in the matter."

"I'm so into this," said Issa, shaking her head. "This is fucking crazy. You're doing it."

Chapter 8

July 3, 2:07 P.M.

"So glad you reached out," said Mike, picking up his napkin and snapping it aggressively through the air to unfurl it, before gingerly spreading it over his thighs. It had been almost a month since he and Ursula had crossed paths at the Indubitably meeting. This time slot—2 P.M. on Friday, July 3—was the only one Mike could swing before October, so Ursula made it work. And because Mike was a billionaire, he knew full well that he could get almost anyone to meet with him anywhere, anytime, for pretty much any reason. "I appreciate you squeezing me in ahead of the holiday weekend," he said, deploying his signature false deference. Or at least, that's how Ursula perceived it.

Holiday traffic didn't concern him, since he would be traveling by private helicopter to East Hampton, where he would spend July Fourth with his second wife and his two teenage children from his first marriage. Holiday traffic didn't concern Ursula, because she had canceled her travel plans (a long weekend at a friend's Catskills cabin) to accommodate this meeting. She didn't lunch with billionaires often, and she was happy to make the sacrifice.

Mike had chosen the restaurant—a Michelin-starred, impossible-to-reserve place on the sixtieth floor of a shiny Financial District skyscraper that evoked a spaceship—and he took the liberty of ordering the seven-course tasting menu for both of them. The meal was a blur of lobster foam, sunchoke purée, hand-foraged moss reduction, dandelion wisps, beet batter, lychee splinters, mushroom mist, arctic char shadows, grass-fed beef breath, Amazonian ant footprints ("They're incredibly good for you," Mike insisted), all seasoned with a sense of exceptionalism. *If you are eating this, you are very important.* Either that, or you're in the presence of someone very important.

Mike left much of this food on his plate, but Ursula couldn't bear to waste a wisp or a stamen. Perhaps it was her frugal upbringing in proximity to the dying industrial towns of the Hudson Valley, or that her mother abhorred ostentation. "Waste not, want not," she learned to say at age two and a half. She ingested every last particle of mushroom mist.

Mike, on the other hand, was a man who had had too much for too long. This meal wasn't remarkable to him, and he counted calories religiously. Although he was in his mid-fifties, his wealth and dog-gedness allowed him to hang on to the appearance of youth. In addi-tion to his Brazilian Jiu-Jitsu habit, he exercised daily with a personal trainer who also coached Olympic decathletes; he fasted quarterly; he practiced transcendental meditation; he took cryotherapy baths; he avoided sugar; he got regular facials and manicures; he took specific supplements to promote the retention of his silver-fox hair. He had a perpetual tan (from the actual sun, which he chased persistently throughout the year via his private jet), and his clothes were crisp and polished, as if they were all brand new. When Ursula complimented his shirt, he explained to her that it was custom-made by a tailor in London, whereas the majority of his suits were custom-made in Rome. When it came to clothes, why waste his time going to anyone other than Alistair and Giancarlo?

Only the best for Mike Rutherford, for whom money was almost inconsequential at this point. But *time*—that was a currency he had yet to master. In a feverish campaign against his own mortality, he was constantly throwing money at anything that might buy him more time. Ursula wondered if she would ever experience that shift for herself. Perhaps "making it" in New York in 2018 meant you had so much money that you were trading in a different commodity altogether: time spent entirely on your own terms. She envisioned herself walking up to a currency exchange office, handing over a bur-lap sack of cash, and receiving vouchers that offered her guilt-free ski weekends, spontaneous jaunts to Barcelona, a multi-week exploration of Mongolia on horseback, perhaps a few years all to herself to draw and write poetry and search for meaning on the Bahian coast.

Ursula didn't like what Mike represented—or what she assumed he represented—but she was happy that they now inhabited the same ecosystem. She had arrived at this lunch with a vague hope of establishing a symbiotic relationship. She remembered learning about these relationships—which took place between two different species—in her seventh-grade science class. Three types of symbiosis were mutualism, where both species benefited from the relationship; commensalism, where one benefited, while the other was not harmed; and parasitism, where one benefited, while the other was harmed. When it came to Mike, she was open to mutualism or commensalism. She drew the line at parasitism—too sinister, too desperate.

"Remember when I told you that you had a great brain at the Indubitably meeting?" asked Mike, getting back to business.

How could she forget?

"Well, I still believe that," he said.

Ursula was glad to hear it, given that it had only been a few weeks since he made the declaration.

"And of course, your work with Coctus speaks for itself. To take a sex-toy company to a $1 billion valuation in three years? Impressive. There was nothing special about their business model—it was all about the marketing. You're talented, but I think you're more than a brand-builder. I think you're a businesswoman. I think you have an eye for the next big thing."

Ursula felt a familiar mixture of pride and anxiety. Just because she'd had a few wins didn't mean she'd be able to repeat them. Or did it? She marveled at her own ability to achieve success, while simultaneously being certain that complete and utter failure was imminent. Her visible accomplishments meant a lot to others, but little to her. What she actually valued in herself was her ability to teeter on the knife edge between earned confidence and persistent anxiety, to maintain her equanimity amid success spikes and moments of devastating self-doubt. "Thank you," she said.

"I wanted to run an idea by you," said Mike, casually flicking a pepita off his finger into the air behind him. "I'm at a point in my life where I don't want to simply make money. Making money is easy. You name it, I've invested in it: energy, lumber, lab-grown meat, spider silk that's stronger than steel. I'm bored. I want to *have fun* while making money. I want to be where the innovators are."

"You want to sit with the cool kids," said Ursula.

"Bingo," said Mike. "I'm looking for early investment opportunities—hot new startups that are disrupting their industries."

Innovation. Disruption. Ursula cringed at how little these words meant nowadays. Just a half century ago, the word "innovation" had been reserved for breakthroughs like landing on the moon or developing a birth control pill that enabled women's liberation. Now, it meant convincing consumers to subscribe to monthly deliveries of razors and goji berry powder; it meant there was an app for everything. There were even apps to manage your apps. The pace of "progress" had accelerated, but the actual results were middling. And yet, this startup-centric culture was Ursula's professional world. She willingly participated, and what's more, she profited.

"But I don't have time to be pitched by every HBS grad under the sun. I need to filter," Mike continued. "Better yet, I want to hunt strategically, and I want you to be the huntress."

Ursula raised her eyebrows. She liked the word "huntress"; she had to give him that. But she wasn't sure what it meant in practice.

The waiter appeared at their table. "Can I get you anything else, Mr. Rutherford?"

"Armagnac?" Mike asked, pointing his index finger at Ursula. Before she could answer, he swirled his wrist in a circle and stuck two fingers up at the waiter. "Two glasses of the Lannaud." To Ursula, he elaborated: "It's a 1942. Trust me, you've never had anything like this." He didn't mention whether *he'd* ever had anything like it, but of course he had. By the time you're fifty-seven and have been a billionaire for two decades, you've had almost everything. And you've had it multiple times.

"Where was I?"

"You want me to be the huntress," Ursula supplied.

"Exactly. You work at what I understand is the city's hottest agency. You're in the mix. You're young. Well, youngish. Young, but not too young. How old are you? Never mind." He swiftly shifted gears. "You're smart, you've got your finger on the pulse, you have an eye, and I assume you're privy to the financials of the companies you work with. All I'm proposing is that you fill me in when you hear about an investment opportunity. For me, it's about time. My team and I could spend all day vetting, or we could count on a trusted advisor to curate opportunities and present us with the most promising ones."

Ursula could be that advisor. That huntress.

"Are you in a position to do this type of consulting?" asked Mike, leaning back and placing his hands behind his head, his elbows jutting out. The Cobra.

"I could be," said Ursula, sitting up straighter, energized by the glimmer of an idea. "I'd have to think about how it would work, how we'd structure it."

"I'm eager to get the ball rolling as soon as possible. Why don't you draft a proposal and send it to me on Monday? Or whenever your schedule will allow." That meant Monday, Ursula understood.

She paused to think. This could be very lucrative, but she would have to carve out time for it, and it might take a few months to get momentum. "I can do that, but since there will be a lot of work up front, I'd need to collect my fee at the outset," she said, shocked by her own audacity.

Mike lowered his hands from his head and crossed them over his chest. He cocked his head to the side and waited for her to offer a number.

"For this type of work . . ." Ursula paused. Did she dare propose $40,000, which would cover The Arc's fee? And if so, why stop there? $50,000? A force overtook her, and she heard herself say, "One hundred thousand dollars annually."

The waiter arrived with a tray and set down two large snifters. "The Lannaud, sir," he said, holding the bottle out. Mike nodded, and the waiter filled each glass partway up with the tawny liquid.

Mike began swirling his glass vigorously. "A hundred thousand dollars," he said slowly, as if trying out the number. He took a deep inhale of the liquid and then looked up. "That won't be a problem."

Ursula maintained her outward composure, but her internal organs began to clench with excited disbelief.

Mike lifted his snifter toward Ursula. "To the hunt."

Chapter 9

July 4, 8:33 P.M.

It had taken Ursula longer than expected to get the grill in her garden going. She'd tried to use one of those charcoal chimneys, but in the end had just squirted a healthy amount of lighter fluid onto the coals. That did the trick.

She was supposed to be upstate right now, with a pack of friends she'd fallen in with over the years—one of those ramshackle New York networks where no one quite remembers how anyone got to know anyone. It was always some combination of a former coworker and someone's old roommate, then the ex-girlfriend of a cousin and her neighbor, who also happened to work with the former coworker. Then it started circling in on itself, until it turned out they all knew each other through multiple connections, some of which had fallen by the wayside. The true origin of the group was hazy, clouded by the happy chaos of life in one's twenties in New York City, with people colliding in ways that had felt serendipitous and meaningful at the time. But as they got older, they realized this was just how life worked: people were in fact just energy blobs bouncing off one another and then circling back again. Now that they were in their mid-thirties (or mid-forties, in some cases), the smoke had cleared, and the problematic members of the group had fallen away. Others had become parents, which prevented them from taking off on spontaneous holiday weekends.

Ursula had been looking forward to this gathering, but she wasn't there. She had stayed in town to accommodate the meeting with Mike, but then had happily discovered that a number of her college friends had stuck around, too. So it was just as well.

Issa and Eric sat at the picnic table in Ursula's small rectangular yard, along with Virginia (Ursula's sophomore-year roommate) and her new fiancé, Matt, who was just okay. He was fine. Eminently tolerable. Virginia could have done much better, but she also could have done much worse. Given her track record with men, Matt landed firmly on the acceptable side. He and Virginia had met eight months ago via a dating app and had just gotten engaged. Ursula knew that Virginia planned to be pregnant within the year. It was unclear if Matt knew that.

Phil, who had been Eric's freshman-year roommate, pointed at his cheeseburger as if he couldn't believe its deliciousness. His hairline had begun to recede a bit, but otherwise, he still had the boyish quality he'd had when they were in college. "You did this?" he asked Ursula. *"You?"*

"I told you I knew how to grill!" said Ursula. "Why does everyone underestimate me?"

Issa reached for a bottle of rosé and filled up all the near-empty glasses on the table. Eric picked a leaf that had fallen from a tree out of his wife's hair. As usual, he was wearing a button-down shirt— tonight it was navy—with the sleeves rolled up to just below his elbows. With his curly brown hair and intellectual air, Eric had always looked like an adult, even long before he was one. He took an organized bite out of his burger and pushed his round, wire-framed glasses higher up the bridge of his nose.

"And it's a happy cow," said Ursula.

Phil looked at his burger skeptically. "You sure?"

"Yes. I'm only buying meat from Rigby's now," Ursula said. She was feeling increasingly conflicted about eating animals these days. The social pressure to embrace vegetarianism was rising, but she wasn't quite ready. For now, Rigby's was her chosen purveyor, because it sourced all of its products from upstate gentlemen farmers and had a sign with thoughtfully designed sans serif font. This felt like a logical stopgap on her journey toward actually admitting that she hated the concept of eating animals. But they were so goddamn delicious.

Steven, Phil's partner, emerged from the back door of Ursula's apartment and ducked under the string of round lights that zigzagged from the wall of her building to an oak tree to the back fence that separated her yard from her neighbor's.

"Did you do those framed animal sketches in the bathroom?" Steven asked.

"Yes, she did!" shouted Issa, who always got louder as she got tipsier.

"They're pretty great," said Steven.

"Thank you," said Ursula. "I'm obsessed with animals. But I just do those for fun."

"But she *could* do it professionally," Issa boasted on Ursula's behalf.

"But I don't *want* to do it professionally," said Ursula, "because then it would no longer be fun."

"Well, work *can* be fun," said Issa, who genuinely enjoyed her job.

"And you know what Oprah says," said Virginia. She sat up straighter, her brown bob framing her elegant swan neck. "Follow your passion. If you do what you love, you'll never work a day in your life!"

"I know, I know," said Ursula. "I'm just really trying not to take advice from billionaires right now. Especially ones like Oprah who are so self-actualized they just shimmer their way through life. Like, they've been at the top of Maslow's pyramid for so long they forget what it's like to be at the bottom, where you're just clinging to the last rung for dear life—and your cat is clinging to *you* for dear life. It's so precarious."

Phil rolled his eyes. "You're on the third rung at least."

"And Oprah hasn't forgotten what it's like to be at the bottom. She's very self-aware," said Virginia defensively. She considered Oprah to be her unofficial mentor and North Star.

"Speaking of billionaires," said Issa. "How did the lunch with Mike Rutherford go? Isn't that why you stayed in the city this weekend?"

"Who's Mike?" Virginia perked up, hopeful that he was a romantic interest. She was one of those people who claimed to "*love* love." Especially new love.

"He's the lead investor for one of my clients, and he wants me to consult for him," said Ursula. "He runs a hedge fund and he's a VC."

"Mike Rutherford?" said Matt, who worked in finance. "He's a legend."

Ursula nodded. "So I've heard. I mean, this isn't really in my wheelhouse, but it would pay well. And there's this thing I've been considering . . ."

"Tell them about The Arc!" Issa clapped her hands together, and Eric gave her shoulder an affectionate squeeze in response to her rising energy.

"I'm tired of talking about it," said Ursula. "You tell them."

Issa happily obliged. After she laid out all the details, Virginia asked, "So there's no choice? You just get paired with the perfect person?"

She and Matt briefly locked eyes, each wondering whether they might have missed an opportunity by using standard dating apps.

"No choice," said Ursula. "They do all the decision-making for you."

"The glorious flipside of freedom," said Steven, processing it. "Sounds like heaven."

"The Arc. Yes, I've heard of it," said Phil, plucking a radish out of his salad and placing it daintily on Steven's plate. "That's how my coworker met her wife. She said it was amazing, but she can't talk about it."

"Why not?" asked Steven.

"There's some NDA you have to sign. It's all super confidential," said Phil. "I don't know why. But she seems really happy, and her wife is great. You'd think they've been together forever, but they actually met like a year ago."

Ursula caught Issa's eyes, which were sparkling with excitement.

"I already told her she has to do it," said Issa.

"Don't you think it's a little creepy?" asked Ursula, looking around the table for someone to talk her out of it. "They really pry into your life. They collect a lot of information. And honestly, if there was a perfect person out there for me, wouldn't I have found him already?"

"Not necessarily," said Phil. "Some women have horrible taste in men."

"Excuse you," said Ursula, fake-offended. The fact that her friends knew her so well gave her a warm rush.

Phil shrugged, unapologetic. He reclaimed the uneaten radish off Steven's plate, sniffed it, took a tiny bite, and put it back down. "Remember that guy Damian?"

Ursula covered her eyes.

"Damian Stallion!" squawked Issa.

"Damian Stallion!" Phil lit up with the recollection. "I walked into my apartment one morning, and Ursula was in *my* bed—god knows how she got into the apartment—and Damian Stallion was on the Flip'n'Fuck."

Matt was trying to follow. "What's the Flip'n'Fuck?"

"Oh, it was this futon thing I had in my living room in my early twenties," said Phil. "For guests."

"And Damian was this very hot, very dumb waiter who worked with me when I was a hostess after college," explained Issa. She'd spent two years working the front of house at a sceney SoHo restaurant before she went back to school to get her architecture degree. "And we were so young and poor. Remember?" Thanks to family money, Issa had never *actually* been poor, but she had feigned it well during her early twenties as she waited for her friends to catch up financially. "All these models would come into the restaurant, and they didn't actually eat. They just pushed their food around their plates. And then Damian would bus the plates back to the kitchen, and we would just eat whatever they left on the plate."

"That's disgusting," said Phil.

Matt nodded in agreement. It *was* pretty disgusting.

"It seemed strategic at the time," said Issa. She turned to Eric, saying, "You would eat Naomi Campbell's leftover salad, wouldn't you?"

Eric paused to mull the concept.

"I wonder where Damian is now . . ." continued Issa.

"He's in LA," said Ursula. She occasionally checked his Instagram out of curiosity and nostalgia. Back in those days, fresh out of college, she had been considered the most responsible of her friends. Eating the cast-off food of supermodels was one of the less questionable things Issa had done during that era. But slowly, over the years, the dynamic had shifted. Now Issa was as passionate about her investment portfolio as she had once been about cocaine. And it was Ursula who was leading a less structured, more impulsive life. That said, none of them did cocaine anymore, which was for the best. If there was one lesson Ursula took from her twenties, it was that nothing constructive happened after 2 A.M. They were all relieved that their long white nights were behind them.

"So, are you going to do it?" asked Virginia.

"Do what?" Ursula was still thinking about Damian Stallion.

"The Arc! What's your hesitation?"

"I just don't know if you can really optimize a relationship. I'm not sure you should even try. I hate that concept: optimization. Who even knows what's optimal? *We* don't know. We might think something is optimal, but then its ramifications turn out to be disastrous. What one generation thinks is optimal is the next generation's pitfall. Right? And even if you knew what was optimal, can you really pre-program love? It seems so unnatural." Fireflies had begun to appear, and one hovered patiently near Ursula's head as she spoke, its bottom half glowing warmly.

"But you said it's not an algorithm. It's not as if a robot is going to matchmake you," said Issa. "They use all different types of tools, many of which are incredibly human. Primal, even. Don't they smell your armpits or something? I think it sounds *very* natural."

"Well, then maybe it's just me. My attitude. Maybe I'm too old and jaded to even be open to finding love—via The Arc or any other method," said Ursula.

"Oh, please. You're spry as a street cat!" said Phil, refusing to let Ursula slither out of this bizarre but exciting opportunity. "Plus, they guarantee it will work."

"But do they always get it right?" asked Steven. "I mean, what's the margin of error?"

Ursula batted a lone cherry tomato around her plate with a fork. "Dr. Vidal said that if they are able to match you—which they can't for everyone—then it's a hundred-percent success rate."

"Dang," said Issa, her mouth full of burger.

"I think it's great," said Phil. "If I could start over, I'd definitely do it."

Steven batted his shoulder. Virginia and Matt exchanged skeptical glances again.

"I don't know," Virginia said. "I *want* to think it could work. It's just hard to *actually* believe it."

"Exactly," Ursula said. "I want to believe it, too."

"Just do it," said Eric, who had been quiet as usual. Though Ursula's personal dramas occasionally exasperated him, he enjoyed the theater of her life. His own existence had always been quite orderly. Having grown up on the Upper West Side in a cerebral Jewish family, he was now the managing editor of a prominent political magazine. "What do you have to lose?"

"Exactly $40,500," said Ursula. "I mean, would you pay that much for him?" Ursula asked Virginia, gesturing to Matt. "And would you pay $50,000 for her?"

They laughed. "Of course," he said, pecking Virginia on the cheek.

Phil looked Steven up and down. "You're worth at least $1.2 million. Maybe $1.3."

"I'd pay $2 million for you," Issa said to Eric. "If I could take out a mortgage."

"Ursula, who's to say what the right way to find love is? None of us know what we're doing!" said Steven, turning to Phil. "Just because this guy turned up at my sister's party five years ago doesn't mean we met the 'right' way."

"It's true," agreed Phil. "Open up your mind, Ursula. You have such a crazy, creative brain. Get a little creative when it comes to your love life."

"All that matters in the end is that you find the right person," said Issa. "It doesn't matter *how* you find him."

"Or *her*," said Phil, holding up his hands to suggest anything could happen.

"And it would be awesome if you found him—or her—through The Arc," said Eric.

Everyone nodded enthusiastically as a deep *bang* reverberated through the darkened sky, followed by a fizzling sound. *Bang, bang, bang.* More fizzles.

They couldn't see the fireworks from Ursula's backyard, but they were too comfortable to go up to the roof for a better view. This felt sufficient—being gathered among best friends around a low-lit table, shoes kicked off, fireflies blinking, the suggestion of fireworks in the distance, and a sense of promise in the hot, still air.

Chapter 10

Mallory was suspicious. Whenever Ursula took her suitcase out of the closet, the cat knew something was afoot. She was either going to be abandoned at home or shoved into her carrier and driven god knows where. Wanting to prevent both outcomes, she alternated between hiding under the couch (to prevent her own kidnapping) and sitting in the suitcase (to keep Ursula from leaving).

"Don't worry, my little dippin' dot," said Ursula, scratching between Mallory's silken ears. "I'm only going to be gone for a little while. One hundred sixty-eight hours, not that you know what an hour is. But don't worry about it. Darrell is going to take care of you." Darrell was their upstairs neighbor, whom Mallory tolerated.

The Arc had sent Ursula explicit instructions about what to bring, what not to bring, and how to prepare for her sojourn. She was to arrive at 9 A.M., having fasted that morning so they could begin with blood work. She needed only a few casual outfits, pajamas, and workout clothes. The instructions said she could include one "comfort item." She looked around her bedroom: the carved-wood moose figurine she'd had since childhood, the hot water bottle that had its own cashmere turtleneck sweater, the malachite pyramid she'd bought from a voodoo priestess in New Orleans. Her eye settled on a tiny rubber wolf—the size of a peanut—that she took on all her travels. She called it "Travel Wolf," and although this wasn't technically a trip, she decided it counted as a journey, during which she would need her trusty companion. She slipped Travel Wolf into her toiletry bag for good luck.

Once packed, Ursula made some chamomile tea and contemplated how much she should reveal in her "Out of Office" message. She had told her clients she was going on a silent yoga retreat in the Adirondacks to justify going dark for an entire week. Since getting her first job after college, she had not gone more than a few days without checking work email; and in recent years, she hadn't gone more than a few hours. She was both stressed and exhilarated by the prospect of fully disconnecting. She typed:

> Thanks for your email. I'm currently in the woods and unreachable—yes, completely unreachable—but will get back to you when I return to the office on Wednesday, July 25.
>
> For urgent matters, please contact my associate Sabrina Davis (sdavis@anonymousandco.com).

She stared at the screen. She had spent the last week prepping Sabrina and assuring her she could handle anything that transpired while Ursula was "out of pocket" (a term they both hated). At twenty-five, Sabrina was one of the most capable people Ursula had ever met, let alone hired (first as an intern when Sabrina was a senior at NYU, and then into the full-time role of "strategic audacity associate" once she graduated). Sabrina worshipped Ursula, and despite her youth, she had an old-school work ethic that set her apart from her peers, who too often expected their entry-level jobs to be fulfilling *and* well-compensated *and* fun *and* soul-nourishing from day one. But not Sabrina. A steely-eyed pragmatist, she was an old soul with a get-it-done approach to everything she was assigned—from administrative tasks like spreadsheet management to creative challenges like tagline brainstorming. And although Ursula was her mentor and ten years her senior, she often felt anchored by Sabrina's steady presence and innate self-assurance. Though she was still at the outset of her career, Sabrina seemed to know that she was valuable, that the agency was lucky to have her— and that replacing her would be effortful and difficult. Ursula was still working to establish that sense of steady confidence in herself, and she admired Sabrina's poise. Ursula was determined to help facilitate her young employee's professional ascent, and she wanted all the same things for Sabrina that she wanted for herself: success, money, love, freedom, peace. A dynamic life without compromise. Feeling a mix of pride and affection, Ursula updated her closing line:

> For urgent matters, please contact my exceedingly capable associate Sabrina Davis (sdavis@anonymousandco.com).

She slapped her laptop shut and picked Mallory up from the couch. "You sleep with me tonight," Ursula whispered, carrying the cat into the bedroom and gently setting her down at the foot of the bed. Mallory waited a moment before hopping down and disappearing into the closet, her preferred place for "me time" and sulking.

At 7 A.M., Ursula's alarm—the song "Once in a Lifetime" by Talking Heads—sounded. Nervous, excited, and already alert, she skipped hitting Snooze and headed to the shower, where she assiduously shaved her legs. Again, she realized she was preparing for her visit to The Arc as if it were a first date. Or perhaps this was more of a second date. She pulled on jeans from a vintage store in LA, a white T-shirt, and a pair of raffia sandals designed by a friend in Morocco. Plum-colored lip stain on her lips. Cruelty-free, lash-amplifying mascara. Rounded sunglasses with thin gold-wire frames. A silk scarf from a vintage store in Copenhagen.

"Good morning, my little squirrel," she said to Mallory as she entered the kitchen. The cat was on the counter, mewling for breakfast. They butted foreheads, as they did every morning. Ursula poured the all-natural, grain-free kibble into a bowl—no time for Mallory's food puzzle today—and set it down on the floor. "I love you, and I'm going to try to find you a father."

In response, the cat buried her face in the kibble.

Ursula scrawled a note for Darrell ("She prefers to be scratched between the ears, but not under the chin—note that this is different from most cats."), grabbed her bag, and tried to ignore the voice in her head that insisted this would never work and that she should temper her hopes. "Shut up," she said to the voice. "You don't know my life." As she walked out the door, her phone lit up with an incoming text from her mother that read: *Daily Death Check!*

It was a ritual they'd begun earlier that year, when Orla had gone to the doctor and been diagnosed with both high and low blood pressure. "It's called labile hypertension. Dr. Nixon said I'm one of the top-ten lability cases he's ever seen," Orla had boasted.

"That's not a good thing, Mom. Are you sure you're taking care of yourself?" Ursula had asked.

"Yes! I can still do a full lotus pose, for crying out loud," said Orla, as if that settled it. "But people my age *do* die. I know some who already have. And if I were to expire in my studio—which could happen—no one would find me. So I think we need a system. How about I text you every day to let you know I'm alive? If you don't hear from me by noon, you text me. And if you don't hear back, it means I'm dead. We'll call it Daily Death Check." Her mother delighted in this type of macabre humor.

Ursula hadn't wanted to tell her mother about The Arc yet, but she now realized she had to let her know they'd need to put their Daily Death Checks on pause for a week. This would require an explanation, so instead of heading to the subway, she called a car, and then dialed her mom's number.

She did her best to explain what The Arc was about, without going into too much detail.

"God, it's so complicated nowadays," said Orla.

"What is?" Ursula asked, as the car pulled up. She handed her bag to the driver and slid into the back of his sedan.

"Mating," said her mother. "I mean, for me it was easy. Efficient, even. Meet, make love, have a baby, and then, *boom*, he was dead by the time you were three, and I was free to do whatever I wanted with the rest of my life. It was bliss."

"Incredibly efficient, Mom. Good work," said Ursula. She loved her mother, but she didn't want her mother's life. She wanted something bigger, wilder, richer, something rife with daily surprise but anchored by a solid, lasting love. If her hypothetical partner died, she wanted to care. She wanted to be devastated.

"I don't mean to be insensitive," said her mother. She had that distracted tone in her voice; Ursula could tell she was painting. "It's just so different now. The logarithms, the chats, the apps."

"Algorithms," Ursula corrected her.

"It's not very *romantic*," said her mother. She wasn't helping.

"The Arc isn't an app, Mom," said Ursula.

"Well, love and capitalism don't mix," said her mother. "Love as a business? I don't like it. You deserve something unhindered by the pressures of the marketplace, something real."

"But hopefully this will yield something real," said Ursula.

"It just doesn't sit right with me," Orla went on. "I know! You should go to one of those ashrams in India. That's where you could find a nice, enlightened man. Just like that woman in *Eat, Pray, Fuck*."

"*Eat, Pray, Love*. And she didn't find him in India. She found him in Bali. And they're divorced now, so . . ." Ursula looked out the window as the car began to climb the bridge, Manhattan sprawling out before her in the brilliant morning sun.

"Oh," said her mother. Then suddenly, with energy: "What about Danny? Don't you want to reconnect with Danny?"

"Danny is gay, Mom," said Ursula, picturing her first high-school boyfriend, who had been incredibly sweet. They were still friends, but she rarely saw him because he now lived in Berlin.

"So? You can be with a gay man. It's 2018—you can do anything!"

"Well, I don't think I want to marry a gay man," said Ursula. "Because I'm a heterosexual woman." She contemplated it for a minute and realized it wouldn't be the worst thing. Actually, it could be kind of great.

"Just think about it," said Orla. There was a clattering noise in the background. "Damn it. Ursula, I have to go. Call me when you're released, and I'll try not to die in the meantime. Love you." The phone went dead.

When Ursula arrived at The Arc, she rode the elevator up, walked down the dim hallway, and waited calmly as the walls slid closed around her. She was a pro now. But this time, instead of the side wall opening into the waiting room, the opposite wall slid open and revealed an elegant concrete staircase that wound down and around to the right. She followed it, and when she reached the bottom, the woman with the slick ponytail—Nadia—greeted her. "Welcome, Ursula," she said warmly, taking her suitcase. "So nice to see you again. I'll show you to your room." Ursula followed her down another lantern-lit hallway. Nadia waved a small metal device over the wall, and a door slid open, revealing an elegant suite within: a bar area, a living room with a large TV, a spacious bathroom with a rain shower and a freestanding soaking tub, and a king-sized bed made up with beautifully arranged ivory-toned bedding—crisp hospital corners, a diamond-textured quilt, four perfectly fluffed pillows. The suite had no windows, but its walls and floors were made from light-hued wood, perhaps ash, that gave the space a bright, earthy, Scandinavian feel. Ursula didn't even miss the sunlight.

"In about ten minutes, my colleague Sasha will come by to explain how everything will work while you're here. Then she'll do your blood work, and then breakfast!" said Nadia. "Oh, before I go, could I ask for your phone and any other Wi-Fi–enabled devices you have? We'll keep them safe until we return them on your final day."

Ursula riffled through her bag. Her phone had a text from Issa that said: *Go get 'em, Tiger! See you on the other side!* She powered it down and handed it over. Nadia smiled and then slipped out the door, which slid closed behind her.

It occurred to Ursula that she had no idea how to open the suite door if she needed to get out, and she began to feel trapped. But the space was so comfortably and tastefully appointed that she quickly relaxed. In fact, this was one of the nicest rooms she'd ever set foot in. She unpacked her few clothes and arranged them in the closet, whose built-in shelves offered more space than necessary. She went into the bathroom to check her makeup, which hadn't shifted since she left her apartment an hour ago. She browsed the bookshelf in the living area, which featured an array of hardcovers ranging from classics to contemporary: *Anna Karenina, Lolita, Jane Eyre, Zen and the Art of Motorcycle Maintenance, Wild, The Power Broker*, and *Men Explain Things to Me*. Against the odds, there was even a copy of her favorite book, *Light Years* by James Salter. She tried to recall if she'd mentioned it to Dr. Vidal or referenced it in any of her correspondence with The Arc, but she was sure she had not.

She heard a soft chime that she guessed was a doorbell.

"Come in?" she called. The rectangular door panel slid open.

A petite woman wearing thick-framed black glasses entered. "Ursula? I'm Sasha. Such a pleasure to meet you." She had a British accent similar to Dr. Vidal's and looked like she could have been related to her, although Sasha was younger—probably in her late twenties.

They shook hands, and Sasha gestured toward the sitting area in the living room.

"So I imagine you probably have questions about what's going to happen over the next seven days," said Sasha, settling into a cane armchair with thick, cream-colored cushions. "Why don't I talk you through the process, and then if anything is unclear, just let me know."

Nervous and excited, Ursula nodded from her spot on the caramel-hued leather couch. This felt like the first day of an incredibly intimidating summer camp.

"On day one—that's today," Sasha explained, "we'll get the basic things out of the way: blood work, some free-response questions just to get you thinking, and we'll set you up with a device that will monitor things like your heart rate, depth of sleep, hydration level, and hormonal surges. Nothing too invasive—we just want to gauge how your mind and body are responding to various situations and stimuli. Then in the afternoon: a treat. You'll get a massage, assuming you'd like one? And in the evening, we'll teach you a specific type of meditation that we'll be employing throughout the rest of the week as we get to know you better. Over the next six days, it's really going to be just a series of conversations, activities, physical challenges, exercises, and meditations that we can use to map who you are and how you vibrate on various levels. And on your final day, day seven, you'll spend some time with Dr. Vidal drilling down into some of the more emotionally demanding parts of this process. We call it Emotional Mining, but just think of it as an in-depth therapy session or a conversation with someone you truly trust. So that's the gist. Any questions?"

Ursula opened her mouth, but Sasha cut her off. "I should emphasize, you don't *have* to have questions. In fact, we think this process works best when there's an air of mystery around it, so no pressure to ask anything."

Ursula paused. She was either going to ask a hundred questions or none, so she went with none. "No questions for now."

"Great!" said Sasha, sounding relieved. She punched something into her smartwatch and then looked up cheerfully. "Alright, so our first stop is the medical lab. You can follow me."

They left Ursula's room, and the wall panel slid closed behind them.

"All of your things are completely secure," Sasha assured her. "But I should let you know: both your suite and the common spaces are equipped with cameras—except for the bathrooms, of course. So everything you do will be recorded. But don't let it worry you. It's just part of our process that helps us paint the fullest possible picture of who you are."

Ursula expected as much. After all, she was here to find a life partner, a perfect match. She understood that couldn't happen unless she was honest and transparent and, yes, closely observed, throughout the process.

"It's going to be a busy seven days," said Sasha. "But most people really enjoy it. There's no right or wrong way to do it. Just be yourself— whatever that may mean. And have fun."

Sasha stopped halfway down the hallway and placed her palm on the wall. A panel opened, revealing a small room with one of those molcajete chairs and some medical equipment—a scale, a blood pressure monitor.

"Just a quick stop so I can draw your blood and take your vitals before breakfast. Please step onto the scale."

Ursula complied. Her weight was the same as always. She'd been a bit heavier in college, but after a series of breakups in her twenties, she'd descended into sadness and inadvertently lost ten pounds that never came back. Heartbreak had its advantages.

"Great. You can take a seat," said Sasha.

Ursula lowered herself into the chair, inhaling uneasily in antici-pation of the blood draw. "I'm never good at this," she said.

"Not to worry," said Sasha. "First, we're just going to cleanse the space." She pushed on the wall, and a small cupboard opened. She pulled out a bundle of dried sage, struck a match, lit the sage, and gently dragged it through the air, back and forth five times, before rest-ing it in an agate ashtray. The room filled with an earthy, herbal haze.

"There we are," Sasha soothed. "I'll just take your blood pressure."

She wrapped a velvet, Velcro-backed band around Ursula's upper arm with intense focus and care. She pumped, waited. "Ninety-six over fifty-two. That's magnificent."

Ursula smiled, proud of her low blood pressure. Sometimes it dipped so low that she briefly saw flashing lights when she stood up after a long period of sitting.

"Okay, ready?" said Sasha, as she tied an elegant gold rubber band around Ursula's arm. "Please make a fist."

Ursula squeezed her eyes shut as she balled up her left hand.

"You have stunning veins," Sasha said, softly running her fingers over Ursula's inner elbow. "Just gorgeous. Release your fist."

Ursula felt a rushing through her forearm and braced herself for pain, but felt nothing. She waited for a few seconds. "Tell me when," she said through clenched teeth.

"Actually, we're almost done," said Sasha, untying the rubber band. She gently withdrew the needle and swabbed Ursula's arm with an alcohol-soaked cotton pad. Then she spritzed Ursula's arm with lavender mist. "That's it!"

Ursula looked down. The needle mark was undetectable. No red-ness or soreness whatsoever. A far cry from her last blood draw at her physician's office, which had left a bruise that lasted for weeks.

"And now the fun part," said Sasha, pushing another area of the wall to release a drawer that contained a tray full of rings in differ-ent sizes and materials—silver, gold, rose gold, matte black, Bakelite.

"Believe it or not, these rings monitor everything from your heart rate to your sleep cycles to your perspiration level. Which one would you like to wear for the remainder of your time here?"

Ursula tried a few on before selecting a gold signet ring that reminded her of the one she'd lost during a drunken make-out session on a Nantucket beach when she was in college; she still felt sad when she thought about it. This new version fit her pinky perfectly.

"Love that on you. Okay! You can follow me," Sasha chirped.

Ursula followed her down the hallway. Another gentle push on the wall, and a panel shifted to reveal a high-ceilinged kitchen with a six-burner gas range and a marble island with three leather stools. There was an attractive man—too attractive, really—standing at the stove, stirring eggs in a cast-iron pan.

"This is my colleague Jack," Sasha explained to Ursula. "And Jack, this is Ursula!"

Jack tossed some chopped chives into the pan, flipped off the burner, and turned to face them. He was dressed in slim sweatpants and a white T-shirt that skimmed his significant pectoral muscles. He wore glasses with tortoiseshell frames, and his thick black hair was a bit disheveled, as if he'd just rolled out of bed after a rigorous morning romp.

"Nice to meet you, Ursula." Jack held out his hand. When she took it, he pulled her into a half hug that lasted a beat longer than she expected. She could feel her heart rate increase, and she thought about the ring on her finger. Did someone in The Arc's control tower now know that she would definitely have sex with Jack if given the opportunity?

"Breakfast is ready," said Jack, as he pulled out of the hug. "Don't be shy. I did scrambled eggs with organic feta and local chives, buttermilk biscuits, fruit, toast, and apple-cider doughnuts from Kenworthy Farm, upstate. But before I go: Coffee? Tea? Latte? Matcha latte? Kombucha?"

"Wow," said Ursula, collecting herself. "Can you do an almond milk latte?"

"Absolutely," said Jack, spinning around. He pulled out a drawer

in the freezer that contained at least a dozen varieties of coffee, ranging from everyday commercial brands to well-known franchises to
obscure coffee-snob favorites. Ursula chose what looked to be a fancy
small-batch variety from Kona.

"Niiiiiice," said Jack. It seemed that The Arc's staff were pro-
grammed to compliment the client's choices. Either that, or Ursula
was passing every test.

Sasha motioned for Ursula to take a seat at the marble island.
"While you have breakfast, you have some work to do," she explained,
pulling a tablet from a hidden drawer in the island. It lit up with a
welcome screen that said: *1,001 Questions for Ursula Byrne.*

"Just a basic questionnaire about some of your interests and preferences," said Sasha. "It's a fun one."

Jack set down a warm plate piled with fluffy scrambled eggs in
front of Ursula and then a small basket of doughnuts. He handed her
a napkin and silverware, and then turned back to get the latte. When
he put the mug down, Ursula noticed that he'd managed to perfectly
render The Arc's minimalist logo in foam, with the tail of the "C"
creating an arc across the surface of the liquid.

"You have about an hour to complete this, or to get as far as you
can. The key is not to overthink any of it," Sasha said, redirecting
Ursula's attention to the tablet. "When you're done, just hit this"—
she indicated a button on the side of the island—"and we'll whisk
you off to your next activity. Have fun with it. And help yourself to
anything in the kitchen."

Jack gave a little wave and he and Sasha exited the kitchen together, leaving Ursula alone, or as alone as one could be within these
walls.

She lifted a forkful of eggs to her mouth. Goddamn, they were
good. Perfect texture (cooked low and slow), perfect seasoning (salt,
pepper, and a mysterious little kick). Jack knew what he was doing.
He knew *exactly* what he was doing. She wondered if she could just
take him home and be done with it. But no. No. That was not how
this worked. There was no shortcut, and she had 166 hours left.

She hit the Begin button on the tablet. The first question was: *How do you feel about picnics?*

Ursula mulled. Her first instinct was to say that she loved them, but then she began to think more specifically about her real-life experiences. She had attempted to stage a number of romantic picnics over the years, only to forget the wine opener, or get swarmed by mosquitos, or spill mustard on her dress, or get into a fight with her picnic partner mere moments after sitting down. In the free-response field, she wrote: I like them in theory, but often find them unfulfilling in practice.

The next few questions all had to do with food. *If your pasta can't be perfect, is it better for it to be one minute undercooked or one minute overcooked?* (One minute undercooked.) *When making corn on the cob, do you bring the water to a boil with the cobs in it, or do you boil the water before adding the cobs?* (Boil the water first.) *Is this something you feel strongly about?* (Yes.) *Have you ever gotten into a debate or altercation about which method is best?* (Yes. On a few occasions.) *In retrospect, was it something worth arguing about?* (Yes. Absolutely.) *What's worse: an underdressed salad or an overdressed salad?* (Overdressed.) *When you make pancakes at home, do you use pure maple syrup, or are the imitation brands just as good?* (Pure. I'm not a barbarian.) *Do you insist that the maple syrup be warmed up?* (When possible.) *Do you post pictures of your food on social media?* (I have a few times in the past, but I regret it. I would not do that now.)

Then there were questions about work. *How do you feel about your current job?* (Committed but conflicted.) *Is your career a significant part of your identity?* (Yes.) *Professionally, do you believe you're doing what you were born to do?* (No.) *Do you "live to work" or "work to live"?* (Live to work. But I'm very intrigued by the inverse.) *What conditions do you require to do your best work?* (Creative autonomy. Silence. Reese's Peanut Butter Cups.) *How does the phrase "Let's touch base" make you feel?* (Annoyed. Aggressive. Anarchistic.) *Do you agree there's no "I" in team?* (It depends on the team.) *What's more important to you: feeling useful or being rich?* (Are those mutually exclusive? I'd prefer to have both.) *Do you expect your partner to make more money than you do?* (Not necessarily, but I wouldn't mind.) *Do you hope to be financially supported by your partner someday?* (No, that's insulting.) *Would you rather be part of a "cute couple" or a "power couple"?* (Power couple. But we can also be cute.)

There were questions related to sleep. *How often do you have nightmares?* (A few times a week.) *What was your last nightmare about?* (I was playing in the US Open finals without a racquet, and Tom Hanks was my opponent. But he was very mean—and then I realized it wasn't Tom Hanks at all. It was a werewolf.) *What single hour of the day is your brain sharpest?* (10–11 A.M.) *What color or pattern do you prefer your sheets to be?* (Bright white.) *Do you sleep with a technological device within three feet of your brain?* (Yes.) *Do you worry about how electromagnetic fields affect your sleep?* (No. Should I?) *What happens if you don't get enough sleep?* (I'm a monster.)

There were questions that felt both random and significant. *Do you let your phone go completely dead before you charge it, or do you plug it in while it still has battery remaining?* (Plug it in while battery remains.) *If you come back as an animal in your next life, what animal would you like to be?* (A maned wolf. They're very rare.) *On a scale from 1 (Cat-averse) to 10 (Cat-enthusiastic), how do you feel about cats?* (10.) *On the same scale, how do you feel about dogs?* (10.) *What's a scarring childhood memory?* (When my mother jokingly held me over the lobster tank at the seafood market, but my foot dipped into it for a second.) *What's something you hate that most other people seem to like?* (Bowling!) *Have you ever used the hashtag #squadgoals?* (No.) *Name three things that are overrated.* (Silicon Valley. The Founding Fathers. Truffles.) *Name three things that are underrated.* (Hearts of palm. Neon yellow. Providence, Rhode Island.) *What are you afraid of?* (Possums.)

Then came sex. *What's your attitude toward sex? If an alien from outer space asked you to describe sex, what would you say? If an alien from outer space asked you to have sex, what would you say? How many people have you kissed? How old were you when you had intercourse for the first time? Would you say you have Victorian values? How many people have you had sex with? What's the most memorable sexual experience you've had, and why? Have you ever engaged in group sex, and, if so, what was the configuration? What is your attitude toward monogamy? Does the idea of a Dionysian bacchanal excite you? Do you ever cry during sex? Do you like to snuggle after sex? What's your attitude toward spooning? Do you ever feel numb or indifferent during sex? When it comes to your sexual preferences, what's something your (platonic) friends would be shocked to learn about you? When it comes to your sexual preferences, what's something you've been shocked to learn about yourself?*

The questions went on, in increasingly random order. *Top three ice cream flavors? What was the last animal you hugged, and why? What's the plant you most relate to? If you were in a permanently nocturnal state, what would you choose as a profession? Do people consistently tell you that you look like a specific celebrity / public figure, and if so, how does this comparison make you feel? Are you attracted to "bad boys"? Regardless of how you answered the previous question, would those who know you well say that you are attracted to "bad boys"? What is your place in your family's birth order, and are you happy with that place? If you had to watch the same film every day for the rest of your life, which film would you choose and why? Have you ever ridden on the back of a mysterious man's motorcycle or moped? Do you ever fall asleep on the couch, but then move to your bed in the middle of the night? To what extent do you worry about your fertility timeline? How does the statement "you're just like your mother" make you feel? When walking down the street with your partner, do you like when he puts his hand in the back pocket of your jeans? What's your single greatest regret in life?*

And on and on. By the time she answered the final question—*Do you believe in love?* (I'm not sure, but I want to.)—Ursula was both exhausted and exhilarated. She had learned things about herself, and she had eaten the full plate of eggs and two and a half doughnuts. She wanted more of everything. She wanted to know more about the depths of her preferences. She got up from her stool and walked around the island to the cabinets. She opened one to reveal a huge array of snacks: Cheetos, organic impostor Cheetos, raw almonds, beef jerky, South African biltong, Goldfish crackers, medjool dates, seaweed strips. She picked up a box of Fruit by the Foot and was instantly transported to her elementary school dining hall. She couldn't help trying one of these, for old times' sake. She reached into the box, tore open a wrapper, and unspooled the three-foot-long fruit strip. She began chomping along its length and was halfway through when one of the panel doors slid open.

"Oooh, Fruit by the Foot," Sasha said, entering the room. "My favorite. Are you ready for a few more exercises?"

Ursula nodded enthusiastically, slurping the final foot of fruit tape into her mouth. She had been at The Arc for just a few hours, and she'd already surrendered her bodily fluids, developed a crush, feasted on eggs and doughnuts, and mulled 1,001 questions that, although random, left her feeling newly curious about herself. She thought back to the dating apps she'd previously tried. The interminable swiping—left, left, left, left, right, left, left, left, left—based on self-reported crumbs of information about the other person. The Arc was a different animal entirely.

Over the next few hours, Ursula completed a battery of tests: IQ (148), Myers-Briggs (INFP), Enneagram (Type 3—The Achiever), and Ayurvedic stress type (Vata). She submitted her exact birth time and location so that The Arc's resident astrologer could read her natal chart. (She knew this information not because she read much into her sign—Aries—but because her mother had often told her the story of her birth, how she had entered the world at one minute past midnight on April 3, during a full moon, no less. And it had happened fast—her mother only labored for seven hours before Ursula shot forth.) Then she was given a tablet with images of faces, and she had one second to respond to each (stating "yes" or "no"), using the following guideline: *Would you be excited to kiss this person?*

After Ursula completed those assessments, Sasha escorted her to a small screening room with just one large leather recliner. She hooked up a number of electrodes to Ursula's head—"just to monitor brain activity and areas of emotional resonance"—and told her to sit back and relax. Over the next hour, Ursula watched a number of video clips that spanned genres and subjects: Eddie Murphy stand-up from the '80s, the pottery wheel scene from *Ghost*, funny animal bloopers, a sopping Colin Firth emerging from the pond in *Pride & Prejudice*, bits from Ken Burns's documentary on national parks, scenes from a Spanish bullfight, footage of an actual vaginal birth, grainy footage of couples skiing in the Swiss Alps circa 1950, a clip of Whitney Houston singing the national anthem at the 1991 Super Bowl (which brought tears to Ursula's eyes), Al Pacino's plane monologue from the film *Scent of a Woman*, dramatic shots of long romantic embraces, abrupt cuts to hard-core pornography, Mao Zedong standing very still, and finally, an aerial scene of a warmly lit village under falling snow.

By the time Sasha came to get her, Ursula felt oddly euphoric. That morning's purge of information had been a catharsis; and the discordant visual stimulation of the last hour had been so discombobulating that she now felt like a worn-out baby, ready for its nap.

"How are you feeling?" Sasha asked, removing the suction cups from Ursula's scalp. "Up for a massage?"

Ursula was thrilled. "That would be amazing."

"Follow me." Sasha led her down the hall and into a wood-walled dressing room that smelled like cedar. "You can leave your clothes here"—she gestured to a large marble cube—"and choose a robe." There were five neutral-toned robes hanging on the wall, all made of slightly different materials in colors that ranged from bright white to dark beige. Ursula couldn't help but quickly name the hues in her head: "Blizzard, Vanilla, Champagne, Sahara, Barley." Once a color-namer, always a color-namer.

Ursula chose the vanilla-colored, waffle-textured, Egyptian-cotton robe.

"Beautiful choice," said Sasha. "Follow me and I'll introduce you to Björn."

Björn was hot. Very hot. Tan, blond, tall, lean, with a strong, trustworthy presence. He looked like he could ride a bike very fast. He was definitely someone's type—but not Ursula's type, which came as a relief.

After she chose her aromatherapy scent—"Winter Wind over Beach Dunes"—Björn told her to lie down, and he placed his warm hands on her spine, rocking her back and forth gently, as if she were a precious and delicate object. He began gliding his hands over her back in smooth, long, melting strokes, and within minutes, she was asleep.

That evening, after Ursula had been allowed an hour of downtime in her suite, where she had eaten a large bowl of butternut squash ravioli, Sasha appeared at her door again.

"How are you feeling?" Sasha asked.

Ursula had never been asked about her feelings so frequently, and after one of the strangest days of her life, she wasn't sure how to articulate them. Overall, there was a pleasantness, a calmness. She missed Mallory, but other than that, she felt she could happily live at The Arc for weeks on end.

"I'm feeling . . . good?"

"It's normal not to know how you're feeling at this point," said Sasha. "And that's exactly what our meditation exercises will help you to explore. Follow me."

Another hallway, another secret door, another windowless room. This one was square, perhaps eight feet by eight feet, with a small mat on the floor. There was a ledge on one wall that held three flickering candles in smoked-glass jars.

"You'll be here for the next hour," said Sasha, "and the audio will guide you, so you'll know exactly what to do. I'll be back in sixty minutes to get you, and then bedtime."

Ursula realized she had no idea what time it actually was. She hadn't seen daylight since she had entered The Arc that morning; and there were no clocks anywhere.

"Just take a seat here." Sasha gestured to the mat. "Lotus position is best." She touched her digital watch again, and then slipped out, the door closing smoothly behind her.

Ursula sat on the mat. After a minute of silence, a man's voice began speaking. She guessed he was older—maybe in his seventies—and Indian. He sounded exactly like her friend Aditi's uncle from Delhi.

"This is day one. Tonight, we will spend time on our earlobes.

We will become completely sensitized to our earlobes—just our ear-lobes. If you start thinking about anything besides your earlobes, stop. Bring your attention back to your earlobes. Now close your eyes. Feel the earlobes. Feel any sensation that arises. Maybe hot, maybe cold. Maybe itching, maybe tingling, maybe pain, maybe something pleas-ant. Do not judge the feeling. Simply notice the sensation on the ear-lobe. Remain nonjudging. Always nonjudging. Always nonjudging."

The man began chanting in a language that Ursula could not iden-tify, and she turned her attention to her ears. It occurred to her that while she had looked at her earlobes many times, she'd never actually made an effort to "feel" them. They felt numb and neutral at first. But then, she noticed warmth, then slight twitching. The man's voice faded out and Ursula was alone in deep silence, in near-darkness except for the candles, alone with her earlobes. She wondered what this was all about. She wondered if she'd be able to sleep tonight. She thought of Jack and his perfect scrambled eggs with the little flecks of chive. Damn it—she was supposed to be feeling her earlobes. She brought her attention back. Her lobes were still there, still feeling warm. Actually, feeling slightly electric now.

This went on for what felt like ages. Her thoughts spiraled but then came back: thoughts, earlobes, thoughts, earlobes. Over and over and over. It was effortful, but boring at the same time. Finally, the man's voice came back. After a few moments of chanting, he said, "Open your eyes. Take rest. Take rest. Take rest."

Ursula opened her eyes as the door behind her slid open. Sasha gave her a warm smile and without a word, led her down the hallway to her suite. "Now, just sleep. Don't worry about waking up in the morning. We'll handle that."

What did that mean? A bucket of water over her head? A song-bird alighting on her shoulder? Ursula was too tired to guess. She stepped into her room, took her clothes off, threw them on a chair, and brushed her teeth. Then, too lazy to put her pajamas on, she crawled naked into the soft white bed. For a moment, she felt uneasy about the fact that she was being watched. But then again, this was what she'd signed up for. She had already let them probe the interior of her brain; was it really such a big deal if they saw her naked? This was an experience of full surrender. And if they saw her boobs, so be it. She reached for the light switch, but before she touched it, the lights in the suite automatically dimmed to complete blackness.

In the morning, she awoke slowly—perhaps over the course of a minute or two, though it was impossible to tell—as the lights in her room slowly brightened and a soundtrack of chirping birds and buzzing insects increased in volume. It sounded tropical and so realistic that she could almost feel the jungle humidity. Once she got out of bed, the sound ceased. She showered, dressed, and then sat on the couch. She turned on the TV and browsed the selection of films that were available on-demand: *How Stella Got Her Groove Back*, *Baby Boom*, *Risky Business*, *The English Patient*, *Lady and the Tramp*, *Love Story*, *Pretty Woman*, *Cast Away*, *Titanic*, *Get Out*, *Y Tu Mamá También*, *Annie Hall*, *Kramer vs. Kramer*, a Danish film called *The Celebration*, Bergman's *Persona*, and Almodóvar's *Women on the Verge of a Nervous Breakdown*. Before long, there was a knock at the door. Sasha again. "Good morning, Ursula. Welcome to day two."

Over the next few days, Ursula drifted through various activities— kundalini yoga, a watercolor session, a Capoeira lesson, an hour dedicated to writing haiku, a workbook of basic arithmetic—each with a different gentleman, all of whom gave her the same initial hug-hold that Jack had. Some of them were attractive to her, some were decidedly not. Some were in the nondescript middle.

On day four—or was it day five?—she was told to put on her athletic clothes and was escorted into a small gymnasium that was outfitted with odd-looking obstacles. There, she participated in various physical challenges: she had to run on all fours on a human hamster wheel, swim in a small pool filled with a thick but pleasant-smelling sludge, and leap between high pillars placed a few feet apart. Her supervisor for this session, Diego, then brought out a harness and hooked her up to a belay rope. She climbed a twenty-five-foot rock wall, and when she got to the top, she was given the option of plummeting into a foam-filled pit. She took a breath and leapt, while Diego shouted encouragement.

Over the course of the week, the frequency and duration of her meditation sessions increased. On day six alone, she meditated for a total of eight hours. The disembodied man's voice had guided her deeper and deeper into the practice. During a few sessions, she was convinced she had entered a trance. Her initial night of earlobe-focus seemed like years ago. She had since moved on to her forehead, her neck, shoulders, armpits, core, pelvis, legs, toes, toenails. She was now scanning her whole body for sensation. What's more, she felt that her life outside these walls had faded entirely. The world now consisted of The Arc's dim hallways and clandestine spaces. But more specifically, when she was meditating, the world consisted of her own body and of subtle feelings she had never noticed before: small electric pulses along her jawline, crawling feelings along her collarbone, warmth in her tailbone, vibrations in her hip joints, searing heat in her femurs, and bubbling energy on the tops of her feet. She felt turned inside out, as if anyone who saw her now would be able to read her life story just by glancing at her.

Prior to this week at The Arc, Ursula had dabbled in meditation but had never been able to stick with the routine. She had friends and colleagues who swore by it, claiming that it had increased their productivity exponentially. But Ursula had a feeling that whatever kind of meditation they did was wholly different from the type The Arc was employing. Was this even meditation? It felt more like hypnosis. But at this point, she had surrendered so completely to the process that the distinction didn't matter to her. She was in touch with her feelings—deep pain, but also deep joy. She had stopped judging and criticizing herself. She *liked* herself.

On her final day, Ursula woke from a heavy, dreamless sleep to the chirping birds and Sasha's gentle knock.

"Congratulations on reaching day seven," said Sasha, wheeling in a cart with a black stone teapot, a large bowl of colorful fruit, and those delicious apple-cider doughnuts from day one. "Take your time getting ready. In about an hour, I'll come get you for your final meditation and your Emotional Mining Session with Dr. Vidal."

Ursula poured herself some tea and went to the closet. She'd been wearing various combinations of leggings and cashmere sweaters for the past few days. Today, she chose her favorite pair of charcoal lounge pants and "Old Reliable," a trusty sweater she'd pilfered from a particularly benign ex-boyfriend.

When Sasha came back, she led Ursula to a room she'd never seen before: a larger meditation space with two mats side by side on the floor. Sasha explained that Ursula would meditate here for two hours by herself, and for the final hour, Dr. Vidal would join her.

With that, she left Ursula in the candlelit room, and the man's voice began chanting. Then silence descended. Ursula had now built up her tolerance for these seemingly endless expanses of quiet. She burrowed into her own body, tracking little frissons here, little electric surges there. She heard a familiar whooshing noise, like the ocean, like the echoing sound that resulted from holding a conch shell up to one's ear. It had confused her when she'd first noticed it on day three, and she'd assumed it was external, but she now recognized it as the sound of her own blood, surging powerfully through her body. She had become focused enough to hear it.

The man's voice came back. "You've tracked your bodily sensations for six days now, and today we will go to new depths. We will go inside. We will explore the darkest recesses of your body. Notice your organs, your heart, your kidneys. Notice your spinal cord. Your pulsing brain. Imagine all the memories, all the pouches of pain, all the areas of tension and repression. Now, imagine that they are all being pierced, released. You are free, liberated. You are flying. You have escaped your own body and are simply floating like a cloud into a sea of loving-kindness." The man began to chant in what Sasha had explained was Pali, the language of the Buddha.

Ursula lost track of time, but felt that her consciousness was expanding and contracting, accessing a plane that was entirely new. Eventually, she felt rivers pouring down her face, and her whole body reverberated with silent sobs. The chanting stopped, and the man said: "Open your eyes. You are now awake for the first time."

She opened her heavy, wet eyelids and was surprised to notice Dr.

Vidal sitting beside her with legs crossed. She must have slipped in noiselessly, but it didn't seem as though two full hours had passed.

"Let's turn and face one another," said Dr. Vidal, shifting herself 90 degrees so that she was facing Ursula's mat.

Ursula shifted. "Wow." She took a deep breath, wiping her slick cheeks. "Sorry."

"There's absolutely no need to apologize," said Dr. Vidal, offering her a small wooden box of Kleenex. "It's wonderful that you've reached a state of deep feeling. That will make our Emotional Mining Process even more effective. But don't focus on the terminology. This is just a conversation."

Ursula nodded, sniffling, wiping away more tears. She still felt out-of-body, as if she were in a half-hypnotized state.

"What's making you emotional? What did you learn in this final meditation session?" said Dr. Vidal.

"I was thinking about . . . love," said Ursula. "And I realized . . . I don't think I've ever experienced real love. But I want to. There is a force inside of me that says not to give up."

"Tell me about that," said Dr. Vidal. "What does it feel like?"

"It's sort of like a wound that never heals, right here," Ursula put her hand on her ribs, on the spot above her stomach but below her heart. "It's like I've been stabbed by a sword. I mean, I've never actually been stabbed, but I imagine that's what it feels like. It's like a melancholy ache, a permanent homesickness, a longing. Yes, it's a longing. And I'm realizing that I've lived with it my whole life."

"And what would happen if you let that longing guide you?" asked Dr. Vidal.

"Well, I guess that's why I'm here," said Ursula. "I think the ache will go away when I find real, lasting love."

"And your past relationships didn't do anything to relieve it?"

"They made it worse."

"How so?"

"I feel like I evaporate in relationships. On my own, I am this well-defined, strong, feminist, career-driven person. And then once

I commit to someone romantically, I start to dissolve. It's like I can't love someone else without abandoning myself. I always end up feeling . . . subjugated, somehow. I hate that feeling."

Dr. Vidal nodded, encouraging her to continue. Ursula began to divulge the evolution and devolution of her relationships, the alternating waves of hope and disillusionment she had experienced over the years.

"Sean was my most recent serious boyfriend. We dated for three years, and I thought we would get married. Although it seems *he* never thought that. I met him through work—he ran an industrial-design studio in Greenpoint. He had a lot of tattoos and a fixed-gear bike. I thought he was really exciting and smart, but he was also kind of a jerk. I have a talent for trying to love people I don't actually *like*. I think on some level, I wanted to teach him how to be my ideal man. But I ended up losing myself in the effort, which led to self-loathing and then a sort of implosion. I wanted a lot more than Sean could give. He probably sensed that, but we weren't very good at communicating. We started fighting, and then before long . . . well, I have a tendency to mentally fast-forward through conflicts before they happen, and then I run the relationship into the ground. It's something that I do: skip over the fighting and go straight to the breakup. A few years before Sean, there was this British guy, Edward. He was a journalist who covered war zones, so he was always traveling. One week he'd be in Sudan; the next week he was in Syria. He needed the adrenaline to feel alive, but as a result, the whole relationship had to take place on his schedule, his terms. We dated for two years, but now that I think about it, we didn't actually spend that much time together. I spent most of those years hoping he was still intact and waiting for his texts to confirm as much. But the time that we did spend was amazing: I met up with him in Zanzibar, and one summer, we took the Trans-Siberian Railway across Russia. Those moments kept me holding on, and although I knew our relationship probably wouldn't last, I suppressed that knowing. One day I finally erupted and told him it was over. He said he felt blindsided, and not long after that, he relocated to Cairo. I haven't talked to him since."

"Hm." Dr. Vidal took it all in.

"Before him was Adam. He was sweet, but he didn't know who he was. He was an investment banker who wanted to be a DJ. And I was trying on different identities, too. And after a year and a half, we realized that our chosen identities didn't mesh. In retrospect, I'm pretty sure he was a closet Republican. Anyway, it was good for a while, but then we started fighting, and that was the beginning of the end. One fight led to another. He told me I was too 'intense,' and I think I had a bit of a meltdown. And that was that. And in college, there were a few brief relationships: There was Jake, who definitely cared more about his car than he did about me. There was Osman, who told me I had tricked him because I 'wasn't as angelic as I looked.' And in high school, I dated a hockey player named Greg. But one day, I learned that my friend Allison had given him a blow job in the chemistry lab. So that was the end of that relationship—and that friendship. My therapist used to say I gravitate toward emotionally closed-off men who I know are incapable of committing because I have an unhealed abandonment wound. I guess I expect to be abandoned, so sometimes I just fast-forward to the inevitable. Because I know what's coming. Maybe I *want* to be abandoned."

Dr. Vidal asked gently. "Why would that be the case?"

"So I can recenter. So I can find my way back to myself. In the past two years, since my breakup with Sean, I just haven't been able to get close to anyone. It's almost like I'm my own boyfriend now. I know that sounds weird."

"Not at all. And you've got a robust career."

"My job is a big part of who I am. But beneath the surface, I am totally preoccupied with love—why I haven't found it yet, and why I'm starting to give up on it."

"Why would you give up?"

"I just feel more secure on my own than I do when I'm entangled with someone else, someone unpredictable. And I think it's because I've always known that I am fundamentally alone: a one-woman operation, an emotional orphan."

"Even as a child?" asked Dr. Vidal.

"Especially as a child." Ursula paused. "I didn't know my dad—he died when I was three. My mom and I had a pretty peaceful dynamic; we didn't fight. She did her own thing; I did mine. Almost like we were roommates. But yeah, when I think of my childhood, I picture myself alone. I'm very comfortable alone."

"Except for the persistent longing," said Dr. Vidal.

"Yes, except for the sword in my ribcage," said Ursula.

And then a memory emerged—or perhaps it was a dream—from her babyhood. She must have been about two years old—old enough to stand in the crib, desperately rattling the square wooden bars, but not old enough to climb out of it. "I was crying and crying, and no one came. And eventually, I just got exhausted and gave up. Looking back, it feels like the saddest moment of my life."

"You weren't receiving what you needed. You were crying for help and no one gave it to you," said Dr. Vidal, gently. "How do you get what you need now?"

"I take care of myself now. I'm self-sufficient. At the very least, I know I'll never let myself down."

"Never?" Dr. Vidal coaxed.

"Well, except when I'm in a relationship, because I start taking care of the other person—and then no one takes care of me. And I'm too preoccupied taking care of the other person to take care of myself. I've never been able to do both, and I've never found anyone who wanted to take care of me as much as I wanted to take care of him."

"Would you like to find someone who *is* capable of that?" asked Dr. Vidal.

"Yes, of course. But I don't even know what that would feel like," said Ursula.

"Let your imagination lead you," said Dr. Vidal. "Tell me about the man you envision yourself with."

Ursula took a deep breath and closed her eyes. "Well, he's incredibly smart," she began. She felt like she was in a trance. "But not pretentious. He doesn't make anyone feel stupid. He's quietly confident but he doesn't have to broadcast his intelligence. It's clear that he's the smartest person in any given room, except for me. We're equally smart, but different kinds of smart." Ursula went on with more confidence, starting to enjoy the vision she was conjuring. "He's politically progressive, of course, but not a liberal automaton. He's a critical thinker, but he always finds the correct moral plane. He has feminist values, but he doesn't brag about being a feminist in that annoying way that some men do, when they're actually just doing it to curry favor with women. He wants children, like I do. Ideally two children, but we can negotiate on that front. He has experience in relationships. He knows how to love deeply—he just hasn't found the right person yet. He's sexually confident *and* emotionally available *and* ready to fall in love. When he meets me, he feels deeply and unmistakably whole—and so do I. His desire to be with anyone else evaporates, because he is so satisfied by me on every level. He would literally rather make pancakes for me than have sex with another woman."

Dr. Vidal nodded encouragingly.

"And I don't have to lose myself to love him. I just know it's right. There's a confidence there, an understanding between us. We balance and stabilize each other. He doesn't have to be around all the time, physically. Like, it's okay if he travels. I like alone time. But I want us to feel connected when we're apart and euphorically in love when we're together. Quality time together; quality time apart. That's my holy grail. Dark hair. Warm, kind eyes. Not those creepy serial-killer eyes. Emotionally generous. Sexually generous, loves to—well, you know. Loves it so much he doesn't even care about reciprocation. Laughs easily. Wry, offbeat sense of humor. Loves animals. Doesn't mind if the cat sleeps on the bed once in a while . . ."

Ursula went on, until she reached her natural conclusion: ". . . not just a partner, but a playmate. A fully present playmate-partner who doesn't think it's weird if I growl like a wolfling when I'm excited or perturbed."

"That's beautiful," said Dr. Vidal, her voice gentle, as if she were the older sister or kindly aunt that Ursula had never been lucky enough to have. She placed a warm, steady hand on Ursula's knee. "But now, Ursula, beyond a relationship, what do you want?"

Ursula squeezed her eyes shut. "I'm looking for . . ." A torrent of feeling rushed through her body. "I want to feel useful and purposeful. I want to feel like I'm in the right place, using my energy in the right ways. I don't want to be scared anymore. I'm scared every second of every day, but I pretend that I'm not. I want to stop running from one empty 'accomplishment' to another. I want to stop feeling like the whole world rests on my shoulders and is slowly crushing me into a tiny, warped, grotesque, compromised little version of myself. I want to stop twisting myself to appease some inner impulse that is driving me to prioritize money—I don't even know where that comes from. My mother is an artist. She's a Trotskyist! So maybe that's where it comes from—my rebellion is being a capitalist." She was surprised to hear herself say this, but it felt accurate. "I want to be like an animal: acting on my instincts and not second-guessing myself. I don't want to have to perform anymore, and I want the man I'm with to understand that. I want security, and I want joy. But most of all, I want peace. I'm exhausted. I don't mind the struggle, but I want to feel confident that I'm on the right path, moving in the right direction, in all aspects of my life."

"Thank you, Ursula," said Dr. Vidal. "Anything else I should know?"

Ursula shook her head. There was nothing else to say. She was completely spent.

"Then we can conclude." Dr. Vidal stood up and extended her hand to Ursula, who allowed herself to be pulled up out of her lotus position and onto her feet. Once the blood rushed back into her legs, she stepped out into the hallway. Sasha was waiting to escort her back to her suite, where an elaborate dinner was laid out in the living room. Too drained to eat, she collapsed into bed and slept for thirteen uninterrupted hours.

The next morning, as Ursula packed her things, Sasha arrived with the final paperwork. Ursula had read this a few weeks ago when they'd sent it via email, so none of the information was new, but now it was time to sign.

Her fee was $40,500. Eighty percent of that would be billed upon initial matching, and the remaining 20 percent would be billed eighteen months later. This delay was an act of good faith, because The Arc guaranteed that all couples "would be together eighteen months after their initial meeting." If for some reason they weren't, the remaining 20 percent would be waived.

There was a required four-month check-in at The Arc's headquarters, plus a required one-year review, exactly 365 days after the couple's first date. During this first year, The Arc required monthly email updates on the progression of the relationship—nothing too time-consuming, just a quick multiple-choice questionnaire on the first of every month.

Then there was an NDA, which enforced mutual confidentiality. Just as The Arc would never release information about its clients to outside parties, they, in turn, were prohibited from talking about the details of their process for the first eighteen months after receiving their match. Beyond that timeframe, they were free to share their stories publicly.

There was also a clause that stated: *In the unlikely event that you and your match experience relational discord of any kind, please contact us. Our dedicated in-house relationship technicians will be happy to assist you. We strongly discourage you from seeking out external resources such as couples therapists, who will not have the requisite background information to grasp the full nature of your relationship.*

The past seven days had been a blur of self-inquiry and meditation and drowsiness and rare dreamless nights and something bordering on serenity. Ursula could barely remember what had happened on which day, or what she had revealed to whom, but she trusted Dr. Vidal and her team to use the information judiciously. She felt known and appreciated as she whipped her hand across the bottom of the contract, signing her name with unusual conviction.

RAFAEL

Chapter 11

August 9, 6:43 P.M.

Rafael held the envelope in his hands, momentarily conflicted about opening it. He knew it contained the name of the woman who was "guaranteed" to be his ideal partner, but ever since the dramatic implosion of his first love (Meredith Sinclair, junior year at boarding school in Connecticut), the beginning of every new relationship had been tinged with a prick of fear. Outwardly, Meredith had appeared entirely innocent, with her straw-blond hair pulled back into a neat French braid. At the beginning of his junior year (and her sophomore year), she had begun lingering on the lawn in front of his brick dormitory every day after her field hockey practice. When he returned from his own soccer practice, she would feign surprise that they had run into each other yet again. By Columbus Day weekend of that fall, they were stealing off to hook up at every opportunity—in the library, by the pond, under the defunct train trestle behind the athletic fields—and by Thanksgiving, Rafael was in love. But Meredith's seraphic looks belied a rebellious spirit. She was the leader of a pack of girls who used to drink cheap gin—disguised in Snapple bottles—behind the chapel on Sunday afternoons. Rafael's first sexual experience—which was not Meredith's first—took place in the school planetarium. (As an admissions tour guide, Meredith had a set of keys to many of the school's normally off-limits spaces.) Rafael was captivated by Meredith's gall, but often irked by what he felt was pressure to go along with it. The fact that she'd already been suspended twice didn't stop Meredith from finding creative new ways to break the school's many rules. (Her father was an alumnus and a trustee, which gave her near-invincibility when it came to repercussions, or so she thought.) Rafael didn't benefit from that protected status, and he knew better than to risk his spotless disciplinary record, especially during junior year, with the college admissions process looming. Come spring, Meredith would show up outside his bedroom window, her wooden lacrosse stick in hand, and try to lure him down to the river to smoke a joint before dinner in the dining hall. He sometimes accompanied her, but never partook. It was nearly the end of spring term when Meredith was caught by a campus security guard while shimmying down a front pillar of Danforth Dormitory at 2 A.M. Rafael did not live in Danforth; he lived in Olcott. Meredith was finally expelled (having exceeded her get-out-of-jail-free cards) on the same morning that Rafael found out she'd had a secondary boyfriend, Riggs Heffernan, the entire time they'd been dating.

But this was different, he remembered, gripping the envelope from The Arc that bore his name: *Rafael Banks*. He was no longer an earnest seventeen-year-old, and there was nothing to fear here. This time, there would be no danger or doubt that it was meant to be. There was built-in peace of mind, and not because it was "destined" or because it "felt right," but because this match was scientifically formulated by experts who knew far better than he what it took to create lasting love. And of course, because he had paid $50,000 for it, and he was determined to get his money's worth. Yes, this would work.

He tore open the envelope, which contained a handwritten note that read:

> Dear Rafael,
> Congratulations on beginning this exciting journey with Ursula Byrne. May your arc entail joy, wonder, growth, and most of all, discovery.
>
> > Your champion in lasting love,
> > Dr. Corinne Vidal

In addition to the contact information for this woman—Ursula Byrne—there was also a photo of her that filled him with a warm flood of emotion, followed by a subtle electric twinge. She was laughing at someone or something out of frame, but not in a false, posed way. This was definitely a real laugh, and she had beautiful, bright teeth. She wasn't wearing makeup, as far as he could tell—although he had learned that women sometimes wore makeup without looking like they were wearing it. Anyway, he couldn't *see* any visible makeup, and he liked that. She was raking her wavy blond hair back with her hand, and it fell messily around her shoulders. Chaotic in a good way. She wore a slouchy sweater and jeans. She seemed confident and relaxed, as if she liked herself. Yes, that was it: *She liked herself.* She was having fun just being herself. And he couldn't quite tell, but it looked like she had nice legs.

He knew that "liking someone on paper" wasn't enough, but this was a promising start. "Yes," Rafael thought. "This might actually work." His heart pounded and he felt slightly light-headed, but there was no stab of anxiety, no hint of melancholy. Just a surreal sense of hope.

He tucked the photo into the inner pocket of his jacket and looked at his watch. There was no time to change. As a lawyer, he almost always wore a suit, even in early August. Outfit-planning was neither his forte nor his passion, and he was grateful to have a well-defined uniform so he didn't have to spend mental energy figuring out what to wear every day. Clothing could be unnecessarily confusing, so he kept his choices simple and straightforward, if a bit formulaic. He paused to look in the mirror by his front door. The day's humidity had made his thick, wavy, almost-black hair a bit rambunctious. He tried to tuck it behind his ear and reminded himself that he needed a haircut. He enjoyed having the least lawyerly hair in his office, but this was pushing it. He removed his tie and undid the top two buttons of his shirt. By this stage of the summer, his naturally bronze skin was always especially tan.

He grabbed his keys and headed out the door of his sixth-floor co-op apartment, which he had bought three years earlier. When the elevator hit the ground floor, he walked swiftly through the lobby and gave a quick wave to Dalmat, his doorman. He was headed to the nearby Explorers Club, where his best friend, Skipp, was giving a lecture on narwhals. Skipp's last few years had been tumultuous—a divorce followed by a disastrous attempt to summit Annapurna, which had left him with an amputated toe—and Rafael was eager to support him however he could.

He ran the few blocks between his Upper East Side building and the club on East Seventieth Street, where he bolted up the two flights of stairs that led to the Trophy Room. He could already hear Skipp's voice—". . . Inuit legend involving a woman who was dragged into the sea and then transformed into a narwhal, her hair becoming its legendary tusk . . ."—and he halted to compose himself in the hallway. He wiped his forehead and then quietly slipped into the room, finding a seat at the back of the small crowd. A taxidermy cheetah partially blocked his view, but that was fine. He had already heard most of Skipp's thoughts on narwhals; tonight, he was just here to be a pal.

Skipp was a natural and enthusiastic orator, and he loved nothing more than holding forth. Tonight, he was in full effect, his pink cheeks blazing with passion. He wore a white linen suit covered in creases. His floppy sand-colored hair looked clean but uncombed, which reminded Rafael of their college years, when Skipp had sported perpetual hat hair from his backward-turned Taft School baseball cap.

"Where would we be without the narwhal?" Skipp concluded. "I shudder to think."

The audience applauded politely, and a few members approached Skipp to ask questions. In no rush, Rafael allowed his friend time to bask in the modest limelight. He strolled the perimeter of the room and examined a taxidermy peacock and what appeared to be an enormous four-foot carrot mounted on a wooden stand. Rafael leaned in to examine the plaque that identified it. It was no carrot—it was the preserved foreskin of a sperm whale.

As the room emptied out, Skipp walked over to Rafael. "You found the whale dong."

"It seems so," Rafael said.

"J. G. Melon's?"

"Yeah, let's do it."

They descended the club's winding wooden staircase and set out into the sticky August night, destined for their favorite burgers.

"This one was really good," said Rafael, who was an unfailing champion of all his friends, but especially of Skipp, who had always marched to his own tune. As the third of four children in a well-known media family, Skipp had struggled to find his professional footing. His older brother ran a respected investigative journalism organization; his older sister was a powerhouse literary agent; and his younger sister was a television news producer. Skipp had completed half of his Ph.D. in earth and environmental sciences, but he had lost momentum and become a freelance journalist. He'd written a few articles for *National Geographic*, but his regular gig was a website called FarFlungMedia.com. The money he spent to personally fund his travels far outweighed the fees he was paid to write about them, but a generous inheritance gave him plenty of financial wiggle room. Despite his moneyed background, he was not ostentatious. He lived in a tiny ground-floor apartment that had been converted from a defunct dentist's office, and he went everywhere on his ten-speed Italian road bike (a mint-colored Bianchi), which he'd had since 1992. Its wheels whirred softly now as he pushed it along the sidewalk beside his friend.

"I like how you added the tie-in to global warming and the implications of the US's leaving the Paris Agreement," said Rafael. "It made the material feel even more relevant."

"Thanks, man," said Skipp, whose love of narwhals predated their current trendiness. It ran deep and had always endeared him to Rafael. "Yeah, it's a constantly moving target. But if the narwhals go . . ." He shook his head, horrified by the idea of a narwhal-less world. "I'm thinking of going to Baffin Island this winter to do some more observation. You want to come?"

"Maybe," said Rafael. He and Skipp used to travel together often. After meeting in college in New Haven, they spent winter breaks, summers, and even an entire year after graduation traipsing through South America and Asia, partaking in everything from psychedelics to ice-climbing to trysts with interesting women they met along the way.

Since his divorce, Skipp seemed eager to return to that time, but Rafael had happily settled into a calmer phase of life. As a partner at his law firm, he was committed to his career, though not defined by it. To him, work was a means to an end, a facilitator of everything else, and at forty-two, he was finally ready for that "everything else": a partner, a nest, and eventually children. This realization had hit abruptly—after a difficult decade that encompassed a painful breakup and the death of his mother—and he wasn't quite sure how to proceed. He was wary of traditional dating apps (too much personal exposure, too time-consuming, too wide a net, too many unknowns), but a work colleague had enthusiastically recommended The Arc after meeting his own wife through the service. After a few months of deliberation, Rafael decided that this was the only modern dating solution that didn't offend his old-soul sensibility, and he had gone for it. He refocused on Skipp's proposition. "Baffin Island this winter . . . sounds cold. We'll see."

They arrived at J. G. Melon's, and Skipp dragged his bike over to a pole to lock it up. Upon entering, they walked past the boisterous bar and nabbed a green-and-white-checked table in the back.

"What's going on with you?" asked Skipp, glancing quickly at the menu but then putting it down. They always ordered the same thing here: cheeseburgers and bourbon on the rocks. Sometimes they got ice cream sundaes if they were feeling indulgent.

"What's going on with me . . ." Rafael tried to remember when they'd last seen each other. It had been a few weeks. Summer in New York always pulled people in different directions—weekends on Long Island or upstate, trips to Europe, annual sojourns to family lake houses—and offered natural breathing room in decades-long friendships such as theirs.

The waiter slid up to their table and took their order.

"You know that thing I told you about?" asked Rafael. "The Arc."

"The dating app," said Skipp. "Yeah, I want to try that. Sounds pretty sweet."

"But it's not an app," said Rafael. "I mean, it's a service. But it's intense. I had to spend seven days being analyzed at their facility.

Remember, I did it back in June when you were in Lapland? It was some shamanic shit."

"Yeah? What did they do to you?" asked Skipp, who loved subversion. The weirder, the better.

The waiter appeared and set down their drinks.

"Hard to say," said Rafael, picking up his bourbon. "I mean, the whole thing was . . . I actually enjoyed it. I learned how to meditate. This really hot woman named Simone made me eggs. I got a few massages. I ran on a human hamster wheel. I played tennis against a glass backboard while they piped in Gregorian chants."

"Whoa," said Skipp, his mouth full of ice cubes.

"I told them everything about my life," said Rafael. *I cried.*

Skipp raised his eyebrows in disbelief.

Rafael nodded affirmatively. "I don't think I've cried that much since . . . ever. Not even when my mom died. Suddenly, I could just feel everything so deeply. But now that I'm trying to remember the details, the whole thing is kind of hazy."

"Shit. Think they hypnotized you?"

The waiter arrived with their burgers. Skipp picked up the ketchup, then halted and offered it to Rafael, who gestured for him to go first.

"Kind of," said Rafael. "I don't really know how to describe it. I talked about things I haven't even thought of for years. And some things I've *never* thought about. At the end, I spent hours with the founder, Dr. Vidal, and I told her *everything.*"

"Like, family stuff?" asked Skipp. He and Rafael had known each other for twenty-four years, so he was well-versed in the contours of his friend's background. Rafael had been adopted from Argentina by Haskell Banks, a business professor at Dartmouth, and Celeste, a former competitive equestrian. Together, the couple had spent the 1975–76 academic year on sabbatical in Uruguay. Toward the end of their stay, they were approached by a local friend who had a shocking proposition. His cousin in Buenos Aires was currently taking care of a six-month-old boy, Rafael, whose parents (Fernanda and Rafael Sr.) had been disappeared by Argentina's murderous military junta, which had overthrown President Isabel Perón just two months before.

She couldn't keep the baby for much longer, and she was looking for someone who could take him out of harm's way. Haskell and Celeste had never succeeded in having children, and although Haskell had two daughters from his first marriage, Celeste had always longed for a baby of her own. While they were not reckless or impulsive people, they agreed that this opportunity felt fated. A few weeks before they were to return to New Hampshire, they traveled with their friend to the Argentinean border to meet his sister, who handed off a quiet baby boy with almost-black hair and long-lashed brown eyes. Though the adoption was off the record, the crumbling bureaucracy in that part of the world made it entirely seamless. Three weeks later, Haskell and Celeste returned to New Hampshire with Rafael in tow, where one of Haskell's professional connections who had a brother at the State Department swiftly helped make their son a naturalized citizen. Convinced that they were leveraging their privilege for the good of the child, they never looked back.

"So yeah, we got into some of the family stuff," Rafael explained to Skipp. "But it was more than that. More than questions of identity. It wasn't just 'who are you and what do you want?' It was a deep exploration of existence. As in, why am I even here? What is my purpose? But through it all, you're doing this meditation that kind of opens you up and soothes you. Honestly, it reminded me of that time you and I did ayahuasca in Peru. Except that I was entirely sober during this whole process. As in, not even a beer."

"When we did ayahuasca, you were haunted by a vision of a bird," said Skipp, squinting as he tried to remember the details.

"Yes! The flamebird! But remember what that bird told me? It told me that I would have *one* transcendent love in my life. *One*. And in the past, I always assumed that was Freja, and it had come and gone. But now I realize it wasn't her."

"That's huge," said Skipp, recalling the ex-girlfriend who had knocked Rafael off balance in their late twenties. "Did you talk about her at The Arc?"

Rafael nodded. Freja was a Swedish photographer who had made her way to New York via Sydney and Shanghai. Rafael had always liked free-thinking, creative women, but Freja was on another level. When he met her, she had tailbone-length rust-colored hair and was working on a series of twenty-six self-portraits called *This Is How You Spell Desire*, in which she contorted her naked body into each letter of the alphabet. Their three years together were a heady whirlwind, during which Freja never once wore a bra. After two years in New York, she spontaneously decided that they should move to Bogotá together; but when Rafael, who was firmly committed to his life and work in New York, resisted, she became defiant. They agreed to consider relocating in the future, but in his heart, Rafael knew that he wanted to stay in the United States near his family. And he loved New York—his life felt intertwined with the city itself. Freja spent their final year as a couple working on a series called *Aftermath*. Each photo featured a different naked man in a rumpled bed, staring directly into the camera with grateful eyes. At the opening of the gallery show, there was a brief Q&A during which an attendee asked, "How did you get your subjects to look so authentically post-coital?"

Freja paused and then said matter-of-factly, "I had sex with them."

This was news to Rafael. Though he had objectively loved the photos—all seventeen of them—this experience shook him deeply. To this day, he could still recall the faces of many of the men whom his girlfriend had seduced during their final year together.

"What?" Freja had asked defensively, as they trudged home through the snow that night after her vernissage. "It wasn't *personal*. It's my *work*." She moved back to Sweden a few months later, and Rafael channeled his heartbreak into *his* work. He took comfort in the methodical pace of his weeks and the content of his job: helping families to plan and organize their trusts and estates, to ward off inter-generational conflict before it could take root. He liked that his job allowed him to work with people, albeit in a highly structured way. Clear parameters. Preemptive measures to prevent future drama. His job was an anchor, holding him steady amid the unpredictable chop of life in New York. He worried for a time that Freja had flooded his emotional engine and left him romantically hobbled. He went on to date a series of nice, albeit too-tame, women with whom he could not seem to fully connect, emotionally. And then when he was thirty-five, his mother was diagnosed with breast cancer. By the time she died four years later, dating was the furthest thing from his mind. But finally, three years hence, he had begun to crave partnership, a family of his own, a sense of home. Although the past decade had rocked him, he was still an optimist at his core, and he began to dream of someday finding a woman with passion and spirit, who could energize his life without destabilizing it.

"Freja, Freja, Freja," said Skipp, shaking his head and putting the final bite of burger into his mouth. "What a character."

"That's one word for her," said Rafael.

"No wonder you overcorrected," said Skipp, referring to the string of bland women Rafael had dated since. "So, what happens next? When do you meet this new love of your life?"

"I got this today," said Rafael, pulling the photo of Ursula out of his pocket and holding it out to Skipp. He felt a bit overwhelmed by the enormity of it all. "This is her. Ursula. But I haven't reached out to her yet."

Skipp took the photo and examined it. He grinned. "Oh, she's a babe," he said. "Definitely your type. A real firecracker."

Rafael felt relieved. The validation helped.

"She looks kind of young." Skipp began analyzing the photo more closely, tilting his head to the side. "Nice sweater puppies."

Rafael snatched the photo out of his friend's hand, feeling protective. Skipp always referred to women's breasts as sweater puppies, but it had never annoyed Rafael until now. "Yeah, she's beautiful. They told me she's thirty-five."

"Seven years younger. That seems good?"

Rafael had typically dated women his own age, but this did seem good. He nodded.

"Yeah, and if you're going to have a kid . . ." said Skipp. "I guess The Arc did the math."

"For $50,000, I would hope so," said Rafael.

"Jesus," said Skipp, choking on his bourbon. "Are you sure it's worth that much to you?"

"If it works, yes," said Rafael.

"You know, I just joined a dating app," said Skipp, wiping liquid off his chin. "It's called The Cum Laude."

"No," said Rafael in disbelief. "That's not real."

"It is. I know, the name is absurd," said Skipp. "But that's how they get your attention nowadays. There are so many apps, they have to break through the noise. Anyway, it's no-strings-attached sex for people who went to Ivy League schools or had GPAs of 3.9 and above."

"Skipp, that sounds terrible," said Rafael. "Like the worst of all worlds. Pretension meets lack of accountability."

Skipp shrugged. "Gonna give it a go."

Rafael and Skipp operated very differently. Skipp had been engaged four times, married twice, and now divorced twice. He fell in love passionately and recklessly, without seeming to consider why he chose the women he did. Or rather, why those types of women chose him. That said, he was endlessly resilient. Rafael, who had been guarded ever since the Freja fiasco, had always admired Skipp's capacity to bounce back.

"Maybe I'll see if she wants to go out this weekend," said Rafael, feeling courageous as he finished his bourbon.

"Do it," said Skipp, sliding from absurdity into sincerity as only he could. "Seriously. It's so awesome that you're doing this. I can't wait to meet her."

"Me too," said Rafael, slightly embarrassed by how giddy he felt. He signaled for the waiter. "Can we have two sundaes? Extra chocolate sauce on his."

"Yessss, Rafa," said Skipp, delighted. When he'd started gaining extra weight at forty, he'd instituted a no-ice-cream-during-the-week rule, but it didn't count if someone else ordered it. Rafael knew the loophole and was encouraged to exploit it.

"And two glasses of port," yelled Skipp as the waiter walked away.

A few moments later, Skipp brandished his port in the air. "To you and, wait, what's her name? You told me. Ursula. That's a weird name."

"It's a cool name," said Rafael, retracting his glass.

Skipp tilted his head, reconsidering. "You're right. It is cool. *Really* cool."

Rafael waited for Skipp's train of thought to settle.

"Sorry," said Skipp, collecting himself. "To you and Ursula."

Chapter 12

August 14, 11:42 A.M.

Rafael stood in front of his dresser wearing only navy boxer briefs. Of course it had to be 89 degrees on the day he was supposed to meet Ursula. Normally on a first date, if he were going somewhere casual, he would wear jeans and a white-and-blue checked button-down. That outfit never failed; he felt like himself in it. But it was way too hot for jeans today. He didn't want to meet this woman in a pool of his own sweat.

He riffled through the drawers and landed on a pair of navy shorts. Those were innocuous. Those would work. He threw them on the bed. Now for a shirt. He wanted to wear a T-shirt, but he also wanted to look like an adult. He *was* an adult, after all, although something about this rendezvous made him feel like he was sixteen and dating for the first time. He needed a watch. That would help. He usually wore his grandfather's old Rolex to work, but he thought that was overkill in this context, so he grabbed his black Casio. Classic, casual, not trying too hard. He decided that if he were wearing shorts, he could do a long-sleeved white button-down as long as he rolled the sleeves up for ventilation.

But shoes. He struggled with shoes in the summer. He stared at his brown boat shoes in the closet. He was meeting Ursula in Brooklyn, and she lived in Brooklyn, which meant she was undoubtedly cooler than he was. Most people in Brooklyn didn't wear boat shoes. He knew this.

It was too late to text either Catherine or Patricia—his half sisters—for help, and they would have had too many opinions anyway. Five and seven years older than he, they'd been dressing him up like a baby-doll ever since he'd arrived in New Hampshire from Argentina in June of 1976. By then, they were spending the school year in Manhattan with their mother, Margaret, who was remarried to a wealthy stockbroker; but they spent summers up in Lyme, where they treated their younger brother like an adored pet. He never minded, especially since he only had to endure their love for a few months at a time. And as he got older, he realized how lucky he was to have grown up with genuinely loving parents, siblings, and a large extended family. His sisters' tales of the dysfunction that unfolded in their mother's Park Avenue penthouse provided a counterpoint to his own relatively peaceful home life. His mother, Celeste, was attentive but not smothering. As a toddler, he had loved accompanying her to their local stable, where she taught him about horse care and he came to love all the animals in the barn: the horses, dogs, cats, even the birds that nested in the rafters. His father, though perpetually busy with his work as an economist and professor at Dartmouth, took his son fishing, skiing, and adventuring whenever possible. Their annual hiking trip in the White Mountains was Rafael's favorite tradition. His childhood had been largely uncomplicated, but adulthood in New York was another story.

Rafael brought his attention back to the task at hand. He furrowed his brow as he pawed at his hair, wishing he'd had the foresight to get a haircut that week. He wondered what Ursula would be like in person. The last woman he had gone on a date with had shown up in those '90s mom jeans that so many women seemed to be wearing lately. He understood they were considered stylish, and it would be fine if Ursula *did* wear them—he just really hoped she didn't. It was abnormally humid, so it was probably too hot for pants like that anyway.

He was getting flustered again. He took a deep breath and walked to the doorway of his bedroom where his pull-up bar was. One, two, three . . . twenty pull-ups later, he felt more in control. He put on the shorts. He put on the white shirt. So far, so good. The boat shoes were a no-go, so he pulled on his sneakers. Not his gym sneakers, but the sneakers he wore when he wanted to look nonchalant. But he didn't look nonchalant. He felt awkward. He kicked them off, and then he stopped. Why was he agonizing? None of this mattered. This was guaranteed to work. He'd paid $50,000 for this to work. Ursula wasn't going to reject him over his choice of shoes. He put on canvas slip-ons that his sisters had insisted he buy last summer in Greece, ran his hand through his hair, and headed into the living room to grab his keys and wallet.

But then he went back into the bedroom to tidy up. He knew Ursula probably wouldn't end up coming here today. He didn't expect to sleep with her on their first date, especially since they were meeting at 1 p.m. And they were supposedly going to spend their lives together, so there was no rush, but his philosophy was "you never know." He straightened up his bed, shoved his laundry hamper into the closet, and checked his watch. He needed to go.

When Rafael had initially texted Ursula, she had written back promptly—no need to play it coy—and they had agreed to meet for lunch that Saturday. During their exchange, they mutually acknowledged how weird the premise for this relationship was, and he had suggested they not put undue pressure on the circumstances of their first date. "What's the first food that comes to mind? No overthinking," he had texted. Within two seconds, Ursula wrote back, "French fries." "Perfect," Rafael had replied. "Let's have French fries." The rest of the conversation flowed freely and easily. They both typed in full sentences with proper punctuation and no emojis—an early sign of compatibility, perhaps. They decided to pair their French fries with lobster rolls, and Ursula suggested a place in Red Hook, not far from where she lived. Although Rafael barely knew where Red Hook was, he enthusiastically supported the idea.

But now, as he made his way from his apartment to the subway to the ferry landing at Thirty-Fourth Street, he started to wonder if he would get there on time. Maybe he had underestimated just how far away Red Hook was. But once on the ferry, he started to relax. The sun was hot, but the wind kept him cool, and he was happy to get out of his usual rut and venture somewhere unfamiliar. By the time the boat docked at the wharf in Brooklyn, he was oddly calm and not as sweaty as he expected, thanks to the breeze off the water. He walked up Van Brunt Street, charmed by its odd, rickety storefronts. There was a small street fair underway, just local vendors: Brooklyn-made whisky, key lime pies, chocolate, ceramics, textiles. Was this the same city he lived in? It felt foreign and quaint. The unrelenting stress and churning tension of Manhattan seemed far away. When he got to the lobster shack, he looked around. No Ursula. At least, not yet. He sat on a bench outside and reached for his phone, but then stopped himself. Was he really going to pretend to be busy? Just answering a quick work email? Checking his stocks? He'd spent $50,000 and 168 hours in observation to facilitate this date. This was no time for feigned nonchalance. He lifted his head, took a deep breath, and looked up the street. And then, there she was.

URSULA AND RAFAEL

Chapter 13

August 14, 1:07 P.M.

Nerves of steel. That's what it took to date in New York City in 2018. Either that or an Ativan prescription. Or both. Ursula had trained for this, but she still felt out-of-body as she left her apartment and headed toward Red Hook. The midday heat was intense. She was glad she'd decided against her favorite pair of jeans—high-waisted vintage Levi's that she'd bought in Tokyo. Instead, she chose a coral-toned floral sundress that skimmed her torso without being tight. She felt good in it, and she wanted to feel good when they met for the first time. She also wore her go-to Moroccan raffia sandals, which she now realized were starting to fray in the toe. Most men didn't notice that kind of thing, but some did. It was too late to do anything about it now, and she decided that a little fraying wouldn't derail a love that was meant to be. Overall, she felt put-together, and she was only a touch too hot.

As she neared Van Brunt, she began vibrating with jitters that made her knees feel untrustworthy. She was both excited and afraid to see Rafael for the first time. There were a few people milling around on the sidewalk; she noticed the small street fair up ahead. Then, suddenly, she saw a silhouette on a bench, and everything else went into slow motion and blurred out.

She had never even considered whether a silhouette could be sexy, but now she knew: it could be, and his was.

When she was a half block away, their eyes met and Rafael slowly stood up from the bench, relaxed, as if he were welcoming her home from a long journey, as if this were inevitable. Ursula smiled and approached, but then jumped back and yelped. She felt something soft, possibly alive, under her foot. They both looked down. It was half of a discarded baguette. Their eyes met again and they both began to laugh hysterically. "It's not funny!" yipped Ursula. "What if I had sprained my ankle on a baguette!"

"It happens. I blew out my knee on a brioche last year," joked Rafael.

Ursula threw her head back and cackled like a baby hyena. He instantly loved her laugh. This was already wildly fun.

"Did The Arc plant that baguette?" asked Rafael, looking over his shoulder. "Are they watching us?"

"Probably," said Ursula, shaking her head. "This is the weirdest day of my life."

"Mine too," said Rafael, happy. A surprising, uncomplicated happiness. He leaned in and kissed her left cheek, then her right. A successful, smooth double kiss—that was a feat unto itself. "It's so great to meet you. And I love how you negotiated that baguette."

Ursula noticed that he radiated warmth. Not just heat—although there was that too—but warmth. Safe, friendly, emotional warmth. He looked just like his photo, but a tiny bit better. He had sensual lips, and even when he wasn't smiling, the corners of his mouth turned up just slightly. It was the opposite of Resting Bitch Face. It was . . . Resting Nice Face? His dark, wavy hair looked a little wild, and Ursula liked that it wasn't too short. Most men were constantly cutting their hair, so they spent at least a third of their lives looking like freshly shorn sheep. Rafael's eyebrows were prominent caterpillars, the left one flecked with a scar at the corner. His eyes were dark wells: deep, but gentle. When he laughed, sweet little wrinkles spread from the corners of his eyes and a subtle vein appeared down the center of his forehead. A little tuft of chest hair was visible at the opening of his white button-down. Ursula could just see the outline of his biceps through his shirt, which was rolled up, revealing the most beautiful forearms she'd ever seen. Again, she'd never really stopped to consider anyone's forearms. But these, she realized, had to be the sexiest forearms in the world. Rafael's appearance wasn't over-the-top in any way, but he was beautiful, healthy, and he seemed happy, optimistic. Ursula couldn't know yet whether that was because of her, or if that was just his way. She hoped it was both.

He wasn't as tall as she'd expected. Based on her own height (5'7"), she guessed he was 5'10", maybe 5'11" on a good day. That surprised her, since she'd told The Arc that her significant ex-boyfriends ranged from six feet to 6'5". But she knew there was a reason; she trusted the master plan. She began to envision their children and liked what she saw, but then she snapped back to reality.

"Shall we?" Rafael asked, gesturing toward the door of the lobster shack.

Ursula slid by him, and Rafael glanced at her butt as she ducked inside. He loved her dress, and the fact that her sandals were a bit frayed in the toe. She looked like joy embodied: vibrant, natural, healthy, glowing. Maybe the glow was sweat, but it was an appealing, natural kind of sweat. She looked just like her photo, but a tiny bit better.

The restaurant was not busy, but they made an easy mutual decision to sit at the bar. Another small sign of compatibility. Ursula loved the bar because she liked the evolution of starting side by side and then gradually angling her way toward her date until her leg was sort of in between his legs, and then he could casually put his hand on hers without anyone having to do anything overt. Rafael liked sitting at the bar because it was friendlier, less stuffy, but also offered potential access to his date's legs, if it was the kind of vibe where she was gradually leaning closer to him and indicating that he should touch her. He didn't know if that would happen today, but he was definitely open to putting his hand on Ursula's thigh if the opportunity presented itself.

Ursula ordered rosé; Rafael ordered an IPA. They debated the merits of Maine-style lobster rolls versus Connecticut-style. Although Rafael had gone to summer camp in Maine as a child, he counterintuitively preferred the butter-bathed Connecticut rolls. And although Ursula generally had an aversion to mayonnaise, she counterintuitively preferred the mayo-laden Maine rolls. However mundane, everything that happened between them felt fascinating. This was the most surreal dating experience of their lives, and they also happened to be electrically attracted to one another.

At first, Ursula was concerned by this current of attraction. Her former therapist (two therapists ago) had urged her to beware of instant chemistry, as it could indicate the beginning of an anxious-avoidant dynamic rooted in trauma bonding. Ursula had dated her share of narcissists who preyed on her natural empathy, and lately she ran from any man who expressed even a glimmer of self-absorption. But this attraction was not rooted in trauma, and Rafael wasn't a narcissist. He couldn't be—The Arc wouldn't have done that to her. Was this love? Actual, healthy love? She wasn't sure how to recognize it, but it felt like this could be it, or the seed of it.

Rafael asked about her name. Where did it come from? Was she named after the writer Ursula Le Guin? Or Ursula Andress, the renowned Bond girl?

"Wow, you know your Ursulas!" she said, impressed. "My mom wanted to give me a German name, because my father was German. And as a *visual person*"—Ursula used air quotes around this term, which she found simplistic—"she liked the form and symmetry of the letter 'U.' So there you have it. But most people find it very shocking. I'd describe my relationship with my name as 'contentious.'"

"Why?" asked Rafael. "It's such a cool name."

"Well, it might have been," said Ursula, dragging a fry through a small pool of ketchup. "If a certain animated movie about mermaids hadn't been released when I was six, henceforth associating me with a well-known sea witch."

"Such a great character though. And a great film in general," said Rafael. "'Under the Sea'? 'Kiss the Girl'? Some of the greatest songs of our time. But I hear you, and I can relate to having an unusual name."

"But there are tons of Rafaels," said Ursula.

"Yes, but not where I grew up. Actually, I think I might have been the only Rafael in the entire state of New Hampshire. And then the Teenage Mutant Ninja Turtles came along, and Rafael wasn't even one of the good ones. Then there's the fact that my family calls me Rafa, which, as you've probably noticed, is the name of a prominent Spanish tennis player. So when I tell people in New England my name is Rafa . . ."

"They immediately think of Nadal," supplied Ursula.

"Exactly," said Rafael. "Which is fine. But yes, most people associate my name with either the lamest Ninja Turtle or the best tennis player in the world."

"Well, *arguably* the best player," said Ursula, who had always been partial to Federer. But this wasn't the time to get into it. "And I always thought Turtle Rafael was sweet, with his little daggers."

Rafael chuckled. "Anyway, I understand what it's like to have a contentious relationship with your own name. But for the record, I love your name." He wasn't just being polite.

"I love *your* name," said Ursula. She wasn't just being polite either. "Although we should probably come up with nicknames for each other at some point. But no urgency on that front."

"I predict I'll have a nickname for you by the end of the day," said Rafael. "A starter nickname, at least."

The bartender popped back to the counter, eyeing their empty glasses. "Another round?"

Ursula started to order an IPA, to match Rafael's order, but he had simultaneously started to order a rosé, to match hers.

"I want to be like you," said Rafael.

"I want to be like you!" said Ursula.

They ordered one of each and agreed to share. By this time, Ursula had fully angled her legs toward Rafael, and his left hand slid naturally onto the outside of her right thigh.

"So how does this work?" asked Ursula.

"How does what work? A date?" asked Rafael.

"Yes, a date," said Ursula. "How does a date work?"

"Well, first you step on a baguette, and after that, it all just flows," said Rafael.

"So we're doing this right."

"Oh, yes," said Rafael.

"And how does a relationship work?"

"That's the $50,000 question. What do you think?"

"Don't ask me. I'm batting . . ." Ursula hesitated, realizing that she'd begun a baseball metaphor she didn't know how to finish. "What's a really bad batting average?"

"Really bad? Zero," supplied Rafael.

"Okay, I'm batting zero," said Ursula.

The bartender set their drinks down.

"Well, here's to improving our batting averages," said Rafael, raising his glass.

Ursula clinked hers against his and took a sip. "I'm still waiting for you to explain how a relationship works," she nudged.

"Okay, let's see," said Rafael, taking a sip of beer and rising to the challenge. "It's like a fire. It starts with a foundation: kindling, newspaper, other combustible materials. So the stage is set. Then there's a spark, which ignites the fire and puts things into motion. Then comes the first flicker, and you have to nurture this part: blow on it, keep the oxygen flowing. Then another flame, then the initial burst as the flames combine. It's beautiful; it's hot; it's exciting; it's atavistic. And then after a little while, the fire settles into itself. Sometimes it dies down a little, but then it flares up again. Embers form, and they keep the heat going even when the flames aren't as strong. So it stays lit, it stays warm, and it evolves. Every fire evolves in its own way, if you keep feeding it."

"You're better at metaphors than I am," Ursula said, impressed. She made a mental note to look up the word "atavistic" later.

"Tell me something weird about your childhood," said Rafael.

Ursula furrowed her brow, and then a memory surfaced. "I haven't thought about this for years, but have you ever played Greased Watermelon? Is that a thing that other people did, or was it just us?"

"Greased Watermelon?"

"Yes. When I was growing up, my neighbor had a pool, which was very exciting and was the focus of great envy. I wanted a pool so badly, even though we had a stream; and in retrospect, the stream was much more charming than the pool. Anyway, every Fourth of July, they would invite all the neighborhood kids over, and we'd play this game called Greased Watermelon. Someone would take a giant melon and coat it in Vaseline. Then they threw it into the pool. There were two teams, and you had to try to get the watermelon over to the opposing team's side of the pool and up onto the ledge. It was a surprisingly violent game—lots of water-swallowing and near drownings. It was a major event."

"Wow," said Rafael. "That's so much weirder than what I hoped you might come up with. Well done, Ursula."

"What about you?"

"I think I have a suitable rebuttal, since we're on the subject of weird games. My uncle Horsley—he's long dead now, but he was around for family gatherings when I was a kid—always made us play this game called 'Are You There, Moriarty?' He told us it was an old parlor game, but it's also very possible he made it up. You have to lie on your stomach, blindfolded, head-to-head (literally) with your opponent—who is also in prone position—and you hold left hands. And then, in your right hand, you hold a rolled-up newspaper, and you say, 'Are you there, Moriarty?' and the other person has to say 'Yes,' and then based on where their voice comes from, the asker has to thwack them on the head with the rolled-up newspaper. The responder can dodge and roll at will, but since he's holding the left hand of the thwacker, he can't get very far. And then it just goes back and forth, with each opponent smacking the other with a newspaper roll while blindfolded and writhing around on the ground."

Ursula was using all of her mental capacity to picture what Rafael was describing. "I think I can envision it?"

"It's hard to articulate. You probably just need to see it in action," said Rafael. "Although I sincerely hope my family never subjects you to that."

"We should play sometime." Ursula smiled. "And that's significantly weirder than Greased Watermelon, so now *I'm* impressed."

Rafael shrugged modestly, pleased that he had amused her.

"I have an idea," said Ursula, signaling the bartender for the check. "Do you like Trivial Pursuit?"

"Love it."

"Do you think it's a bad idea for us to compete with one another this early in the relationship?" she asked.

"No, I think it's a great idea," he said. He wanted to do a lot of things with her. He wanted to do *all* the things. But he was completely willing to let her determine which things they did in which order and at what pace. Rafael loved anticipation as much as—or perhaps more than—whatever followed it.

The bartender dropped the bill and Rafael snapped it up, checked it, and then quickly handed over his credit card before Ursula could protest, which she appreciated. She always felt she should split the bill with her dates and often did, but she secretly loved being paid for, and she didn't care if that wasn't progressive. She gave herself permission to contradict her own principles at times; that was a modern feminist's right. In these moments, she often thought of the Walt Whitman refrain: "Do I contradict myself? Very well, then I contradict myself, I am large, I contain multitudes." Rafael had done well in paying before she could kick up a fake fuss.

As they left the lobster shack, Rafael lightly touched the small of her back. It was now 4 P.M., three hours since they'd entered, and a heavy haze had settled over the Brooklyn afternoon. She took his hand. It was such an innocent thing—hand-holding—but somehow, in their slightly tipsy state, in the sticky, dead-of-summer wind, it felt incredibly intimate. Maybe too intimate. She began dragging him down the block to her favorite dive bar, where they could duck out of the heat. Inside, the bar's wooden banquettes provided a cool, dark refuge.

"What would you like?" Rafael asked Ursula as he approached the bar.

"A pilsner, please," she said, as she scanned the shelf of board games by the door. She reached toward the top, grabbing the tattered, booze-stained box that contained Trivial Pursuit. She slid into the corner table and began setting up the board.

Rafael returned and placed her glass delicately in front of her, careful not to disturb her set-up process.

"Millennium Edition, huh?" said Rafael, noting the box and sliding into the booth so he could sit at 90 degrees to Ursula, sharing the same corner of the table.

"I prefer my trivia to be twenty years out of date," she said, reaching for the blue pie.

"Uh-oh," said Rafael, faking concern. "I'm always blue."

Ursula held out the piece to him, but he held up his hand in an act of deference, then reached for the yellow pie.

"Now that's chivalry." Ursula smiled.

They rolled to see who would go first, and Rafael prevailed, rolling a five to her two. Ursula felt a spike of competitive aggression, which she enjoyed. Rafael pushed his sleeves up over his elbows, rolled a three, and then moved his piece to a Science & Nature space. Ursula reached for a card, but before she could say anything, a man bumped against the far corner of their table.

Ursula had seen him here before. He was always drunk, but on this Saturday afternoon, he was extra drunk.

"Well, look at this." He swayed and caught his balance on a chair. "Look at you lovebirds with your *board games*. So *happy*. You make me sick."

It was true—they were happy, and they did look like lovebirds. Rafael put his hand over Ursula's and gave her a gentle squeeze. The man wasn't a threat, but Rafael wanted Ursula to feel subtly shielded.

"You," the man said, pointing at Rafael. "You better marry this girl." He swung his hand so that his finger was a foot from Ursula's forehead. "You know why?"

Ursula and Rafael waited to hear why.

"You know *why*?!" the man asked again, more urgently. "Because I didn't. I let *my* girl get away. We used to play board games. All that shit . . ." He pointed at the Trivial Pursuit board, sounding both disgusted and nostalgic. "Fuckin' lovebirds."

He looked at the board, then at Rafael. He pointed to Ursula once more and then hobbled off toward the bathroom, mumbling, "Lovebirds, dingbirds, dingbats . . ."

"Wow," said Ursula. "There you have it."

Rafael nodded, amused, taking it in. "So, should we get married?"

"Yeah, let's do it." Ursula giggled.

"Great," said Rafael, turning his attention back to the board.

Ursula plucked a creased card from the pile and read, "What is the world's deepest lake?"

Before she could supply the multiple-choice responses, Rafael said, "Lake Baikal. Too easy." He rolled again and landed on a square that could earn him a pie wedge.

Ursula read: "What All-India Institute of Medicine alumnus penned the mega-selling *Ageless Body, Timeless Mind*?"

Rafael made a face, then ventured: "Deepak Chopra?"

"Yes!" said Ursula, impressed and excited to learn that Rafael was such a worthy opponent.

Seventy-two minutes later, Rafael had earned five pie wedges to Ursula's four, but she was on a hot streak. She rolled a three and squeaked excitedly, tapping out the spaces and plunking her pie down on the wedge space. She was poised to tie it up.

Rafael picked up a card and read: "This 1906 novel by Upton Sinclair exposed the horrors of the US meatpacking industry to the American public."

"*The Jungle*," said Ursula confidently, not waiting for confirmation before dropping a fifth wedge into her pie.

Rafael nodded his head and smiled. She was going to beat him; he could feel it. He suspected that she was smarter than he was, and he liked that. Ursula held the die in her hand, and just as she threw it, their drunken friend careened into their table again, slamming it with his hip and knocking the pieces all over the floor.

He looked down, then up at them, then down at the floor again. "You better marry the fuck out of her," he reminded Rafael, and then he wobbled off.

Ursula and Rafael decided to conclude the game in a friendly tie. Everyone wins. They collected the stray pieces, put the weathered box back on the shelf, and then emerged out of the dim bar into the evening light of the street. It was 6 P.M., and the street-fair vendors were packing up.

"Cricket-infused bourbon?" A woman held out her final samples to them.

"Yum," said Ursula, knocking hers back. It burned, and she reacted with a low growl. "Raarrrrr!"

Rafael grabbed her hand. "Come on, jungle cat."

She followed willingly, but fifteen feet later, she stopped to point at a blob of fur sitting on one of the fair tables.

"What is this?" Ursula asked, thrilled.

"That's our angora rabbit, Bobbitt," the vendor said. "Want to hold him?"

"Of course." Ursula held out her arms, and the man dropped Bobbitt into them.

"Wow, I can feel his legs," said Ursula, fascinated and slightly disturbed by the stick-like objects hidden in the cloud of fur. "Rafael, he has bones under all this fluff!"

"Thank god," said Rafael, amused by this display.

"Wait, how many legs does he have?" Ursula seemed genuinely confused and attempted to sift through Bobbitt's unruly coat.

"Should be four in there," the other owner said.

"Ursula! Bobbitt!" Rafael called for their attention. He had his phone out, and he snapped a photo of a beaming Ursula and a blurry Bobbitt, Van Brunt Street stretching behind them, the sky a pale peach.

"Wait, you be in it, too! Would you mind?" Ursula asked Bobbitt's owner. He happily held out his hand for the phone, and Ursula snuggled into Rafael's shoulder as Bobbitt wriggled in her arms. They looked like a happy family with an unusual fur-covered child.

Ursula kissed Bobbitt on the head and set him down on his owner's table. Rafael slipped his hand into hers again, and they continued down the street.

"I can't *not* hug an animal when I see it," said Ursula. "I just can't help it."

"I understand, and I support all of your animal-hugging endeavors. Unless it's an apex predator or something," he said. "No shark-hugging."

Ursula's heart felt warm, and she squeezed his hand. They ambled, and she pointed out some of her favorite stores, a gallery where her friend was having a photography show next month, the bar where she had celebrated multiple birthdays. They continued, their momentum carrying them as if they were floating down a lazy river. Up ahead, a band played. "I love this song!" Ursula said. Suddenly, she felt pulled in two directions: a wave of nostalgia for something lost collided with the feeling that she was in exactly the right place with exactly the right person. "Bruce Springsteen wrote this for Elvis," she explained, "but then Elvis died, so Bruce recorded it."

Rafael watched as she dance-walked, dipping her hips, and then she whirled around and grabbed his hands.

> *I'm driving in my car,*
> *I turn on the radio,*
> *I'm pulling you close,*
> *You just say no.*

Rafael was a good dancer, a natural dancer. Though he'd grown up in New England, a land of rhythmically challenged white people, he had an innate smoothness.

> *You say you don't like it*
> *But girl, I know you're a liar*
> *Cause when we kiss*
> *Ooo-ooh, fire.*

He pulled her into him, and they danced slowly, noticing where their bodies aligned and parted, where they were one versus two. She looked up at him, laughing, radiating, free, her limbs liquid with joy.

> *Late at night*
> *I'm taking you home*
> *When I say I wanna stay*
> *You say you wanna be alone*

The music got louder as they reached the band, breaking away from one another and then coming back together seamlessly.

> *You say you don't love me*
> *Girl, you can't hide your desire*
> *And when we kiss,*
> *Ooo-ooh, fire.*

Rafael lifted Ursula off the ground, crossing his solid arms behind her thighs, so her face was just a few inches higher than his. He held her there for a few seconds so she could look down into his eyes and he could look up into hers. Then he lowered her slowly, inch by inch, until her lips met and melted into his—first sizzling and surreal, and then soft. It wasn't an out-of-body experience, or even a shared-body experience. It was more palpable than that: like gently dissolving and powerfully exploding at the same time.

He set her down, and she took a step back, feeling faint, electric, feverish, alive. She inhaled deeply, and then drifted into Rafael again, riding the kiss back to the alternate universe they could only access via each other. This went on for a while, and by the time they stopped kissing, the band members were dismantling their equipment. The sky had deepened into a shade of deep, vibrant coral.

"Do you want to get on a boat?" Rafael asked.

Ursula nodded. In that moment, she would have boarded the *Titanic*. She would have gotten on a spaceship to Mars. She would have done literally anything he asked; fortunately, Rafael was an honorable man. An honorable man with subtle bad-boy vibes. Ursula couldn't believe her good fortune.

Because everything was going uncannily smoothly, the ferry arrived just as they got to the dock in Red Hook. Ursula insisted on paying for their tickets, and then she took Rafael's hand, guiding him along the mini gangplank that led to the big white boat. They leaned against the back railing of the upper deck as the ferry reversed, churning up the East River. Pink and orange clouds, ragged like claw marks, tore the sky over the southern tip of Manhattan. A warm summer wind swirled through Ursula's hair.

"Does my head look like a squirrel's nest?" she shouted as the boat picked up speed, attempting to run her fingers through her tangles.

"Yes," said Rafael, grabbing the railing on the other side of her so that he was behind her, encircling her with his arms as they looked out at the river. The boat shifted forward, and Ursula felt Rafael's muscles tense in order to stabilize them both. Ellis Island was visible in the distance, and the Statue of Liberty jutted her torch toward them with what seemed like intention—and possibly even approval.

Ursula turned her head to peck Rafael on the cheek. He smelled like something she could only describe as "magical man musk." It was as if you poured molasses over a block of raw cedar and then lit the whole thing on fire to keep it warm and alive. That's what Rafael smelled like. She tried to describe it to him, but realized she wasn't making sense.

"No, it makes sense," he said. "And you smell like . . ."

He buried his nose into the top of her head and then stopped to consider. He wanted to get this right. "Eau d'East River."

She slapped his arm playfully.

"No, you smell like the combination of a really subtle flower and a tiny kitten and a scone," he said with conviction. Yes, he felt good about this description.

"A scone?"

"Yeah, like a raspberry scone. But there's only a hint of that. It's much more kitten-forward, with strong honeysuckle notes and a fluffy finish, like the tip of a kitten's tail." Rafael had an idea. "That's what I'm going to call you tonight: tail tip."

Ursula felt truly "seen," as her comrades at The Stake would say. She turned and stood on her toes to kiss Rafael's lips, her hair whipping both of their faces.

By the time they disembarked in Manhattan, they realized they were hungry again.

"What's your relationship with the mob like?" asked Rafael.

"Cordial, respectful," said Ursula.

"Perfect," said Rafael. "I want to take you to one of the strangest restaurants I know." He whistled loudly and a taxi dramatically swerved over to the curb in front of them.

Ursula was momentarily stunned, and then said, "I didn't realize that was still a thing." In the world of app-enabled car services, she thought of taxis as a last resort. And the idea of effortlessly summoning one with a whistle? That was the stuff of movies. But there they were, clambering into the back seat of the yellow cab, and Ursula realized that the sight of Rafael whistling and successfully hailing one was more than novel—it was sexy. What else could he make happen with a subtle, assertive gesture?

Suddenly Ursula registered: she was officially in lust with him. She had to do something about it. She had to pull the emergency brake.

"Rafael," she said gently.

"Yes, tail tip?" he looked into her eyes.

"I know we're heading uptown, and I know you live uptown," said Ursula. "And I'm sure we're going to have a really nice time at dinner, and I'm going to want to sleep with you after, but I also need you to know: I don't sleep with anyone on the first date. It's just a policy I have. So don't be offended later when I don't sleep with you."

"Thank you for the warning," said Rafael, making that happy-glow face that indicated he was laughing on the inside but remaining equanimous on the outside. "Any other policies I should know about?"

"Just that one for now," said Ursula. "What about you? Any policies?"

Rafael paused and then joked, "I never sleep with anyone on the first date." He leaned over and kissed her, their heads bobbing as the taxi dipped and swooped up FDR Drive. They laughed, but kept kissing. Kiss-laughing would soon become one of their signature moves.

The taxi deposited them on the corner of Seventy-fourth Street and First Avenue. Rafael helped Ursula out of the back seat and then held the restaurant door open as she stepped inside. The maître d' quickly materialized, saying, "*Signorina*, good evening." When he spotted Rafael behind her, his eyes lit up. *"Buona sera, Signor Banks. Bentornato!"*

They shook hands heartily, and the maître d' snapped his fingers toward a waiter, who scurried off to prepare one of the good tables in the back.

Ursula loved it here already. The walls were covered in dark wood panels adorned with kitschy Tuscan landscapes and signed-and-framed photos of celebrities who had visited the establishment.

The maître d' led them to the table in the corner so they could sit on the same banquette rather than across from one another. Ursula and Rafael settled in and the maître d' lifted the wineglasses off of the white linen tablecloth to clear space.

"Anything you want," he waved his hand in the air to indicate the infinite possibilities, "we take good care of you."

He walked away, and an eager waiter slid into the spot where his boss had been. They both ordered Manhattans, and although Ursula knew this was probably not a wise choice for her after the panoply of drinks she had already had that day, she didn't care. This place was the antithesis of the typical Brooklyn restaurants she frequented, with their overly familiar waiters ("Hey, I'm Kyle. What can I get for you guys tonight? Love your jumpsuit, by the way!") and aggressively homey environs (suspended Edison bulbs and rough-hewn wooden tables that always rocked back and forth). She had grown accustomed to beginning every meal by asking the waiter to jam a shim under the leg of her table to steady it, but not here. Ursula loved being in this foreign world of deferential middle-aged waiters, white linen, and solid tables that didn't budge.

She looked around. It did indeed feel like a mafia hideout. From her perch on the red-leather banquette she could envision being threatened by a pinstripe-clad mob boss, and she liked it. The other patrons seemed to be a mix of older businessmen, octogenarians from the neighborhood, and a few men in their fifties and sixties accompanied by short-skirted, synthetic-lipped escorts.

"This place is amazing," said Ursula.

"You should see it on Thursdays," said Rafael. "That's mistress night."

Ursula looked confused.

"Like, see all these guys who are here with their wives?" Rafael nodded discreetly at a few tables. "On Thursdays, those wives are replaced with their mistresses."

The waiter set their cocktails down. Ursula picked up her icy cold Manhattan and said, "Oh, we're definitely coming back for mistress night."

Rafael looked at her and carefully clinked his full glass against hers, maintaining eye contact as he took a sip. He felt so unabashedly happy. Everything was working; everything was flowing. They hadn't made any plans for the day beyond meeting at the lobster shack, but here they were, eight hours later, cozied up in a mob den. Rafael usually felt skeptical when things were too perfect; he kept his expectations moderate, but this was different. The Arc was simply delivering on what it had promised. And this woman was not Freja. He looked at Ursula, whose wind-whipped hair had settled around her shoulders in messy waves. She kept clawing at it, but he thought she looked magical.

After dinner, as they walked west along Seventy-fourth Street toward Central Park, Ursula said, "You know what's too bad?"

"The fact that we both have a no-sex-on-the-first-date policy?" asked Rafael.

Ursula slapped his upper arm playfully for the second time that evening. "Fresh!" she fake-scolded him, then refocused. "No. It's that no one says 'Frenching' anymore."

"Frenching. As in French-kissing," Rafael clarified.

"Yes! When I was younger, that was one of our most-used words. Like, 'Ooh, you guys totally Frenched.' Or, 'We were Frenching and his parents walked in!' But now, it has completely fallen out of the vernacular."

"Are you crazy? I say it all the time," teased Rafael. He now understood that almost everything Ursula said was a joke, and he felt fully capable of playing along, and even one-upping her on occasion. His challenge, he realized, would be to get beyond her playful surface into her more emotional depths. Could Ursula ever be serious? He would find out. But for now, he just said, "I'm planning to French you all night."

She laughed. He stopped but held her hand as she kept walking, so the momentum of her own body swung her back around toward him. He tilted her head back slightly, and they kissed. No, they Frenched. They missed the Walk sign. They continued for a good thirty seconds, exploring the feeling of it, and finally Ursula pulled back to breathe.

"Look at us," said Rafael. "Frenching right here on sin-ridden Seventy-fourth Street."

Although they were properly drunk by now, they decided to go for a nightcap at Ursula's favorite uptown bar, Bemelmans. Despite living just three blocks away, Rafael had never been there. Ursula acted scandalized when she heard this, and she insisted they go. When they arrived, their uncommonly good luck continued—there was one free table at the banquette across from the piano. Ursula loved this bar, whose extraordinarily expensive cocktails were justified by the rarefied ambiance: whimsical murals on the walls, scrumptious bar snacks, and perfectly calibrated live jazz.

"I don't want to get too meta," said Ursula, once they were settled at their table. "I mean, I don't want to self-analyze while we're in the midst of this weird-but-amazing experience. But, what made you decide to do The Arc?"

Rafael didn't really want to talk about his romantic past yet, but it was a fair question. "I reached a point where I realized I was ready for a real partnership with someone extraordinary."

"But why are you still single?" Ursula knew this was the most annoying question of all time. The only thing more annoying than asking it was having to answer it. She hoped he didn't fire it back at her.

"Well, I haven't always been single," said Rafael. "I mean, I've had relationships. Mostly good relationships. But nothing that ended up feeling sustainable." It was vague, but it was the truth. He wondered whether to ask her the same question. It was an annoying question. He wanted to spare her, but then curiosity got the better of him. "What about you?"

"The same, I guess," said Ursula. Vague, but true. "I read some-where that dating in your thirties and forties is just a process of wondering how this amazing person could still be single—and then eventually finding out why."

Rafael choked on his drink, laughing.

"I guess I could begin with my family, the forces that shaped me, the relationships that taught me things but weren't quite right, etcet-era. Various fears. Various moments of bravery and cowardice that moved me in and out of singledom. Now here I am, and I'm glad we're single at the same time. Single but also *ready* at the same time."

Rafael nodded. That actually was a satisfying answer.

"I guess the expense of The Arc didn't deter you?" Ursula asked.

"It gave me pause at first," said Rafael, sipping his bourbon. "But I decided that if it worked, it would be well worth the cost. I still have a hard time believing that they can really do what they claim to do, but I'm fascinated. And tonight, I really do feel like I'm exactly where I'm supposed to be."

Ursula felt that warm rush—familiar now—that Rafael could cre-ate within her, just by saying something sweet and well considered. And she was relieved he didn't ask her about her financial strategy when it came to The Arc. Mike Rutherford had wired $100,000 into her account back in July, kicking off her consulting contract, but there was no reason to introduce the topic of her new patron. At least not right now.

"So, Ursula," said Rafael, and then corrected himself. "I mean, tail tip. I know you have a no-sex-on-the-first-date policy, which I absolutely respect. But my next question is: do you have a policy that prohibits you from coming to my apartment so we can listen to music and eat ice cream?"

Ursula smiled. "I actually have a policy that dictates I *must* accept all ice cream offerings." Of course she wanted to listen to music and eat ice cream at his apartment. She also wanted to have sex with him—and she had no problem violating her own policy on this par-ticular occasion. But she didn't need to let him know that yet.

Leaving Bemelmans, they squeezed into the same section of the revolving door, rushing out onto the street in a blissful tornado. The wind was gone, so the night's heat was now still and thick. Cars crawled up Madison, a man walked a greyhound on a leash, and a few human voices floated in the air. Rafael felt as if they were caught in a suspension, like a summer snow globe, but instead of snow, they were floating in humidity and pleasant anticipation.

They walked the few blocks to his apartment, where Dalmat opened the door and smiled when he saw Rafael. "Evening, sir." It was after midnight.

"Evening, Dalmat." Rafael nodded a friendly hello as they entered. It was a dignified building—aged marble floors, wooden moldings, a creaky old elevator with round protruding buttons. They stepped inside and started ascending. Ursula loved that Rafael lived here. Nothing was overly new or sleek. It was like somewhere a fancy old man would live. Rafael sort of *was* a fancy old man, in a hot forty-two-year-old body. The elevator jolted to a stop, and the door sighed open. The landing had three doors; Rafael's was to the right. He turned the key and pushed the door in. "After you."

Ursula loved his gentility. It wasn't that she hadn't experienced good manners on other dates, but many men's attempts at chivalry came off as affected, awkward, and overly studied, as if they wanted a Medal of Valor for holding open a door or pulling out a chair. Rafael's gestures were genuine, natural, automatic, bred deeply into him. He was, miraculously, a true gentleman. Then again, Ursula had once read that "a gentleman is simply a patient wolf." But that didn't sound so bad, either.

The apartment was decorated sparsely with a mix of new and antique furniture, stylish but not overly trendy. "This is lovely," she said.

"Thank you," said Rafael. "My sister Catherine is an interior designer. She intervenes before I have a chance to buy anything too hideous."

Ursula beelined for the built-in bookshelves to see what Rafael's library held: Howard Zinn's *A People's History of the United States*, Neruda, Updike, Twain, plenty of Margaret Atwood (which pleased

Ursula immensely), Borges, more Borges, more Borges, some James Baldwin, an antique-looking edition of the complete works of Dickens, and even a few Roald Dahl titles. This was promising. The crackle of vinyl filled the room as Rafael wandered away from the record player and into the kitchen, and she recognized the opening chords of "Breakdown" by Tom Petty. She made her away across the room to the shelf that held his records, and she began leafing through them: Tracy Chapman, Jorge Ben, Bonnie Raitt, Charlie Parker, Mulatu Astatke, Khruangbin, Roxy Music, Fleetwood Mac, Ellis Marsalis, Led Zeppelin, Sam Cooke. Ursula had noted that many men her age and younger took up record collecting as an affectation, a self-conscious signal of their appreciation for a bygone analog age. But Rafael was forty-two, and she could instantly tell that he'd been listening to vinyl since long before it resurged as a trend.

"Tail tip!" Rafael called to her from the open kitchen. Ursula halted her examination of his books and records—he had passed with flying colors—and approached the kitchen, where Rafael pointed toward the open freezer drawer. It contained at least twenty pints of ice cream, ranging in brands and flavors, although the selection was heavy on the extra-indulgent varieties like Marshmallow Meltdown and Double Brownie Apocalypse.

"I'm a simple man," said Rafael, "but I am rich in ice cream."

Ursula put her hand over her mouth in delighted disbelief. After she collected herself, she pointed to a particular pint that spoke to her: Midnight Mint Cookies and Cream.

"Great choice," said Rafael, grabbing Ursula's selection and what looked to be a Dutch dark chocolate flavor. He grabbed two tumblers from a cabinet and proceeded to scoop the ice cream into each. As he pulled open a drawer, Ursula noticed his arms again: his lean muscles were visible beneath a layer of soft black hair. Rafael took two spoons and plopped them into the glasses of ice cream, then held Ursula's out to her.

She took a bite and allowed the coldness to melt in her mouth. It was delicious, but suddenly, she couldn't care less about ice cream. She looked at Rafael, but his eyes were down and focused. He was deeply immersed in his own glass, and he was an efficient ice-cream eater. He had already devoured half of it; this wouldn't take long. Ursula took one more slow bite and waited for him to take his last spoonful. When he finally looked up, she took his glass out of his hand and kissed him deeply. There it all was: mint, chocolate, an entire day's worth of sexual tension, an entire life's worth of wondering if she would ever find someone that made her feel like this.

"I've updated my policy," Ursula said.

"Is that right?" Rafael wrapped his arms around her waist. "Tell me more."

"Effective immediately, I always have sex on the first date."

Rafael laughed.

There was no rush, and yet Ursula felt a pleasant urgency. Had The Arc architected this? This perfect tension between security and excitement? She felt both in control and delightfully out of control. Ursula wanted to seduce Rafael as if he would disappear tomorrow, even though she knew she was contracted to be with him eighteen months from now—and probably forever after that.

"As you wish," said Rafael. "You're the policy expert in this relationship."

Ursula started to unbutton Rafael's shirt. He looked down at her fingers and his heart sped up as she undid one button, then another. He slid his fingers up her thigh and under the flouncy hem of her dress, something he'd been wanting to do all day.

Ursula tilted her head back and bit her lip, distracted from her unbuttoning mission.

Rafael looked into her green eyes like she was the most remarkable thing he had ever seen and then picked her up—her legs wrapping around him—and carried her toward the bedroom.

Chapter 14

Ursula awoke feeling surprisingly good. A bit thirsty, but no detectable hangover, which was a miracle given the array of drinks she'd had the day before. Rafael was still asleep. Unlike Ursula, who slept in an asymmetrical swirl—like a human who'd been trapped and preserved in volcanic ash—Rafael was more organized. He slept on his back, with his arms crossed and his hands tucked neatly into his armpits. It was a bit mummy-like, but Ursula found it beautiful. She pressed herself into his side, and he made a little grunt of recognition, turning so he could spoon her.

Yes. Oh, hell yes. Ursula remembered this from last night. He was the ideal big spoon to her little spoon. They were perfect puzzle pieces. As his body heat enveloped her, it dawned on her: The Arc had nailed it. She had indicated in her intake assessment that snuggling was almost as important to her as sex. She realized that's why Rafael was 5'10" to her 5'7". They were perfectly proportioned to spoon. Suddenly, she wondered why she had ever dated anyone over six feet, because this—*this right here*—was heaven. And on top of the size and shape compatibility, Rafael had the most amazing skin. She wanted to say it was like silk, but actually, it was much, much smoother than silk, like something in between solid and liquid.

She felt something harden against the back of her legs.

"You have an amazing ding-dang," she said, reaching back to touch it.

"Oh, thanks, my savanna cat." Rafael laughed. "That's a great term for it—no one has ever called my dick a ding-dang before."

"No? That's the standard term in my household. It's from the Old English." Ursula smiled.

"Ah, I see I've got a linguist on my hands. I guess it's time for me to get more descriptive when talking about your . . ." He slid his hand from her ribcage downward, and then stopped to contemplate.

Ursula was feeling incredibly frisky but also eager to see what he would come up with.

"Your Viggo Mortensen," said Rafael, saying the first thing that popped into his head, perhaps because he had recently watched *Eastern Promises*.

"Did you just call my vagina Viggo Mortensen?" Ursula asked in a neutral voice.

"No," said Rafael calmly. "I called it '*your* viggo mortensen,' as in, not a proper noun. Not *the* Viggo Mortensen, the man. Just a run-of-the-mill term for a vagina—which I just made up."

Silence followed. Rafael held Ursula in a tight spoon. He felt fairly confident that he understood her sense of humor, but then again, he'd only known her for twenty hours. Maybe he had overstepped.

Then, Ursula convulsed with laughter in his arms. "I love it so much," she said, delighted by how this man could simultaneously be so sexy and so unpredictably odd. "You nailed it." She giggled for a good while and then turned to face him and said, "Let's fuck."

The sober morning sex was even better than the first-time (middle-of-the-night, booze-and-ice-cream-fueled) sex. How, how, *how* was the sex this satisfying? In Ursula's experience, sex with nice men was always *okay*, while sex with scoundrels was significantly better. But this was the best of all. *How had The Arc pulled it off?* Ursula wanted to understand, but at the same time, she didn't care. Two orgasms later, she fell back to sleep. And when she woke up again, this time at 11 A.M., Rafael was gone. She heard dishes clacking in the kitchen.

She got up, feeling a bit wobbly, and walked over to look at herself in the large round mirror above his Scandinavian-style dresser. She looked decent. Definitely sex-frazzled, but in an acceptable way. She scanned the room for her underwear, bra, and dress, which Rafael had left in a neat pile on a chair. She dressed and then scurried into the bathroom to run some toothpaste around her mouth with a finger. Feeling refreshed, she strutted into the kitchen, where Rafael was cooking eggs, low and slow in a cast-iron skillet.

"Morning, my creature," he said.

"Morning, capybara," said Ursula.

"I'm assuming you like eggs, but I could be wrong," said Rafael, as four pieces of toast popped from the toaster.

"I don't like them. I *love* them," said Ursula. She also loved Rafael. That hadn't taken long. "Is there a coffee situation?"

"I forgot about that." Rafael winced. "I mean, I didn't know you were going to sleep here, and I don't drink coffee. I can get some; I just don't have any right now."

Interesting—a difference. But a difference that Ursula could definitely live with.

"Don't worry about it," said Ursula. "I consume too much caffeine anyway. And I feel pleasantly out-of-it right now."

"I do, too," said Rafael. He'd been in a euphoric haze since yesterday afternoon. Whereas Ursula had dipped in and out of enjoyment and analysis as they'd learned more about each other, Rafael had simply been present. This was working, which wasn't surprising, because it was supposed to work. He really, really liked this woman. She was weird as hell, but captivating. He couldn't imagine ever not liking her, and he hoped that, soon enough, he would love her. Ever since he'd been burned by Freja, that possibility—love, attachment, emotional dependence—had stressed him out. But now, it felt like something to look forward to.

After they ate the eggs and toast (sourdough—which they discovered was a mutual favorite), they lounged on the couch, where Ursula lay her head on Rafael's lap.

"Wait, what about your cat?" asked Rafael. "Doesn't she need to be fed?"

Ursula was touched that Rafael was already looking out for Mallory's needs. "I gave her a giant lunch yesterday. She'll be a bit mad when I get home, but she's okay. I should go soon, though. I have to meet my friend Issa in a few hours at this club we belong to, The Stake."

"Like S-T-E-A-K?" asked Rafael, hopeful.

"Close," said Ursula. "S-T-A-K-E."

"Like what you use to kill a vampire?"

"Yes, and also where witches were burned," said Ursula. "But at *this* Stake, no witches are burned. Instead, we reclaim our feminine power and we rage against the patriarchy."

"That sounds nice," said Rafael.

Ursula needed to go, but she didn't want to burst their first-date bubble. She was so happy that it scared her. They lounged in silence for a few minutes, Rafael gently stroking her hair.

"The Arc," Ursula mused. "They really know what they're doing."

"They sure do," said Rafael, looking down at her. Her makeup had rubbed off during the night, and he noticed that the tips of her eyelashes were blond.

"What's this?" Ursula said, reaching up to touch the scar on Rafael's left eyebrow. She had wanted to ask him last night, but had abstained, aware that while many scar stories were fun, others were tethered to unpleasant memories. Now, she felt ready to receive the story, whatever its origin.

Rafael smiled and touched the spot with his finger. "My sister Patricia was trying to teach me a dance routine when I was two, and I fell into the edge of a glass table."

"Yikes."

"Yeah, they weren't big on baby-proofing in the seventies."

"Times have definitely changed," said Ursula, envisioning the maniacally protective parents who dominated her neighborhood with their designer strollers. Then she smiled, thinking of a toddling Rafael, learning the ropes of life from two older sisters. "It must be nice to have siblings."

"It is," Rafael said. "My sisters are a little nuts, but they keep things interesting."

Ursula smiled up into his brown eyes. "I'm trying not to overthink right now, but I just have one question. Is it okay for me to be enjoying you this much? I mean, can I just let myself fall into this? Because I want to. But am I safe with you?"

"Oh, swan tuft," Rafael had just started calling her random things at this point, which she loved. "You're very safe with me."

She felt the warm rush thing, and she pulled herself up so that she was sitting in his lap. They kissed. Not a French; just a long, strong, lip-to-lip kiss. A solid kiss that felt like a promise.

Then Ursula got up to pull herself together, and Rafael started rinsing the dishes.

"Thank you for an amazing first date," she said, leaning against the counter.

"Thank you for updating your no-sex policy," said Rafael, drying his hands so he could pull her into his arms. He kissed her gently, and then asked casually, "Can I see you again sometime?"

She playfully slapped his arm—already a recurring theme in their relationship—and said, "I'll think about it."

Chapter 15

"Yes, he is funny," Ursula responded to Issa. "But that word doesn't really capture it. He's weird-funny. Low-key funny. He's droll. Yes, that's it. He's droll."

Ursula had gone home to feed Mallory and change, and now they were at The Stake doing a body treatment called The Awakening, where they lay naked on side-by-side tables in a room that was effectively a giant shower, while two spa specialists sloughed off the top layers of their skin using fruit acids and rough sea sponges. It was both painful and exhilarating, and was designed to create a feeling of physical and spiritual rebirth. Ursula's skin burned; she tried to breathe through it.

"Droll," said Issa, trying out the word. "I like it."

"You talk about new man?" asked one of the spa specialists, Svetlana, in a deep Russian accent.

Before Ursula could answer, Svetlana continued. "I tell you how to judge new man. Is simple. All you need is listen to four inner compass: head, heart, gut, wagina." She pointed to each body part on herself as she said it. "If wagina say yes, but gut say no, run. If head and heart say yes, but wagina say no, von't vork. If you have two of four, or three of four, you can do it for a vhile. You try. But you vant lifelong love? You need four of four. *Must have* four of four—no compromise. Must trust compass. Flip!" She slapped Ursula's thigh.

Ursula and Issa rolled from their backs onto their fronts, slipping around like seals on the acid-and-oil-covered tables. Svetlana and the other attendant began sloughing off the skin on their legs and backs.

"You're a sage, Svetlana," said Issa.

"Not sage," said Svetlana, dumping a bucket of warm water over Ursula's back. "Just voman who has lived."

"Did your four compasses lead you to lifelong love?" asked Ursula. "Did you find your man?"

"Yes. He dead now," said Svetlana, without emotion. "But it was great love."

Ursula and Issa made momentary eye contact. As ridiculous as The Stake was, they always gained something by coming here. Two huge buckets were dumped over their heads.

"And . . . done!" said Svetlana, patting Ursula on the butt cheek. "Like fresh-born babe."

She and the other attendant left the room, and Issa and Ursula got up to towel off.

"I do feel like fresh-born babe," said Ursula, slipping into a white robe. "And not just my skin. Everything, everything feels clean. The literal and emotional filth has lifted. I'm innocent and pure like a baby again."

"You do look really good," said Issa. "And you seem happy. You have a whole different energy today."

"Oh my god, Issa. Am I in love?" asked Ursula, grabbing her friend's robed arm to steady herself. "I'm in love!"

"You're definitely in *something*," said Issa. "You've got that oxytocin thing going on. And Rafael sounds great. But easy, tiger. Take it slow."

Ursula took a deep breath and pointed to each area of her body as she slowly and solemnly repeated: "Head. Heart. Gut. Wagina."

Chapter 16

"That's the wild thing," Rafael said to Skipp as they approached the basketball court where they met most Sunday afternoons. "There was so much pressure that there was actually *no* pressure."

"The pressure was so immense that it consumed itself and liberated you," said Skipp.

"Exactly," said Rafael, walking onto the court. He dribbled the ball a few times and then took a free throw. The ball dropped through the netless hoop without touching the rim. "See? What was that?! Did you see that? The entire date was like that shot. Seamless. Zero friction."

"Maybe too seamless?" asked Skipp, who preferred his romances full of friction.

"Maybe. I don't know. Supposedly The Arc knows more than I do, and I'm starting to really believe that's true." Rafael watched as Skipp bricked his shot, retrieved the rebound, missed the layup, and then finally made a four-foot jump shot. Basketball was not Skipp's sport. It wasn't really Rafael's either, which made their games fun and low-stakes. Squash was another story: despite being twenty pounds heavier than he wanted to be, Skipp could destroy Rafael on the squash court. To this day, Skipp's right arm (in which he held his racquet) was significantly more muscular than his left—a relic of his years as a New England junior champion. He often joked that he looked like a fiddler crab.

"So what's Ursula like?" asked Skipp.

"She's smart," said Rafael. "And she's just the right amount of weird."

"What kind of weird?" asked Skipp.

"It's hard to describe," said Rafael, attempting a three-pointer but missing. "She growled a few times—like a jungle cat. She picked up a rabbit on the street. And she called my dick a ding-dang."

"This is very promising," said Skipp.

"Right?" confirmed Rafael. "And then I called her vagina her viggo mortensen, and she thought that was hysterical."

"You what?"

"She liked it! She was totally on board with it."

"Wow. You guys are *both* fuckin' weird," said Skipp, finally making a free throw. "But that's great. She sounds cool. Most girls wouldn't go for the old 'viggo mortensen as vagina' routine. That was a risk."

"I know," said Rafael. "But I sort of knew she would appreciate it."

"So you were, as they might say, 'being yourself'?" Skipp bounced a pass over to Rafael.

"I guess so," said Rafael, dribbling a few times and then making another frictionless free throw.

"Because sometimes being yourself can backfire," said Skipp, who knew from experience.

The two friends had been playing at this court for twenty years. Throughout their friendship, Skipp and Rafael had always felt closest when they were side by side, or sprinting around one another, rather than when they were face to face.

"I don't know why I'm surprised that it was so great," said Rafael. "It's supposed to be, right? That's what I signed up for."

"Fifty thousand dollars' worth of greatness," said Skipp, driving hard toward the basket and accidentally slamming the ball into the underside of the rim.

"Still got it." Rafael laughed at his friend, grabbing the ball and dribbling along the three-point line.

Skipp began commentating in his Marv Albert sports-announcer voice. "And here's Jordan from way downtown!"

That was Rafael's cue to shoot. He sank the three-pointer.

"Damnnnnn," said Skipp, his hands on his knees as he tried to catch his breath. "Alright, I'm gassed."

Rafael grabbed the ball and started walking toward the bench where they'd left their things, calling over his shoulder, "Pizza?"

"Zig-a-zig-zaaaaa," sang Skipp, combining his favorite Spice Girls song with his favorite food.

That meant yes.

Chapter 17

Late Summer into Autumn

Ursula and Rafael did not take it slow. Emboldened by The Arc's guarantee of success, they dove in with the wild abandon of teenagers, as if drunk with the thrill of first love. They didn't take this feeling for granted: people of their age rarely got to experience the initial phase of a relationship without trepidation, without navigating their own emotional tripwires, without batting away the ever-present specter of disaster. But The Arc had solved for all that. Both Rafael and Ursula had directed their skepticism toward The Arc itself during their early deliberations about whether to use the service, but now that they had taken the plunge—and it had worked!—there was no reason not to trust the process. Theirs was more than a great love; it was a triumph.

On their second date, Rafael showed up at Ursula's door with an elaborate bouquet of herbs that he had grown on his balcony: fragrant mint, abundant basil, bright cilantro. Ursula led him inside, poured him a drink, and proceeded to make the most impressive meal she knew how to cook: heirloom tomatoes and burrata with aged balsamic, lemon-roasted chicken, herby green salad with tangy Dijon vinaigrette, and chocolate mousse. They split a bottle of Côtes du Rhône and spent three hours languishing at the wooden table in her garden. By the time they finished, the fireflies were out.

"What's that photo on your fridge of you in the cheetah suit?" Rafael asked.

He must have noticed the picture from Ursula's friend's Save the Amazon fund-raiser.

"First of all, it's a leopard suit," said Ursula, scolding him. "Know your big cats."

Rafael put his hands up in atonement.

"It was a fund-raiser to help protect the rainforest, and we were told to dress up as our favorite jungle animal," said Ursula. "It's a shame there aren't more occasions to wear that thing."

"Do you need an occasion?" said Rafael.

Ursula paused to consider. She liked his subtle way of recognizing who she was without judgment, and then encouraging her to lean even further into her instincts, to be even more herself.

"You know, the other night, you admitted that you sing songs to your cat," said Rafael. "Do you remember that?"

"Did I?" said Ursula casually. Of course she remembered. She felt as though she spent half her life singing to her cat.

"You did." He smiled, pouring the last of the wine into their glasses. "When do I get to hear one of these songs?"

"Well, they aren't really meant for public consumption," said Ursula. "They're for Mallory. It's just this thing that's between her and me."

"I'm not the public," said Rafael. "I want to be part of this exclusive musical world."

Ursula was nervous, but healthy-nervous. This felt like a true gateway into the oddness that pervaded her home life, her inner life. She hadn't expected to let Rafael in on this so soon, but what the hell. "One moment, please."

She got up from the table and went inside. Rafael watched her. She was barefoot and wearing a yellow wrap-dress with tiny flowers on it. Her hair was in a braid, or a braid-like thing, where half of it was up and half of it was down. He wasn't sure what to call it—a microbraid?—but he liked it. He liked everything about her so far, including the fact that she had served him burrata and roast chicken, two of his favorite things, and then artfully incorporated the herbs he had brought into her salad. Their conversations were fun and unexpected, and she gave off an air of having no agenda. Of course, there *was* an agenda. The Arc experience was an agenda unto itself. But within that agenda, they had established an unhurried, natural equilibrium. Their interactions so far felt light, unburdened. Ironically, they felt much lighter than the "casual" dating that Rafael had done in the previous few years. Most of his first dates had begun with the woman subtly grilling him to deduce how much money he made, whether he was emotionally available, and when he would be ready to procreate and rear children with her. He wasn't against sharing that information, but he didn't like having it extracted from him in such a transparent way. He was always put off by it. But with Ursula, there was no need to talk about those things yet, and he was sure the conversation would unfold smoothly when they did. Maybe The Arc had ironed out any potential pitfalls, and the entirety of their relationship would be as seamless as these early encounters. Rafael realized with some amazement that he was happier than he'd ever been.

The screen door swung open and Ursula stepped back into the yard, holding Mallory's balled up body in her arms.

"Are you sure about this?" said Ursula, stopping abruptly and cocking her head to the side.

"Completely sure," said Rafael. He liked how Ursula put up little resistances, but easily relented when he encouraged her.

She took a few steps closer to him and then looked down into the cat's face. She sang in a way that was both earnest and aware of how ridiculous she must have sounded:

> *Are you a cat? Or are you a seal?*
> *I don't believe you're even real.*
> *Instead of flippers, you've got feet,*
> *But fish is what you love to eat.*
> *Take your flippers, hold them up,*
> *I knew it, Mal! You're my seal pup.*

"Just stuff like that," said Ursula, spinning around and retreating through the screen door to put Mallory back inside.

Rafael clapped enthusiastically. "Did you just make that up?"

"Yes," said Ursula, scampering over to him on her toes. "It wasn't a very good one, actually."

"You're a real talent," he said. "Seriously, you have a future as a cat troubadour. There's a lot of money in that."

Ursula flopped onto Rafael's lap and helped herself to the last sip from his wineglass. She set it down, kissed him, and then pulled back. "It's a pretty big deal that you got to see that," she said. Her heart was beating fast—he could feel it.

"I know," said Rafael. "It's a great honor."

On their third date, they went to Jalisco, a kitschy but legit Mexican restaurant in Rafael's neighborhood. Rafael got there first and installed himself at the corner table. Six minutes later, Ursula walked in wearing her leopard suit. There were a handful of other patrons in the restaurant, and they looked at her with shock before turning back to their conversations and quesadillas.

Ursula grinned at Rafael from the doorway. He held out his arms to her, and she slinked into them. "Who is this leopardess?!" he asked, loving her wildness. She looked incredibly sexy.

Ursula liked this developing element of their relationship. She liked shock-and-aweing him. He appreciated her efforts, and she loved making him laugh.

The waiter came over to take their order. As Ursula deliberated, Rafael said, "Tequila rocks with a lime."

"And for the panther?" asked the waiter, turning to Ursula. A margarita for the panther.

The waiters comped them for most of their meal. Ursula wanted to think it was because of her outfit, but she realized that all the waiters here knew Rafael. In fact, the employees at most of the establishments in his neighborhood seemed to know—and like—Rafael.

"This is a beautiful couple," said the owner to no one in particular, gesturing toward Ursula and Rafael as they made their way toward the door after dinner. It seemed the whole world was cheering them on.

Rafael's building was up the block, and as soon as they got in the elevator, Rafael peeled off the top half of Ursula's leopard suit and began kissing her neck and collarbone.

"Jesus," he said, inhaling her skin.

Ursula had never experienced this kind of sizzling chemistry before. The closest she'd come was with the reprobates of her younger years, whose asshole behavior somehow fueled the intensity of their sexual encounters. But this was different, because Rafael wasn't an asshole, nor a reprobate. He was simply a mystery. She wanted to know him. But more than anything, she wanted to please him, to enthrall him, to never disappoint him.

On their fifth date, they strolled through the roses at the Brooklyn Botanic Garden, laughing at the oddly named varieties under a golden September sun.

"I'm very into the Julia Child," said Rafael.

"I'm liking the Michael Bolton," said Ursula.

"The Michael Bolton! Who comes up with these names? And why stop there? Let's see if there's a Genghis Khan."

"I'll be over here looking for the Ruth Bader Ginsburg," said Ursula.

Eventually, they settled onto a bench near the cherry trees, which had shed their flowers months before, but still created shady thoroughfares for those strolling the garden.

An awkward man jogged past them. He was wearing poofy jeans and listening to a Walkman.

"What in God's name . . ." said Ursula.

"Are you even allowed to run in here?"

"I don't think so."

"And he has an incredibly dysfunctional gait," said Rafael. A former college athlete, he couldn't help but analyze such things. "He's going to injure himself."

"Maybe that's because he's wearing mom jeans," said Ursula. But then she started thinking about her own form. She turned to Rafael. "Will you assess my gait?"

Rafael had not expected this request, but it delighted him. "I would love to."

Ursula got up and walked a few meters to the left, until she was hidden by a high hedge.

"Ready?" she yelled.

"Ready!"

When she emerged, she was cantering like a horse. Of course she was.

"Now that's a fine gait," he said. "That filly is ready for the dressage ring."

Ursula pulled the reins on her canter and turned. "Okay, but for real this time," she said, disappearing behind the hedge again.

Rafael waited. This time, Ursula emerged backward, moonwalking skillfully. He shook his head in awe.

"Okay, but for *real* real this time," said Ursula, disappearing once more.

This time, she ran in her normal, natural way.

"Your gait's actually pretty good," said Rafael, being honest, but feeling a brief nostalgia for her antics. "I prefer you as a show pony, though."

Their seventh date fell on Mallory's adopt-a-versary, so they decided to bake a cake. Rafael pointed to a random page in a cookbook that Ursula had never used and landed on a photo of a cake with an elaborate sculpted-sugar owl on top.

"Mallory would love that," said Ursula. "She's obsessed with birds."

"Have you ever made anything like this before?" Rafael asked.

"A cake? Yes," said Ursula. "A sculpted-sugar owl? Absolutely not. But you make me feel ambitious. You make me feel like I could win *The Great British Bake Off.*"

They spent the afternoon carefully melting sugar into puddles on parchment paper and then using toothpicks to swirl it into approximations of wings, feathers, a head, eyes.

Throughout the process, Rafael adopted a fake persona named Gunther von Schmidt, an Austrian specialist in the sugar arts.

When Ursula critiqued his technique, he said things like: "I trained *mit* Axel Freigenstadt. Don't question me."

At one point, Ursula touched the molten sugar and yelped.

"Are you okay?" Rafael said, breaking character to put her finger to his mouth. Then slipping back into Gunther: "Sugar sculpting is very dangerous. My classmate in Austria lost both her hands making a croquembouche."

When they had created something that resembled an owl, they carefully placed it on top of the cake and stood back. It looked more like a raccoon than a bird, but they both felt jubilant. No matter what they did together, they had what felt like an obscene amount of fun.

On their ninth date, they snuck into an apartment building near the Brooklyn waterfront that Ursula had briefly lived in years ago, for which she still possessed the key to the front door. Its roof had a water tower that made it one of the tallest buildings in the neighborhood. The roof was not particularly safe, but it afforded the best view of Manhattan that Ursula had ever seen.

After climbing up the rickety ladder, they sat on the ledge of the tower, their legs hanging down. Manhattan sparkled across the East River, so picturesque that it looked almost fake: a toy city illuminated by the bright pearl of the October moon, high and full.

"Do you think we ever looked at the same full moon before we knew each other?" Ursula asked.

"Like at the same time?" said Rafael.

"Yes, but in different places," said Ursula.

"Of course we did."

"I think so, too."

"This view almost makes me want to move to Brooklyn," said

Rafael. "Almost." They had playfully sparred over the fact that they lived in rival boroughs, although neither was particularly attached to theirs. Ursula had loved Brooklyn for years, but recently felt that its self-satisfied bourgeoisie was perhaps even more insufferable than the Manhattan snobs she'd once sought to avoid. Rafael had always lived on the Upper East Side, save for a handful of years in the East Village when he was in his twenties. For him, his chosen neighborhood was not a statement of identity, but rather a matter of convenience: he worked in Midtown and did business with the suit-wearing crowd, most of whom still lived uptown.

Despite the roughly forty-five minutes it took to get from her apartment to Rafael's by subway, Ursula liked visiting him; and he liked visiting her in Carroll Gardens. They thrived on the thrill of entering each other's worlds, but then retreating to the familiarity of their own.

"Everyone loves the Chrysler Building," said Rafael. "And it is beautiful, but is it really the *most* beautiful?"

"Thank you!" said Ursula, raising her hands in victory. "I've been saying this for years! New Yorkers get so sentimental about the Chrysler Building, and then act like the Empire State Building is a Walmart or something, just because it's frequented by the masses. It's not right. There's significant pretension at work there."

"You might be onto something," said Rafael. "I'm not going to hop on the Chrysler train just because it's the sophisticated choice. If you're talking art deco, I just don't think you can do better than the Empire State. Especially when the lights are all white, like tonight."

"I am completely with you on that," said Ursula. "I was having this exact debate with a client the other day."

"Ursula, I have to ask you something." Rafael paused, and then said, "What exactly is it that you do? I mean, I know you're a force and everyone worships you. But what *is* branding? What do you *do* all day? In detail."

She laughed. "That's a good question. The public-facing answer is: I help clients, mostly startups, build or pivot their brands to make them more relevant and resonant. The real answer is: I sell my soul and deplete my creative resources so that others can profit from them. I go to a zillion meetings, and I try to prevent my clients from making major marketing faux pas. And once in a while, I get a chance to actually build a brand or a campaign from the ground up. That part is fun." She took a breath. "Storytelling. That's the word we use in my industry. We deploy 'storytelling' to help build brands and make money. But most of us on the creative side would prefer to be telling our own stories on our own terms."

"Yes. That pesky need to make a living . . ." said Rafael, picking up on one of Ursula's core frustrations.

"The worst, right?" she responded. "But that's exactly it. Ever since I started working, I've felt this tension. I want to succeed and rise to the top of wherever it is I work, but I also want to flee and build my own thing in my own way. It's this cycle of motivation and frustration that seems to repeat endlessly."

Rafael grinned.

"What?" Ursula asked. "What's funny?!"

"Nothing, we're just different in that way," Rafael said. "I really admire what you do. Even if some of your clients are delusional lunatics. The fact that your work is creative—I wouldn't be able to do that every day."

"I guess I'm used to it," said Ursula. "I grew up with a mother who flung her body onto canvasses for fun. Everything was creative— maybe unnecessarily creative. She would sometimes make big bowls of fruit salad, and she'd arrange the top layer of fruit to look like classic paintings. She once made Van Gogh's *Starry Night* using peaches, bananas, and blueberries. And parsley for the cypress tree."

"Yum?"

Ursula laughed. "'Yum?' is exactly the right way to describe it. But yes, it was an odd childhood. I think I've always felt like a bit of an outsider, an underdog. Confident in my ideas but suspicious of the system. Intrigued by the Game but repelled by the Man."

Rafael looked at her, amused. "Am I the Man?"

"I don't think so," said Ursula. "Although I was a little surprised to learn that my ideal mate was a *lawyer*. And a trust-and-estates lawyer, at that. So tell me: What do *you* do all day, Rafael? What are you typically doing at 2:08 P.M.?"

"At 2:08 P.M.? That's when I'm usually staring out the window and wondering why I didn't become a wildlife photographer," said Rafael, joking. "No, the public-facing answer is: I help families and individuals navigate the process of managing assets and planning for the future, for the unknown. The real answer is: I mitigate conflict among rich people who are fighting over their dead parents' wealth. I know it sounds . . ."

"Dry?" Ursula supplied.

"Sure." Rafael smiled. "Aspects of it are very dry. But there's also the human component: getting to see families at their best and their worst, seeing the effects of both extreme generosity and extreme selfishness play out. And I suppose there's some creativity to it as well. I have one client who structured his will like a scavenger hunt for his children. Who were forty-nine and forty-four, by the way."

Ursula's jaw dropped. "That's amazing. I'm going to do that."

"I think I like having the opportunity to witness the drama of other peoples' lives, while keeping my own life relatively drama-free. I chose trusts and estates because it's reliable—families will never stop feuding over money. It's old-school, but I like to think I introduce new-school ways of thinking about it. And I knew I could have autonomy and become a partner at a small outfit without being beholden to a giant corporate firm and all the pressure that comes with that," he explained. "But yeah, at 2:08 P.M. on the average day, nothing too exciting is happening. It's mostly the same process over and over."

"You don't get bored?" asked Ursula, who relied on the churning chaos of the branding and startup worlds to keep her on her toes.

"No," said Rafael. "It's just my job."

Ursula laughed, then she realized he was serious. "*Just* your job?"

"I mean it's just one facet of my life," said Rafael. "It's not the whole picture, mercifully. I can leave my work at work, so to speak."

"That's very European of you," said Ursula. "Very British. At the pub by 5:30. Excellent work-life boundaries."

"Five thirty might be pushing it," said Rafael. "But yes. There's a balance."

"In my industry, there's no pub. We just drink in the office and then go home at 10 P.M.," said Ursula. "Work is both the office and the pub."

"Your generation is so confused," said Rafael lightly, joking about their meager age difference. "And I'm sure my philosophy sounds exceedingly pragmatic and boring and not romantic to you."

"No, it doesn't," said Ursula. "Just the opposite. There's nothing wrong with pragmatism or boundaries. I *wish* I were more pragmatic. Sometimes I conflate my job with my identity, and things get confusing. The irony here is that I think one of the reasons I'm so obsessive about my career is because my mom never really got hers off the ground. And the reason *that* matters is because we didn't have a lot of money. There was an inheritance dispute that ended up alienating her from her family."

Rafael gave her a knowing glance and then looked out toward the river. "This stuff runs deep. What happened with your mom's family?"

Ursula explained the financial snub that had propelled her mother east, the frugal life she had known as a child. The fact that her uncles had been tasked with managing the Byrne family wealth, but had eventually run their father's company into the ground. Luckily, they had created a college fund for her before all this happened, but she had developed a deep sense of ambivalence when it came to the role of money in providing a sense of "security." Once you had enough to survive, she often wondered whether it created more problems than it solved.

Rafael listened. When she finished, he didn't offer his professional opinion. He merely nodded and said, "Money is an emotional currency—how and when we spend it, withhold it, invest it, hoard it, squander it, seek it. Decisions that seem pragmatic are often reactions rooted in deep-seated biases and conditioning. I like to examine how generations organize themselves materially, because it's always about more than the money. Families are complicated, and I'm as interested in emotional inheritance as much as financial inheritance. I like untangling all of that. But most of all, I like to help keep the peace."

"Ah, so you're not *really* a lawyer," concluded Ursula. "You're a psychologist and a peacekeeper. You're the VP of fiscal and psychological untangling."

He smiled as if she had cracked some kind of code.

"That's good." She nodded, proud of her own sleuthing. "Because I'm a bit of a rabble-rouser."

"I would expect no less from the VP of strategic audacity," said Rafael, putting his hand on her knee. "I think we have a lot to learn from each other."

She examined his profile in the half darkness. He was so goddamn handsome and smart and even-keeled. She loved that he was mature and solid, but still a little bit unformed. There was still room for her to influence him, and vice versa. He had a way of getting her to open up more than she usually would. He rode out her jokes and then pivoted into more earnest conversations, taking her with him, which she needed. Earnestness was uncomfortable for her, but it was refreshing to dwell there with him.

"I'm already learning things from you," said Ursula.

"Like what?"

"Like, I need to write a scavenger-hunt will ASAP or else my kids will never know where to find the family fortune."

"*Our* kids," corrected Rafael. The notion filled Ursula with a calm, bubbling feeling.

"And I also need to generate the family fortune," said Ursula.

"We can work on that together."

"Should we do everything together?" The calm, bubbling feeling rose higher.

"We should definitely do everything together," he said, leaning over to kiss her.

She pushed him gently onto his back, undid his belt, released the top button of his jeans, and then slid slowly down his torso.

Rafael lay back, watching Ursula, her hair falling around his hips, the Empire State Building luminous in the distance. If he weren't living this moment, he wouldn't have believed it was possible.

Their eleventh date did not go as planned. They were supposed to attend Ursula's friend's movement-art performance, but the morning of, Ursula woke with an oppressive cold. She texted Rafael to alert him to her condition: "My eyeballs are hot and squishy. My head is an ominous storm cloud. My nostrils are tunnels to hell."

Rafael texted back: "Oh, poor water moccasin. Are you at home resting?"

Ursula texted: "Yes, sea snake."

Rafael responded: "Good. We don't need you sniffling all over the office with those hot eyeballs. Make sure you drink a lot of water today." He remembered that she disliked drinking water, so he added: "Or whatever qualifies as a lot for you."

Ursula appreciated this attention to detail: "I've done at least six big sips. A new record."

Rafael responded: "I'll stop by your place this evening to check on you."

She knew the term "stopping by" was generous, since her apartment was nowhere near Rafael's office, but at 7 p.m., he showed up at her door. She loved seeing him in his work clothes. In her professional world, people were stylish but casual. So there was something about a man in a well-cut suit that immediately turned her on. She was attracted to the novelty of it.

She, however, looked atrocious, her hair tangled and unwashed. When she opened her door, Rafael set a bag of groceries down, picked her up, carried her over to the couch, laid her down gently, and tucked a blanket around her.

"I brought some soup," he said. "I'm going to heat it up, okay?"

"Yes, please," said Ursula. She couldn't remember the last time someone had taken care of her when she was sick. Her mother had never been much of a nurturer. And her exes had all said things like,

"Oh, that sucks. Let me know when you're on the mend." No one had willingly—lovingly—subjected themselves to her pathogens. But Rafael was not daunted. Because The Arc had matched her with a perfect man who knew exactly how to take care of her. She watched as he looked through her cabinets for a pot. He mostly knew his way around her apartment by now, but he still had things to discover. He put the soup on the stove, stirring it slowly. He tested it to make sure it wasn't too hot, and then put it in a bowl and brought it to Ursula on the couch.

"Hey, glockenspiel. What if I light a fire?" he said. It was late October, and although it was still warm in New York, the evenings had turned brisk.

"Oooh, yes," said Ursula. She watched blearily as he prepared the fireplace with the precision of a surgeon, balling up newspaper first, then layering on small twigs, then larger kindling, then a birch log. He checked to make sure the flue was open—he was no amateur—and then struck a match, lighting a few of the newspaper balls. He sat back on his heels, one knee up, as he assessed the fire. The newspaper burst into flames, then the kindling caught, and finally, the bark of the big log started to smoke and pop. Rafael took a deep breath and blew on the embers, encouraging the flames a bit higher, and then, satisfied, he got up and clapped the dust off his hands.

Ursula was in heaven. With the exception of her throbbing head and sore throat, this was heaven.

Rafael wandered over to the bookshelf and examined the titles, eventually pulling a collection of poetry from a middle shelf. "'When the Himalayan peasant meets the he-bear in his pride, He shouts to scare the monster, who will often turn aside . . .'" he read from Kipling's "The Female of the Species" as he returned to the couch. Ursula sat up to make room for him and then lay back across his lap. Mallory hopped up from the floor and wedged herself in between them, wanting to be in the center of things.

Ursula remembered what she had heard somewhere (though she couldn't remember where or when): "Pay attention to how a man treats you when you're sick. It's telling." She closed her eyes and let the sounds of the room wash over her: the pop of the fire, the vibration of Mallory's purr, and the rumbling of Rafael's voice through his chest. Realizing that she was no longer merely in lust, but deeply and peacefully in love, she drifted into sleep, lulled by the poem's rhythm: ". . . But the she-bear thus accosted rends the peasant tooth and nail, For the female of the species is more deadly than the male . . .'"

Chapter 18

After a raucous dinner in Brooklyn (at which Issa and Eric met Rafael for the first time, and Ursula met Skipp for the first time), the five of them ended up in a dingy pool hall on a side street off Flatbush Avenue in Prospect Heights. Though their ages ranged from thirty-five to forty-two, they felt like college kids again, the clack of pool balls and the garish lights reactivating the exuberance of their youth.

"Beers? Shots?" Rafael asked the group.

"Oh, you don't have to do that," said Issa, but Rafael was already headed to the bar.

"He likes doing this," Skipp explained about his friend's generosity. "It gives him a distinct thrill."

"Works for me," said Issa, giving Ursula a look of approval.

"Air hockey?" Skipp asked Issa. They had formed a quick affinity for one another at dinner, and they walked off to explore the tables along the far wall.

"Has Rafael met Orla?" Eric asked. Ursula's mother had a particular fondness for him, because he had everything she adored: curls, glasses, an excellent vocabulary, a socialist-leaning outlook.

"Not yet," said Ursula. "She was pretty skeptical about The Arc in general." Ursula had a feeling Orla would be aghast that she had been matched with a lawyer, as opposed to, say, an interpretive dancer. Orla was always pushing her daughter to be more countercultural. Ursula didn't think of Rafael as representing the establishment, but Orla might.

"I can't imagine anyone not liking him," said Eric of Rafael.

Ursula wrapped her arm around Eric and gave his shoulder a grateful squeeze, hoping he was right.

Rafael arrived with their beers, and the three of them claimed a pool table.

Off in the corner, Issa and Skipp were engaged in a dizzying game of air hockey, the puck zipping back and forth between them across the table.

"You have a very distinct playing style," yelled Issa, smacking the puck into the wall of the table, where it ricocheted into Skipp's goal.

"Nice shot, mademoiselle!" Skipp nodded with respect.

"I've played some air hockey in my time." Issa shrugged, cool as a cucumber, as Skipp knocked the puck back into play.

"Rafael and I used to have epic air-hockey games in college," said Skipp. "It's one of the few sports I can beat him in."

"He's good at sports?"

"The best," said Skipp. "He was the captain of the soccer team at Yale."

"What a stud," said Issa, delighted for Ursula.

"I would marry him myself if he'd have me," Skipp joked, although in many ways, Rafael *had* been his primary partner in life. Adopting his sports-commentator voice, he said: "He fakes left, dodges right, banks it off the . . ." He leaned in and jabbed his arm at the puck, launching it entirely off the table. He held his hand up in a gesture of apology to the woman whose shoulder it had hit. She smiled and threw it back.

"Should we go see what they're up to?" Issa pointed toward Ursula, Eric, and Rafael, who were now standing near the Pop-A-Shot baskets.

"Yep, Ursula might need my expertise," said Skipp.

Issa winced playfully. "Just a word of warning: Ursula doesn't like unsolicited 'advice' or 'help' of any kind."

"Got it," said Skipp. "Note to self: do not advise Ursula."

"Exactly. Never try to help Ursula," said Issa, adopting Skipp's clinical tone.

"Assist Ursula at your own risk," riffed Skipp.

As he and Issa approached, they realized that Ursula was sinking basket after basket, while Eric and Rafael looked on. The points on the digital scoreboard increased with each shot she made, and Eric and Rafael became more animated as they realized she had a chance at breaking the existing record, which was displayed in illuminated red numbers above the basket.

"She's in the zone," said Rafael as Issa and Skipp approached.

Swish. Swish. Swish. She broke the record with time still left on the clock. She kept going, and as the clock counted down, she reached for one final ball, throwing it effortlessly through the hoop.

Issa did a shoulder shimmy and whooped loudly.

"Damn," said Skipp to Eric. "Ursula can ball."

Eric nodded and Rafael grinned with pride as Ursula spun around to face her audience. "What the . . . ?!" she exclaimed, slightly out of breath and surprised by her own skill. She had never played Pop-A-Shot before, but she was indeed in the zone.

Chapter 19

Ursula stood at the stove in her little galley kitchen, trying to gauge whether her risotto was too liquidy or not liquidy enough, when Rafael came up behind her and pressed his boner against her butt.

"Let's get humpy," he said.

She threw her head back against his shoulder, laughing.

"Rafael, I'm engaged in something right now. You realize risotto is one of those dishes you have to continually stir while you're making it?" she said. "I can't get humpy for at least twenty-five minutes."

"Sure you can," he said, lacing his arms around her aproned waist.

"I think we need to work on your seduction logistics," she said. "And on the timing of your sensuality."

He leaned into her ear and whispered: "You wouldn't know sensuality if a dick slapped you in the face." And then he sauntered off into the living room, leaving Ursula laughing so hard that her eyes started leaking.

She heard Rafael turn on a nature documentary. As David Attenborough's trustworthy voice wafted into the kitchen, she silently thanked the universe—and The Arc—for bringing her this magical man.

After dinner, they lounged on the couch listening to jazz and reading magazines (or in Ursula's case, a Design Within Reach catalog). She paused to scroll through her inbox and realized she'd forgotten to fill out her monthly update for The Arc. By this point, however, it seemed futile—she'd given the exact same glowing report each month. She began whipping through the survey.

On a scale of 1–10, where 1 is "Not at all" and 10 is "Completely" . . .

*How satisfied are you with your choice to become a client
of The Arc?* 10.
How satisfied are you with your match? 10.
How confident are you that you've found your life partner?
10.
*How likely are you to recommend The Arc to a friend or
colleague?* 10.
Anything else you'd like to tell us?

Normally, Ursula skipped the free response box, but tonight, she felt especially effusive: *This is more than a successful match—it's a minor miracle! A relational triumph! You've pulled off the impossible. Thank you.*

"I just gave you another A+ on your monthly report," Ursula said, hitting Send and looking up at Rafael.

"Thank you, but you're late. It's the third!" said Rafael, mock-scolding her. He sent all his reports promptly on the first of the month.

"I know! But I've got a lot on my plate. I'm an incredibly important and busy executive, you know," said Ursula, joking but also realizing how tired she was.

"Did you see *The* Mike Rutherford today?" asked Rafael, looking up from the copy of the *Economist* he was reading.

"I did," said Ursula. Since July, she'd been meeting with Mike every few weeks. Her mandate was to keep an eye out for startups in need of funding, vet investment opportunities, and make strategic introductions for Mike. She'd already secured his participation in The Stake's latest raise, and he'd led the round, investing $15 million so the club could begin its global expansion: The Stake LA, The Stake London, and The Stake São Paulo were all due to break ground next year. It was a good investment on Mike's part, although the irony was not lost on Ursula that all of the funding for this feminist-wellness empire came from middle-aged men hoping to profit from it. But she couldn't allow herself to dwell on things like that for too long, or else her entire world would come toppling down. She would never get out of bed in the morning if she started following the chain of money to its problematic source. This was just how capitalism worked.

Plus, Mike wasn't as insufferable as she had initially thought. She liked him, and she was learning from him. He was smart, in some ways. Smart enough to make a billion dollars anyway. And he was kind—not just to her, but to almost everyone she had seen him interact with. Although, earlier that day, when she had mentioned Rafael, she thought she perceived a shift in Mike's tone. "So you're off the market. That's wonderful," he had said, his smile frozen as his eyes turned icy. Ursula didn't flinch. Love made her brazen, and in her mind, Mike Rutherford—*The* Mike Rutherford—worked for her now. She got a subtle thrill from feeling she had some kind of rising power over him.

"Lunch was good," Ursula elaborated to Rafael. "Have you heard of CitiBloke?"

"CitiBloke?" Rafael furrowed his brow.

"It's a service where you can essentially rent a local guy to be your date for events," said Ursula. "And the female version is called Citi-Babe. No joke."

"So, it's an escort service," said Rafael, chuckling and shaking his head.

"Pretty much," said Ursula. "Mike wants to invest, of course. But I don't know. It feels like these startup concepts are spiraling out of control. All of these aspiring entrepreneurs trying to manipulate and streamline every aspect of our lives, but they end up making us even more stressed out than before. Like we're losing sight of the bigger picture. And so many of these new products are supposedly about saving time, but you know what would save me time? Not having 75,000 apps on my phone that are shooting lasers into my brain. And you know what would *really* save me time? Not having one of these at all!" She threw her smartphone onto the far armchair, startling Mallory, who was napping in a nearby cardboard box.

"Easy there, tapenade," said Rafael, kissing the top of her head. "Maybe you should just delete some apps."

She looked up at him. "I'm so glad I got you rather than a CitiBloke. How am I so happy? How did we pull this off?"

"I don't want to upset you," said Rafael. "But there's this company called The Arc . . ."

"I guess I can't complain about the unbearable proliferation of bullshit optimization services, when I have a bullshit optimization service to thank for our relationship. For *you*." She leaned toward him on the couch and ran her finger along his sideburn.

"Yeah, there's some irony there," said Rafael, giving her that look: sincere affection paired with deep internal amusement. She knew he wasn't laughing at her. He was just radiating with the wild energy current that had animated their entire relationship thus far. This whole thing was completely manufactured, rooted in psychological calculus, and yet it continued to feel like an inexplicable miracle. Ursula and Rafael hugged each other with ferocity, delight, desperation. The guarantee of lasting love—and it did, by now, feel solidly guaranteed—was overwhelming.

Chapter 20

When Ursula walked into Anonymous & Co.'s open office, the other forty-four employees started applauding. She rolled her eyes, assuming that Roger, who was both her boss and the agency's founder, had put them up to this to shame her for her lateness. She usually got in by 10 A.M., but she'd spent last night uptown at Rafael's apartment, and they'd taken their time getting out of bed this morning. She realized she hadn't even checked her email yet as she swiftly made her way across the loft to her nook. Not even the five most senior executives at Anonymous & Co.—of which she was one—had offices with actual doors. (Doors were deemed too elitist, too psychologically dismissive.) Instead, the execs at Anonymous sat in glass-walled "nooks," which were essentially transparent cubes that ran along one wall of the open space. Ursula's made her feel like a turtle in a terrarium. She longed for opaque walls and a door she could close, or perhaps even slam on special occasions.

Ursula had only made it halfway to her nook when Roger jumped up on someone's desk and shouted, "Ursula Byrne!"

The clapping subsided and Ursula turned around, confused. She wanted to respond by shouting "Roger Desjardins!" back at him, but she resisted. What was he up to?

"As most of you know, but it seems Ursula doesn't—*because she's too important to check her email now*—she has been nominated for a 2018 Brandy!" announced Roger, dramatically.

Ursula's jaw dropped. In the wider world, no one cared about the

Brandy Awards. But in her industry and adjacent industries, they were a Big Fucking Deal. In this room, *she* was a Big Fucking Deal.

"For Cruisify?" asked Ursula, naming her client that operated small, high-end cruises for young affluent folk who wouldn't be caught dead on a traditional cruise ship. The campaign, "Cruisify Yourself," had featured Instagram influencers sunbathing in poses that evoked crucifixion. It was controversial (which was Ursula's intent), and had boosted Cruisify's revenue by 400 percent since it debuted. This was part of her skillset: having good taste, but knowing exactly how and when to compromise it in order to drive value for her clients. Industry insiders agreed it was a risky but brilliant campaign.

Roger held out his hand and someone offered him a bottle of Dom Pérignon.

"Saber it!" an employee yelled from the far corner by the kombucha fridge.

"HR doesn't let me do that anymore." Roger grinned. He twisted the cork cleanly—a perfect pop, no spillage—and threw it toward an unsuspecting employee for disposal before hopping down and following Ursula to her nook, which was located in the far corner of the office. He grabbed two glasses off her bar cart and filled them, tipping them just so to prevent the foam from overflowing onto Ursula's Moroccan shag rug.

"Ursula, I've said it before. I'll say it many times again: you're a genius," said Roger. "You make me proud—proud of myself for hiring you. So maybe *I'm* the genius. Anyway, you make Anonymous & Co. look good. Amazing work this year."

Ursula smiled. Roger could be obnoxious, but as far as bosses went, he wasn't the worst. He knew how to hire smart people and then stay out of their way, incentivizing them as necessary to keep them working around the clock on his behalf. He was curious, hungry, and generally open-minded, if a bit condescending. He wore thick-framed, olive-toned round glasses, and his head was shaven clean to prevent any discussion of whether his hairline was receding or not. (It was.) He was always impeccably dressed in understated but luxurious pieces from Loro Piana that fell perfectly on his tall frame; and he seemed younger than his forty-nine years, perhaps because he had a shiny-haired, thirty-eight-year-old wife who had once been a fashion editor but who now made money by pushing a steady stream of products on her 275,000 Instagram followers. Together, they made an intimidatingly well-heeled pair—as did their four-year-old twin boys, who occasionally modeled for Ralph Lauren. Roger sat on Ursula's couch and put his feet up on her coffee table. "Nice table. Someday we'll get you a real Noguchi," he said, referring to the fact that Ursula's was a knockoff of the well-known designer. Roger had a distinct way of complimenting people while simultaneously negging them; Ursula always felt both praised and slightly burned by him, and she knew this was his intention.

Roger's new assistant, Addison, poked her head into the nook and held up a few printouts: "Roger? Fonts for you to review."

Roger held out his hand and waved for her to give him the papers, which he then snatched impatiently.

"Congrats, Ursula," Addison said shyly and turned to leave.

"Stay," Roger barked, not looking up from the papers. Addison whipped back into the entryway.

"No. No. No. No," Roger leafed through the pages. "Maybe. Maybe. Maybe. Maybe." He handed them in two bunches back to Addison. "I told those guys no more sans serif. Minimalism is played out. I want to swing hard in the opposite direction—I want the most serify serif you've ever seen. I want Shakespearean script. I want fucking Elizabethan flourishes. No, I want Middle Ages. Think *Beowulf*. Give me Grendel in font form. Tell Kei's team I want to see another round by EOD, and if I catch even a glimpse of sans serif, I swear to god . . ."

He didn't need to finish. Addison nodded and started to scamper off, but Roger added, "And what is that copy? I hope that's just dummy copy and not something we're actually working on. It sounds like a poor man's Dr. Seuss. Very derivative. Do better."

Addison nodded again and then practically leapt back into the safety of the open office.

"You don't have to terrorize people, you know." Ursula looked at Roger.

"Yes, I do," he replied. "That's my thing."

"Ah," said Ursula, rolling her eyes.

"It works. I terrorized you for years, and look at you now: on top of your game." Roger took a long swig of his champagne and let out a satisfied exhale. "What's the latest with Rutherford?"

Before embarking on her consulting gig with Mike, Ursula had cleared it with Roger, assuring him there was no conflict of interest. If anything, her two parallel gigs complemented one another: clients of Anonymous & Co. were often looking for investors; and the companies Mike funded were often looking for help with branding and positioning. Ursula had convinced Roger she could manage it all without getting her professional wires crossed, and he had given his blessing, deploying his signature sarcasm by saying, "I don't know what Rutherford sees in *you*, but go for it." He assumed it couldn't hurt to have a direct line, via Ursula, to one of New York's preeminent financiers.

"All good with Mike," Ursula said breezily. "He's putting $2 million into CitiBloke. I'm talking to them about working with us when they're ready for a rebrand."

"Good. That logo is hideous," said Roger, taking a deep breath and running his hand over his bald head, as if the logo itself were a source of great stress. "And how's Mr. Banks?"

Ursula's face lit up, which happened automatically whenever someone mentioned Rafael. "So good," she said. "I think we're going to go to Mexico for New Year's."

"Nice," said Roger. "Punta Mita? Stay at the Four Seasons, not the St. Regis."

"No, Roger," Ursula said with exasperation. "We're not really Punta Mita people."

Roger shrugged. He'd both inherited and made money, and he sometimes had trouble calibrating what was out of reach for others.

"I think we're going to Oaxaca—to a little surf town and then to the city," said Ursula.

"Nice," he responded. "My buddy Miguel can get you the best rugs in Teotitlán del Valle." Roger knew everyone, everywhere, and he demonstrated it constantly. He finished his champagne and put the glass down. "Ursula, congrats."

"Wait, who else is nominated?" she asked, finally opening her laptop and seeing the email Roger had sent to the company about her nomination. She paid only passing attention to her competitors in the industry, but she was curious.

"Doesn't matter." Roger waved his hand as he walked out of the nook. "Start drafting your acceptance speech."

Chapter 21

Issa and Eric leaned against the bar in the ballroom of the University Club, watching Ursula and Rafael sway to the music, completely engrossed in each other, even more so than the bride and groom they were there to fête. Many of those on the dance floor were older relatives or young kids, flopping around playfully, out of sync with the rhythm of the song. But Ursula and Rafael were in their own world, interlocked, dancing in a way that was right on the line of inappropriate, given the stuffiness of the venue. Issa knew that Ursula didn't care. In fact, Ursula loved to make this kind of minor scene.

"Do you realize what they are?" said Issa, who wore a vintage YSL smoking jacket and black silk trousers. She and Eric were essentially both wearing tuxedos, although Issa's was decidedly more risqué, since she wasn't wearing a shirt with hers. (She and Ursula had agreed that it was fine to flash subtle side-boob in a black-tie setting.) "They are *that* couple. That freakishly in-love couple that makes all other couples realize they aren't in that mode anymore." It wasn't jealousy she felt; it was more like nostalgia. Watching Ursula fall in love with Rafael had been a beautiful thing to witness over the past few months, but it did make Issa more aware—for better or worse—of the holding pattern that she and Eric were in.

"Aren't *we* freakishly in love?" said Eric, putting his hand on Issa's hip.

She gave him an efficient kiss. "Of course we are," she said. "It's just different. They're in the phase where the other person is like a drug. And who knows? Maybe they'll be in that phase forever. That's what's so interesting about this Arc thing. Their relationship was manufactured for success. Maybe it won't go through the phases that normal relationships do."

Issa had no doubt that she had married the right person, and she was totally committed to Eric. But it's true that when they had gotten together ten years earlier, there was no Arc. There was no swiping on dating apps. There was no talk of optimizing compatibility. You met someone and you fell for them; and then you either broke up or you didn't. Issa and Eric had always been solid, but Issa had wondered, over these past few months, what it would be like to live an alternate life where she could go to The Arc and present herself as the thirty-five-year-old she was now, rather than the twenty-five-year-old she had been when she'd started dating Eric. Whom would The Arc choose for her? Still Eric? Someone Eric-like? Or someone completely different from Eric? If she thought about it for too long, it made her nauseous.

"I think we should just enjoy it with her," said Eric. "She's so happy. She hasn't cried on our couch for months—that's a record. This is a good thing for everyone."

Ursula and Rafael were now shamelessly making out. Eric plucked Issa's empty glass from her hand, put it on the bar, and led her onto the dance floor, where he slyly steered her into Rafael and Ursula, interrupting their passionate encounter. The band began playing a not-terrible rendition of Ginuwine's "Pony," and the four of them broke into an ecstatic group dance.

That was another of Rafael's winning qualities, thought Ursula. He fit so seamlessly into her group of friends. He could be seducing her one minute and then pony-dancing with Issa the next. He and Eric had only met a few times, but they had instantly slipped into an easy rapport. Everything was flowing. After a few songs, they all gravitated toward the enormous dessert table, laden with cake, of course, but also with gilded doughnut holes, a tower made of French macarons, rows of regal-looking petit fours, and spun-sugar statues in the shape of the bride's horse, whose name was Perchance to Dream.

Ursula felt a hand on her shoulder, and she turned around to see

Mike Rutherford. She didn't know he would be here, and she hadn't noticed him until now. He answered her question before she could ask it: "I did some business with the groom's father years ago." She turned to make the requisite introductions, but Rafael and Eric were already enraptured by the dessert table, analyzing the offerings as Issa seemed to be taking one of everything.

Mike waved his hand as if to indicate that he didn't need to meet them now. There would be time for that later.

"Dance with me?" he asked, though Ursula wondered if it was more of a command. Sensing her hesitation, he added: "Strictly business. A business dance."

She looked back at Rafael, but figured he wouldn't mind. He didn't get jealous, and there was nothing to be jealous about. Mike was just a cog in the machinery of Ursula's personal economy, albeit a big cog.

The band was playing something slow and jazzy. The horn section sounded lazy, in a pleasant way. It reminded her of her favorite song, "Bird of Paradise" by Charlie Parker. Mike gingerly led Ursula onto the dance floor, placed his hand on her waist, and took her other hand in his. "I heard about your Brandy nomination. Congratulations."

She was working on accepting praise graciously but not awkwardly. "Thank you," she said, surprised that he even knew what the Brandys were.

"And how do you know Brooks and Tabitha?" he asked as the bride and groom shimmied by them.

"College," said Ursula. "Tabitha was my freshman-year roommate."

Mike nodded. He had done the required small talk and now he wanted to discuss what was actually on his mind. It turned out he wasn't flirting with her—this truly was a business dance. "I forgot to mention at our last lunch: I'm planning on going to Jackson." He was referring to the Jackson Hole Investment Summit, known to insiders simply as "Jackson" and attended by financial luminaries like him, but also, more recently, by startup founders and other self-described disruptors. "You should be there."

Ursula had always been curious about the legendary summit, but had never been able to finagle an invitation.

"When is it?"

"February. I'll have Jed send you the info," said Mike. "Just make sure to hold that weekend."

He didn't specify what weekend, but that was fine; Ursula would hold all of her weekends in February. He looked behind her, where Eric and Rafael were huddled, taking not-so-discreet glances at them. "Your wolf pack awaits," said Mike, releasing her. As he walked away, he said over his shoulder, "Great dress, by the way."

Ursula looked down at her slinky crimson gown, smoothing the silk around her hips. *Was* he flirting with her? She couldn't tell. Maybe she was so conditioned to receive (and rebuff) inappropriate advances that she was seeing something that wasn't there. She decided to give him the benefit of the doubt. She walked over to her friends and leaned into Rafael, plucking a sugar horse off his plate.

". . . but *is* this a great country? No really, is it? " Issa was on a tear, talking to a gray-haired man that Ursula didn't know. "The foundation of our economy was built on the backs of slaves. And nowadays, it runs on the labor of undocumented people who live in fear of deportation every day of their lives. You're telling me that's greatness? I think America is number one in *avoidance*, in averting our gaze so that we don't have to confront the exploitative supply chains that generate most of our wealth. America is number one in hypocrisy!"

Ursula bit Perchance to Dream's sugary head off and put the rest of his body back on Rafael's plate. "She's right." Ursula nodded, glad to have caught the tail end of Issa's diatribe.

"So that's Gordon Gekko?" asked Eric, nodding in Mike's direction.

"That's him," said Ursula, still chewing. By now, all of her friends knew about her second vocation as Mike's consigliere. She smiled at Rafael, who smiled back. "So . . . supply chains? Hypocrisy? Where were we?"

Rafael squeezed Ursula's waist. He still wasn't sure how he felt about Mike Rutherford, but he was impressed and amused by Ursula's irrepressible hustle. He felt a sense of pride to be by her side tonight, watching her charm everyone she crossed. The experience of finding exactly what he wanted in her, after all these years, both soothed and scared him. It was one thing to go through life wondering if this kind of love was really achievable, but now that he knew it was, he couldn't help but wonder: What would it be like to lose it? To return to living without it?

Chapter 22

November 14, 4:07 P.M.

"What did you think of their concept?" Sabrina's curly brown hair was pulled into a low ponytail, and her red lipstick had left a faint crescent on the white espresso cup in front of her.

She and Ursula were seated in the corner of Freud, their go-to coffee spot near the office. The space's perfectly considered details—cognac-hued leather, white marble, brass hardware, birch stools, assiduously whipped foam, an array of esoteric milks—made it clear that at Freud coffee was not merely a beverage or even a socially acceptable addiction; it was an art, a lifestyle, a state of mind, a belief system. On one of the walls, thick black letters read: "Out of your vulnerabilities will come your strength. *But first, coffee.*"—Sigmund Freud

Ursula glanced up at the bastardized quote, whose glib addendum pained her, and then turned her attention back to Sabrina. "Super impressive. I love their approach. I love *them*. They're very smart."

The two women had just come from a meeting that Sabrina had set up with a new company called Nine to Five that made gender-neutral, job-themed play kits for children. It was founded by two sisters, Juliana and Alejandra, whom Sabrina had met when she and Juliana were classmates at NYU. Juliana and Alejandra had grown up in the Bronx, where they still lived, and had come up with the idea for Nine to Five when Alejandra became frustrated with the overly gendered toys she kept receiving after having her daughter, who was now four.

Ursula loved the specificity of their product, which went far beyond the typical doctor or fireman accessories on the market. Their line included air-flight traffic controller, human rights lawyer, epidemiologist, documentary filmmaker, senator, horse trainer, even physiotherapist. Each kit came with the requisite outfit and accessories, technical equipment, and a degree (if relevant) to hang on the child's wall. They also included official "contracts" that outlined things like benefits and parental leave in simple terms. Some of the professions even came with certificates delineating equity in the form of company shares. Nine to Five's tagline was *Work hard. Play smarter.* And its mission was to set the stage not just for imaginative play, but also for ambitious expectations around what workplace culture looked and felt like for both boys and girls. Ursula loved the idea of children play-negotiating for equity.

"Right? It's so creative, so empowering," said Sabrina. And yet, Juliana and Alejandra were having trouble securing funding for their next stage of growth. When they did manage to get in the room with investors (the majority of whom were older white males), they heard one of two refrains: either the product didn't "resonate," or their operating plan was impractical (their goal was to keep their manufacturing local, and to build their business within their community). Ursula suspected that the subtext of this feedback, which was so often the case, was that many investors liked to "see themselves" in those they funded. They liked to go with their gut. And because so many investors were white men from privileged backgrounds, this "gut instinct" kept the money circulating within a very specific group. Funding flowed freely to the Brads and Daves and Jacks of the world, but Juliana and Alejandra didn't enjoy the same automatic access.

"My cousin's daughter has three of them and she's obsessed," said Sabrina of the Nine to Five kits. "She rotates between the pilot, the dental assistant, and the philosophy professor."

"I want to rotate through jobs!" said Ursula, not exactly joking. In a way, this was what her double professional life—balancing Anonymous & Co. with her consulting gig—allowed her to do. But still, she fantasized about the possibility of endless shape-shifting; she wanted to wear a different uniform every day of the week, to try on a different kit, so to speak. "It really resonates with me, that desire to inhabit different identities. I like the idea of giving kids more ways to envision what working could look like."

Sabrina nodded. "Exactly. They just need to build out the brand and get it in front of people. It's a bummer that their marketing budget is so low. They spent this entire year trying to fund-raise but didn't get any traction. So I guess that's a dealbreaker."

"Why a dealbreaker?" asked Ursula.

"In terms of Anonymous doing their branding," said Sabrina. "I doubt they can afford our $15,000-a-month minimum."

"There might be a way," said Ursula.

Sabrina raised her thick, on-trend eyebrows in anticipation.

"Option one is that we convince Roger to let us take them on at a lower rate," said Ursula.

Sabrina looked skeptical.

"Which is a long shot," conceded Ursula. "Option two is we help introduce Juliana and Alejandra to a new pool of potential investors, and we hope they allocate their branding budget to us in the future."

"How do we do that?" asked Sabrina. "The investor part."

"I'll ask around," said Ursula. This was her big chance to connect all the dots: to help fund a female-founded company she believed in, to bring Mike a ground-floor opportunity, to drum up future business for Anonymous & Co., and most importantly in this moment, to help bring Sabrina along. She'd been taking her mentee to new business meetings since the beginning of the year, but this was the first opportunity Sabrina had brought to her, and she didn't want it to fizzle unnecessarily. Meager marketing budget be damned.

Sabrina was alert. "So, it could happen? I could land a client?"

"It could absolutely happen," affirmed Ursula. "It just might take some time."

"That would be so exciting," said Sabrina. "I think Juliana and Alejandra are building something amazing. We need to be part of it."

"It would be refreshing," said Ursula. Anonymous & Co. currently only had a few female-run companies on their client list.

"Refreshing to not work with a bunch of bros with mediocre products but lots of funding?" said Sabrina.

Ursula dropped her jaw in fake astonishment at her young charge's insight, then laughed. "Yes. Pretty much."

"I just think the best ideas and the smartest people should rise to the top," Sabrina continued.

"Hear! Hear!" said Ursula, clinking her mug against Sabrina's espresso cup.

Sabrina was on a roll. "The arc of history can't 'bend toward justice' until the VC money starts flowing toward a more diverse pool of entrepreneurs, right?"

"Oh hello! Sabrina Davis, casually dropping MLK quotes at our coffee catchup," said Ursula, impressed.

"But really, how do we distribute investment more equitably?" pressed Sabrina, proud of herself.

"That's the million-dollar question, my friend," said Ursula. She deeply wished she had an answer, that startup money would naturally flow toward the most deserving ideas and the hardest-working people. But the current venture capital structure wasn't set up for that. It was set up to channel money to the best-connected, the savviest, the people who gave investors a "good feeling," which was code for those who reminded them of their younger, more idealistic selves. In 2018, the majority of those rooms were still full of young white men pitching ideas to slightly older and better-established white men. And for all the talk of "data-driven" concepts, much of the decision-making was still blatantly subjective. But maybe that could change. Ursula felt a twinge of triumph when she realized she was finally in a position, via her consulting gig with Mike, to shift the balance, to channel money in more diverse directions. She picked up her phone and made a note to reach out to Mike about investing in Nine to Five. Then she looked back up at Sabrina. "Your instincts are right. We'll get the money flowing toward justice someday. It's a slog, but you have to stay in the game. *We* have to stay in the game."

"It's a frustrating game," said Sabrina.

Ursula smiled, charmed by how Sabrina could simultaneously

wear her integrity, her naivete, and her ambition on her sleeve. For a second, she wanted to be twenty-five again. Just for a second.

"There are a lot of interests in the mix," said Ursula, debating how much of her own career-related angst she wanted to reveal to her mentee.

"Yeah. I mean, I love working with you," said Sabrina. "When I think about what it means to be a working woman and a feminist, you're the person I think of. You're so good at your job. But it also seems like . . ."

Ursula waited for her to go on, both flattered and concerned. She both aspired to be a role model and dreaded the responsibility.

"Sorry. I mean . . ." Sabrina hesitated, weighing her words. "It just looks like it takes a lot of energy to do what you do. Like to deal with Roger, and then to deal with all the clients, and to oversee me, and to run those Women-at-Work seminars that you organize. It's like you're managing things in eight different directions. Like an octopus." She waved her arms as if through water.

"Like my tentacles are just all over the place," said Ursula, joining in the arm waving but accidentally swatting a man sitting to her right on the banquette. She gestured an apology.

"Yeah." Sabrina laughed, pleased that her octopus metaphor had gone over well.

"That's how I feel," said Ursula. "It's such a tangle: carving out space for yourself to have ideas, fighting for those ideas, but also accommodating other peoples' opinions, keeping an eye on the market, reading the tone of the culture as it constantly shifts. You're right. It's pretty exhausting."

"But how do you have energy left to do the actual work? How do you have time to come up with creative ideas?"

Ursula considered the question. "I don't have time. I get most of my ideas on the subway."

"Like Cruisify? You thought of that on the *subway*?"

"Yep. Subway," confirmed Ursula. "I mean, we brainstormed earlier that week. But it crystallized on the subway."

"Coctus?"

"Also subway."

"So . . . you do your *actual* job on the subway," said Sabrina, trying to make sense of it. "And then when you're at work or in meetings, you're just dealing with all of the personalities who either facilitate or block that work. You're managing the swirl of people and opinions. It's like there are two different Ursulas."

Ursula nodded, slightly jarred by how on-point Sabrina's description was. She had never thought of it in such stark terms, but yes, all of her breakthroughs happened either in transit or in the shower.

"If I were you, I'd just stay on the subway." Sabrina laughed. "I want to be the version of you that never gets off the subway."

Ursula indulged the fantasy, adding, "Just blow right past Broadway-Lafayette. Take the F all the way out to Jamaica and then back down to Coney Island. Just skip Manhattan altogether."

Maybe Sabrina was on to something. The part Ursula loved most about her job was the time she spent in her own head, privately wrestling with ideas, brainstorming, letting her notorious "audacity" lead her. It was the subsequent part that pained her: when others' opinions started to trickle in, diluting and distorting her ideas. She understood that teamwork and cooperation were widely considered to be "good," and she did her best to cultivate a collaborative mentality at work, to make mental room for others. But ever since she was a child, she'd been her own favorite collaborator, the only cook in the kitchen. Having to compromise her ideas and "scale" her creativity felt unnatural to her, and although she pushed herself to play nice at work, she was always relieved when she stepped into the anonymity of a subway car. Cocooned by strangers, flowing with the current of the city, she could retreat into her own mind and let her eccentricity carry her, without the need to calibrate or strategize or cooperate. She could be as outlandish as she wanted. She could remember who she was.

"I mean, I want to do what you do, someday," said Sabrina, as she spun her espresso cup slowly between her fingers. "But I don't know if I want to deal with the people swirl."

"I'm not sure I want to deal with it either," said Ursula, setting down her empty mug. "If you figure out how to escape it, take me with you. But for now, we soldier on."

Sabrina nodded with conviction and repeated: "We soldier on."

"Shall we?" Ursula pointed toward the door. As she got up to put her rust-colored cashmere coat on, Sabrina took their mugs over to the plastic bin at the side of the room, placing them carefully so they wouldn't fall or crash. She also wore a rust-colored coat (no doubt inspired by Ursula's, though she hadn't admitted as much), and as she followed her boss out into the misty November afternoon, it was clear they were part of the same tribe.

Chapter 23

It was late when Ursula and Rafael got back into the city, and even later when they finally found a parking spot for their rental car. But despite the traffic and the late hour, they were running on their typical love fumes. They'd spent the weekend upstate, where they'd rented a modern (and fully heated) tree house to celebrate their almost-four-month anniversary. The early December weather had been cold and wet, so they'd nested: coffee in bed, thick wool blankets, classic novels they'd been meaning to read for ages (*Anna Karenina* for Ursula, *David Copperfield* for Rafael), leisurely woods walks, and luxuriously unhurried sex.

Now back in the city, Ursula had opted to stay at Rafael's for the night. She began searching his cabinets to see if there was anything cookable, but he was down to an incongruent mix of crackers and hot sauces.

Ursula put her arms on Rafael's shoulders and looked deeply into his eyes. "Tacos," she said.

"That's my girl," said Rafael. He called down to Jalisco, and because they made everything astonishingly quickly, he put his coat on to go pick up the order.

While Rafael was out, Ursula leafed through the mail he'd thrown onto the counter. It was mostly catalogs selling different variations of the rugged outdoor lifestyle that so many nature-starved urban men seemed to crave. Brands like Swift Mark, Lustig & Sons, and Altitude. She had done a project with Lustig & Sons years ago to bolster the struggling sales of their $498 birdhouses. Then something caught her eye: a mailer from Granite State Ridgeback Ranch. She picked it up. It was a dog breeder, and on the front was a proud-looking Rhodesian Ridgeback with her litter of five floppy pups. Ursula smiled. She knew Rafael came from a "Ridgeback family." He'd had at least four throughout his childhood: Boomer, Bolt, Nipper, and she couldn't remember the other one. The front door opened and Rafael came in, setting the plastic bag down on the counter.

"Getting a Ridgeback?" said Ursula, jokingly holding up the mailer.

"Maybe," said Rafael, not joking. Ursula looked at him, and he looked up. "What?"

"Well," said Ursula. "Um . . ."

"I was going to talk to you about it," said Rafael. "It's not something I would do without discussing it first."

"No, it's not that," said Ursula. "I want a dog. I've always wanted a dog. I'm just surprised you'd want to get one from a breeder."

"As opposed to . . . ?" asked Rafael.

"As opposed to adopting one of the zillion dogs that need homes right here in New York," said Ursula. She'd spent a few years in her early twenties volunteering at a shelter, and she felt strongly about the Adopt, Don't Shop movement.

"Yeah," said Rafael. "That's a thought, but Ridgebacks are hard to find. And you know I grew up with Ridgebacks."

"I know."

"And I always assumed that when I got my own dog, it would be a Ridgeback. Now that I think about it, I can't really imagine having anything else. At least, not as a first dog."

Ursula didn't say anything. She wasn't upset; she was just surprised. She felt something unfamiliar: not outright discord, but a divergence of energy, a flattening of the mood. Normally they were so in sync.

"Is that a problem?" said Rafael, confused about why this felt contentious. He grabbed two plates from the cupboard and started unpacking the tacos.

"I don't know," said Ursula. "I mean, no. It's not a problem. It's just something for us to talk about. I guess this is one of those areas where we don't naturally agree."

"Look, I think adopting dogs is great," said Rafael, pulling her toward him. "I think adopting *cats* is even better." Ursula smiled. "But I just love Ridgebacks, and if I get a dog, that's what I want."

"So you wouldn't even consider adopting? What about just going to an event to see what's out there?" said Ursula, realizing she felt more strongly about this than she'd initially thought. "It just feels like the first important decision we're potentially making together. Or, I guess it would be your dog, so it's your decision. But it would be my stepdog. I just wish we agreed."

"So, it's not really about adopting or not adopting," said Rafael. "You just wish we agreed? You don't want to disagree."

Ursula nodded.

"We're not going to agree on everything forever, mouse trap," said Rafael, casually tapping her on the butt and carrying his plate over to the couch.

"I know," said Ursula. "It just makes me a little sad."

"Really?" asked Rafael from the couch. "Why sad?"

Ursula didn't know how to articulate it. She felt a familiar ache in her ribs at the place where all of her insecurity lived: the sword wound. She felt as if they had just stumbled onto the fault line that, although insignificant-looking now, could eventually threaten their relationship. This is how it had always happened in her previous romances: a small disagreement, then a bigger one, then a fight, then a series of fights, then the end. She always felt the initial tremor in her body—a warning of the seismic shift to come.

"Why is this such a big deal to you?" Rafael looked at her, perplexed.

"I just . . ." Ursula stopped. She knew it would sound crazy to say aloud the fear that had just taken root: that this benign disagreement about dogs would soon beget a series of spats that would eventually turn them into foes, miserable and lost. Determined not to let the situation escalate, Ursula relented. "It's not really a big deal. You should get the dog you want."

It felt like a forfeiture, but she preferred that to a fight. Or did she? Was this the beginning of the self-sacrifice that would eventually lead to total self-abandonment? She had vowed not to do that to herself again. Suddenly, she felt both defensive and defiant. "I just think we should adopt a vulnerable dog that needs a home, rather than get a WASPy, New Hampshire dog that already has a guaranteed good life."

Rafael stopped to let this land. "A WASPy New Hampshire dog?"

Ursula shrugged. Her brain felt tangled, and now she wished she hadn't said it.

"Can dogs be WASPs? Or are you just accusing *me* of being a snob?" asked Rafael coldly. Suddenly, he was reminded of some of his conversations with Freja, who had often accused him of being overly bourgeois. He knew that it wasn't fair to connect the two—Freja and Ursula were so different—but a familiar fear crawled to the surface of his consciousness. He wanted to retreat, to steady himself.

"I don't know. Never mind," said Ursula. It was the first time she had heard him use such a sharp tone. "I'm not making sense."

"No, you're not," said Rafael, aggressively shaking hot sauce onto his tacos. He turned on the TV and scanned his recordings, looking for the Bundesliga game he'd saved while they were away. After a few minutes, Ursula realized the conversation was over. He was done talking. She felt a chill down her spine. She now understood that she had the capacity to wound him—or at least alienate him—even if unintentionally. A low-level self-loathing began to churn in her stomach. She had stirred up discord and burst their perfect love bubble; she'd made him sad, or was he mad? He seemed sad-mad.

Ursula knew she had to back off, but she felt unsatisfied. She sat down and leaned into Rafael's shoulder, but he didn't move to accommodate her the way he normally did, so she wriggled over to the other side of the couch and turned her attention to her tacos. She felt she deserved this—to be punished with soccer and silence. Before long, she fell asleep to the sound of the commentators and the loud German crowd, their cheers rising and falling like waves on the sea.

Ursula woke abruptly at 3 A.M. She was in Rafael's bed, though she didn't remember being carried there. He was in his usual sleeping position: on his back, arms crossed, hands tucked into his armpits. His face was serene, and he took long, steady breaths.

There was an icy sadness in Ursula's stomach. The joyful, smooth surface of their relationship had cracked. She knew that this was not the ideal hour for mulling, but she was wide-awake, her heart pounding. She tried to emulate Rafael, assuming his sleep position. She wanted to know what it felt like to be him, so still, so at peace. She tucked her hands into her armpits and took deep breaths: in, out, in, out. But her breaths were ragged and uneven, and after a minute, her back felt tight and she couldn't hold the position anymore. She flipped onto her stomach, kicked her left knee out to the side, and hugged her pillow for comfort. Her anxiety began to feel like a hot web under her skin, heating her insides and making the surface of her limbs feel prickly. She wished for sleep. After five minutes, she took a loud, exasperated sigh, hoping Rafael would wake and pull her into a spoon, reassuring her that everything was okay. But he made no movement, so she tried to focus on her earlobes, as she'd learned to do during her intake week at The Arc. Eventually, hungrily, emptily, she slipped into sleep.

Chapter 24

December 14, 3:32 P.M.

A week and a half later, Ursula and Rafael went to The Arc for their requisite four-month check-in. They'd gotten past the Ridgeback conversation and had had a handful of sweet moments since the night of their spat. Ursula felt ridiculous for letting the incident rock her to such an extent; in the end, they'd rebounded easily, buoyed by the knowledge that theirs was an unassailable love. Ursula felt even closer to Rafael, and even more determined to protect their rare connection.

Today, they were ushered into yet another of The Arc's wood-paneled rooms, this one outfitted with a wooden bench and two of the familiar volcanic-rock chairs.

"I love these seats," said Rafael. "They're like molcajetes."

"Yes!" said Ursula, delighted that they'd made the same connection. "So unexpectedly comfy, right?"

The door panel slid open, and a young man with aviator-shaped optical glasses entered. He shook both of their hands and introduced himself as Rich before sitting on the bench and crossing his legs.

"So nice to see you both. We've loved the monthly updates you've filed since August. Although it looks like . . ." He looked down at the tablet in his hands. "Ursula, you still owe us your December update."

"I do," Ursula confirmed. She was late again. Although, what was the point? It was the same questionnaire every month, and her answers had been unanimously glowing each time: everything perfect, no concerns, full marks, huge success. There was a clear trend. But to Rich, she said, "I'll get on that."

He smiled warmly. "Sounds like you're having a lot of fun. Every-thing is going well?"

Ursula and Rafael exchanged a proud look and then turned back to Rich, nodding.

"It's been amazing," said Ursula. "We don't know how you guys pulled this off."

"It's what we do," said Rich, sounding satisfied and assured. "So, anything you want to discuss? Anything on your minds? Any ques-tions about the course of your relationship so far?"

"I don't think so," said Rafael, turning to Ursula, who shook her head.

"Any conflict? Anything you'd like to talk through with an objec-tive third party?"

"We don't have conflict," said Ursula, feeling accomplished.

"Huh," said Rich, making a note. He smiled. "Must be nice."

"It is. We've literally only had one fight, and it wasn't even a fight. It was a disagreement over a dog." Ursula laughed. Not that it was a competition, but she wouldn't have been surprised to hear that she and Rafael were the greatest success story The Arc had ever spawned.

"More of a misunderstanding, really," Rafael added, wanting to emphasize the triviality of the incident.

"Hm." Rich tilted his head, casual but curious. "Tell me about that."

"It wasn't even a thing," said Rafael, waving his hand.

"I'm sure it wasn't," Rich agreed. "But I'd love to hear about it."

Ursula and Rafael recounted the night they'd returned from up-state and had the conversation about adoptive dogs versus breeder-sourced dogs. Ursula tensed up as she admitted to having suggested there was something snobbish about Rafael's preference. He patted her knee to comfort her and signal that all was forgiven. He really was over it.

Rich made a few notes on his tablet, and then looked up. "And that's the first time you've discussed pet acquisition?"

They nodded.

"How about any other significant joint commitments? Buying property? Marriage? Children?"

"We haven't discussed those in any detail," said Rafael. It's not that he didn't want those things with Ursula—he did—but he wasn't in a rush. He figured if they were going to be together forever, what was the hurry? "It's only been four months."

Ursula tensed a tiny bit, worried that this might be an early glimmer of a commitment-phobia that would manifest more clearly down the road. She knew they'd only been dating for four months, but if they were going to be together forever, why not proceed full-speed ahead? She took a breath and tried to dispel her anxiety, reminding herself that Rafael was not Sean. He was not any of her exes.

Rich scribbled something onto his tablet. "Okay. Sounds like it was just a little hiccup. Nothing to be concerned about. I'm just going to take a quick look at your file. I'll be back shortly."

Once Rich left the room, Rafael held out his arms, and Ursula maneuvered out of her chair and settled into his lap. "Cocoon me," she said, and he was happy to oblige.

"He's a little weird," said Rafael.

"Aren't *all* the Arc employees a little weird?"

"They are," Rafael agreed. "But this is good. I'm glad we had to do this check-in. He's just going to come back and tell you that we're getting a Ridgeback from the breeder, and we'll be on our way."

Ursula smirked at Rafael and nuzzled into him, but after a beat, she pulled back to look at him.

"You *do* want to marry me, right?" she asked.

"Of course," he said, brushing her wild hair out of her face. "I just want it to be on our timeline and our terms."

It felt like the joy was flooding back into their shared emotional system. But after about five minutes, Rafael realized that Ursula was cutting off the circulation in his arm. They both stood up.

"I wonder how long this is going to take," said Ursula, looking at her phone. She was supposed to go back to work that afternoon for a management meeting where they would be discussing upcoming promotions. She shot off a quick text to Roger, letting him know he should proceed without her, but reminding him that Sabrina was due for a raise and title change. (She was being bumped up to *senior associate of strategic audacity*.)

She then bent herself into a downward-facing dog, lifted one leg, and swung it forward into a half-pigeon pose, her shin at a right angle to her body. "I carry all of my existential angst in my hips," she said.

Rafael had removed his suit jacket, and he was now in a plank pose, flexing his feet one at a time to stretch his perpetually tight calves. He'd been a college soccer star, but for the past ten years, his body had been in a slow-motion state of subtle breakdown. It seemed that no amount of stretching or foam-rolling could stave off the aging process.

"Nice biceps," said Ursula.

"Nice butt," said Rafael on his next exhale.

After they'd stretched for a while, they returned to their respective chairs. It had been a longer wait than they had expected.

Finally, after twenty-seven minutes had elapsed, the door slid open. Rich entered, followed by a young woman and Dr. Vidal herself. None of them emanated warmth this time. They filed in and sat side by side on the bench, facing Ursula and Rafael.

Ursula peered at the young woman. She seemed so familiar, but Ursula couldn't place her. Maybe she just had a generic face? Except she didn't. She had a pointy nose, sharp horizontal eyebrows, and short, bleached hair that was slicked back. Ursula's pulse quickened. It was the woman from the Purple Rain room at The Stake—the one who had given her The Arc's card. The one who had set this entire process in motion. This time, she wasn't wearing a bathrobe; she was wearing a white lab coat.

"Ursula. Rafael. I apologize for keeping you waiting," said Dr. Vidal without smiling. "I know you've already spoken to Rich. And this"—she gestured toward the blond woman—"is Renata, one of our psychological architects."

Ursula caught Renata's eye, and Renata gave a smile of recognition.

"First, I want to emphasize that you are one of the most exciting couples we've ever worked with," said Dr. Vidal. "A beautiful example of how two exceptional individuals can be made even more exceptional when matched with the right partner."

Ursula flushed with pride. Here it was—they were about to win some kind of award, or perhaps they'd broken a record for most in-love couple of the year.

"But unfortunately, there's a problem," continued Dr. Vidal. "Rich filled us in on your conflict concerning the possible acquisition of a dog, and when we looked at the data to see what might be at the root of this conflict, we discovered an error in our initial analysis."

Ursula and Rafael both sat up straighter, suddenly anxious.

"You are indeed perfectly balanced along 99 percent of our axes, but there is one crucial area, Emotional Reverberation—we call it ER for short—where we failed to realize that you are diametrically opposed, and for this particular metric, that's an insurmountable conflict. You see . . ."

"Wait, wait." Rafael held up his hand, stopping her. He looked at the floor and tried to collect himself. "What is Emotional Reverberation?"

Dr. Vidal nodded, eager to clarify. "Emotional Reverberation is a psychological category that is incredibly helpful in allowing us to understand how two individuals will relate to one another over time. To put it somewhat crudely, it's how you emotionally bounce off each other, and how those echoes affect the longevity of your relationship, for better or worse."

"But how does it work? How do you calibrate that?" Rafael wanted specifics.

"It's a measure that's proprietary to The Arc, so I can't divulge the exact inputs that we use to calculate it, but it's a very powerful indicator of whether a relationship will succeed or fail in the long run."

Ursula and Rafael looked at one another, and then looked back at Dr. Vidal. Ursula felt her heart split in two: half devastation, half indignation.

Dr. Vidal went on. "The level of so-called chemistry you two have achieved is higher than expected. In fact, it is among the highest we've ever tracked, and I imagine you've felt the beauty of this chemistry. But you see, there is an underlying danger. It's impossible to achieve that level of synergy without also experiencing volatility. You've gotten a small glimpse of that volatility, which is what you divulged to Rich earlier. And I wish I could tell you there was a simple solution, but unfortunately, based on what we've uncovered, this disagreement—about the dog—is just the tip of the iceberg, so to speak. It's a taste of what's to come, should you choose to stay together. And as you seek to make larger decisions—about family, career, wealth management, medical needs—the conflicts will only increase."

Rafael and Ursula froze, absorbing the information while also resisting it.

"When it came to balancing your ER, we misjudged the calibration. We created a relationship that would deliver the highest of highs, but also the lowest of lows. Essentially, we created the perfect storm."

"You flooded the engine," Ursula said flatly.

"That's a good analogy. We flooded the engine. I want to be very clear that the error was entirely ours," said Dr. Vidal. "Nothing like this has ever happened in the distinguished history of The Arc."

Rafael choke-laughed.

"Well, what now?" Ursula pressed Dr. Vidal. "We've been dating for four months. We're in love."

"Completely in love. I love you, Ursula," said Rafael, for the first time.

"I love *you*," she reciprocated, wondering why it had taken this crisis for them to articulate what was so obvious to both of them.

They stared into each other's eyes, simultaneously buzzing with affection for one another while chilled by the information they were receiving.

Rafael addressed Dr. Vidal. "So how do you calibrate for the fact that we're now completely fucking irreversibly in love?"

Rafael rarely swore, and Ursula was exhilarated by it when he did.

"We understand your frustration, Rafael," said Dr. Vidal, gently pressing her hands together in front of her heart. "And we have a recommendation. It's what we call an Emotional Detachment Procedure, or an EDP. It's the best way to ensure that your relationship doesn't spiral into a place where it begins to compromise other aspects of your life: your professions, your friendships, your mental health. It takes twelve hours, and we conduct the procedure here at our facility. Again, it's a proprietary process, but it will help facilitate your separation from each other, rendering it much less painful."

Ursula and Rafael looked at each other, panicked by the idea of disappearing from one another's lives.

"And as recompense, we will arrange for you to have new matches, if you'd like to attempt our service again. A fresh start." Ursula and Rafael looked horrified at the thought of being rematched, and Dr. Vidal quickly changed her tack. "Or if not, we'll provide a full refund. And Ursula," she turned and looked deeply into Ursula's eyes, "we are fully aware that our oversight may have implications for your reproductive planning timeline, which we know is of concern to you. To offset that inconvenience, we would cover the cost of immediate egg freezing."

Jesus. This was some serious damage control.

"But." Ursula's breath was shallow and sharp. "We're in love. We don't want to detach. Do we?"

Rafael shook his head. "No. Absolutely not."

"We understand your resistance to the idea," said Dr. Vidal. "And I assure you: This conversation and the decision is the most painful part. After this, the Emotional Detachment Procedure will be nothing. I do want to reiterate and emphasize that the EDP is our recommendation. And the sooner the better, to prevent any possible emotional scar tissue."

Rafael put his head in his hands. Ursula felt tears rise to the surface of her eyes and pool before falling heavily down her cheeks.

"Wait," said Rafael, putting his hand up and squeezing his eyes shut as he tried to reason. "This seems very, very dramatic. Let's back up. We had a tiny fight. Not even a fight. We had a disagreement about a hypothetical dog. It was completely inconsequential. And now you're telling us to void our relationship? This was the first time we've even disagreed!"

"It's a great point." Dr. Vidal had a way of saying patronizing things without sounding patronizing. "I understand the anger and frustration. I do. To reiterate: This isn't about the fight itself. It's about what the fight portends. It's about what's to come—the storm on the horizon that you can't yet see."

"I can't believe this." Ursula's throat tightened.

"I know it's hard to wrap your head around why you would want to terminate what feels like a great thing," said Dr. Vidal. "But this is a prophylactic recommendation."

"Prophylactic!" Rafael laughed. "Prophylactic? Four months after telling us we were perfect for each other? We are in so deep. *So* deep. I'd expect a woman who can invent the term Emotional Reverberation to choose her words more carefully. Prophylactic . . ." He shook his head.

Dr. Vidal allowed his dig to land. She sat patiently, and after a brief pause, said calmly, "Why don't we leave you two alone for a moment? Say, fifteen minutes. This is a lot to take in, and I imagine you'd like to discuss it in private. I should let you know that, should you opt to stay together and not undertake the detachment procedure at this time, you'll still be obligated to fulfill any necessary elements of your initial contract, and we won't be able to return your fee."

"The $50,000 fee," Rafael clarified. "Each. So the $100,000 fee."

"Ursula's fee was $40,500 because we calibrate for . . ."

"The gender wage gap. Yeah, yeah. Got it," Rafael said.

"That's correct," said Dr. Vidal. "We would keep the combined fee of $90,500. But if you do proceed with detachment now, you'll get a full refund and will be completely released from your contract."

Rafael shook his head and pinched the bridge of his nose.

"We'll let you have some time, and then we can discuss next steps." Dr. Vidal rose and nodded at Rich and Renata, indicating they should follow her out of the room. The wall panel slid closed behind them, leaving Ursula and Rafael in the warmly lit space, the air now heavy with silence.

They sat for a minute, staring at each other. Then Rafael got up, and he pulled Ursula out of her chair. She crumpled into his arms and cried, and he rocked her from side to side.

"This is surreal," he said.

"What do we do?" Ursula's normal tendency toward control had faltered. She wanted someone else to tell her how to proceed. She was having a hard time relinquishing the faith that she'd had in The Arc and its mysteriously infinite wisdom, but she did not want to surrender her relationship at Dr. Vidal's recommendation.

"We have to make a calculation," said Rafael. "They're essentially asking us to decide whether keeping our current relationship is worth $90K to us. Are we willing to gamble that amount on a now uncertain future? Or do we want to cut our losses and start again?"

Ursula pushed back from his embrace. "A calculation? How can you be so clinical about this?"

"I'm just trying to see it from their perspective," he said, holding her hands to his chest. "*They're* being clinical. They're running a calculation. And to be clear, I don't want to do this procedure. I am not willing to lose you for any amount."

The hope flooded back into Ursula's heart. But then she stopped to recenter herself. In prior relationships, she had been in a constant state of reactivity—happy if her mate was happy, anxious if he was distant, relieved when he rewarmed to her. She needed to do more than merely react to Rafael's feelings. She needed to know where she stood, irrespective of his stance. Did she feel the same way? It was true that she didn't want to lose Rafael, but there were so many factors to consider.

"But what if they're right about our future being doomed?" she fretted. Then she voiced a chilling prospect: "What if we lose the money, and then we lose each other anyway? They knew enough to match us, and honestly, they did a good job. A *brilliant* job. I know we've only been together for four months, but you are unequivocally the love of my life. But I'm worried that they know what they're talking about. They've been right about everything else."

Her eyes filled, and she blinked out a few heavy tears.

"They knew enough to match us," said Rafael. "But Ursula, we know more than they do now. We are the ones in this relationship. The Arc is not in this relationship."

"You're right," she said, but she wasn't sure. Wasn't The Arc in the relationship, to some extent? She took a long exhale. "I know how I feel about you. There's no way that's going to just evaporate, even if we do have more conflict in the future."

"Every relationship has conflict," said Rafael. "I don't know what kind of sinister horizon they're looking toward, but I don't see it. I don't accept it. How bad could it be? Look at us. We have already come so far. You resuscitated me. You fulfilled the flamebird's prophecy of transcendent love."

"What?" said Ursula. This was the first she'd heard about a flamebird.

"I'll tell you about it later," said Rafael, not wanting to get into the details of his long-ago ayahuasca trip. "I love you so much, tree top."

"I love you so much, buffalo nape," said Ursula, burrowing into his collarbone. "Fuck them."

"Fuck them," repeated Rafael. "I'm not losing you. I bought you! For $50,000!"

"And I bought *you* for $40,500! What a bargain!"

They were laughing again. They were hugging again. They were breathing again. A lightness began to dispel the heavy air.

There was a knock at the door.

Dr. Vidal, Rich, and Renata filed back in. This time, they all wore the same expression—cordial smiles—in an attempt to infuse pleasantness back into the room. They took their seats on the bench, and Ursula and Rafael settled back into their chairs.

"We're not doing the Emotional Detachment Procedure," Ursula said decisively. "You can keep our money."

Dr. Vidal frowned but then regained her neutrality. "Fair enough. Are you absolutely sure?" She raised her eyebrows and shifted her gaze to Rafael. "Both of you?"

"We don't want anything more to do with this sham of a service," said Rafael, resolute.

"I understand," said Dr. Vidal, stiffening. "We truly regret this outcome."

Rafael and Ursula stood up to leave.

"One last thing," said Dr. Vidal. "Remember that you are still under the NDA until your first eighteen months together have elapsed, so that will take us to"—she did a quick calculation on her fingers—"not this February, but the following February. Your first date was August 14, yes? So February 14 of 2020. Valentine's Day!" Her energy rose a bit at the coincidence. "And you'll have to come in for your one-year check-in next August 14th. If you have questions or want to check in between now and then, we are always here. Since we're retaining your fees, we'll still consider you our clients. Our *top* clients. Rich can fit you into my schedule anytime." Dr. Vidal looked to Rich and nodded, prompting Rich to confirm by nodding even more vigorously.

"I said we don't want anything more to do with this service," repeated Rafael. His eyes widened and fixed on the floor as he reached the limit of his patience.

"I heard you, Rafael," said Dr. Vidal. "And that is completely your choice. But sometimes, with the passage of time, people change their minds. Things evolve. If you *do* experience a level of conflict you can't control, you can always come back to get the Emotional Detachment Procedure at that time."

Rafael raised his dark, angry eyes to meet hers. She put her hands up defensively to indicate she was just covering her bases.

"Again, I'm so sorry about this. We truly wish you both the best. I hope you prove us wrong. After all, anything is possible," said Dr. Vidal, standing and holding out her hand as a final olive branch.

Ursula and Rafael stood, grabbed each other's hands, and walked toward the door, but then realized they had no idea how to open it. Renata scurried over and tapped a spot on the wall, and they charged past her without glancing back at Dr. Vidal, whom they never wanted to see again.

Once on the street, Ursula felt a rush of relief. Rafael had chosen her, and she had chosen him. They were free, autonomous, out from under the scrutiny of The Arc.

"I didn't realize until now how oppressive the whole thing felt,"

Rafael said. "Not you, but The Arc—requiring those monthly up-dates, tracking our progress."

Ursula nodded. "It's like a weight has been lifted. I feel like I'm floating."

Rafael checked his watch. "Wow, we were there for two hours. It's 5:30."

Ursula had already missed her meeting. "Jalisco?" she suggested. The thought of blowing off the final hours of the workday and drink-ing tequila with her one true love wasn't just appealing—it was heav-enly. She began to feel euphoric. "There is nowhere else I'd rather be right now than in a dank Mexican restaurant sipping margs with my bobcat."

Rafael did the sexy whistle thing and a taxi pulled up to the curb, hitting a puddle of slush. Rafael tugged Ursula toward him so she wouldn't get sprayed.

"I love you, kickstand," said Ursula.

"Love you too, cheese knife," said Rafael.

It was thirty slow, wet, wintry blocks to Jalisco. They kissed all the way there, feeling like giddy teenagers who had broken curfew and gotten away with it.

Chapter 25

Rafael had just gotten out of the shower when his buzzer sounded.

"Catherine is here," said the doorman through the intercom.

"Great. Send her up," said Rafael. He opened the front door a crack and ran into his room to throw on sweatpants and a T-shirt. Catherine would be dressed to the nines, as usual, but he didn't feel the need to gussy up for his sister. She'd texted him earlier in the day to ask if she could come over for a drink tonight, which she usually only did when she was emotionally hemorrhaging.

"Rafa!" Catherine called from the entryway. He heard her heels clacking toward the kitchen.

"Hola, hermana," he called in Spanish, which he had learned in school and then honed during a semester abroad in Madrid. Catherine was known as the family basket case. Although she was five years older than Rafael, he had long ago assumed the role of older brother in her life.

"Whisky. Now," she said, rummaging through his cabinets. She wore tight leather pants and an oversized black cashmere sweater, which contrasted with her icy blond hair.

"It's over here," said Rafael, grabbing a bottle off the built-in shelf he had designated as the bar. He pointed to the couch. "Sit."

He took two glasses out of the cabinet and opened the freezer drawer. Behind his twenty pints of ice cream was the special tray that made giant, manly ice cubes. He popped two out and dropped them in the glasses, then poured four fingers of bourbon into each. He sensed this was just the beginning of what would be a long evening.

"He has a wife," Catherine said, grabbing her glass from his hand and taking a long, hungry sip. She looked both beautiful and terrible: her eyes were red and swollen from crying, but she had a natural elegance that never deserted her. She had always been long and wispy, with shoulder-length blond hair that evoked an old-school politician's wife. And although she was forty-seven, she did whatever it was that wealthy women did to their skin to make it look mostly ageless—fractals or lasers or jackhammers or something. She had learned these practices from her mother, Margaret, whose face had been nearly motionless since the mid-'90s. Catherine had also followed in her mother's footsteps professionally by becoming an interior decorator whose clientele consisted mostly of her immediate friends.

Rafael paused to figure out who Catherine was talking about. It must have been the British finance guy she'd been dating for about six months—Derek? No. Daniel? Yes, Daniel.

"We're talking about Daniel?"

"*Dashiell*," she corrected him. Dashiell spent half the year in New York and half in London.

"Didn't he always have a wife?" asked Rafael, trying to get his bearings. It had been a few weeks since he'd seen Catherine, and at the time, she'd been deliriously happy.

"Yes, but he's supposed to be divorcing her," said Catherine, choking back tears as she drank more bourbon. "They've been separated for a year. And now . . ."

She took a dramatic inhale and then an even more dramatic exhale. "He tells me they're *reconciling*." She said it as if it were the most hateful thing one could do, and then burst into heavy sobs.

Rafael waited. He knew it was best to let Catherine implode for a minute before trying to respond. And he had to hand it to her: for a forty-seven-year-old woman, she was still living with the unbridled passion and drama of a twenty-five-year-old. Some might call that immaturity or instability, but he appreciated her rambunctious spirit, especially in contrast to their elder sister's relentlessly ordered life. Patricia, who was fifty, lived in Washington, DC, and actually *was* a politician's wife. And although Patricia was never disparaging,

Rafael knew that she looked at her unmarried younger siblings with bewilderment. Whenever they visited her, she treated them with curious caution, the way you might approach a pair of coyotes that had wandered into your yard.

Rafael enjoyed having Catherine in the same city, even if that meant he was responsible for providing her with emotional tune-ups a few times a year.

"I'm sorry. That sounds frustrating," he said, getting up to fetch the bottle from the counter. He returned and refilled her glass. "He seemed like a nice enough guy."

"He is *perfect*." Catherine sniffed.

Rafael had met Dashiell, and though "perfect" was a clear overstatement, he knew better than to contradict his sister when she was in this state.

"That's always a tricky thing," said Rafael. "Dating a newly divorced—or not even divorced—person. It's a big transition. People rarely know what they actually want or what they're capable of at that stage, even if they think they do."

"He just seemed . . . *ugh*," said Catherine. "He seemed ready. He said he was ready."

"Sometimes people don't know what they're saying," said Rafael, who despite not always knowing what he wanted, had always been careful with his words and promises. He erred toward silence when he wasn't sure what his heart desired.

"I just love that newly single man energy," said Catherine. She put her hand over her face as the realization sunk in. "I did it again, didn't I? I dated another emotionally unavailable man."

Rafael clenched his lips in solemn confirmation.

For all her faults, Catherine did have a certain amount of self-awareness. At this point, she'd done enough therapy to be her own therapist, but it didn't stop her from making spectacularly bad choices. Again and again, the thrill always outweighed the consequences. She was reckless, but endlessly resilient; Rafael respected this about her.

"I was ready to live the transatlantic life with him." She wiped away a tear and then appeared to flick it onto the floor aggressively.

This was a good sign. She was making the transition from sadness to anger exceptionally quickly this time. "I was ready to change my life!"

Rafael shook his head. "But he didn't earn that. He doesn't deserve that."

"You're goddamn *right* he doesn't," said Catherine. Now she was truly pissed.

"Catherine," said Rafael. "I know this part is hard. But just remember: There will be something better in your future. It might happen sooner than you think. But first you have to let this go."

"This too shall pass," said Catherine, nodding.

"Exactly," said Rafael. "This too shall pass."

"The only way out is through," she self-soothed.

"The only way out is through," Rafael repeated.

"Wooooooohhhh." Catherine let out a long, exaggerated, yoga-trained exhale. "You're so right. Such a sage." She massaged her temples for a few seconds and then looked up, as if seeing him for the first time. "You look amazing."

It was true. He did. Rafael had always been considered good-looking, but since meeting Ursula, he had acquired a luminous quality. He noticed women on the street not just looking at him, but *staring* at him, wantonly. He had that irresistible, "I'm happily taken" energy.

"Thanks," he said. It normally took Catherine at least an hour to stop talking about herself and turn her attention to him, so this was quicker than expected.

"I'm still dating Ursula," said Rafael.

"Such a darling," Catherine said of Ursula, whom she had met briefly. Then her eyes lit up. "Ohhhh my god! Should *I* do it? Should I do The Arc?"

Rafael couldn't envision Catherine achieving what he and Ursula had achieved, but more importantly, he was now loath to recommend The Arc to anyone.

"No," said Rafael. "I mean, Ursula is incredible, so I guess I'll always be indebted to The Arc for that. But they completely screwed us over."

"What? How?"

"I signed an NDA, so I'm not supposed to talk about it, but essentially, they told us they botched whatever proprietary formula they used to match us, and they say our relationship is doomed."

Catherine gasped and opened her eyes as wide as they could go—which wasn't that wide, given her recent filler injection.

"It's ridiculous," said Rafael. "They told us our relationship is untenable after we had one disagreement. *One* disagreement in four months. And it was about dogs."

"Dogs?"

"About what kind of dog to get."

"A Ridgeback," Catherine said automatically, as if it were the only breed worth considering. Then she quickly became serious. "Ursula doesn't want a Ridgeback? Doesn't she know we're Ridgeback people?"

"Yes. That's not really . . . it's not important," said Rafael. "The point is, The Arc is a fraudulent, sinister operation, and it's the last thing you need right now."

"Hmmm," said Catherine pensively. Rafael had a feeling she might try it anyway.

"So, when do I get to see the fabulous Ursula again?" she finally asked.

"Anytime," said Rafael. "We're going to Oaxaca for New Year's, but we'll be back on the sixth."

"*Oaxaca*," said Catherine, trying out the word. "How exotic."

Suddenly her phone pulsed. She looked at it and sat up straighter, electrified. "It's him. It's *him*! It's Dashiell."

She looked at the text message. "He wants to talk."

Rafael raised his eyebrows skeptically, but it was a foregone conclusion.

Catherine got up, pecked Rafael on the cheek, and then walked toward the entryway while typing feverishly into her phone. "Thanks, Rafa," she said. "Love you."

She grabbed her coat and walked out the door. Rafael could hear her flirtatious "Hello, *you*" as she waited for the elevator.

Rafael sat back on the couch, dumping the remainder of Catherine's bourbon into his own. Suddenly the disagreement about where to get their dog—Ridgeback or not—seemed wholly inconsequential. He was in love with the most incredible woman in the world, and what they had together was almost impossible to find. Nothing else mattered.

Chapter 26

They hiked up a hill, along a ridge, and then down to a sapphire lagoon that swelled with Pacific sea water. Rafael sat on a warm rock, shirtless, easily absorbing the Mexican sun. Ursula had thrown her hiking clothes off and was slowly wading into the water, her skin glowing beneath the surface. They had celebrated the night before, drinking margaritas and eating a whole roasted fish at the terrace restaurant of their little hotel. A local surfer had played the guitar, first soothingly, then more dramatically as the sky darkened. At midnight, underneath sharp, clear stars, they had walked down to the beach and swum out into the ocean, past the breaking waves. Not too far, but far enough to feel that the world was theirs alone.

Now, in the generous warmth of mid-afternoon, they again felt alone on the earth. The lagoon was entirely theirs, save for a few cormorants swirling overhead. Ursula moved deeper into the cold water, feeling it rise up over her knees, her thighs. A wave surged into the surrounding rocks and water shot through the opening that fed the lagoon, causing a swell around her. She inhaled sharply as the water rose to her belly button.

Turning to look at Rafael on his rock, she felt a surge of happiness, followed by a shadow of dull dread. The happier she got, the more she feared the loss of that happiness, the downward slide she knew so well. She tried to tell herself it wasn't inevitable, and that this shadow of anxiety was a vestige of the failed relationships of her past. Still, she wanted to hold on to this peace, to hit Pause and live in this moment forever: in a secluded Mexican lagoon, on the first day of a new year, with her long-sought love. They could sleep in a cave, eat fish, and cut each other's hair with sharp rocks. She wanted desperately to preserve this moment.

"Do the mermaid," said Rafael through squinted eyes, requesting the move that Ursula had debuted a few days prior.

She smiled and took a deep breath, dipping her head forward into the water before whipping it back so that her hair sprayed a dramatic arc through the air.

"Your best one yet!"

Ursula did it one more time, and then took a break so as to avoid whiplash.

"Lose the suit," she yelled, with only her head visible above the surface.

Rafael got up, slipped his trunks off, and walked steadily into the blue water, diving once he was deep enough and swimming all the way out to where Ursula was now floating on her back. He pulled her feet toward him, and she wrapped her legs around his waist.

"Do you think 2019 will be a good year?" she asked him.

"It will be the best year so far," he responded with certainty.

The way their bodies intertwined in the water felt natural, elemental, primal. He kissed her salty lips, and his mind went pleasantly blank, moving neither forward, nor backward, but simply resting, like a slow exhale. He had never experienced this kind of stillness, and he knew to enjoy it while he could.

Chapter 27

January 4, 4:32 P.M.

"I love this one," said Ursula, pointing at a large woven rug hanging on the wall. It was predominantly red, with accents of black and white. "The red ones are so optimistic."

"It's really nice," said Rafael. "What about the blue?" He wandered over to the opposite corner of the little shop in Teotitlán del Valle. They had, in spite of themselves, sought out Roger's buddy Miguel, and he did, in fact, sell some of the most beautiful rugs they'd ever seen. Rafael started to look through a tall pile, flipping up the corner of each rug to see the one beneath.

"*¿Podemos ver ésta?*" he asked Miguel, who, with the help of his assistant, pulled the rug from the middle of the pile. It was a brilliant royal blue, with slashes of red, white, and green.

"This one." Rafael looked at Ursula for approval.

"Great. Let's get it," she replied.

"*And* the red one?" Rafael wondered.

"I don't know," said Ursula. "I mean, where are these going?"

"Well, I think this could go in my living room, under the dining table," said Rafael about the blue rug. "Right?"

Ursula didn't say anything.

"No?"

"I'm just trying to think."

"Agh, I hate when you think," joked Rafael, trying to lighten the mood. He could see she was starting to agonize about something.

"I mean, is this *your* rug? Are these *our* rugs? Are we buying them together? Are we each buying one on our own? I guess . . . what's the plan?"

"The plan," said Rafael, thinking for a minute. "I don't have a plan. I just like this rug. I like both rugs."

"I guess I just want to visualize where each is going," said Ursula. "And if they're going to stay in those places, or if eventually we'd have two of these rugs in one apartment . . ."

"I see what you mean," said Rafael. "We just haven't talked about that yet."

"No, we haven't," said Ursula, her stomach tightening. But why not? Had he not envisioned moving in with her? The possibility that he hadn't even considered it wounded her. Then again, she hadn't brought it up, either.

"I don't know, monkfish," he said. "I mean, are we negotiating future assets? We can talk about all of this. But for now, can we just buy some rugs? We can each take one for now, and we can use them elsewhere in the future."

"Sure," said Ursula. "Yes, let's buy the rugs."

"Both?"

Suddenly, she felt pulled in two directions, panicked both by the idea of moving in with Rafael and the idea of *not* moving in with him. Part of her froze at the thought of sharing a rug, giving up her apartment, saying goodbye to her independent life, compromising about where the rug would go, losing rug autonomy, then eventually losing *all* autonomy. "Your life is no longer your own," she'd heard her married friends say of melding their lives with another's, and the thought always knocked the wind out of her. *If it's not my own, then whose is it?* she always wondered. At the same time, she wanted Rafael to want to live with her. In fact, she was secretly relying on him to advocate for and initiate that next phase. She couldn't do this without him; she needed him to take the lead.

"Yes, let's just get both," she said, starting to approach the small table that served as a check-out counter near the open door of the store.

Rafael wondered why she seemed so flustered. "I'll get it," he said, reaching for his wallet.

"Are you sure?"

He nodded. He liked buying things for her, providing for her, taking care of her. It made him feel useful, even when she was confusing him. Especially when she was confusing him.

As Ursula stepped outside into the golden sunlight, she heard Rafael chatting cheerily with Miguel, paying and arranging for the rugs to be shipped to New York—one to his apartment, the other to hers. It was perfectly warm in the afternoon sun, but her body was flooded with a cold fear, her lean frame casting a slanted shadow on the saffron-colored façade of the shop.

Chapter 28

Ever since Ursula and Rafael had returned from Oaxaca, they'd been squabbling. Nothing major, just little bouts of bickering. They agreed that they were entering that phase where you stop letting everything slide and start being more confrontational about little things that bother you. Ursula had to constantly remind herself that this was nothing to panic about. Not a sign of relationship demise. Just a normal part of the evolution of a deepening connection. In a sense, it was a sign of progress. The bickering was a good thing, they agreed.

On this particular Tuesday, they woke up at Ursula's apartment in Brooklyn. In an attempt to counteract what had been an indulgent holiday season, Ursula had been foregoing her usual morning lattes for ginger tea with lemon. She popped her head into the bathroom just in time to see Rafael do that thing he always did when he brushed his teeth: rather than lowering his head and spitting the toothpaste out near the drain, he held his head high and let the foam fall in a long, lazy stream from his mouth.

"God, that's so gross," said Ursula. "Do you want some ginger tea?"

"No thanks," said Rafael. He didn't believe in momentary health kicks. He tried to eat responsibly year-round, with the exception of his ice cream habit. He rewrapped his towel snugly around his waist and anticipated what was going to happen next: Ursula would chop up the lemons and the ginger, and then she would leave the rinds and the shavings on the cutting board on the counter, where they would sit all day. When she came home that night or the next day, they would be dried up, and only then would she dispose of them. Her delayed approach to tidying up irked him. He put deodorant on and ran some waxy pomade through his hair.

When he got to the living room, Ursula was on the couch, checking her email and drinking her tea.

She realized too late that Rafael was going to do that infuriating thing he always did: sweep the fruit remnants off the counter into the trash. She'd asked him at least a dozen times to remember to compost.

"Rafael," she said sternly. She shot him a disapproving look. He realized his error.

"I'm cleaning up your scraps. You could say thank you," he said, walking to the freezer. "Why do you keep the compost bag in here, anyway? How am I supposed to remember to do this if it's in the back of your freezer?"

"Well, if I leave the bag out, the stuff will rot," said Ursula.

"But you always leave the scraps on your counter for at least a day anyway, and they rot there," said Rafael. "So it's not really a question of *whether* they'll rot—it's just *where* they'll rot."

"Your Emotional Reverberations are annoying me right now," said Ursula. They'd been joking about the term ever since leaving The Arc back in December, but little by little, Ursula had begun to worry if there were something legitimate there.

Rafael pulled the compost bag out of the freezer and fished through the garbage for the lemon rinds and ginger scraps, dropping them carefully into the bag, which he then returned to the freezer. For just a second, he hated her. It was less than a second. A flash. A flicker. An electric surge that was gone as soon as it had registered. But for the first time, he realized with some horror that he had the capacity to hate her. What if he were to let it take hold and grow?

He reacted to the feeling by trying to force himself in the other direction. "I love you," he said.

"I love you, too," she said, hazily, not looking up from her laptop.

"Writing your memoir?" he asked.

That got her attention. "No," she said. "I'm writing yours. *Obsessive-Compulsive Scrap Gathering: The Rafael Banks Story.*"

"Weird, because I'm working on yours: *How to End Up Alone with Your Cat: The Ursula Byrne Story.*"

"Well, now I'm working on our joint memoir," Ursula responded.

"Yeah? What's that one called?"

She stood up from the couch and walked over to where he was in the kitchen. *"Intent to Fuck: The Ursula and Rafael Saga."*

She pulled off his towel and threw it behind her. They were going to be late for work again.

Chapter 29

January 11, 9:13 A.M.

As Ursula stepped out of the subway car and onto the platform, an agitated man with a tattered shopping bag pushed past her, yelling, "Stop fucking playing with me, New York! Stop playing with me, you stupid-ass city."

Ursula could relate. Like every New Yorker, she knew what it was like to feel defeated by the city itself: train delays, unexpected downpours, creepy catcallers, slow walkers, exceedingly long lines, rats underfoot, deceptively deep slush puddles, the rudeness of other New Yorkers who were having an even worse day than you. The list was endless. Then again, the city could lift you up just as easily as it could slap you down. On any given day, on any given subway platform, the exultant were brushing shoulders with the downtrodden, knowing they'd be in each other's shoes soon enough.

Ursula silently wished the man well and thanked the city for its stark contrasts: she was having the best day she'd had in a while. She made her way up the subway stairs, crossed the intersection at Broadway and Houston, and breezed into the SoHo building where the Anonymous & Co. office occupied the entire sixth floor. Bursting out of the elevator, she scanned the open space for Sabrina. After two months, Ursula had finally persuaded Mike to invest in Nine to Five, the company Sabrina had introduced her to, and she'd received an email from him that morning confirming the amount: $3 million. Although this development was completely separate from their work at Anonymous, Ursula knew Sabrina would be proud that she had helped a female-founded fledgling company secure a crucial round of funding. And hopefully Nine to Five would now have a big enough budget to hire Ursula's team to blow out their brand in a big way. She was dying to celebrate, but Sabrina wasn't at her desk, so Ursula scribbled on Sabrina's notepad: *Come find me! U*

Ursula wandered over to the espresso machine. Her ginger tea wasn't cutting it, so she made herself a double shot, and then strolled across the office to her nook. On days like this, she felt like everything was falling into place: She was both succeeding within the system and challenging it. She was making her own way, and helping to clear a path for others. She was playing the game, but also questioning it. She was threading the needle perfectly, as only she could. Rafael was right: 2019 was going to be the best year yet. She hung up her coat, plopped her bag on the floor, sat down at her desk, and opened her laptop.

There was an email from Roger, sent twenty minutes prior, with the subject line, "Drum roll, please . . . 2019 Promotions." Ursula clicked on it and scrolled past Roger's introductory paragraph—". . . such great work . . . huge congratulations . . . well-deserved . . . taking Anonymous to the next level . . ."—in search of the blurb she had submitted to announce Sabrina's jump from "associate" to "senior associate" of strategic audacity. But Sabrina wasn't on the list. Only four people had been promoted this cycle—two in the art department, one in HR, and one in digital strategy.

Ursula shot off a quick response to Roger: *I assume this is an oversight? You missed Sabrina. Could you send around an addendum? Or I can. Thx.*

Two minutes later, an email from Roger popped up. *Not an oversight.*

Ursula peered at her laptop in disbelief. She got up, walked out of her nook, and made her way across the office, gathering speed as she went. By the time she got to Roger's nook, she was almost jogging.

"What the hell?" she asked from the space where a door would have been if this were a real office.

Roger gave her a look as if he didn't know what she was talking about.

"Sabrina was . . ." She realized she was shouting and lowered her voice. "Sabrina was supposed to be promoted. We talked about it."

"You missed the promotion meeting," said Roger.

"Something came up!" Ursula said, flipping her palm up in protest. "It shouldn't negate *her* work. She earned this."

"Listen," said Roger sternly. "If you'd been at the meeting, you would have learned that 2018 wasn't as big a year as we'd hoped. After we closed the books, we decided we had to scale back the promotions. It's still fair: We promoted two men, two women. We're all good. Everything's egalitarian."

"Oh, so you hit your female quota?" Ursula said icily. "Why didn't you give me a heads-up?"

"Because I'm the boss, and it's my decision," said Roger. "Relax. She'll get promoted next year."

"Next year? You know that's basically an eternity for a twenty-five-year-old," said Ursula, remembering her own impatience and will to succeed at that age. "But more importantly, she deserves it *now*."

"She'll get there. Tell her to keep doing good work."

"Is giving her a $10,000 raise really going to break your budget?"

"Yes," Roger said calmly, not willing to negotiate. "And it's already done. The email is out."

"Well, you should have let me know," said Ursula. "I already pretty much told her she was getting promoted."

"So *un*tell her," said Roger. "That's on you."

"This is bullshit."

"Retract your claws, Ms. Byrne," said Roger with finality. "Go get a massage or something. Go to The Stake and get your aura waxed." He smirked.

"Fuck you, Roger." Ursula turned and walked out, devastated, as if she herself had been passed over. But this was worse, because the disappointment was accompanied by guilt. When she got to her nook, Sabrina was there, waiting.

Ursula gave her an aggrieved look.

"Is everything okay?" asked Sabrina, looking uncertain. "You wanted to see me?"

Suddenly, Ursula remembered the good news from Mike. But she had to address this first.

"Did you see Roger's email?"

Sabrina nodded. "Yeah, I'm confused."

"I'm so sorry," said Ursula. "This is my bad. I vouched for you to be promoted, but there was a miscommunication. It turns out we didn't have the budget, and it's going to have to wait until next promotion cycle."

"Okay," Sabrina said calmly, taking it in.

"It's okay if you're disappointed," said Ursula. "*I'm* disappointed. Not in you, just in the situation."

"No, I'm okay," said Sabrina. She seemed a little down, but fine. "So it's not a reflection of my work? There's nothing more I could have done?"

"Of course not. You're invaluable to me. And I did fight for you."

"I appreciate that," said Sabrina, shifting into a reassuring tone. "It's okay, Ursula. Really."

Ursula leaned her head on her palm.

Sabrina looked at her boss. "We soldier on, right?"

Ursula smiled, and Sabrina rose to get up.

"Oh, wait! Now the good news. I got an email from Mike," said Ursula. "He's going to invest in Nine to Five."

Sabrina's face lit up. "Really? That's amazing!"

"You played a big role in making it happen," said Ursula. "You helped connect the dots."

"Ah, that's awesome," said Sabrina, seeming relieved. "That makes up for the promotion thing."

"Have you been in touch with Juliana and Alejandra?" said Ursula.

"A few emails," said Sabrina. "Can I reach out to congratulate them?"

"Yes, go for it. And congratulations to you, too."

Sabrina flashed Ursula an understanding smile before heading out of the nook and back to her own desk.

Ursula stared at her computer numbly. At this point in her career, her own continued success was assured, assuming she didn't rock the boat too much. But the more she achieved as a lone wolf, the more isolated she felt. If she couldn't successfully bring other deserving women along with her, was she really succeeding at all? She could feel her sense of purpose shifting on its axis. The stream of promotions and awards and pats-on-the-back weren't sustaining her the way they used to. It wasn't enough to be Roger's MVP or Mike's secret weapon or even a rising industry star. She was tired of being the intrepid exception who was doing nothing to improve the system—and was perhaps, inadvertently, reinforcing its dysfunction by continuing to play the game. She looked around her glassy nook. For the first time in a long time, she felt like a failure.

Chapter 30

Ursula had been hiccupping throughout their entire walk home, interrupting her own story at regular intervals. They'd attended a dinner with the other partners of Rafael's firm and their significant others at the Fifth Avenue duplex of Ira Crane, the firm's founder and chairman. It was as fun as an evening among lawyers could be, but it had been long. Most of Rafael's colleagues were men in their fifties or sixties with college-aged children. The group had spent at least fifteen minutes comforting Tip Chastain, whose son had not been recruited by the Princeton squash coach as was anticipated. His chances at an Ivy now looked grim. Ursula tried out at least a dozen facial expressions as she attempted to feign sympathy. She had no idea how much wine she'd had, but the rough answer was a lot.

As they approached Rafael's building, Dalmat was waiting to open the door. "Evening, Mr. Banks," he said, nodding to Rafael. And then: "Good evening, Miss Byrne."

Ursula opened her mouth to respond to Dalmat, whom she liked very much, but all she could do was hiccup.

"Don't mind her," said Rafael. He loved Ursula when she was in this state of docile inebriation.

Once they got into the elevator, Ursula opened Rafael's coat and wriggled into it. She liked being enveloped in this way, as if she were a barnacle and Rafael's warm, sturdy body was the ship carrying her home. "Do you think our child will make the Princeton squash team?"

"Definitely not," said Rafael. "Our child will be too busy leading a post-capitalist feminist revolution to worry about things like racquet sports."

"Mmmmm, let's hug like this forever," Ursula said, drooping against him.

The elevator door opened.

"We can hug forever," said Rafael. "But let's do it on the couch so we don't have to worry so much about gravity." He steered her through the door, removed her rust-colored coat, and then guided her over to the couch where she collapsed into a surprisingly elegant heap in her silk dress. Rafael lay down beside her and they squirmed a bit before settling into a comfortable jumble. Ursula hiccupped again.

"Do you need to be burped?" Rafael laughed.

"Probably."

He patted her back, which she found genuinely comforting. She leaned into him and imagined the love transferring from her skin directly into his, wordlessly. At times like this, their shared energy felt so good, as if they were simultaneously feeding off and replenishing one another's life force.

"How do you work with those guys?" she mused.

"What guys? My colleagues?" said Rafael. "They're fine. It's not a chore."

"I'd die," said Ursula.

"Well, then it's a good thing you don't have to work with them," said Rafael, reaching for the remote. "Should we finish *Titans of the Savannah*?"

"They're just so bland," Ursula continued. "And the wives . . . I'd never be a lawyer's wife."

"Is that so?" said Rafael, looking at her.

"You know what I mean," said Ursula. "I'd never be *just* a lawyer's wife."

"Okay, well no one called you a lawyer's wife," said Rafael. "You should be so lucky."

"And you're not a real lawyer," she went on.

Rafael furrowed his brow.

"That's a compliment! I mean, you don't *act* like a lawyer. You're like an undercover lawyer."

"Well, being a lawyer isn't my identity; it's my work. I'm not playing a role; I'm not undercover. I'm just doing my job."

"I just don't know how you hang out with those guys all day every day."

"We don't 'hang out.' They're not my best friends; they're my co-workers," said Rafael, starting to get annoyed. "I'm sorry they bore you. Do *I* bore you?"

"No!" said Ursula. "But your coworkers do."

"Then you're lucky you get to spend your days with people like Brad the toilet-paper tycoon," said Rafael. "I know I'm not a war journalist like your ex, and I'm not a billionaire like Mike. But I'm perfectly content with my career—and I don't take that for granted. Not everyone has to spend their workdays in a cortisol-fueled frenzy or a state of torturous existential angst."

"Who spends their days in a state of torturous existential angst?"

Rafael looked at her as if it were obvious. The week prior, she had cried hysterically after the Sabrina promotion fiasco; had labeled herself a "failed mentor"; and had referred to her boss, Roger, as a "pretentious, poison-souled taskmaster."

"Me? I'm tortured?" asked Ursula, realizing that's what he was getting at.

Rafael chose his words carefully. "You have a tortured relationship with your job, yes."

"Well maybe that's why I'm good at it," said Ursula.

"Maybe," acknowledged Rafael. "But do you like it? Are you happy? Or do you just do it because you're good at it?"

Ursula paused. She'd asked herself the same question many times, especially lately, but she'd never arrived at a satisfying answer, and no one else had ever pressed her on it. When you're good at your job, people usually assume you like it.

"I'm just saying, you're deflecting," said Rafael. "You don't need to tell me you'd be bored if you had my job. I *know* that you'd be bored if you had my job. That's beside the point. You're avoiding the fact that you're unhappy at *your own* job. Or jobs, plural."

Ursula was growing tense. He was right, but she suddenly felt defensive. She'd poured too much energy into her career to admit that she might be veering off course.

"You just seem overwhelmed lately," said Rafael, "and I think you're projecting your frustration onto me. But you don't need to—I'm all good. I like my job."

"Congratulations," said Ursula. The wine had made her surly, and he was hitting a nerve.

"What about taking a break? A sabbatical?" said Rafael, thinking he might be able to provide her with an unexplored option.

"A break?" Ursula recoiled. The idea was unfathomable.

"It could be good," said Rafael, trying to help. "I can take care of things financially if you want to just breathe for a while, figure out what it is you'd be happier doing. And you don't have to keep consulting with Mike if you don't want to."

"I *do* want to," said Ursula, feeling protective of something she couldn't quite name.

"But didn't you take that gig just so you could pay for The Arc? And that's done."

"I did, at first. But now it's kind of exciting. And my contract with Mike isn't up until July. And I like making money. And I like Mike."

"Oh yeah? Since when do you like Mike?" asked Rafael, feeling a spike of jealousy.

"Well, it's evolving. He's an interesting person."

"He's your ATM."

Ursula laughed, but Rafael was annoyed now. Not at her, but at himself. Annoyed that he felt jealous of Mike, and annoyed that he couldn't seem to help Ursula navigate her professional woes. He persisted. "I have money. *We* have money. Maybe not Rutherford money, but you don't need to work yourself to death just to prove something."

"I'm not. I like my job," Ursula insisted.

"If you liked your job, you wouldn't be having an affair with another job," said Rafael. "The Mike Rutherford thing is more than a side hustle."

Ursula shrugged. Lately, she had lost track of exactly how much time she was allocating to her consulting gig versus her actual job at Anonymous & Co. The lines were beginning to blur. "I like being busy."

"I know you do. I'm just not sure you're happy."

Ursula took this in. Happiness felt like something she could get to later, once she had ensured her own survival.

"I'm just saying, you *can* take your foot off the gas for a second," said Rafael. "No one will think less of you."

"*I* will!" Ursula suddenly exploded. "I will think less of me."

"Why?"

"Because!" said Ursula, as if it were obvious. "I need to make my own money. I need to be independent. My career is the only thing that keeps me safe. Why would I just start financially depending on someone else *now*? After I've worked so hard to be self-sufficient?"

"Well, it's not just 'someone else,'" said Rafael. "It's *me*. And that's what partnership is—leaning on each other. Creating space for each other."

"Well, what if you leave?" said Ursula, caught in a wave of anxiety.

"I'm not leaving."

"Well, what if *I* leave?" said Ursula. She said it to provoke him, to test him. But it was true that she'd made hasty exits from previous relationships when they became too difficult to navigate.

"What are you talking about?" Rafael said, his anxiety ignited by hers.

"I'm just saying, nothing is certain," said Ursula. "Expecting someone else to take care of you is the most dangerous thing you can do. A woman needs to make and control her own money."

"You're sounding a lot like your mom," he said. "Or what I imagine your mom sounds like."

"Well, you're sounding a lot like a chauvinist," said Ursula, her eyes widening. "Did you think I was going to quit my job and become one of those wives from dinner?! Oh my god—do you just want a trophy wife?"

Rafael rubbed his brow with his hand, physically and now mentally exhausted. It was 12:45 A.M., and he had a meeting at 8:30 the next morning. "You're putting words in my mouth. And you're overthinking."

"Maybe you're underthinking!" she sniped.

"Ursula, you think I would pick a wild little pit viper like you to be my trophy wife?" Rafael said, trying to lighten the mood. "I have *never* wanted a trophy wife. And if I did, you would be an interesting choice."

"Excuse me!" said Ursula, needing to win the conversation. "I'd make a great trophy wife—if I wanted to!"

Rafael buried his face in his hands. "I'm not telling you to abandon your career, and this isn't about gender or power or subjugation. I'm trying to offer some balance. I know you don't *need* help. I'm just trying to say that I'm here for you, financially and otherwise. I'm trying to be supportive."

"Well, I can support myself," said Ursula. "And I feel like you're not taking my career seriously."

"I think you're taking it *too* seriously," said Rafael.

"Women have to take their careers seriously or else no one else will," yelled Ursula. "I don't get to just sashay into a conference room and command instant respect because my name is *Rafael Banks* and I'm wearing Tod's."

"Give me some fucking credit, Ursula," Rafael said. "And don't take this out on my loafers."

"Fine." She relented. "Sorry. I just don't think you understand what women are up against. You make it look so easy."

"What looks easy?"

"Your career. Your relationship with work. It's so seamless."

"Well, I just don't take it as personally as you do."

"I don't think you understand the pressure I feel."

"But you're putting that pressure on yourself. The world is not against you—it really isn't. You don't have to singlehandedly solve for the ills of the capitalist system, and you don't have to win Most Valuable Feminist every year," said Rafael.

His hyperbole annoyed her, but he was right that she felt she was at war with the structures in which she operated.

"Isn't feminism about freedom of choice, anyway?" he asked. "Aren't feminists allowed to take breaks, too?"

"Yes," she conceded.

"I think everything is getting tangled in here, tadpole." He tapped her head. "You've got so much going on. We need to get you untangled."

Silence fell between them, and after a moment, Ursula admitted, "I feel alone. Isolated."

"I'm trying to reach out to you right now. But you won't let me."

Ursula didn't respond.

"I think you *like* feeling isolated because it helps you feel special, unique, set apart," said Rafael. "I think you're terrified to be mediocre. But guess what? Being mediocre is kind of nice."

"How would you know? You're not mediocre," said Ursula.

"Well, I aspire to be."

Ursula smiled at the concept: an aspiration to mediocrity. It felt revolutionary, somehow.

She closed her eyes, exhausted and overwhelmed. She had lost track of what was agitating her. It wasn't actually anything he had said. It was something bigger that was surfacing, something she had been denying for too long. He was right. She needed more than a break; she needed a personal reckoning. But she had spent so much time and energy cultivating this current version of herself that she didn't know which parts to retain versus which parts to cede. She knew how to build her own "brand," so to speak, but she didn't necessarily know how to deconstruct it. And yes, she was disgruntled at work, but she was worried that if she let go professionally, she might never find her way again. And if she began to depend on Rafael, she might melt into him and lose herself entirely.

"I want you to feel empowered to do whatever you want to do," said Rafael. "But if we're going to be together, you need to rely on me sometimes." He yearned to know he was needed, whatever form that took.

"*If* we're going to be together?" Ursula asked. This was the first time she had heard him qualify their future. Her stomach clenched. It was happening—the turning point before the gradual slide. The "whens" were becoming "ifs."

"If. When. Whatever. You're wearing me out." Rafael stood up and went over to the side table. He opened the drawer and removed a bronze canister where he kept his assiduously rolled joints, selected one, and walked toward the terrace of his apartment.

Ursula remained on the couch. She felt something inside of her retreat, curling into a self-protective ball. The outline of their future, once bright and brilliant and guaranteed, now felt hazy. She had no-where to turn for answers—not to him, not to herself, and certainly not to The Arc. They had crossed into a new realm where there were no more guarantees.

Chapter 31

January 22, 1:58 P.M.

"He doesn't want you to work?" asked Issa. "That doesn't sound like something he'd say, or even believe."

"Well, he didn't say that exactly," said Ursula. "He said I should take a step back, take a break. No, he said I *could* take a break, a sabbatical. If I wanted to. And that he could take care of things financially."

"That sounds kind of amazing," said Issa.

"But insulting, no?" said Ursula. "Like he's trying to undermine my career."

"Not necessarily. You *do* complain about your job a lot."

"But everyone complains about their job," said Ursula. Then she amended: "Except you. And Rafael."

"Everyone has gripes, yes," Issa responded. "But your grievances seem deeper, more existential."

"Damn it," said Ursula. "Rafael used that word, too."

They sat cross-legged on their respective yoga mats in the exercise studio at The Stake, stretching out their triceps. The class instructor, Cass, walked the perimeter of the space, taking deep breaths and gently waving a stick of smoldering Palo Santo. A former model and dancer, she had a long, lithe body, and she wore beige leggings and a loose white crop top. The nonchalant neutral tones of her outfit and her long, curly hair hinted at her liberated inner state. This woman had the answers.

"I can't just quit my job," said Ursula. "What would I do? Reinvent myself? I'm thirty-five!"

"People do it all the time," said Issa.

"Yeah, other people," said Ursula. "People who know what they actually want to do. If I quit, I'll just drift into oblivion and no one will ever hear from me again."

"It could be kind of exciting to start over," said Issa, pushing her hand against her left knee as she twisted to the right. Her back cracked. "A blank canvas."

"Like a rebirth," Ursula murmured, suddenly overcome by a vision of her mom leaving her life on the West Coast to chart her own course as an artist. She only knew the 2.0 version of her mother; the California version was a total enigma.

"I mean, it doesn't have to be a *rebirth*. You don't have to emerge from primal ooze," said Issa. "But it does sound like Rafael hit a nerve."

"I guess he did," conceded Ursula. "And things have been a little tense lately. These conflict bubbles keep popping."

"Conflict bubbles?" Issa squinted her eyes as she tried to interpret the phrase. "You mean fights?"

"Maybe that's what they are," said Ursula.

"Oh, that's right," Issa remembered. "You fight like a weirdo."

"What do you mean?"

Issa thought for a second. "Well, you don't really fight. Or rather, when you're upset with someone, you try to work it out in your own head, without letting them participate. You kind of have the fight with yourself, and you play both parts, so you can be in control. Then by the time you finally address the issue with the other person, you've already kind of written their script, and you don't actually take in what they're saying."

"Me? I do this?"

"Yeah. Or sometimes, you're not even fighting with the person. You're fighting with a concept, and the other person is just a sounding board for your objections to that concept."

"Whoa," said Ursula, turning toward her friend. "Am I insufferable?"

Issa smiled and shook her head. "Don't worry. You have plenty of redeeming qualities."

Cass dimmed the lights and took her place at the front of the room as a loud track of African drums came on. They were at The Stake's "Heart-Healing Implosion" class, which combined elements of talk therapy with rigorous calisthenics and cardio.

"Welcome, welcome, welcome," said Cass, calmly, smoothly, and then she began to raise her voice as the music intensified. "Welcome to the searchers! The seekers! The curious! The courageous! Place your hands on your embattled heart and just *feel*. Whatever comes up in the next sixty minutes—the pain, the strength, the yearning, the regret, the shame—just feeeeeeeeel it!" she roared, as she began tapping her heels to the drums. The whole room of women pulsed in rhythmic bounces.

"We hurt! We heal! We hurt! We heal!" shouted Cass. "Let's go ladies. Turn inward. This is about you and only you. Buckle your seat belts, beauties. THIS IS ABOUT TO GET GNARLY!"

She dropped down into a forceful squat, and when she straightened her knees and rose, she growled viciously. The entire class followed suit—thirty jaguars squatting and roaring in unison.

When the next song came on, Cass lay down on her back and pulsed her hips up toward the ceiling. Up, down, up, down. Smooth, even, purposeful thrusts. "Ask yourself: What have you been carrying lately? Who have you been performing for? What mask have you been wearing? How exhausted is it making you? Stop performing, ladies. Take the fucking masks off. It's time to get realllllllll! Rrraaarrrrrrrrrr!" Again, Cass roared her hips up to the ceiling and the room exploded with growls.

This particular class was designed to provide an emotional purge, an opportunity to use the body as a vessel to clean the mind and help the spirit come unstuck. But on this day, no matter how gutturally she roared, or how loudly she howled (during the wolf sequence), Ursula could not shed her worries. What if The Arc was right? What if she and Rafael were beginning a spiral that would only worsen? What if she had poisoned their relationship with her stubbornness and professional convictions? But wait, why had those convictions shaken him so? The thoughts circled round and round as Ursula moved between lunges, burpees, and finally, into the culminating component of the class, which was The Stake's proprietary exercise move: Heart Immolation.

Ursula kneeled and slapped her chest with her hands, alternating between left and right, as Cass yelled, "Feel the fire! Let it consume you! Let your heart burn down into an ashy little mound! Burn! Burn! Burn! Let it fuckin' burn, bitches! Let that broken heart burn, baby!!!!! And now . . . stillness."

The music cut out and the thirty class-goers slipped into sweaty silence. Droplets slid down their necks; tears slipped from their eyes. The room was thick with humidity and the sound of weeping.

"First you hurt, then you heal. First you break, then you build. Hurt. Heal. Break. Build," said Cass, breathily. "You are here; you are whole. You are here; you are whole. Namaste." She bent down and pressed her forehead firmly onto the floor, then sat up, re-lit her Palo Santo stick, and stalked silently out of the room, trailing fragrant smoke behind her perfect body, which looked even more toned now that her taut skin gleamed with sweat.

Issa rocked back onto her heels from her namaste. "That was a great class," she said. "I needed that." She looked over at Ursula, whose mascara had run in sludgy black rivers down her cheeks. "Jesus."

"I feel sad," said Ursula. "That dark, scary stomach feeling."

"It's okay," said Issa, pulling her friend into a sweaty, one-armed hug. "Relationships aren't supposed to be smooth all the time. Not even ultra-modern, super-optimized, Arc-generated relationships. You still have to put in the work."

"But what if Dr. Vidal is right?" moaned Ursula. "What if we're doomed?"

"You're not doomed," countered Issa. "You guys just need to talk through this stuff. You have more control than you think."

Ursula hoped Issa was right, but her confidence was shaken.

Chapter 32

February 9, 9:13 P.M.

Ursula threw a pair of thick wool socks into her suitcase. Mallory looked at them and then back at Ursula, before hopping up onto the bed next to Rafael.

"So, tell me again what happens at this thing?" he asked.

"Elite schmoozing," said Ursula. She would spend the next four days with Mike Rutherford at the Jackson Hole Investment Summit. "A bunch of VCs, founders, a few hangers-on who just like 'startup culture,' whatever that means. And a few strategically audacious rapscallions like me."

Rafael stroked Mallory's head and tried to look as neutral as possible.

Ursula stared at him. "You're sad. You have Resting Sad Face."

"I'm not sad," said Rafael.

"Well, I think *I'm* sad," said Ursula. "And my sadness bounced off your face back to me."

"I think that's called projecting," noted Rafael. "But you do have a way with words."

"I don't want to leave you," said Ursula, sitting on the bed beside him. "What if our Emotional Reverberation goes haywire while I'm away?"

Rafael let out an exasperated sigh. "Ursula, two months ago, we had never even heard of Emotional Reverberation—probably because it's not a real thing. So instead of letting it terrorize us, maybe we should just forget we ever learned about it."

"We can't just slide back into ignorance," said Ursula. "We need to figure this out! Why did everything used to feel so hopeful and now it feels colder and scarier?"

"Maybe because we talk about Emotional Reverberation all the time," said Rafael. "It's just a concept, a lens. It's not the only lens. Remember how excited we were when we left The Arc on that day in December? Ready to build this relationship on our own terms?"

Ursula felt a pang of nostalgia. Their unified front had dissipated over the past few weeks as doubt—Hers? His? Theirs?—had seeped into their every day.

"Let's stop worrying. I'm freaked out by how freaked out you are," said Rafael. "And I'm sorry if I've been snarky about Mike or your work in general. I'm glad you're going to Jackson. It will be interesting, and I'm looking forward to missing you."

"I'm excited to miss you, too." Ursula smiled and kissed the upturned corner of his mouth. Maybe this was just a blip. Totally normal. Like Issa said, all relationships had blips.

Rafael squeezed her knee. "You know when you did your intake week at The Arc, and they asked about the Love Lexicon?" he asked, citing the pop-psychology test that had been part of their initial assessment. "Like, which are your top two Love Lexicons: Words of Affection, Selfless Acts, Surprise Gestures . . . ?"

"Yes," said Ursula.

"Well, maybe there's something to that," said Rafael. "Like maybe we're speaking different languages and we don't even know it."

"Like the other night? When you told me you want a trophy wife?"

"Yes, exactly." Rafael smiled and rolled his eyes. "But seriously, communication is never easy, even when it seems easy. So how did you respond to the Love Lexicon question?"

"I refused to choose two," said Ursula. "Honestly, who settles for just two of six? Who is like, 'I'm happy because my husband gives me gifts and does the dishes, even though he never says anything nice to me, spends time with me, or touches me!'? That's the recipe for relationship success?"

"I knew you wouldn't answer it like a normal person," said Rafael. "But what *did* you put?"

"I put 'Other: Rat Chat,'" said Ursula. "It's a language I made up with my childhood friend, Susie. We pretended we were the only humans who knew it, and we could use it to communicate with any rodent."

Rafael shook his head in amusement. Of course, Ursula had to resist the system and write in her own answer.

"What did you put?" asked Ursula.

"I don't even remember," said Rafael.

"It doesn't matter," said Ursula. "I figured out what your Love Lexicon is a long time ago."

"Oh yeah?"

"Blow jobs."

"That's what I'm talking about," he said, pulling her into his arms. "But I'm more than willing to learn Rat Chat, if it will help."

It was still dark when Rafael woke up in Ursula's bed the next morning, but she had already left for Teterboro, the small airport where Mike kept his private jet. He liked to be in the air as early as possible—ahead of the plebeians.

Mallory sat on Ursula's abandoned pillow, staring at him. He reached out and scratched the cat's ears, avoiding her sensitive, downy chin. He had arranged to work from home this morning so that he could transport Mallory from Carroll Gardens to his apartment, where he would take care of her for the next few days.

"Do you think you're ready for the East River Ferry?" he asked. No response. "Not a water cat? Okay, we'll take a car."

Rafael got out of bed and went into the kitchen for a glass of water, and then wandered into the living room. There were two photos on Ursula's mantel: one of her as a child, grinning while holding a hammer, and then the one of Ursula, Rafael, and Bobbitt, the rabbit from their first date.

Ursula's Hudson's Bay blanket lay in a disorderly pile on her couch, as usual. She almost never folded it, and it drove Rafael crazy. He picked up the blanket, folded it into neat quarters, then artfully draped it over one arm of the couch. He immediately felt better. Then he looked around for other opportunities to neaten things up. Had Ursula been here, she would have laughed at his efforts, but she wasn't here. This was his opportunity. He straightened a few of her frames, picked some cat-hair tumbleweeds off the rug, dusted the creepy bronze statue with the melting face, straightened the doormat, and moved the three dirty glasses that were in the sink into the dishwasher. He headed back into the bedroom, where he assiduously made the bed and scrawled a note—"Welcome back, timber wolf"— which he left on Ursula's pillow.

He rummaged through her closet to find the cat carrier, and as soon as Mallory spotted it in his hands, she bolted under the bed, unreachable. Rafael spent the next seventeen minutes coaxing her out with various treats and other psychological traps. He finally got her into the carrier, where she grumbled menacingly.

Maybe he had overstepped in suggesting Ursula should rethink her relationship with her job. He was self-aware enough to know that a man's professional experience was not the same as a woman's, and Ursula seemed particularly protective of the professional web she had weaved. Hopefully he could smooth things over by being a stellar cat dad this weekend. He ordered a car, and as they waited on Ursula's stoop, he held the carrier up so he could make eye contact with Mallory, whose meows had finally ceased. He had come to love this tiny cat over the past few months, and he was pretty sure she loved him back.

That evening when Rafael got home from his run, he received a flurry of texts from Ursula.

The eagle has landed! We should really get a private jet. How's Mallory? Does she like the Upper East Side?

Mike is a decent skier. Not as good as you. But he has very, very fancy equipment. Also, he's getting a divorce (again). So, he's moody about that.

We have a dinner tonight and then I'm going to sleep forever. I'm exhausted.

I miss you, my hyrax. What's the news from NYC? Give Mallory a hug for me, but don't squeeze TOO hard.

Rafael felt a wave of love. It was nice to be apart, and his feeling of longing for Ursula reassured him. Later that night, as he lay in bed rereading a John Le Carré novel that he had already read at least three times, he got another text from her.

It was a selfie of her in a big, fluffy white bed. She was lying on her stomach, her messy hair falling around her collar bone. In the background over her shoulder, he could see the curve of her naked butt.

He knew exactly how to respond. Ursula was not the type to want a "sexy" photo of him, which was good, because he was not the type to take a sexy photo of himself. But he knew how to please her, and pleasing her had long ago become his favorite pastime.

He held the phone above him and took an aerial shot of himself, lying down, his head cut off, with Mallory sprawled across his chest, her eyes closed dreamily. He sent it.

Ursula responded: *My heart is soaring. This makes me so happy. I miss her, and I miss you even more.*

Rafael texted back:

Miss you too, runt of the litter.

He went back to reading and decided to let Mallory sleep on the bed, just this once.

The next day was a Friday. When Rafael got home from work around 7 P.M., Mallory had mauled a copy of the *New York Times* and left scraps throughout the living room. He respected the fact that she had interests—namely, shredding—and he gathered the remainder of the newspaper and put it in a corner where she could easily resume her hobby as she wished. It was unexpectedly comforting to have Mallory in his apartment. Being responsible for her gave him a sense that he was needed and necessary. It tethered him to Ursula and helped offset the subtle current of anxiety running through his core. Should he be worried that Ursula was in Jackson Hole with Mike? It wasn't normal for him to be jealous, but their recent tension had knocked him off balance. And he had never dated a woman whose existence was intertwined with a soon-to-be-single billionaire's. Maybe Ursula wanted a bigger life than he did, even if she didn't know it yet. Maybe she harbored an insatiability that he would never be able to satisfy. He had been half-serious when he said he aspired to mediocrity. Of course, he wanted a comfortable life, and he wanted to be able to provide one for his future family. But he was happy with routine, consistency, predictability. Life was complicated enough—he didn't need to rock the boat unnecessarily. But Ursula was different. She seemed to delight in extremes: one moment, she was deriding the capitalist system, and the next, she was on a billionaire's jet. Rafael enjoyed her contradictions and her ability to move between worlds, but sometimes she shape-shifted so rapidly that he wondered who she really was. One version of her seemed to need him, and another seemed determined to prove that she didn't need anyone. She both energized and exasperated him, delighted and drained him. He was a patient person, but sometimes she gave him whiplash.

Suddenly, Rafael realized how relieved he was to have a few days alone. His bachelordom now seemed far behind him, and though he didn't actively miss that phase of life, he occasionally became nostalgic for it. This weekend felt like a return to a former version of himself, like a reunion with an old friend. He turned on a nature documentary—*Crocodiles: Sages of the Shallows*—and poured himself some bourbon. He began chopping onions and garlic. He didn't know what he was going to cook yet, but he had learned that everything good started with onions and garlic. Mallory jumped up on the counter, knocked a shallot onto the floor, and then hopped off to chase it.

"Make yourself at home, Mallory," Rafael said. His phone vibrated with a text.

Ursula: *So far, so good. Had a massage this morning, which was heaven. Went to a bunch of presentations by startup guys in the afternoon, which was tolerable. What are you and M up to?*

Rafael: *I'm chopping garlic and she's playing soccer with a shallot on the floor.*

Ursula: *I wish I were chopping and playing shallot soccer with you.*

Rafael: *Dalmat says hi. He asked where you've been lately and I told him you turned into a cat, and then I held up Mallory. He liked that.*

Ursula: *I wish I were a cat.*

Rafael: *What's happening tonight?*

Ursula: *Another dinner with some of Mike's investor friends, then an after-party thing, which I may or may not go to. What about you?*

Rafael: *Laying low tonight. Might do something with Catherine and Skipp tomorrow.*

Ursula: *Tell them I say hi. Need to hop in the shower. Will text you later before I go to bed.*

Rafael: *Have fun, chipwich. Behave yourself.*

By the time Ursula texted at 3:24 A.M., Rafael was asleep, so he didn't see the message (*Lovy you so mucH my beautiful fox kit. Xoxx-Oxoxo*) until the next morning.

Chapter 33

"Urminator!" Ursula heard someone call out as she leaned her skis against the rack and hooked the loops of her poles over the tips. She turned to see Kyle Hastings slide to a stop, his smooth cheeks pink from windburn. He was a cofounder of Bro-lex, a San Francisco–based watch company, whom she'd met last night when the summit invitees had convened at a local watering hole where the bar stools had western saddles instead of seats. Ursula had felt ridiculous when Mike directed her to "mount up," patting the saddle next to his, but ultimately, she had gotten into the spirit of things and ended up having a fun night. The three Bro-lex guys, who were all twenty-four and had founded their company while still in college, had given her a hard time for drinking her beer too slowly—dubbing her "Nursula"—and ordered a round of shots of the most expensive blanco tequila the bar offered. She took one, and then discreetly instructed the bartender to fill her subsequent shots with water. No one picked up on her ruse, and after four water shots, she earned both respect and a new nickname: The Urminator.

"Hey, Kyle," she said, as his cofounders, Tom and Angus, swished up beside him.

"Howdy, cowgirl," said Angus, popping out of his bindings. He was wearing a fluorescent pink-and-yellow one-piece ski suit that recalled the early '90s. "How's the hangover?"

"Actually, I'm good." Ursula smiled, taking off her helmet and fluffing her hair. "You guys feeling it?"

She could tell from their bleary eyes that they were. Kyle and Tom both had cameras attached to their helmets, whereas Angus had one that was strapped to the front of his pelvis.

"What's going on there?" Ursula nodded toward Angus's camera.

The three cofounders exchanged mischievous glances. "What? You've never heard of a wang-cam?" asked Angus, looking proudly toward his crotch as his buddies dissolved into laughter.

Ursula raised her eyebrows.

"You haven't heard of it," Angus continued, "because I just invented it."

"It's not a real prototype," Tom clarified. "It's just his chest strap that he moved down so he could film . . . from a wang's-eye view."

They were cracking themselves up.

"That's innovative," said Ursula. She imagined this was what it must be like to have a gaggle of younger brothers, and she kind of liked the feeling. She had spent plenty of time with these types of guys when she was in high school and college, and she'd built up a tolerance for this kind of banter. She had even been called a "guy's girl" on occasion, but that didn't quite encapsulate it. Ursula knew how to appeal to anyone when she wanted to. In school, she had moved between worlds, and she had never related to the simplistic, Hollywood-fueled dichotomy of nerds versus jocks, outcasts versus popular kids. Her experience had been more nuanced: she hung with athletes who were also cerebral, and thespians who were also in frats. If she'd *had* to choose between the artists and the jocks, she would have chosen the artists. But she didn't have to choose, because life wasn't a movie. She knew how to relate to all kinds of people, and therein lay the rub: she could be anything. At the heart of her social life lay an existential question: who was she, *really*?

But school was long behind her, and although she knew how to snap back into that collegiate mode of relating, she resented having to in a professional context. After all, these were not her college buddies. They were her peers at the summit, here to potentially raise millions of dollars to bring their ideas to market. These guys were considered by many to be "the future," and this realization made her fear for the world.

"You hitting the Moose?" asked Kyle, referring to the Mangy Moose, a popular après-ski spot at the base of the mountain.

"I am," said Ursula.

"Us too," said Tom. "I need a little hair of the doggo."

"After you," said Tom, practicing his chivalry and indicating that Ursula should lead the way. She sidled along the path that led to the door of the Mangy Moose, careful not to slip on the snow in her stiff ski boots. The last thing she wanted was to face-plant in front of the Bro-lex crew.

The saloon was warmly lit and full of western bric-a-brac: antlers, snowshoes, vintage posters. A taxidermy moose pulling a sleigh was suspended from the ceiling. Ursula spotted Mike in one of the wooden booths. He sat at one end in his hands-behind-the-head Cobra position while a group of four energetic young guys gesticulated, their eyes flitting between Mike and another man at the opposite side of the booth, who was also leaning back with his arms behind his head. Was he trying to out-Cobra Mike? Ursula wondered who he was.

"I'll catch you guys later," Ursula said to the Bro-lex boys, who had claimed a table under the suspended moose.

She heel-toed her way over to Mike's table, where he greeted her cheerfully. He was wearing a gray wool sweater with a band of navy snowflakes across the chest.

"Guys, this is Ursula Byrne, my secret weapon," said Mike, using the moniker that was so often applied to her by the various men who paid her. "She vets all my startup investments, so she's the one you need to impress."

As they made room for her at the table, he introduced Bruce and Dave Hinkley, a pair of Seattle-based brothers who were launching a butler service for the urban everyman called Thanks Alfred. Then there were partners Josh Berkowitz and Sutton Hunt, whose concept for the "world's most efficient water purification system" was going to revolutionize global health—they were sure of it. The product wasn't quite there yet, and the development process was proprietary, but they were close. They could feel it. All they needed was $25 million to build a lab and hire a team of engineers who could work out the kinks and realize the product they could see so clearly in their minds. "We'll send you our deck," Sutton said to Mike. Then he turned to Ursula, assuming she handled Mike's scheduling. "And we'd love to get some time on his calendar next time we're in New York."

"You can reach out to my assistant Jed about that," clarified Mike.

Finally, Mike introduced the man at the end of the table as investor Carl Hoff, a nondescript sextagenarian who Ursula later learned was worth $13 billion. Instead of moving to shake her hand as the younger men had, Carl left his fingers interlaced behind his head and gave her a cursory nod, as if he'd agreed to tolerate her presence but had no intention of enjoying it. Ursula was accustomed to being underestimated in rooms (or in this case, tables) full of men, but she was still shocked when the most powerful among them—the ones who set the tone for the others—couldn't be more magnanimous. She appreciated that about Mike: he always sought, albeit sometimes clumsily, to make others feel they were worth his time. Or did he only do that for her?

By the time she and Mike left the Mangy Moose, the sky had grown dim. They'd need to make a quick turnaround in order to board the snowcat that would take them up the mountain for dinner atop one of the peaks. Ursula and Mike made their way across the base of the mountain to the Four Seasons. Ursula had planned to get her own room, but Mike insisted she take one of the rooms in the four-bedroom penthouse he had rented, which also had two living rooms, a full kitchen, and an outdoor terrace. They could easily cohabitate there without getting in each other's way or crossing any lines. Ursula took a quick shower, pulled on a cashmere sweater dress that she deemed suitably alpine-chic, and applied deep red lipstick. She figured if she was going to rub elbows with the Carl Hoffs of the world, she might as well do it with fierce-looking lips. She looked at her phone, debating whether to check in with Rafael. But she wouldn't have time to respond if he wrote back, so she decided to text him later, assuming she survived the night.

A fleet of snowcats carried the investment summit's one hundred attendees up the mountain, depositing them at a beautifully lit heated tent that had been erected for the evening—no doubt at vast expense. Elk heads adorned the walls of the rustic-chic space, and flannel-clad servers passed around trays of champagne and canapés.

"Urminatorrrrr!"

Ursula waved to the Bro-lex boys, but turned in the opposite direction, making her way out of the tent toward a massive bonfire surrounded by wooden Adirondack chairs. She spotted Sutton and joined him by the edge of the fire.

"Cheers." He held out his glass to hers.

Ursula clinked, remarking on the opulence surrounding them. "They've outdone themselves."

Sutton tilted his head to the side. "It's okay." He seemed unimpressed. "Sun Valley was better."

"I missed Sun Valley last year," said Ursula, but Sutton didn't catch her sarcasm. She didn't like this guy, and she didn't believe he would actually be able to execute or monetize his water purification scheme, but she tried her best to play nice. "Your concept is really interesting. I'm rooting for you guys."

"We'll get funded," said Sutton, staring fixedly into the bonfire, as if his success was inevitable. "I'm just bummed the heavy hitters aren't here. Buffett, Bezos. This feels kind of bush league."

Ursula felt a pang of defensiveness. "Carl Hoff's $13 billion doesn't cut it?"

"A billion isn't that much these days," said Sutton, his eyes now scanning the growing crowd at the entrance to the tent. He nodded at someone in greeting, then turned back toward the bonfire and shrugged nonchalantly. "But yeah. This kind of thing is always fun."

She knew that Sutton's posturing was an ill-executed attempt to impress her, but she still found it deeply annoying.

He continued. "The VCs are basically handing out cash these days."

To some people, thought Ursula. Many female founders could not find investors willing to "gamble" on their visions, which, if they didn't personally resonate with the men holding the money, felt too risky. The same VC might deem a women's healthcare startup too "niche," but would happily invest in a Viagra delivery service because he "had a good feeling about it."

She looked around at the summit attendees. She'd counted nine other women so far, but the vast majority were men of a certain ilk. As far as she could tell, the trait they had in common was not business experience or ingenuity or even entrepreneurial instinct. It was simply an unwavering confidence in themselves—and an assuredness that the system would never fail them.

Sutton turned to look her in the eyes for the first time. "So, are you and Mike Rutherford boning?"

Ursula wanted to slap him. Instead, she drained her champagne glass and said, "Good luck raising that Series B," before striding back toward the tent.

People were starting to take their seats for dinner, and when Ursula found her chair, she noticed that the place card next to hers read "Shilpa Thakur." She'd heard about Shilpa—an engineer-turned-entrepreneur-turned-VC who was based in Vancouver. A few minutes later, when she approached, Ursula got up to introduce herself.

"Sit, sit, sit," Shilpa said as if they were old friends, "I know who you are. I was just chatting with Mike." She nodded toward where he sat, across the table and a few seats over, laughing at something Josh Berkowitz had said.

"I think you're the first woman I've spoken to all weekend," said Ursula, feeling herself relax into her chair.

"Same," said Shilpa, who looked to be about fifty, with dark, friendly eyes and black shoulder-length hair that had a chic white streak in the front. "It won't faze you after a while."

"Is that a good thing?" Ursula asked.

"No," said Shilpa with a laugh. "Definitely not."

A red-and-black-buffalo-checked arm reached between them to fill their wineglasses.

As the evening went on, Ursula learned about Shilpa's career trajectory—born in a village outside of Mumbai, educated as a bio-medical engineer in Delhi and London, moved to Vancouver to marry a Canadian, invented a groundbreaking cardioscope, built a company, sold that company, then embarked on a second career as an investor. Plus, she'd had two kids along the way.

"And you?" Shilpa asked. "Mike tells me you have a lot of exciting things going on."

There was a time when Ursula had loved to talk about her career, but tonight, she didn't know where to start: The highlights of her resume? Her current angst? The fact that she was outwardly thriving but internally melting down? She provided the broad strokes of her work at Anonymous & Co. and her consulting arrangement with Mike, but something about Shilpa's undivided attention—and the wine—made her feel that she could safely reveal more.

"Honestly, I'm more confused than I've ever been," said Ursula. "I always thought my goal was simply to succeed, but I don't think I ever slowed down enough to figure out what that meant to me. I just caught a wave in my twenties that I've been surfing ever since. The thing is, it might be the wrong wave. Does that make sense?"

Shilpa nodded. "Great metaphor."

"I'm competitive, so if you throw a ball out, I'll chase it. But sometimes I wonder if I'm playing the wrong game altogether. Case in point"—Ursula looked around her—"I don't belong here."

Shilpa took a sip of wine, then said, "Sounds like you're going through your dark night of the soul."

Ursula widened her eyes. "Is *that* what this is? I feel like I'm losing my mind. Like I don't even know what's important to me anymore. And I'm *tired*."

Shilpa looked thrilled. "It's a beautiful phase."

Ursula laughed. "It doesn't feel beautiful inside my brain."

"I understand that. But you're at a wonderful age. When I was thirty-five"—Shilpa pressed her hand to her heart and leaned toward Ursula conspiratorially—"I had a complete breakdown."

"Oh thank god," thought Ursula, soothed by this revelation. Shilpa hadn't mentioned the breakdown when she initially described her career story.

"And it was the best thing that ever happened to me," Shilpa continued. "Two years later, I went out on my own, founded my company, met my husband, and was on the cover of *Maclean's*. That's a big deal—in Canada."

Ursula chuckled at Shilpa's qualifier. "I like you. I wish I had a mentor like you."

"But you do have one," said Shilpa, cocking her head.

Ursula looked at her, confused. She'd never had a mentor in her life.

"Mike," Shilpa said, as if it were obvious. "He thinks the world of you."

Ursula felt flushed with warmth. She had always been slightly wary of Mike, convinced he was judging her or using her for something. She had never considered the possibility that he might be *mentoring* her. "How sneaky," she thought.

"He was the first person to invest in my company, you know. Way back when," said Shilpa. "I'm not going to say 'I wouldn't be here without him,' because I believe we make our own luck, and if I hadn't gotten funding from him, I would have eventually gotten it elsewhere. But he was the first person to step up, and that was meaningful to me. He's a good person to have on your team."

After dinner, Mike made his way over to their chairs, placing his hand on Shilpa's shoulder. "You two are having too much fun," he said. "Ursula, stay focused. Remember, you're the huntress. We're here to find the next big thing."

Ursula looked around the room, which buzzed with the energy of the rich, the even richer, and the soon-to-be-rich, all basking in each other's glow, content with their insularity. She was feeling sassy. "Mike, the next big thing isn't here."

"How can you be so sure?" he asked, lightly rejecting her cynicism. "You're here. What if it's *you*?"

Chapter 34

Rafael opened his front door, and Skipp entered carrying two pounds of elk meat. He'd acquired it during a research trip last summer in Saskatchewan, and it had been lying in wait in his freezer. Tonight was the night: elk burgers. Rafael had been leaning pescatarian lately, but he knew this was important to Skipp.

Mallory hopped up onto the counter to sniff at the meat.

"Should she be on the counter?" asked Skipp.

"Probably not," said Rafael. "But she makes her own rules, just like her mom."

Mallory gave Skipp a skeptical look and then hopped down and scampered into the bedroom.

Catherine showed up an hour later, a bottle of champagne in hand.

"Captain!" bellowed Skipp, using his nickname for Catherine.

"Oh hey, you," she said, delicately double-air-kissing him without actually touching him. Rafael wondered why she insisted on erecting this illusion of a barrier when it came to Skipp. He suspected they had slept together numerous times over the years, always when one of them was reeling from a breakup and feeling down-and-out.

Catherine threw her vicuña-wool coat over the back of a chair and began unwiring the champagne cork. Despite Rafael's protestations—"None for me, Cath"—she pulled three glasses out of the cabinet, insisting: "Come on, participate. Just a splash." She twisted the cork with the precision of a surgeon, not flinching at the *pop*, and deftly tilted each glass to minimize foam as she poured. Her nonchalance suggested that she did this as often as she poured herself a glass of water—perhaps more often.

"Remind me. Where's Ursula this weekend?" Skipp asked. He loved Ursula. It was possible that he was even slightly *in* love with Ursula, but not in a way that was actually threatening to Rafael.

"Jackson Hole," said Rafael. "At an investment summit."

"With that millionaire?" asked Catherine.

"Billionaire," corrected Skipp.

"That's the one," said Rafael. He looked up from the tray of cooked burgers that he was arranging. They were both staring at him. "Am I supposed to feel insecure? Is not being a billionaire something we're ashamed of now?"

"You have nothing to worry about," said Skipp. "The Arc already sealed your destiny."

Rafael hadn't told Catherine or Skipp about the recent friction with Ursula, and he worried that voicing it would somehow confirm its significance. He made his way over to the table.

"Are you guys still worried about this Emotional Reverberation thing?" said Catherine. "Sounds like something my Reiki guy could remove."

Skipp laughed, pulling out Catherine's chair for her.

"I'm serious," said Catherine as she lowered herself. "He's amazing."

"No need for Reiki. Emotional Reverberation isn't even a real thing," said Rafael, determined to convince himself. "The Arc is a sham."

"But they must have done something right. I mean, you two are perfect," said Skipp. "It's real. If I've ever seen love, it's what you have."

"Well, that's the thing," said Rafael. "It is. We do. The relationship is real, but The Arc tried to convince us it wasn't—or rather, that it was doomed. And we had to ignore that in order to stay together. So I don't know—what do we make of that? We owe this relationship to The Arc, but they also tried to sabotage us. I'm grateful to The Arc, but . . . I'm angry. They messed with us. We paid them $90,000 to fuck with us."

"But you got the girl," said Catherine. "Isn't that the whole point? Who cares what their methods are?"

"It just feels manipulative," said Rafael. "I still don't know what to think about the whole thing."

"But you found your gray wolf," said Skipp, noting the monogamous nature of this particular type of wolf, which often mates for life.

"She *is* my gray wolf," said Rafael. "She's the most amazing woman I've ever known—no offense, Cath—let alone dated."

Catherine held her hand up—no offense taken—and took a long swig of champagne.

"But you know what?" Rafael continued from behind his burger. "I *am* annoyed that she's in Jackson Hole with Mike Asshat Rutherford. Sure, it's her job. But *why* is that her job? She talks about it as if it's not a voluntary arrangement, as if she's indentured to him. I don't like it one fucking bit. I've been convincing myself that I'm fine with the whole thing, but I'm not." He took an angry bite.

"Who's taking care of her baby while she's away?" asked Catherine.

"Mallory? I am," said Rafael, looking around for the cat, who had been out of sight since Catherine arrived. "Where'd she go?"

"I saw her in the bedroom when I was having a cigarette," said Skipp.

"Why were you smoking a cigarette in my bedroom?"

"It's freezing! You want me to go out on the terrace in this?" Skipp motioned to the windows and the black, sleet-filled sky beyond.

Rafael got up and went into the bedroom. "Skipp!" he yelled. "You left the window open!"

"I did?" Skipp's mouthful of elk burger muffled his words.

Rafael ran back into the living room. "Where is she? Mallory!" He kneeled down to peer under the couch. Nothing. He worked his way around the open living and dining room, checking under furniture. Skipp and Catherine watched him without getting up from the table. Rafael opened the coat closet and dug deeply into the back of it. No cat. He went into the office and did a thorough check, his pulse quickening. Back in his bedroom, he looked through the closet, under the bed, and even riffled through his drawers. No sign of Mallory.

"She's not here!" he called, walking back into the living room, where Skipp had finally gotten up from the table. "Was she in here when you were smoking? Did she go out the window?" The fire escape would have given Mallory access to the floor above, and ultimately the roof of the building, had she desired a means of egress.

"I saw her for a second, but then she went under the bed," said Skipp, now more serious. "She doesn't like me."

"We have to find her," said Rafael. It was now 9:30 in New York, so 7:30 in Jackson Hole. Rafael hadn't heard from Ursula since that morning, and now he desperately hoped she'd wait a little longer to be in touch. He ran to the window and called, "Mallory! Mallory Fantastica Byrne! Mallory!"

There was no sign of her, and the fire escape was slick with sleet.

"She either went up or down," said Rafael. "You guys go down to the street. Tell Dalmat what happened. Ask if he's seen her. I'm going up."

"Up the fire escape?!" Catherine yelped, standing and grabbing the champagne bottle. She loved this kind of drama.

"The penthouse has a roof garden," said Rafael. "She might be up there."

"How about knocking on their front door instead of scaling their walls?" asked Skipp.

"The Deringers? They're away all winter," said Rafael. "They're old. They have to fly south or else they become desiccated. Get your coats on. Go!"

He was angry now, but also determined and moving with purpose. He pulled his sneakers on and then pushed his bedroom window open wide enough to crawl through. The fire escape was slippery. Why would anyone, human or feline, voluntarily go out in this?

"Mallory!" Rafael carefully climbed the steep steps up to the next level. He looked through the darkened windows of his upstairs neighbors' unit. A single lamp glowed dimly on a table beside the couch. Otherwise, there was total darkness. Mallory would have used various window ledges and moldings to reach the roof garden, but Rafael, limited by his human proportions, would have to climb an iron ladder and then hoist himself over the brick precipice. He could do it. There was no real danger as long as he didn't lose focus.

Starting his climb, he realized he should have worn gloves, but it was too late now. His fingers stung against the surface of the ice-coated ladder. When he got to the top, he threw his arms over the ledge, pulled himself up, and slid forward onto the terrace, like a seal sliding off an ice floe into the water. The rooftop was beautiful, but it had a ghostly aspect to it: a large grill and a few chaise longues were covered for the winter. Large planters lined the perimeter, but the trees that grew in them were now skeletal, their wispy branches coated in translucent ice.

"Mallory!" Rafael yelled, knowing the cat didn't respond to her name. He didn't see her anywhere, and there weren't many places where she could hide. Nonetheless, he conducted an assiduous search. He lifted the slipcover off the grill and even opened its lid. It was unlikely that Mallory could have weaseled her way into the grill itself, but he knew that cats sometimes did strange, physics-defying things. She wasn't there. She wasn't under any of the chaises. She wasn't behind any of the planters. She wasn't tucked in a corner or curled in a shadow. She wasn't here at all.

For a moment, he considered the possibility that she had fallen, but it was too horrific to dwell on that image. If that were true, everything would be over. Ursula would be devastated, and he would be the cause. He took a final glance around the winter-slick rooftop and then carefully climbed over the ledge and back down the ladder to his own fire escape landing. Had she somehow gone down? If she had successfully reached the ground, she was now long gone. He clambered inside his window and walked into the living room just as Catherine and Skipp came back through the front door.

"Dalmat hasn't seen her, but he's going to keep an eye on the street," said Skipp.

Rafael sunk into the couch and put his hands on his face, stress humming through his body.

"I'm sorry, Rafa," said Skipp. "I'm going to stop smoking."

By now it was 10:30. Rafael dreaded the nightly text from Ursula.

He didn't know whether to tell her and involve her in the search, or spare her the stress until he'd exhausted all possible avenues. He would decide when the time came.

"What do you want us to do?" asked Catherine.

"I don't know," said Rafael. "Why don't you guys just stay here? Keep an eye on the window. Eat elk. Clean up. I'm going to look around the block."

He went to the foyer and pulled on his boots, his coat, a hat, gloves. Once in the hallway, he hit the elevator button and looked around. There were dried fir needles everywhere. He mildly respected the fact that his neighbors, the Ernsts, had waited until mid-February to get rid of their Christmas tree, but they could have done a better job of cleaning up the debris. It was too late to knock on their door; he decided to check with them tomorrow to see if they'd seen the cat. He spent the next hour roaming the five-block radius around his apartment. The sleet had let up, and now everything was dark and slippery. "Mallory!" His breath created puffs of mist in the wet, cold air. Why on earth would a cat want to leave the warmth of his apartment for this? He wanted to be mad at Skipp, but what was the point? Ultimately, Mallory was his responsibility. He hated the thought of letting anyone down, most of all Ursula.

When he returned to his apartment cat-less around midnight, Catherine and Skipp were both asleep on the couch. Ursula had not texted, which was odd, but Rafael was grateful, given the situation. He changed out of his wet clothes, brushed his teeth, and got into bed, leaving the window open in case Mallory decided to come back. He tucked his head under the covers, knowing that he was in for an uncomfortably cold night. The stress felt like poison coursing through his veins. He tried a breathing exercise he'd learned at The Arc—breathe in for eight, hold for four, out for four—and eventually fell into a worried, fitful sleep.

Chapter 35

When Rafael woke, he had an apologetic text message from Skipp, who had left in the night. But there was no message from Ursula. He felt a spike of anxiety. Where was she? At the same time, he was relieved to have a bit more time. If he spoke to Ursula before he found the cat, he would either have to lie by omission or send her into a panic when she was thousands of miles away, neither of which he wanted to do. He got out of bed and shut the window against the icy air—just for now. He pulled on his college sweats and went to the kitchen to make some green tea. Catherine was gone as well, although she had left a note on the counter that said:

Hope you find the 🐱

He put the kettle on the stove, aware of a growing internal bifurcation. He felt he was operating as two distinct people: the hopeful search-party leader who knew the cat was just fine, but also the somber realist who knew he might have to prepare for the worst. His thoughts flitted between both outcomes, exhausting him.

Then something occurred to him: Maybe Mallory *was* here. Maybe she had been hiding the whole time. Cats did that kind of thing, didn't they? He vaguely recalled a story he'd heard about a cat that spent an entire week inside a mattress, and he began a frantic search through his apartment, tearing through the front-hall closet, looking under the couch cushions, opening drawers. By the time the kettle squealed, he had flung every kitchen cabinet open, even the high ones that were almost out of his reach. No cat.

His phone lit up and his breath caught in his throat, but it was just Skipp again: *Hoops later?*

Rafael didn't respond. He sat on the couch and started calling various local vets and shelters. They wouldn't be open yet, but he left messages. He longed to pick up Mallory by her fluffy armpits and feel the little pendulum of her torso swinging back and forth. He had to find her—there was no other option. He wondered if there were search-and-rescue services for cats. How much was he willing to pay to have her back? Another $50,000? No, that was ridiculous. But then again, what is the price of relief? Of not breaking your girlfriend's heart?

Maybe it was time to call Ursula. She might have insights about Mallory's escapist urges or likely hiding spots; she might be able to relieve some of the guilt that was consuming him. But it was still only 6 A.M. for her. He decided to give it a bit longer, although he wondered why she hadn't texted him goodnight. It had been almost twenty-four hours since they'd been in touch. Where the *hell* was she?

He couldn't sit still, so he put on his running clothes and did another search of the neighborhood. It was freezing. He couldn't imagine how a dainty little house cat like Mallory could have survived a night in this cold. But again, he stopped himself before he got carried away by macabre thoughts.

When he got back to his building, Dalmat was there. "Any luck?"

Rafael shook his head. "Have you seen the Ernsts today or yesterday? Did they mention anything about seeing a cat?"

"They left early this morning for the Hamptons," said Dalmat. "But I'm keeping an eye out for Mallory."

Rafael sighed. "Okay, thanks."

He took the elevator up. When he got to the landing and stepped onto the carpet, still strewn with fir needles, he realized something. The needles were all over the hallway between their apartments, but there were none in the elevator. It was possible Dalmat had cleaned the elevator, but it was also possible that the tree had been too tall to fit, and it had been taken out via the service stairs.

Rafael walked across the landing to the service door and opened it, peering down the stairwell, which was indeed covered with dry needles. "Mallory? Mallory!" His voice was strong with hope again.

He heard a low chirp. *"Mrrrrreeeooowww."*

Rafael looked down and saw a form curled at the base of the stairs two floors below.

"Mallory!" He hurtled down the steps, startling the cat when he finally reached her. She looked relaxed, as if she'd had a nice winter's nap.

He picked her up and hugged her, feeling her squirm and then relent, clinging to his shoulder. A waterfall of relief flushed through his body. "Thank god," said Rafael, feeling transcendent, superhuman. "You sweet, sweet creature. You little fucking fuzzball. How did you get in here?!" He couldn't figure it out. She must have slipped out into the hallway when Catherine arrived the night before (his sister had a habit of not fully closing doors) and then followed the Ernsts into the stairwell when they dragged their tree down.

He shook his head. Why had he scaled the side of his building before thinking to check the service stairs?

The world was beautiful. Life was beautiful. Everything was right. He carried the cat back to his apartment, where she began yowling for food. He filled a cereal bowl with her kibble. It was more than she was supposed to get, but this was a celebration. He took a swig of bourbon out of the bottle, despite the early hour. His nerves radiated with residual stress, but all was well. He texted Skipp and Catherine to let them know he had solved the case, and then he collapsed on the couch and fell into a heavy, relieved sleep.

When he woke at 11:30, he was spooning Mallory. He checked his phone. Skipp had replied, *Dang, cats are sneaky motherfuckers,* and Catherine had sent three champagne-bottle emojis and a cat with heart-eyes. But there was still no word from Ursula, which made him mad. He sent her a message: *I have a story for you. By the way, where are you? Swallowed by an avalanche? Call me. We miss you.*

Ursula finally called an hour later. Her voice sounded low and husky with sleep. Rafael rattled off the entire story and then braced himself for her to yell at him, but she didn't.

"That's so stressful, Raf," she said. "I'm so glad you found her."

"That's it? You're glad I found her? You're not mad I lost her in the first place?"

"Well, Skipp lost her," said Ursula. "Or Catherine lost her. Someone who isn't you left the door open and lost her."

Rafael realized that Ursula was fully letting him off the hook, and he wondered why. "Wait a minute," he said. "Where were you all night? You never texted. What if I had needed to get a hold of you?"

"Ugh, I know," Ursula rasped. "I'm sorry. I meant to text you before dinner, but I was running late. And then I had no service, because dinner was on top of the mountain and we went there by snowcat. And I was out super late and then I figured you'd be asleep. I'm sorry."

"You could have sent a text."

"I'm sorry. Why didn't *you* text *me*?"

"Because I was scaling my building and roaming the streets looking for your cat!"

"Thank you for finding her," Ursula replied. "I can't wait to get home to you both. This has been . . . a lot."

"Why?" asked Rafael. "What's Mike up to?"

"Nothing," said Ursula quickly. "It's just an intense group of people. A lot of food, drinking, skiing, staying out late. There's this energy in the air, like all these startup founders either know or hope they're on the verge of getting really rich, and it makes them act like assholes. It's exhausting to be around."

"See? This is what I mean," said Rafael. "It's as if you're doing this job against your will."

"Well, there's a lot to process," said Ursula. "Some of it's exciting; some of it is nauseating. I'll tell you all about it when I'm back tomorrow."

"Tomorrow?" said Rafael. "I thought you were coming back tonight."

"I know. Things just shifted. Mike wants to stay until tomorrow, and he's my ride home, so I don't think I have a choice."

Rafael didn't say anything.

"Is that okay? Can you keep Mallory for one more night?"

"Yeah, that's fine," said Rafael. "I'll see you tomorrow night."

"Do you want me to come to you?"

"No, Mallory and I will come to you." Rafael didn't bother to ask whether Ursula knew or cared that tomorrow was Valentine's Day. He could tell she'd forgotten.

Chapter 36

"See you, guys. Safe trip," said Mike, closing the penthouse door behind the founders of skateboard-sharing company SweetRyde, who had stopped by to meet with him and Ursula. He walked back out onto the terrace, where Ursula was throwing another log into the iron fire pit. She stood back as the sparks flew and said, "I like them."

"Very nice guys," Mike said, refilling her wineglass and then his own before settling back into his Adirondack chair.

"And I can't wait to see you try one of their skateboards when we get back to New York," joked Ursula.

"Might need to take out another insurance policy before that happens," said Mike, as the fire crackled at his feet.

Ursula smiled. "This weekend is making my head spin. Some of the people I've met are so interesting and have genuinely great ideas, and some of them are just the absolute worst."

"There's a range. But isn't that always true?" asked Mike, who looked every bit the billionaire-at-leisure with his luxurious navy zip-up sweater, his Patek Philippe watch, and his unshaven face.

"The A-hole quotient is higher here," said Ursula. "Sutton Hunt, the water-purification guy, is terrible. You're not going to invest there, are you?"

"You tell me. What do you think?"

"We can look at his deck when he sends it, but I don't think he has a viable product. I think it's smoke and mirrors," said Ursula.

"He already raised $50 million in his Series A," said Mike.

"So? You know that doesn't mean anything, other than he's

managed to persuade some poor souls to buy into his ruse," said Ursula. "And after this weekend, I now understand who those people are. People with bad taste and money to burn. But still, why would anyone blindly invest in a product they haven't even seen? A product that *no one* has seen, because it doesn't exist and never will?"

Mike smiled. "That's why you'll make a good investor someday."

"Because I have common sense?"

Mike nodded.

"Well, I can't be an investor, Mike, because I don't have serious money."

"Not yet, but you could."

"I don't know if I want serious money," said Ursula honestly. "The more rich people I meet, the more skeptical I become. No offense."

Mike laughed softly.

Ursula sipped her wine. "Did I tell you what Sutton said to me last night?"

Mike shook his head.

"He asked if you and I were *boning*."

Mike threw his head back and clapped his hands, hysterical with laughter. Then he collected himself. "I'm sorry. That's very disrespectful. He shouldn't have said that to you."

"Totally. But it's kind of funny, too," Ursula admitted.

"So what did you say? To Sutton?"

"I didn't dignify his question with a response."

"You didn't tell him you are a happily in-love woman?"

"No," said Ursula, wondering if that descriptor still fit, given the recent turmoil in her relationship.

"Well, I'm glad you found a good guy," said Mike softly.

He seemed sincere. It was beginning to dawn on Ursula that what she had previously interpreted as disingenuousness or power-posturing from Mike was actually just awkwardness: the efforts of a former-nerd-turned-billionaire who was trying to look cool and approachable in front of a woman twenty years his junior.

"Mike, why am I here?" asked Ursula.

"You work with me," said Mike.

"But *why* do I work with you?" she pressed. "I mean, you have a huge team supporting you. And it's pretty clear you don't really need me to make introductions for you. Do you?"

Mike tilted his head to the side, as if mulling. "Not really."

"So, what is this arrangement actually about? I mean, why is it worth it to you?" She no longer worried that Mike was romantically intrigued by her, but she still couldn't quite gauge his motivation.

"Remember that meeting when we first met?" he asked.

"At Indubitably? Of course."

"I thought you were impressive, smart, funny, different," said Mike, recrossing his feet on the concrete ledge that surrounded the fire pit. "Sometimes you meet someone, and you just want them in your orbit."

"But why did you *hire* me?"

"I liked how you operated. A lot of people in my world have trouble telling me the truth, leveling with me."

"Because of your money? They just want to appease you?"

"Yes. It's predictable and it's transparent. But you're not like that. You're more . . . prickly. And honest. Maybe because you're not impressed by 'serious money.'"

"So you hired me to call you on your bullshit?"

Mike laughed. "That's one way to describe it. I knew you'd be able to teach me things, broaden my perspective. And you have. I know it's taken me a little while to come around, but I hear you about the need to invest in those who typically get overlooked. I see now that's where the real opportunity is. Nine to Five was a great find."

Ursula felt a rush of pride and redemption. It felt like a huge win to have influenced someone like Mike.

"I've always thought of my work as a game, and it's one I love to play," he continued. "But I realize that there's more to it than winning. Or rather, there are multiple ways to win. I used to take the most direct path to profit, regardless of the consequences—environmental, social, et cetera. Now, I want to be more thoughtful about where I invest, what the ramifications are, what the *implications* are. I like that you've pushed me to be more egalitarian."

Ursula beamed, flattered. It felt so good to hear this acknowledgement from him. She couldn't quite figure out what he was to her—A brother? A father? A mentor? A champion?—but it was something she had never had before.

"And I also just like you," he said. "You're weird and fun."

"Ah, so you hired me just to hang out with me!"

Mike paused and looked out toward the now-shadowed peaks, firelight illuminating his face. "That's been a pleasant by-product."

It had never occurred to Ursula that Mike might have vulnerabilities, that he might just need a friend. She had always assumed people with that much money were bulletproof. "Are you lonely?" she ventured.

He pursed his lips. "I wouldn't say that. I'm too busy to be lonely. But it has been a hard year, with the divorce."

He was definitely lonely, Ursula realized.

"Anyway, you asked me why you were here," Mike said. "I think that's for you to answer at this point. Initially, I didn't know exactly how we would work together. But now that I know you better, I really value your perspective. And I care about you. Not just about our work together. But about you, as a person. Not everything is a transaction."

Ursula was surprised to hear this. But then again, she'd been consulting for him for six months—it wasn't so shocking that he'd developed some level of affection for her. Technically, she'd known Mike longer than she'd known Rafael.

He pointed his thumb toward the mountain. "This scene is fun for me. As I said, I see it as a game. But if it's not your thing, that's okay. I just hope you find the game that you love, and then enjoy it. Because you have a lot to offer."

Ursula was touched, and she didn't know how to respond. Finally, she said, "Sometimes I feel like I'm still figuring out what I care about professionally. I'm still figuring out who I am."

"We all are," said Mike. "But you might as well have fun while you do it."

Chapter 37

The next evening after work, Rafael got to Ursula's apartment before she did. He let himself in, let Mallory out of her carrier, and put the light-pink roses he'd bought in a vase. He had never put much stock in Valentine's Day, which he saw as a brazen commercialization of love; but he was slightly concerned that Ursula didn't seem to care about it, either. It seemed to him that at least *one* of them should care; otherwise, were they lacking some essential emotional glue?

He settled onto the couch, and for a moment, his eyes rested on the bronze sculpture made by Ursula's father, its face twisted in a deeply unsettling expression. Rafael wondered if it was healthy for her to live in the same space as that haunted thing, but he knew better than to suggest she move it. She was particular about her décor, and she mostly avoided talking about her father, other than to say, "I barely knew him."

Rafael unrolled his copy of the *Economist* and began to read. Thirteen minutes later, he heard Ursula battling with the door, and she lurched in looking pleasantly disheveled: hair up in a topknot, glasses on, cashmere shawl wrapped around her neck and halfway up her face so that it covered her mouth. She dropped her bags and scampered over to Rafael, flopping down next to him. Rafael leaned in and kissed her hair, which smelled like smoke. "Woodsy," he said.

"I'm *very* woodsy now," said Ursula, excited to debrief with him. "I want to tell you all about it, and I want to hear more about Mallory's adventure, but I have to pee. Be right back."

As soon as she closed the door to the bathroom, her phone, which she'd left on the coffee table, began vibrating. One, two, three texts from Mike Rutherford.

u make it home . . . what a weekend . . .

i stand corrected. u can build a bonfire . . .

where should we do lunch on Thursday with the SweetRyde guys . . .

Rafael caught a glimpse of the texts. Something about the ellipses irked him. Ursula emerged from the bathroom and scooped Mallory up in her arms. "You scared us half to death, you little mongrel," she said, kissing the cat between her ears. Then she saw Rafael's expression. "What's wrong?"

He nodded to her phone. "You're getting texts from Mike, who apparently doesn't know how to use punctuation."

Ursula picked up the phone and scanned the messages. "Yeah, he's not great with grammar."

"Ursula, where were you Saturday night and Sunday morning?" asked Rafael, trying to stay calm, but feeling increasingly unsettled. "You went AWOL."

"I told you," she said. "Saturday night spiraled and I didn't have cell service on the mountain, and by the time I got home, it was really late here. I'm sorry—I didn't mean to worry you. I was just in another mode."

Rafael's eyes looked sad, and she didn't understand why.

"Another mode," he said slowly. "Is that the mode where you're having an affair with Mike Rutherford?"

"What?" Ursula's jaw dropped.

"What are those texts?" asked Rafael.

Ursula studied her phone. "I guess it does seem a little sketchy, the way he wrote it. But he's just an awkward texter."

"It doesn't *seem* sketchy," said Rafael. "It *is* sketchy."

Ursula reread the messages, trying to process them from Rafael's point of view.

"Did you have sex with Mike Rutherford by a bonfire while I traipsed through an ice storm looking for your damn cat?"

"No!" yelled Ursula. "Of course not." The concept was so

ridiculous that she couldn't help but laugh. Stress-wrinkles appeared on Rafael's forehead. He hated being laughed at when he was already feeling down.

"Raf, no," said Ursula, becoming serious. At this point, the thought of sex with anyone besides Rafael repulsed her. "The bonfire thing . . . A few of these guys from a startup came to our suite last night, and I built a fire in the firepit on the terrace. It was no big deal, but they were all amazed because they don't think women can do that kind of thing and . . ."

"Whoa, whoa, whoa," said Rafael. "Your suite? That you shared with Mike? At the Four Seasons in Jackson Hole?"

"It was huge," said Ursula, so focused on defending herself that she didn't have the energy to get mad at Rafael for perusing her texts. "I might as well have been staying down the hall from him. In fact, I *did* stay down the hall from him, because the suite had multiple hallways, four bedrooms, five bathrooms. Ugh, my god. You have nothing to worry about."

"If I had nothing to worry about, I wouldn't feel like this," Rafael sniped. "You're hungover. You smell like smoke. And Mike Dipshit Rutherford is sending you sexual innuendos about bonfires."

"You're right that I'm hungover," said Ursula. "And it's a compounded megahangover, because this summit was basically a four-day frat party. But I didn't do—would *never* do—anything with Mike! He's actually . . . I'm realizing he's a good guy, despite what I initially thought."

"Great," said Rafael, perturbed by the shift in her attitude toward Mike, and worried about what might have caused it.

"Oh my god, there's *nothing* going on between us," said Ursula emphatically. "Some of the *other* guys at the summit were flirting with me, if you must know, but that's par for the course in that context."

"Even better," said Rafael, his pulse quickening. "So, let me get this straight. You hate your work, except when you're partying with random guys who are flirting with you?"

"No," said Ursula. "I don't hate my work. I'm trying to figure out which elements I like, versus which are bogging me down. I'm trying to untangle it all, like you said I should."

"And Mike is helping?" said Rafael.

"Yes," said Ursula with a smile. "He was actually really supportive. He thinks I have a lot to offer."

"I told you the same thing," said Rafael. "But I guess it sounds more compelling coming from Mike."

"No," said Ursula. "You told me I seemed overwhelmed and should think about quitting my job."

"That's not what I said," said Rafael. "You're twisting my words."

"Well, that's what I heard. It felt discouraging, the way you said it," said Ursula. "It felt like . . . a forfeiture. Like you want my life to contract rather than expand."

"Well, I don't have a billion dollars, if that's the kind of expansion you're looking for," said Rafael coldly.

"Since when did you become so fixated on Mike's money?" asked Ursula, sounding more defiant.

"Since *you* became fixated on it!" said Rafael. "It's like my perspective on your career is unwelcome, or even offensive to you. But then you go off for the weekend with Mike and come back with new clarity. What's that about?"

"He's my mentor!"

"Since when? I thought you hated the guy!"

"I don't hate him," said Ursula. "I've never said I hated him. There's more to him than I thought, that's my point. But that doesn't mean I'm having an affair with him!"

"Not yet," said Rafael, then backed off, sensing he'd gone too far. "I'm sorry. This weekend was stressful, and I feel really far away from you right now."

"We're eighteen inches apart," said Ursula, now seated on the couch beside him, trying to lighten the mood.

"Stop joking," said Rafael, exasperated. "Stop fucking joking about everything."

"Okay," she said, hurt that he seemed to want to fight. "I'm sorry that I'm getting professional advice from someone who isn't you?"

Rafael hated it when she made her declaratives sound like questions, as if she was simply trying to say the right thing, and it wasn't what she actually felt.

"I'm sorry that I've been flailing, and I'm doing my best to figure it out?" she went on.

"You're allowed to flail," said Rafael, trying to keep his composure.

"But I have to flail in a way that's comfortable for you?" said Ursula.

"No," said Rafael, annoyed that she was running ahead with the conversation, voicing both sides before he could even process his own thoughts.

"I'm sorry I don't tailor my flailing to accommodate others?"

"No," said Rafael, cutting her off before she could put more words in his mouth. "We all know you don't do anything to accommodate others."

Ursula's face fell. She turned inward and began flashing back, as if watching a flip book, to all the little things she had done to delight him (writing him love poems, drawing a portrait of him as a fox with a top hat on), to accommodate him (hauling a bagful of clothes and beauty products from Brooklyn to the Upper East Side every few days to sleep at his place), to support him (the dinner with his colleagues), and to make room for him in her life (she'd ceded two dresser drawers to him). Had he not noticed these things? Was she not enough? It had been years since she had put this much effort into a relationship— maybe *that* was why her career seemed to be faltering. Maybe she was accommodating the relationship *too* much, and letting the rest of her life slide, which was exactly what she had been afraid of doing.

"I don't do *anything* to accommodate others?" said Ursula. "That seems extreme."

Rafael paused. "What I mean is, sometimes I don't feel like we're a team. I feel like I'm just here on the sidelines watching you writhe around in your own chaos."

"Yeah, well that's how I process things: by myself," said Ursula. "I practice self-reliance."

"Self-reliance? Who are you, Ralph Waldo Emerson?"

"Yes!" yelled Ursula. "What's wrong with that? Do you want an invitation into every meltdown I have?"

"Yes, I do! It doesn't scare me. You think I've never seen a meltdown before? Have you met my sister?"

It was true that Rafael's friends and family relied on him for all kinds of support. But that was different. Those people were already solidly entrenched in his life. Ursula felt she was still being evaluated, and she knew—or at least feared—she couldn't share the messiness of her brain without alienating him. Whenever she had sought support from boyfriends in the past, she'd ended up regretting it and feeling even more exposed and alone. Over time, she had become ever more protective of her own internal chaos and contradictions, assuming no one else would ever really understand or empathize with her. "I need space to figure this out by myself," she said.

"By yourself, but with Mike."

"Yes, if I want to," said Ursula. "Why are you so threatened by this? You can't just expect me to become dependent on you." But he had a point. For some reason, she saw Mike as a safe sounding board. The distance between them—in age, outlook, economic standing—somehow gave her breathing room, and she felt she had nothing to gain nor lose by being honest with him. With Rafael, the stakes were higher. His future was tangled up in hers, and she didn't want to scare him with her doubts or her darkness. He was too precious to her. "My career is not your responsibility. And I don't like feeling as though I'm a problem you need to fix. You're acting like you ended up with a lemon and now you have buyer's remorse."

"Buyer's remorse? You're the lemon?" asked Rafael.

"Yes. Do you even want to marry me?"

"We're talking about marriage right now?" He put his palm on his forehead.

"Well, you used to talk about it. But you haven't for a while. So do you still want to? Marry me?"

"I thought I did," said Rafael.

"*Thought?* Really?"

"Look, I signed up for The Arc, too. Would I have paid $50,000 if

I didn't want to find my partner? And would I have walked away from the offer of a refund and a rematch if I didn't want *you*?" he asked.

"I'm just starting to wonder if you still love me, now that you're really getting to know me. Or do you just feel obligated to love me because of everything we've invested in this financially and emotionally?"

Rafael lost his breath. He felt like he demonstrated his love all the time—taking care of her cat, tending to her when she was sick, folding her blankets, composting her gross fruit scraps, picking up every phone call, answering every text—and it wasn't out of obligation. Wasn't that clear to her? Or was she projecting her own feelings onto him?

"If I'm becoming too much for you, and you don't actually love me anymore, just say so," Ursula went on, voicing what she feared was happening. "No one would blame you for leaving. I seem to have that effect on men."

"Do you feel obligated to love *me*?" he asked, trying to understand where she was coming from.

Ursula couldn't lie. "Yes, I do. I love you deeply, but ever since we walked away from The Arc, I've felt like this *has* to work. We *have* to make it work—and there's no breathing room. It's a lot of pressure. I feel like things are starting to unravel, and I'm terrified that The Arc was right. I don't want to fail at love again, and I don't want to drag you down with me."

Rafael nodded, realizing she was right. The anxiety was affecting him, too. Since they'd walked away from The Arc two months earlier, the smallest of conflicts had felt grave and foreboding for both of them. He had been trying to counteract the strain by offering her extra support, but it seemed to be pushing her further away.

"Well, the last thing I want to be is an obligation," he said.

"I didn't mean it that way," she replied. "I just never expected things to get this confusing."

"It's not what you signed up for," said Rafael.

"Not really," she admitted. It wasn't that *he* had disappointed her; but the process had.

"Me neither," he said. "What did you think you were signing up for?"

"Something smooth and easy," she said. "Like the way things were last fall, before we knew we were doomed."

"Something manufactured to be seamless," said Rafael. "Because you don't like dealing with conflict."

"Yes! Exactly," she said, relieved that he understood. "What did you think you were signing up for?"

"I thought I was signing up for a partnership that could withstand conflict," he said. "With someone who doesn't always need everything to be smooth and easy."

Ursula felt a pain below her heart. He seemed to be crafting a narrative that confirmed her greatest fear: She was the problem. She probably always had been. Her expectations were out of whack, and that's why all her relationships derailed, even those that were manufactured for success by luxury relationship architects. Not even Rafael, with all of his patience and kindness, could prevent her from doing what she did best: self-sabotage.

"I'm going to die alone with my cat," she said quietly.

"What?"

"I just feel like a failure. Like I'm the weak link here."

"You're not a failure," said Rafael. "You're a perfectionist who is tormented by the possibility of failure."

Ursula knew he was right. She was difficult to satisfy—at work, in relationships, everywhere—and when things started to disappoint her or go awry, she often couldn't resist the appeal of a clean slate. But when she disappointed herself, there was nowhere to run. Ursula's phone lit up with a new text from Mike.

BTW are you and sutton hunt boning . . .

Rafael saw it and felt a violent chill run through his body. "Are you fucking kidding me, Ursula? You *are* cheating on me. Which means you're also lying to me." It was like Meredith Sinclair all over again. It was like Freja all over again.

"Ughhhhh," Ursula groaned, burying her face in her hands. Sutton Hunt had struck again. "There is a simple but also convoluted explanation for this. There's this terrible guy, Sutton Hunt, and . . ."

"Yeah, there's always some terrible guy, and it's always his fault."

"I'm not cheating on you!" yelled Ursula, feeling like they were going in circles. "It's a joke, and I'll explain it to you if you'll let me."

"I don't care if you're not cheating. You're doing something. You're *allowing* something. And it's not okay." Rafael turned away from her.

"I don't have to work for Mike anymore if it bothers you that much!" Ursula relented.

"It's not just Mike!" yelled Rafael, reaching a reservoir of frustration he hadn't realized was pooling inside of him. "Do you realize you've structured your whole career around working with the exact type of men you find insufferable? Are you some kind of workplace vigilante? Or do you just have Stockholm Syndrome?"

"Ah yes, so that's what this is," said Ursula sarcastically. "Are you here to rescue me, Rafael? Thank god."

"Okay, Ursula," said Rafael. "You're right. You don't need my help."

"I can't just refuse to work with people because they don't meet my standards," said Ursula. "No one meets my standards! Not even me."

"Well, maybe you should do your own thing," said Rafael. "Or draw clearer boundaries. What are you trying to prove by spending all your energy on people and projects you don't really believe in?"

"What's happening right now?" Ursula asked. "What are we even fighting about?"

They were missing each other's point, over and over. They were on different planes.

"I think this is spiraling," Rafael said. "Dr. Vidal was right. This relationship has a fatal flaw."

"Doesn't every relationship have a fatal flaw?" asked Ursula, panicked, as if she were slipping uncontrollably toward an abyss.

"It seems so," said Rafael, defeated. "But in this case, it's clear what it is: you."

"That's not fair," said Ursula, although she agreed with him. She was the problem and always had been. But even so, she wanted him to fight for her, to tell her he would never abandon her. Tears welled in her eyes as she realized he wasn't going to say those things, and she didn't know how to ask for them.

Rafael's eyes were glassy, and he didn't speak.

Ursula felt panicked and cornered. Her gut told her their breakup was inevitable, so she decided to accelerate through the pain, to give Rafael an easy out. "Maybe we should go back to The Arc to get the Emotional Detachment Procedure. I know it's too late for a refund, but maybe we should do the procedure anyway."

"Is that what you want?" asked Rafael.

"I don't want this to get any more painful or confusing," said Ursula. "And I don't know what else to do."

"It sounds like you've already given up," said Rafael, depleted, exhausted.

"Well, haven't you?" She waited, praying his answer would be no.

He hadn't given up until that moment, but now all he felt was despair. "I think we've hit an impasse."

"Meaning we should get the procedure?" she asked, hoping she had misunderstood him. Hoping he would push back. "You're really done?"

"No," he said. "We're really done."

Ursula felt herself disintegrate. A smooth, swift emptying of the heart, like sand through an hourglass. She was left empty and echoing.

Rafael sidestepped past the coffee table, moving toward the chair where he had left his coat. Mallory was now asleep on top of it, and he delicately pulled it from beneath her, pouring her body onto the armchair as gently as he could. He looked pale, and a few gray hairs were visible at his temples, which gave him a distinguished look that Ursula loved. As he passed the side table, she finally noticed the flowers he had put there.

"What are those?" she asked. But he was already through the door. She heard his footsteps and then the creak of the front gate. "Evening," she heard Rafael say politely to a neighbor who must have just entered. Then she heard the closing of the gate—a final metallic *clang*—as he headed into the freezing black of the night.

Chapter 38

When Ursula got to The Arc, Rafael was already there. She was a few minutes early, which meant he had been even earlier. This made her incredibly sad, since she interpreted it as a sign that he was extra-eager to get rid of her. Part of her had hoped he would call the whole thing off that morning, but he hadn't. Since their fight three nights ago, they'd spoken twice, but only briefly and about logistics. Rafael had sent Skipp to pick up his things from Ursula's apartment, and to drop off the things she had left at his. The Arc had immediately responded to their request for the Emotional Detachment Procedure, but they weren't told what it would entail. They'd been instructed to bring a simple overnight bag, to arrive at The Arc at 8 P.M., and to be prepared to sleep there.

In the entry hallway, Ursula and Rafael hugged a long hello, but said nothing. Sasha silently led them into a room that contained two circular platforms, each about three feet across, and each with a four-foot-tall, T-shaped handle on one side. She asked them to step onto the platforms: Ursula on the right, Rafael on the left.

Sasha left the room, and Dr. Vidal entered, quietly, confidently, almost triumphantly. Her manner suggested that she approved of their decision to go through with this procedure.

"Ursula, Rafael," she said deferentially. "I think you're making a wise choice for yourselves—and for your future happiness. For this procedure, we typically provide as little upfront information as possible, though you'll be guided throughout. We're going to begin with a vibration therapy that will activate your nervous systems and loosen any areas of emotional tension, and then you'll be separated for the night. You'll sleep in pods, and during your sleep, we'll infuse your subconscious with messages that will help you to process and let go of your relationship. It's not brainwashing, and we're certainly not erasing any of your memories. We're simply soothing your limbic system and implanting ideas that will make it less painful for you to go your separate ways as individuals. It requires absolutely no effort on your part. You just have to vibrate—and then sleep. The effort will come later, once you leave here tomorrow at 8 A.M. It may be tempting to contact one another, but we highly—*highly*—discourage you from staying in touch once we separate you tonight. It will only slow your healing and inhibit your path to finding the love you seek."

Rafael shook his head slowly. What love could he possibly seek now?

"Are we ready to begin?" asked Dr. Vidal.

Rafael and Ursula looked at each other, their eyes glazed with tears. Then they nodded silently.

"Please hold hands across your platforms, and then place your outside hand on the T-bar in front of you. Close your eyes and keep them closed for the remainder of the evening, until we tell you to open them. You're going to feel a subtle vibration that will gradually increase over the next fifteen minutes. You can lean on each other or the handles for stability, but once you hear the word 'release,' you must drop each other's hands and place both of your hands on your own T-bar. Let's begin."

Ursula closed her eyes and focused on the painful lump in her throat. The platform began to shake softly. Rafael closed his eyes and leaned on his handle. He didn't want to exert any pressure on Ursula or throw her off balance. He felt the heat of his own hand against the coolness of hers. Her appendages always got cold when she was scared. Little by little, the shaking of the platform became a buzzing vibration that radiated up their legs, through their pelvises and into their stomachs. It intensified, shaking their rib cages, their hearts, their lungs, their esophagi. Eventually, Ursula's jawline began tingling with vibration, then her nostrils, her hairline, her scalp. The inside of her ear canals prickled. It felt both good and scary, as if her energy was being exfoliated from the inside out.

The noise of the vibration increased along with the sensation. Ursula could no longer hear anything but the thrum of the machines and her own teeth clattering. Her lips buzzed. Her hair follicles stood up. Rafael felt his sadness catch in his throat, then loosen, and then dissipate.

The intensity of the vibration made it hard to feel or focus on anything except bodily sensation. It was all getting shaken up, confused. It felt both pleasant and terrible, cathartic and chaotic.

"RELEASE!" commanded Dr. Vidal.

Rafael felt Ursula's small hand squeeze his one last time and then drop away. He let out a silent sob at the raw finality of it, and leaned both hands against his T-bar for stability. He felt his platform start to move and realized that he was being wheeled out of the room, then down what felt like a long hallway, then into another room. The platform stopped, and the vibration ended abruptly.

"You can open your eyes," said Rich, who had apparently guided Rafael's platform down the hall and into this room. "This is your sleeping pod."

The space was empty except for a sink, a toilet, and a large object that looked like an oyster shell but was the size of a minivan.

"You have fifteen minutes to get ready for bed, and then just crawl into your pod and pull the lid down with this strap." Rich gestured. "If you need anything in the night, press this button. Otherwise, just rest. You may hear music, you may hear chanting, you may hear poetry, you may hear various orations. Just let it wash over you. The recordings will penetrate your brain and do the work for you. I'll be back at 8 A.M. to retrieve you. Until then, please don't leave the pod."

"Is this like hypnosis? Subliminal messaging?" asked Rafael.

"We don't use those labels," said Rich. "Think of it as a helpful rewiring of your subconscious beliefs. You'll wake up with a whole new outlook."

Rafael didn't like the sound of it, but after all that vibrating, he was too tired to protest.

Down another hallway, in another room, beside another pod, Ursula was getting the same spiel from Sasha. She nodded to indicate that she understood the instructions, and then watched as Sasha wheeled the vibration platform out of the room. The door slid shut behind her. Ursula realized this was the last time she would be sealed into a room at The Arc, which felt bittersweet. Being at The Arc was somehow comforting, even though this place was the root of her current sadness. She brushed her teeth, washed her face, removed her contacts, and put on the linen pajamas she had brought with her.

She grabbed Travel Wolf, whom she had brought for moral support, and crawled into the pod, whose interior was a cloud-like bed with various pillows of different densities. She pulled the strap to lower the top. The interior lights of the pod slowly dimmed to black, and Ursula heard a soft voice: *Sometimes we think we are in love, but it is only a test. A test that awakens us and makes us aware of what we really want, what we really desire, what we really deserve. Sometimes, love is not what it seems. We think we are traveling in one direction, but really, we are preparing to go the opposite way. One path leads to another, and we don't know which part of which path we're on. But if we have faith that a larger, wiser force is guiding us . . .*

Ursula let out one final, ragged sob, and then drifted into an uncharacteristically deep, still sleep.

URSULA

Chapter 39

February 18, 1:03 P.M.

Ursula knew that her mother was trying to help. "I knew you shouldn't have joined that cult," said Orla.

"It's not a cult, mom. It's a relationship solution." Ursula sniffled into the phone. She was still in bed even though it was early afternoon.

"Well, I'm just glad you had the wherewithal to extricate yourself," Orla continued. "Cults are powerful things. Now you can reset."

Ursula didn't want to reset. She wanted to rewind to the time before she'd known about The Arc. She wished she could have just met Rafael by chance in the city, and that they could have fallen in love organically, like normal people. Just a normal New York love story.

"You'll be okay," said Orla. "You know, you've always been very focused on control. Remember when you used to play Tool Families? You loved that you got to decide exactly how all the interactions played out. The Arc was a little bit like that, no? They promised you a perfect relationship; then they choreographed your separation. But real life isn't like that."

It certainly wasn't. Ursula felt that she was quickly losing control of everything.

"Maybe this is a good thing!" insisted Orla. "Maybe it's time to stop white-knuckling your way through life. Just let go and see what happens. Let things take their own course! I know you've always felt vulnerable and resisted instability, and that's probably my fault. But as far as I can tell, the wind has always been at your back. It's very possible that the universe is conspiring to give you what you need, exactly when you need it. That's what happened for me."

"When?"

"When I had you!" said Orla. "You weren't part of any kind of plan. There was no plan, other than to get away from my batshit-crazy family. But you were the best thing I ever did."

Ursula couldn't hold back her tears of both delight and sadness. She was relieved to know her mother saw her that way, but she now felt even more devastated by the idea that she might never have her own child because she had waited too long and sabotaged her chances. She had failed as a mother before she'd even tried.

"Oh, please," said Orla, in response to Ursula's mournful admission. "You haven't failed at all. Far from it. This is the art of living. You're creative, right? So get creative. Open your mind. Just because this relationship didn't go as planned doesn't mean everything is for naught. You can have a baby with a sperm donor. Or have a baby with Danny!"

Danny again. "I'm not having a baby with Danny! He's married to his husband!" Ursula shouted.

"Well, maybe they need an egg donor!" Orla shouted back.

"Okay, Mom," said Ursula, reeling her mother in. She had been the recipient of Orla's spontaneous philosophical orations her whole life. And while they always included threads of wisdom, they often ended on a ridiculously specific and prescriptive note.

Ursula could hear barking in the background, and she heard her mother's rushed footsteps on the wooden floorboards of her house.

"Oh no," said Orla breathily. Ursula could tell she was looking out the window at her dog. "I think Hellion might have eaten one of the chickens. Call me in two hours if you're still crying. Bye, love."

Ursula knew she had to get out of bed. She'd been rotating through various versions of the fetal position for the last twenty-four hours, ever since she returned from The Arc, and she wondered when the so-called emotional anesthetic would kick in. For now, this felt like a real breakup—the most horrendous breakup imaginable. Her insides felt seared from her throat all the way to her tailbone. She Googled

"How to get over losing the love of your life" and scanned the articles, almost all of which emphasized self-care: take hot baths, hug your pet, drink tea, write in a journal, join a group, don't drink too much alcohol, become the love of your own life. Voilà, you're healed.

Two hours later, Ursula was facedown on a massage table at The Stake, a long trail of snot oozing from her nose through the table's face cradle onto the floor of her treatment room. She couldn't help it. Her eyes, her nose, even her mouth seemed to be erupting with the juices of sadness.

"I'm sorry," she said, picking her head up to wipe her nose. "I'm a mess."

"Is normal," said Svetlana. Ever since she had introduced Ursula to the concept of the four inner compasses, Ursula sought her out whenever she did a spa treatment at The Stake. "Let it go. You need let boogers go. Is what Meltdown Massage for."

The Meltdown Massage was for those experiencing extreme emotional upheaval. Svetlana alternated smooth strokes with swift, unexpected blows to shake up the psychic state. The recipient could choose from a variety of ultra-specific soundtracks, all designed to soothe: summer thunderstorm, ocean waves, cricket chirps, the music of a single panpipe, cows lowing. Ursula had selected "Equestrian Outing," and she let the elements wash over her: cantering hooves, snorts, and vocal clicks signaling giddyup.

"Shhhhhh," soothed Svetlana.

"But he was it," sobbed Ursula. "My compasses—my head, my heart, my gut, my wagina—they all liked him. They all loved him. He was *it*."

"Then vhat change?" asked Svetlana, thwacking Ursula beneath her right scapula. "Vhat happen?"

"We were told we were doomed. And then we started to have doubts and fight. And then it fell apart." Ursula began to wail. *"And he didn't fight for me."*

Svetlana slowly pressed a finger into the base of Ursula's skull, saying, "Some love has end. Or sometimes just need breathe. Like vine, needs breathe. If really all four compass, you find your way back."

"I'm not supposed to," said Ursula. "I'm not allowed."

"Say who?" Svetlana protested. "You are boss. You are mistress of your life."

"Yes." Ursula sniffed and burbled in hopeful agreement. "I *am* mistress of my life."

When she left her massage room, Issa was waiting outside. Ursula flopped against her and began crying into her friend's smooth collarbone. Issa gently stroked her head.

"It feels like my body has been turned inside out," howled Ursula. "And everyone can see my heart pulsing with pain and my organs are all mangled and I'm bleeding out all over the floor. Everyone can see that I'm just barely staying alive."

"No one can see that," said Issa softly. "Do you want to go into a Sobbing Pod for a while? There's a free one."

Ursula shook her head. "I need air. Let's go walk outside."

It was the gloaming, and the sky glowed with pale orange light. Though it had been full winter just a few days ago, today felt like the first suggestion of spring. The snowmelt had begun, and the air was warm and wet.

"It's supposed to hurt," said Issa as they strolled through Madison Square Park. "That's what breakups do. They hurt. I think you guys did a really mature thing. You mutually decided that it wasn't working, and you spared each other pain by breaking up before it got worse. You consciously uncoupled, just like Gwyneth and Chris."

"But do I want to be like Gwyneth Paltrow?" Ursula sniffled. "Or do I want to be the opposite of Gwyneth Paltrow?"

"That is the question of our time," said Issa. "Only you can answer it."

Ursula looked down at her white sneakers. One was untied, but she didn't have the energy to do anything about it. "I feel alone."

"You're not alone," said Issa, stopping and bending down to tie Ursula's shoelace, which looked like a wet little worm. "You have a million friends who love you."

"I don't have Rafael," said Ursula. "Maybe I never did. Maybe The Arc was just fucking with me. Maybe I'm being punished for some sin I committed in a past life. Karmic retribution."

"You're going to be okay," said Issa. "This is the sucky part, but it won't feel like this forever."

"I just don't understand," said Ursula, no longer crying but extremely puffy-faced. "The detachment procedure was supposed to buffer this pain. But this feels like a full-on heart massacre."

"Maybe it will just take a little time?" offered Issa.

Ursula halted and stiffened. "Oh fuck," she said. "No, no, no. Please no." She spun around and looked for something to duck behind, but they were mid-path, out in the open, and he was already too close. "It's James," Ursula hissed, quiet and panicked. "The guy I threw up on—well, next to—when we were in the car. On a first date. Remember?"

Issa looked up. "Okay, stay calm. Maybe he won't . . ."

"Ursula?" James furrowed his brow as if he was shocked but delighted to see her.

She took a breath and attempted a carefree smile. "James! How are you?"

"I'm great," he said slowly and thoughtfully. He did seem great—it was radiating from him. "And you?"

Ursula paused, opened her mouth to speak, closed it, and then burst into tears.

"She's also great," Issa quickly answered for her. "She just gets emotional around Presidents' Day. So nice to meet you."

James looked confused, and Issa ushered Ursula along the path. When they were far enough away, Issa said, "He's very cute."

"Shit," said Ursula, examining her face with her fingers. "How do I look?"

"You look . . . good, fine," said Issa. "You look mostly fine. And you didn't even vomit this time! Things are looking up."

She hoped Issa was right, and she spent the next few weeks in survival mode: going to work, forcing nutrients into her body, and then drinking half a bottle of wine every evening to quiet her brain and numb her heart. She thought about Rafael on an hourly basis. If she was in this much pain having gotten the Emotional Detachment Procedure, she couldn't imagine what the breakup would have felt like without it. She found herself feeling grateful to The Arc, but only for an instant.

She knew this wasn't a sustainable state. Earlier that week, she'd had a freak-out at work. She'd been pushing for an idea that was a bit outside the box—even for her—and Roger had insisted they further test it before moving forward, saying, "Let's look at the data on this one."

Offended that he would question her instincts, Ursula had snarled, "Screw your data, you goddamn data whore!"

The room went silent, but after a beat, Roger started laughing hysterically. So Ursula started laughing hysterically, appalled by her own outburst and relieved that Roger had a soft spot for insolent creatives.

Although that crisis was averted, a much larger one presented itself the next day: Sabrina quit. As always, she was gracious and grateful for everything Ursula had taught her, but she had realized the agency world wasn't for her.

"What are you going to do?"

"Actually, I got hired by Nine to Five," Sabrina had disclosed. "I'm going to be their head of business strategy. Help them build the company from the ground up."

Ursula felt herself pulled in so many different directions: proud of her young charge for knowing herself and following her instincts; frustrated with herself for not doing enough to keep Sabrina motivated to stay; and panicked about who would fill Sabrina's unfillable shoes. Finally, she also felt a twinge of jealousy that Sabrina was moving on to a new opportunity and leaving her behind.

"Is this because of the promotion thing?" asked Ursula. "Is there anything I can do to convince you to stay?"

Sabrina shook her head and smiled shyly, as if she knew she was off to a brighter future but was sorry to be abandoning Ursula. "I'm not upset about that. The timing actually worked out really well."

"Did you negotiate your salary?" Ursula couldn't help but ask. "Are you going to make more?"

Sabrina nodded proudly. "Significantly more."

In an unforeseen twist of events, Mike Rutherford's $3 million investment in Nine to Five had allowed Juliana and Alejandra to hire Sabrina at a salary she deserved. This was a great loss for Anonymous & Co., and Ursula couldn't tell whether she had failed or succeeded as a mentor. But she accepted Sabrina's news with as much magnanimity as she could muster, and then she went home and cried.

Chapter 40

Now that it was late March, the weather had begun to warm up slightly, but Ursula felt tense and clammy all the time. Mallory seemed especially restless and jolty as well, so Ursula decided to take her for a Sunday afternoon walk. Rafael had given her this cat harness and leash set as a joke, but what did she have to lose now? She let her thoughts go dark. "My fertile years are waning, my chance at love has passed, my cat is my greatest asset," she thought. She knew she wasn't supposed to travel these bleak mental tunnels, but she couldn't help it.

Mallory seemed skeptical of the harness, but eventually she relaxed her body and allowed Ursula to wrestle her into it and clip the little tartan-plaid vest over her body. Ursula carried her out of the apartment, and once they were on the sidewalk, she set the little cat down. Mallory did an odd lunge, then collapsed onto her side. She rolled onto her back, feet askew, tangling herself up in the leash. Ursula bent down to extricate her as a woman passed them, saying, "Look at that little itty-bitty, weird-ass dog."

"It's a cat," Ursula responded indignantly. She got Mallory up onto her feet, and the cat took a few steps forward, and then listed to the side again. Ursula's phone buzzed with a text message. Every time this happened, she found herself yearning to see Rafael's name on the screen. Every time it wasn't him—and it was never him—her heart stung.

It was Mike: *ready for the Brandys on Thursday . . .*

She knew this was a question, but she wasn't sure how to respond.

By now, the nomination seemed inconsequential; her career seemed inconsequential; her life seemed inconsequential. She had lost love before, but now that she had lost her One Great Love, she didn't know where to direct her energy. The life force continually leeched out of her. Her therapist called it a "double depression," but Ursula knew it was more than that. It was a surrender to the chaos of life, to the randomness. It was a total relinquishing of ambition or plans or goals. She didn't care what happened to her now. She texted back:

Ursula: *I suppose so. You?*

Mike: *wouldn't miss it . . .*

Ever since Jackson Hole, when she had started to see Mike as a multidimensional human and, in turn, opened up to him, he had started extending himself, showing up for her in small ways. There was no professional reason he needed to come to the Brandys, but Ursula didn't want to go alone, and Issa was busy. Mike had seemed thrilled when she invited him, which was sweet. But it killed her to know that the person she really wanted to take as her plus-one was the very person she had pushed out of her life. She half-dragged Mallory home, unharnessed her, and sank into the couch. It was only then that she realized she was crying—again. This had been happening to her over the last few weeks. She called them Sneaky Leaks: tears that she often didn't detect until her cheeks were already soaked.

Chapter 41

April 2, 7:12 P.M.

Ursula arrived at the Brandys in her pale-gold silk slip dress. The odd thing about feeling miserable was that it sometimes made people look kind of glamorous. Ursula welcomed that incongruity tonight, and she walked into the industrial-chic lobby of this particular Williamsburg hotel knowing that she looked good, despite feeling like a despondent hellcat on the inside.

She didn't want to talk to anyone yet, so she headed straight for the bar and ordered a Hendrick's martini, straight up, with a twist. Probably a bad idea, but she needed to get through this thing.

"There's our girl!" she heard someone say, and she turned to see Roger and Mike, both in expensive suits, grinning at her.

"I'm worried about what will happen to you guys if I don't win," said Ursula. "Please don't be devastated."

"You'll win," said Roger.

People were starting to take their seats at various tables around the room. A C-list comedian was emceeing, and he was trying to corral and hush the crowd. Over the next forty-five minutes, Ursula ate half a filet mignon, drank another martini (definitely a bad idea), looked at her phone seventeen times, and wondered where Rafael was, what he was doing, and whom he was with. Then she heard the comedian say, "And for Campaign of the Year, the nominees are . . ." When he got to Ursula's name, Mike, who was seated to Ursula's right, gave her a thumbs-up.

She felt a jolt of panic and then total numbness. She couldn't even tell if she wanted to win. Did she want to succeed in this industry?

Did she want to be in this room at all? What was she supposed to want? She couldn't remember. Was it that she wanted to work on her own terms? What *were* her terms, again? She pulled at her dress, thinking, "Strapless bras are the devil."

"And the award goes to . . . Ursula Byrne of Anonymous & Co. for the 'Cruisify Yourself' campaign!"

Roger shot his hands up and threw his head back, giving a victory yelp. Mike pulled Ursula in for a hug. She didn't know why everyone was acting as if she'd just won an Oscar. She rose from her seat and began to walk toward the stage as the campaign's theme song played. It was a rendition of Tori Amos's "Crucify," but in this version, the lyrics went, "Why don't we . . . Cruisify ourselves?" and played over a video of self-made social media titans holding their arms out, Christ-like, while they drank rosé on the deck of a yacht.

When Ursula got to the stage, the comedian handed her the Brandy statuette, which was a small block with illuminated neon letters that read "YOLO" (as in, "You Only Live Once").

"Thanks so much," said Ursula, taking the neon statuette.

Even from up on the stage, she could hear Roger hollering in triumph.

"Well, thank you so much," Ursula took a deep breath as the room quieted. She looked at the neon YOLO glowing obnoxiously in her hands. "Wow, look at this thing. I don't know if I deserve this. I mean, I don't know if I'm the nominee who would most appreciate it. I mean, I do appreciate it, I'm just wondering . . . why the fuck are you giving me an award for this?" She gestured toward the screen that featured the campaign's ad. "Why is my client called Cruisify in the first place? Why did we take Tori Amos's beautiful song and deform it? And why are we using a crucifixion pun to break through the noise of the current marketing environment? Why are we continually catering to the lowest denominator, against our better instincts? I guess when it comes to the creative, it doesn't matter if it makes sense anymore, as long as it makes money. And you know what? This award doesn't even make sense." She paused to look at the statuette again, and then addressed it. "'YOLO'? 'You only live once'? Are we sure? And if we're sure, do I really want to use my one life promoting cruises and toilet paper? YOLO . . . I'll tell you about fucking YOLO . . ."

By this time, Roger had reached the stage and was dashing toward her. He pulled her away from the podium and began leading her offstage. Then he paused, ran back, and said into the microphone: "Thank you so much for this honor. We really do appreciate it."

He locked his hand in a vise grip around Ursula's upper arm and pulled her firmly across the stage as if he were leading a disobedient child to a time-out. The crowd murmured and the speakers blasted, "Why don't we . . . Cruisify ourselves?!"

When they got to the lobby of the hotel, Roger released her arm. "What the *hell* was that?"

"I don't know," said Ursula, unable to prevent the truth from erupting. "I'm just . . . I don't believe in what we do, Roger. I don't want to do this anymore."

"*Now* you realize this? You know, if you don't want the goddamn award, you could just graciously decline to accept it. You don't have to burn the whole industry down."

"I wasn't trying to . . ." Ursula stopped. She didn't even understand her own intention. She was imploding.

"I don't want to talk to you right now," said Roger. Then he pointed a finger into Ursula's face. "But I want you in my office at 8 A.M. tomorrow. Now go home."

"I'll take her home," said Mike, approaching with Ursula's coat and bag in hand.

Roger nodded deferentially. Then he became stern and turned back to Ursula. "8 A.M." He stomped off, grabbing a glass of champagne off a passing tray and drinking it in one angry gulp.

Ursula and Mike walked out into the fresh spring air. Mike's driver was waiting. The last time she'd been in Mike's car, it had been an armored Hummer, but tonight, he had come in his Tesla SUV. Being outside felt good, as did breathing. Ursula took a long inhale and then ducked her head and got into the car, which pulled out and sped off, passing the former warehouses that now housed North Williamsburg's hipster-flooded bars and boutiques.

"I think I just lost my shit," said Ursula.

"You think?!" Mike's eyes were wide and sparkling. She could tell he was trying to hide his amusement, but she could also tell she'd just given him a welcome adrenaline rush.

"Oh my god." Ursula covered her mouth with her hand in disbelief.

"That's the Ursula I like," he said. "Unfiltered. Speaking truth to power."

"I just set my career on fire," she said. "What the hell am I doing?"

Ursula looked out her window. High and bright above her, the full moon hung like a spotlight, and she wondered whether Rafael had noticed it and thought of her. She started to laugh at the ridiculousness of it all, but her cackle soon morphed into a sob as she felt a surge of sadness well up inside of her. There was no stopping it, and she was too overwhelmed to be embarrassed. She let herself lean against Mike's masterfully tailored shoulder as she wept. He reached over and attempted to smooth her wild hair.

"We'll take care of you, kiddo," he said. "There are a lot of people looking out for you."

By the time they pulled up outside of Ursula's apartment, she had calmed down. Mike looked around as if he were on a foreign planet. "So this is Carroll Gardens? Very bohemian."

He insisted on walking her into her apartment, and once in her living room, he looked around again as if he had never encountered such a place—thin windowpanes, antiquated radiators that intermittently hissed and clanked, only 742 square feet. Once he acclimated, he was thrilled by the exoticism of it.

"You going to be okay?" he asked, looking down into her eyes, which shined with new tears.

"Yes." Ursula nodded, oddly moved by his ability to comfort her. She felt like an exhausted infant, and all she could think to say was, "Thanks for being my friend, Mike."

"Of course. Thanks for letting me." He squeezed the back of her neck gently, and then headed toward the door. "For the record, you're my coolest friend by far."

When Ursula opened her eyes at 7:17 A.M., she was already late. It was a miracle that she had woken up at all, since she had forgotten to set her alarm. She walked to the bathroom and stood in front of the mirror. Not good. She looked as if she'd had multiple martinis, a mental breakdown, and a protracted fight with a honey badger.

Back in her room, she hazily pulled on black jeans, a white silk shirt, and her python-skin loafers. She slicked on bloodred matte lipstick—a protective force field—and grabbed her vintage cat-eye sunglasses. Her body vibrated with the incongruent effects of her brutal hangover, her post-rant embarrassment, and her pre-meeting nerves. She didn't know what Roger was going to say to her, but it wasn't going to be good.

The office was empty when she arrived at 8:21 A.M. except for Roger, who was in his nook waiting.

"You're late," he said as she approached.

"I know. I'm sorry. About everything. I'm going through a really rough phase, Roger."

"Yeah, I noticed. The breakup, yada yada yada." Her award was on his desk, illuminated. *YOLO.*

"It's more than that. I think I'm having an existential meltdown," said Ursula. "A personal reckoning."

"Not a personal one. A public one," said Roger, unamused. "Very public. You just compromised this agency's reputation—*my* reputation—in front of our clients, our competitors, and everyone who matters in this industry."

"I know."

"I would ask you why, but you were pretty clear last night: You don't want this job. You don't believe in our work anymore." His dour expression scared her, and she tried to retrace her steps.

"I know I said that, but I didn't mean it," said Ursula. She had meant it, of course, but she didn't want to lose her job. She wasn't ready to leap off that cliff yet. She had to salvage the situation. "I just lost sight of things for a minute."

"Understatement of the year," said Roger.

"I will make up for this so quickly, you won't even remember that it happened," said Ursula.

"How?"

"We can spin it. Pretend it was all part of the campaign! Or maybe it can become part of Anonymous's new brand: Real-time experiential scandal! Meltdowns with a message! That could be a new offering for us."

Roger remained unimpressed.

"I'll fix it. I'll do what I do. You said it yourself: I'm your MVP. I'm your secret weapon."

"You were," Roger said stonily. "But you just made yourself a liability."

Ursula sighed. She hadn't had time to get coffee, and her energy was dissipating.

"I'm exhausted. I need a break, a sabbatical," she said, missing Rafael desperately in this moment. Wishing he could help her navigate this. "I need to take my foot off the gas for a minute. Do you know what it's like to be in this industry as a woman? To have to tolerate these tech bros, these VCs, these founders who all think they're the next Mark Zuckerberg?"

"So you freaked out and publicly insulted our client because it's hard being a woman in this industry? Ursula, listen. Your whole 'woke feminist' shtick has gone a little far," said Roger. "It was charming at first—I'll admit that—the way you rallied all the women in the office and told them they needed to 'step into their power.' But I think you've overstepped yours."

"I've overstepped my power? What power?!" Ursula said angrily. "What power do I have in this world?"

"Don't pull that," said Roger.

"Pull *what*?" asked Ursula.

"That empowered-but-not thing. That demi-empowered thing. That fragile self-esteem thing," he said.

290 TORY HENWOOD HOEN

"You *like* working with people who have fragile self-esteem, Roger," Ursula responded. "You thrive on it."

"Yes, I do!" said Roger. "And when I hired you seven years ago, you had fragile self-esteem. That's what made you such a great employee. You worked your ass off, and you never complained. But little by little, you've slipped into this place of . . . I don't know. All this stuff."

"What stuff?" asked Ursula, genuinely confused.

"You know, like 'advocating for yourself' and 'speaking your mind' and demanding things."

"Self-confidence?" asked Ursula, defiant that Roger saw her growth as a threat.

"Acting like you deserve more and more, while you deliver less and less," said Roger. "It's getting old. And what you pulled last night . . ."

To the right of Roger's desk hung a blown-up copy of an article he'd been featured in called "What #MeToo Means to Me: Our Male Allies Speak." Ursula had been so proud to work for him when that piece came out, but like many of the men she knew, his enthusiasm for the cause and his openness to "doing better" had flagged in the last year. He had reverted to the self-interested chauvinist he'd always been. His current attitude suggested that he'd done his part for a while, and now he'd like to rest, to not be so stressed all the time, worrying if he was going to offend some woman. God, it was tiring.

"I'm not delivering?" asked Ursula, wishing she'd had the foresight to record this conversation. "I just won Campaign of the Year. Are you kidding me?"

"Are you kidding *me*?" Roger said.

"Are you kidding *me*?" Ursula repeated, now enjoying the verbal Ping-Pong.

"Are you ki . . ." Roger stopped, realizing that he was being mocked. "I'll get to the point."

She knew what was coming. She crossed her arms and waited.

"Ursula, you're fired."

Chapter 42

May 7, 6:12 P.M.

"That was . . . different," said Issa, in response to the sound bath they'd just taken, which involved their lying on the floor with ten other members of The Stake while a woman walked around the room playing a didgeridoo, hovering the end of the long instrument over the participants' reclined bodies. The Stake had titled the session "Don't Mind if I Didgeridoo: An Hour with the World's Most Controversial Instrument"—citing the aboriginal tradition of only allowing men to play the instrument in ceremonial settings. At The Stake, women reclaimed the didgeridoo. Some called it extreme cultural insensitivity; others called it vibrational empowerment.

They made their way up to The Stake's roof deck, which was crowded on this warm May evening. Issa went to the bar to get drinks, while Ursula claimed a hanging rattan nest big enough for two. She had just managed to reach equilibrium in the swinging nest when she heard her name.

"Ursula? Ursula Byrne!" It was Lisa Hutchens, from college, wearing a beige linen jumpsuit.

"Lisa!" Ursula deployed her faux-excited voice.

"What a trip! It's been ages!" Lisa had always used phrases like "what a trip," which made her seem like a woman from another era.

"What have you been up to?" asked Ursula, though she already knew the answer.

"You haven't heard? I'm a Whole Heart Coach. I have my own practice, helping women cultivate love. Speaking of which, are you still single?"

Ursula resented the use of "still," as if her single status were an illness she couldn't quite kick. She also didn't know the answer to that question. Technically she was single, but she still felt energetically bound to Rafael. The idea of dating anyone else made her nauseous. "Well . . ."

"Sounds like a yes to me," said Lisa authoritatively. "Hesitation means yes."

"I'm focusing on my career at the moment," said Ursula, which was not true. In fact, this was the most unemployed she had been since landing her first job at age twelve (weeding gardens in her hometown). She had even terminated her work with Mike, who had technically paid her through July but agreed to let her off the hook for the sake of her mental health—a gesture that both touched and mortified her. But she accepted it, knowing that she needed a full mental reset, a clean slate, a moment to wallow in her dark night of the soul without any outside pressure. She calculated that she had enough savings to carry her for six months without working, if she chose. And although her first week of aimlessness had been unbearable, she was now settling into a rhythm. During the day, she rode the subway to random parts of the city and walked miles through unfamiliar neighborhoods, over bridges, through parks— avoiding anywhere she had ever been with Rafael. Her goal was to create a new mental map of the city, and moving her legs prevented her from descending into sadness too early in the day. Nights were for crying and sketching. She alternated between drawing woodland creatures and portraits of women she admired: Gloria Steinem, Dr. Ruth, Sojourner Truth, Dolly Parton, Issa, Sabrina. She even did one of Shilpa Thakur, using a photo from the summit in Jackson as a reference.

"Career and love don't need to compete," Lisa asserted. "They can coexist and even augment each other."

Ursula deeply wished that Lisa would shut up, and she felt pure joy when Issa returned carrying two highball glasses.

"Lisa!" Issa had a faux-excited voice, too.

"Well, Issa Takahashi. As I live and breathe!" said Lisa. "I was just telling Ursula she could benefit from my Whole Heart Coaching. I have a new workshop on Intentional Yearning."

"This Ursula?" Issa feigned confusion. "Her yearning is always intentional. Yeah, she doesn't just yearn aimlessly."

Lisa smirked and then asked, "What are those?"

Issa looked at the pink-hued cocktails in her hands. "Moon-Water Spritzes."

On one ledge of the roof deck, there were barrels of water that The Stake's shaman put out every twenty-nine days—on the full moon—to absorb lunar energy. The liquid was later mixed into $17 cocktails.

"Sounds like a good way to get rabies," said Lisa.

"Oh, we've been rabid for years." Issa shrugged, handing Ursula her glass. "Great seeing you, Lisa."

"Great seeing *you*, chickadees," said Lisa, taking the hint. She began to walk away, but then stopped, turned, and pulled two business cards out of the pocket of her jumpsuit. "Just in case."

Once she was out of view and earshot, Ursula hugged Issa. This was the first time they'd been out together since Ursula was fired, and she was starting to feel human again.

The roof of The Stake was lovely, with lights strung around its perimeter, but the two friends wondered if the firepit was a bit much. It had an actual stake in the center that supported a sign rendered in wrought iron that said "The Patriarchy," which was continually licked by flames from below.

"I think fourth-wave feminism has veered a little off course," said Issa as they drank their moon water and stared into the flames.

"Everything has veered off course," said Ursula.

She felt a sudden urge to text Rafael, to call him, to curl up on his doormat and wait there until he got home. "I did a weird thing," she admitted.

"Uh-oh. Do I want to know?" Issa sipped her drink and raised her eyebrows.

"I bought Rafael's cologne and started wearing it when I miss him. And I miss him every day, so I wear it every day. Is that weird?"

"You do smell good," said Issa, sniffing Ursula's shoulder. "And I understand the impulse, but I'm not sure that's going to help you get over him."

"What if I don't want to get over him?" said Ursula. "I'm serious. I keep trying to force myself to let go, but then I cling desperately to what's left." She held her hand up like a claw. "Yesterday, I found one of his socks under my bed, and I couldn't throw it out."

"What did you do with it?"

"I put it in the Abyss," Ursula said, referring to the box where she kept unclaimed items from various boyfriends of yore: a lighter with Axl Rose on it, a money clip, a Japanese shibori handkerchief, a Mallorcan pocketknife, a stray pheasant feather, and now Rafael's sock.

"And did I tell you what arrived last week?"

Issa shook her head.

"The rug we bought in Oaxaca," said Ursula, recalling the day when she had felt so rattled by the question of how many rugs to buy and where to put them and what it all meant. "So now it's just rolled up in the corner. I don't know what to do with it. I don't know what to do with myself."

"You don't have to know," said Issa. "You're going through a huge transition. I'm not surprised you feel disoriented. But you can't just sit at home staring at a rolled-up rug. Let's unfurl it. I want to see it."

"Now? Tonight?" asked Ursula.

"Why not? We're both freshly Didgeridoo-ed. Let's go deal with the rug."

An hour later, they walked into Ursula's living room, which hadn't been cleaned for a while. Her sketches were all over the coffee table and couch, except for the one on the floor, which Mallory was shredding with practiced efficiency.

"These are good," said Issa, ignoring the mess and focusing on

Ursula's artistic output. She picked up one that was unmistakably Rafael.

"I think it was a mistake," said Ursula. "The breakup."

"Really?"

"I think so—I don't know."

"Well, what does your gut tell you?"

"I have multiple guts, and they tell me conflicting things."

"What does the most persistent one say? The one you want to ignore but can't?"

"That I'm the problem. That no matter who I'm with, I push him away. And even though I paid $40,000 to meet the perfect person, I still pushed him away. I've really outdone myself this time."

Issa looked at her friend, who had lost weight and let her hair grow into an extra-wild mane.

"I started to get really anxious when we began fighting, because I believed The Arc. I believed it was the death knell of our relationship. And I figured, if he's starting to act like a jerk now, he'll be a jerk forever."

"So? Everyone's a jerk," said Issa.

"Forever?"

"Yeah, kind of," said Issa, nodding. "Everyone's a jerk forever, just in different ways."

"I mean he wasn't *that* much of a jerk," said Ursula. "I just got scared of being locked into something that felt increasingly out of control. I thought if I talked to him about all the things I was mentally wrestling with, he wouldn't like or respect me anymore. But now he's gone, and I still feel out of control. So maybe it was me. Maybe this is just a breakdown that's been a long time coming, and our relationship was collateral damage."

"Maybe," said Issa, hopeful. "But why don't you call him? Talk to him!"

"I can't now,'" said Ursula. "The Arc already detached us."

Issa rolled her eyes. "Enough about the goddamn Arc. Screw The Arc. You know Rafael is still out there. He still exists."

"Yeah, but he's probably over it now. He's probably moving on and feeling relieved that he doesn't have to deal with me anymore. I wouldn't blame him."

"Maybe, or maybe he misses you just as much as you miss him."

Ursula felt a frisson of hope. "Maybe."

Issa looked toward the corner of the room, where the rug was propped up next to Ursula's bronze sculpture.

"I know I came here to help you with the rug, but can we talk about this thing?" Issa pointed to the sculpture. "I know your dad made it and it has sentimental value, but it's horrifying."

Ursula laughed. She had been waiting for someone to finally say this to her, rather than continuing to be polite about the statue. "I know!"

"So why is it in the middle of your space? Haven't you heard of feng shui?"

"You're right. I hate it."

"Can we put it in the closet or something?"

Ursula pursed her lips, looking at the statue. She'd hung onto it all these years because it was the only physical thing she had inherited from her father; but at the same time, his entire artistic philosophy had been to practice nonattachment by scattering his works around the world.

"Actually, isn't it supposed to chart its own course?" Issa asked.

Ursula nodded, her eyes flickering with an idea. "Yes. It's time. Where should we put it?"

"Cobble Hill Park?" suggested Issa.

"Too bourgeois."

"Should it hitchhike? We could leave it on the side of the BQE?" Issa mulled, referring to the eyesore of an elevated highway that bordered Ursula's neighborhood.

"I want to put it somewhere I can check on it," said Ursula. "In case I change my mind and want to bring it back. What about the canal?"

Issa nodded. "Perfect."

They spent the next fifteen minutes plotting logistics, and once the sky fully darkened, they called a car and hauled the statue onto the street. It weighed at least sixty pounds, but between the two of them, they could manage it for a short distance. Their Uber driver skeptically dropped them at a dead end by edge of the Gowanus Canal, where they planned to crawl onto an embankment and leave the statue by the water's edge.

"Mmmm, the Gowanus," said Issa, catching a whiff of the pungent, contaminated water. "I'd know her scent anywhere."

"Let's put it there," said Ursula, pointing to a rocky outcropping. Across the canal, raccoons were skittering along the fence of a construction site where a luxury high-rise was being developed. In response to this gentrification, someone had graffitied "Welcome to Venice jerko" in huge letters on a nearby crumbling cement wall.

"This is our spot," Ursula said, feeling more purposeful than she had in a long time. She threw her leg over a fence and made the three-foot drop onto the rocks, holding up her arms so that Issa could feed the sculpture down to her. Then Issa hopped down to join her, and together, they maneuvered the sculpture toward the edge of the water, choosing a spot where the rocks jutted out to form a little jetty. They propped the sculpture up and carefully backed away from it, hands on hips, admiring their work.

"Yesssss," said Issa, finding her balance on the rocks and appreciating the way the ambient city lights bounced off the water and illuminated the bronze figure. "It's actually really beautiful in this context."

Ursula nodded. "This is where it belongs, for sure." She cocked her head. "Except, don't you think we should turn it around? So it can face the water?"

She stepped toward the statue and began to rotate it in little jerks.

"Hold on," Issa said, "you need help."

"No, I think I got it," said Ursula, but as soon as she said it, the statue tipped toward the water, and she latched onto it, trying to save it.

"Ursula!" Issa screamed, grabbing for her friend's legs, but it was too late. The statue pulled Ursula headfirst into the murky canal, and it wasn't until she was fully submerged that she finally let go.

Issa waited on the edge of the rocks, her hands on her head in disbelief.

Ursula thrashed her way back onto the shore, screaming but also trying to keep the water out of her mouth.

"Holy shit!" yelled Issa.

"Holy shit!" repeated Ursula, collapsing at her friend's feet and looking at her hands as if they were covered in nuclear waste.

"What the fuck do I do?!"

"I don't know!"

"Am I going to die?"

"I don't know!" repeated Issa, catching her breath and trying to think. "You need to rinse. Um . . . take your shirt off."

"What?"

"You're covered in sludge."

Ursula pulled her sweatshirt over her head and flung it onto the rocks.

"We need to get home," said Issa. "Don't touch anything."

They scrambled up the embankment, over the fence, and ran the six blocks to Ursula's apartment.

"Ow-owwww!" someone howled as they ran past, Issa leading the way and Ursula following, wearing just a bra on top. When they got to her apartment, she left all her clothes in the entryway and sprinted into the backyard, where Issa followed her.

"Hose me down!" yelled Ursula, pointing to the spigot.

Issa cranked the knob and pointed the hose at Ursula, blasting her with a forceful jet.

"Ouch, not that one," said Ursula. "The shower setting."

Issa tried again, holding the spray steady as Ursula whirled in a circle. Once rinsed, she sprinted inside and jumped into the actual shower, turning it as hot as it would go and smearing half a bottle of bodywash all over herself.

When she finally emerged from the bathroom in her floral robe, Issa was sitting on the couch, calm but wide-eyed. "You okay?"

Ursula let out a long exhale. Stone-faced, she said, "You realize that falling into the Gowanus is every Brooklynite's worst nightmare, right?"

Issa nodded, trying to hold it together.

"Am I going to melt? Am I going to turn into a mutant?"

Issa nodded again, now dissolving into laughter. "You're a canal creature."

"Fuck, I knew I should have frozen my eggs." Ursula collapsed onto the couch, laughing until her abs hurt and she had to gasp for breath. It took them both a few minutes to collect themselves.

"So . . . that went well," said Issa.

"Oops," said Ursula, casually pushing her hair behind her ear.

"Welp, that thing is definitely charting its own course now."

"It probably already dissolved." Ursula giggled, feeling a sense of levity. "Gross. I wonder what else is down there."

"The Gowanus is full of secrets," said Issa. "But seriously, are you okay? Do you want to call a doctor or something?"

Ursula inspected her hands, front and back, and then gazed around her apartment, as if seeing it for the first time. She looked back at Issa and said, "Honestly, I feel amazing. Let's unroll the rug."

Suddenly, to her own surprise, she felt a subtle but undeniable shift toward optimism.

RAFAEL

Chapter 43

June 16, 7:57 P.M.

The first date was off to a slow start. This woman, Brooke, kept talking about how she was an ENTJ (Extrovert/Intuitive/Thinking/Judging) on the Myers-Briggs scale, and how deeply she identified with that type. Rafael also happened to be an ENTJ, but he didn't deeply identify with it, and he chose not to reveal his type to Brooke, for fear that it would lead to another twenty minutes of analysis on her part. Moreover, he loathed the idea of dating himself in female form. In an attempt to shake things up, he asked the kind of question Ursula, who was an INFP (Introvert/Intuitive/Feeling/Perceiving), might ask.

"What do you mean 'if I were an animal'?" Brooke seemed confused by his question.

"If you could choose any animal and switch lives with it," Rafael tried to clarify. "Which would you choose?"

"Switch lives permanently?"

"Sure."

"I guess . . . a dog?" said Brooke. She wasn't ready to take this hypothetical mental journey with him. "Yeah, a cute dog. What about you?"

"I'm tempted to go with a Canadian lynx," said Rafael. "But the cold might get to me. So maybe a jaguar. An Amazonian jaguar. One of the black ones, which I understand are quite rare."

Brooke cocked her head to the side. "You're funny," she said, though she wasn't smiling.

Rafael was confused. After a few months of moping and railing against The Arc and its unfulfilled promises, he came to the conclusion that Dr. Vidal owed him something. She owed him a return on his investment. When he finally reached out in early June, she emphasized how thrilled she was to hear from him, and she apologized again for her team's unprecedented miscalculation. As an act of goodwill, she offered to find him a new match at no extra charge. This momentarily satisfied Rafael, and using the information from his previous intake assessment, they were able to rematch him quickly. In the lead-up to his first date with Brooke, he had felt excited, even hopeful, for the first time in months. But the second she walked into the Midtown restaurant, which she had selected for its city views but that he found overly fussy, his heart sank. He didn't know why: Brooke was undeniably beautiful in a polished, symmetrical, blow-dried, expensive kind of way. She was a management consultant at a big global firm. She had a delicate way of speaking and impeccable manners—the type of woman many men would adore. When he leaned in to kiss her cheek, she smelled like flowers and money. But now, twenty-seven minutes into their date, all Rafael felt was a sense of internal resistance, like his heart was a damp wick that refused to ignite.

"Are you annoyed that I don't know what animal I want to be?" Brooke seemed concerned.

"No, no, no." Rafael tried to rebound. He smiled, but it felt weird, as if his cheeks were fighting his mouth's attempt to turn upward, and therefore the planes of his face were moving in two opposing directions.

"So what was your experience at Yale like?" Brooke asked. "I loved Duke, but all the clichés you've heard are true. Absolutely true." This she laughed at.

Rafael didn't want to talk about Yale, and he didn't want to hear about Duke. He didn't want to be here at all. Whatever his fate was, he felt Brooke was leading him further from it. He was off course; he felt it in his gut.

It didn't help that Ursula was always in his thoughts, and although it had been four months since they'd broken up, he felt more enamored with her than ever. He wondered when it would stop, if it would stop. No matter where he was, or whom he was with, he wished

Ursula was there, too. He wished she were on this date, right now. He wished he were facing Brooke with Ursula by his side, and he knew that was strange.

He gritted his teeth, determined to get through the evening, employing coping techniques he'd developed as a child when his mother dragged him to church or garden club meetings. He knew how to stay focused and mostly quiet, but still keep a conversation going, without actually expending emotional energy. He had to hoard his inner resources now. He successfully pulled it off through appetizers and the main course, but then there was an excruciating lull, and the waiter kept passing their table without stopping to check in.

"Rafael?" Brooke was snapping her fingers in front of his face to get his attention. "Are you . . . *bored*?"

"No," said Rafael matter-of-factly. He wasn't bored, because he'd been thinking about Ursula, who was not boring. And then he had been thinking about the hiking trip he was about to take with Skipp, which also wouldn't be boring. But yes, Brooke bored him.

"I don't believe this," she said, her composure starting to crack. "What a waste of money. What a waste of *time*."

She slammed her napkin onto the table and stood up, smoothing her skirt, and moving toward the exit. Then she whipped around to say, "I'll let Dr. Vidal know they must have made a mistake in matching us."

Rafael sat, stunned. He was relieved that she had summoned the courage to say what he hadn't been able to, but he was also disappointed in himself. Had he overestimated his own ability to remain cordial? Had he been rude? Would the memory of Ursula haunt every date he would ever go on? He ordered a piece of flourless chocolate cake, which he ate while overlooking the Midtown skyline. He considered New York to be the world's greatest city, and maybe because its lights were exceptionally resplendent on this sublime June night, or maybe because he had dodged the Brooke bullet and veered back in the direction of his fate, he suddenly, unexpectedly, felt a soupçon of hope.

Chapter 44

Rafael's feet hit the gravel in a steady rhythm, and he picked up his pace as he climbed the long, sloped road to his father's house, finally sprinting across the driveway, past the old horse barn, and onto the sprawling lawn that overlooked the rolling hills of Lyme, New Hampshire.

"Strong to the finish!" his father, Haskell, yelled from the stone patio, where he was cleaning off the grill with a large brush. He began to sing the theme from *Chariots of Fire* as Rafael approached, gleaming with sweat.

"Can I do anything?" offered Rafael, fully out of breath as he stretched his quads.

"Nope, I've got this under control," said Haskell. "But your sister might need help—psychological help!" He laughed at his own joke.

"Nothing new there," said Rafael as he opened the screen door and joined Catherine in the kitchen, where she was using scissors to snip chives into a salad bowl brimming with greens. Rafael leaned over her to inspect her work.

"Gross," she said when she noticed how sweaty he was. "Go shower. Dinner is in thirty minutes."

Rafael made his way up the back stairs to the bedroom that had been his since the day he and his parents arrived in New Hampshire from Argentina. His bookshelf was still full of childhood classics like *The Hardy Boys* and the *Lord of the Rings* series, and its top shelf was cluttered with his trophies: soccer, tennis, swimming, skiing. He enjoyed the time-warp experience of visiting this room, of remembering his former self. The interior of his closet still had the glow-in-the-dark stars and Garbage Pail Kids stickers he had collected as a kid. And his *Mad* magazines were still piled on a shelf.

Ever since his mother's death four years before, his father had been making noises about selling the house. "Too big, too rambling, too echoing, too lonely." But Rafael knew it was an empty threat. None of them liked change, and the loss of his mother had been change enough. The house represented the glue that still held them all together—a place to convene and remember who they were, or who they had been.

When he looked out his window at the lawn, Rafael caught himself picturing his mom leading her last horse, Jacques, across the grass. He still couldn't quite accept her death. Every time he bounded down the stairs into the kitchen or rounded the corner into the living room, he expected to see her arranging flowers, wiping up mud the dog had tracked through the hall, or sipping tea while she wrote letters by hand. His longing for her was acute and painful. It was different than the other, foundational longing he experienced, which was quieter and harder to pin down. For as long as he could remember, he'd carried a sense of nostalgia for a life he did not actually know. It was a gentle and vague feeling that he had grown accustomed to, one which he even nurtured from time to time: every now and then, he would let himself wonder about the alternative life he might have led in Argentina, had he not been adopted. Sometimes he even imagined that his body had merely split in two—that there was another Rafael leading a parallel existence with the same hopes, aspirations, aversions, and desires.

But the sharp longing he felt for his mother, Celeste, was another beast altogether, like a conversation cut off mid-sentence. He knew he had inherited much of his gentleness and patience from her. And although they looked nothing alike, most people, upon meeting them, never doubted that he was her biological son. They shared an energy, and Rafael could feel it still, especially when he was home. She had always told him he was the "exact and only son she had ever wanted" and that she would "always, always be here," and he grew up believing it to be true, believing that family—however constituted—was the source from which individual strength sprung. When he met Ursula, he could envision her fitting into this family structure perfectly—an outspoken, openhearted spitfire that could balance him and appreciate the ways he balanced her. And it seemed they had achieved that balance, that it came naturally—at first. It was The Arc's prophecy that had thrown them off. For the first time, it occurred to Rafael that perhaps the reassurance Ursula needed to hear was exactly that which had carried him his whole life: that she was the exact and only one he wanted, and that he would always, always be there.

After showering in his too-small bathroom with the too-low showerhead and the notably bad water pressure, Rafael descended the stairs and joined his father and Catherine on the patio, where the sun was beginning to set behind the pines.

"Ah, that's good." His father exhaled, sipping a Campari spritzer that Catherine had made him.

"Told you," she said. Rafael noted that she looked well: tan, not too thin, her hair wavy from a lack of blow-drying, her gray-brown roots starting to show a bit, but not in an unkempt way. After properly splitting up with Dashiell in the spring, she had decided to spend the summer with their dad in New Hampshire, and the change of scene had mellowed her.

"You look skinny," she said to Rafael as they took their seats around the table, and Haskell placed a large citronella candle on the stone wall that ran around the patio. "Good, but skinny. So you must still be in the first phase of the breakup diet. Next, you'll get fat."

"Looking forward to that," said Rafael, serving salmon onto his father's plate, then Catherine's, then his own.

"What a love story," said Haskell, who had only heard sporadic details until this week, which Rafael had taken off from work to come north. "The best love story I've ever heard, except for my own."

"Which one? You had two," said Catherine, whose mother had broken Haskell's heart by running off with a stockbroker, leading to their divorce.

"The second one," Haskell said decisively, referring to Rafael's mother.

"Maybe I'll get a second one," said Rafael.

"Of course you will," said Haskell. "You'll get as many as you want. The heart is endlessly resilient."

Rafael hoped his father was right, though his heart felt cramped and wary. Just then, they heard the pop of tires on gravel, and the side of the barn was illuminated by the headlights of Skipp's ancient Saab convertible.

"Mr. Skipp has arrived!" said Haskell, as if greeting his second son.

They heard the car door slam, and Skipp rounded the corner of the house and threw his arms up, victorious after his drive from New York. "Only one speeding ticket to speak of!"

"Nice work," said Rafael, and Catherine applauded.

Skipp wrapped his arms clumsily around Haskell, saying, "Good evening, fine sir."

"Sit, sit," said Rafael's father. "Have some of Catherine's famous salmon."

Skipp pulled out the empty chair at the table and sat down with the people he considered to be his second family—and the one he preferred to his own. He helped himself to sizeable servings of salmon, salad, and potatoes.

"Any adventures on the horizon?" Haskell asked Skipp, who enthusiastically launched into his plans for an upcoming trip to Borneo. For a moment, Rafael felt youthful again, as if he and Skipp were just home for a visit from college. The weight of his responsibilities and regrets lifted, and he felt supported by an intangible force.

After dinner, Rafael and Skipp commandeered the table to peruse topographical maps of the White Mountains. The hike they were planning for the next day was well-marked and required no real orienteering, but they enjoyed approaching it like actual mountaineers.

"Who's coming hiking with us tomorrow?" Skipp called to Catherine and Haskell, who were tidying up in the kitchen.

"Alas, my hiking days are over," Haskell responded. "You'll have to take up the charge."

Catherine wandered back onto the patio and stood over them, glancing down at the map of Mount Lafayette, which Skipp was examining with an antique magnifying glass by the light of a kerosene lantern.

"Well this is adorable," she said of the scene. "Very Indiana Jones."

"You bring your boots, Catherine?" asked Skipp. "Got your moleskin?"

"God no," Catherine said. "The last time I went hiking with Rafael, I was attacked by a squirrel."

"It briefly followed you," Rafael corrected her.

"It *chased* me," Catherine insisted. "But you two have fun."

She retreated to the kitchen, leaving the two men to their plans as the chirps of crickets filled the warm summer air.

Chapter 45

"Beautiful day," said the white-haired man, leaning on his hiking poles at the side of the trail as he let Rafael and Skipp pass him.

Rafael let out an affirmative grunt and Skipp called out, "Indeed!"

When they had ascended a bit higher and were out of earshot of the old man, Rafael said, "After all these years, I still haven't mastered the trail small talk."

"Yeah, you get pretty awkward," said Skipp, his red bandana damp with sweat. "But it's an art."

"I just never know what's going to come at me," said Rafael. "'What a day!' 'Windy up here!' 'How about that view?'—and you have to respond on the spot. It's a lot of pressure."

"You just need a few go-tos you can deploy: 'Sure is,' 'Doesn't get better than this,' 'Can't complain.'" Skipp rattled off various options. "And you can almost always go with 'You can say that again.'"

"A classic." Rafael nodded. They were nearing the summit of Mount Lafayette. Rafael had hiked this area, the Franconia Range, with his father almost every year since he was a child. This peak was high enough that it occasionally hailed at the summit, even during summer, but on this day, the sky was completely clear. It was the solstice, and he and Skipp still had plenty of daylight left to make it down the opposite side and over to the hikers' hut at Lonesome Lake, where they'd spend the night.

Skipp ran the final few yards of the trail, his metal water bottle dinging against his backpack. Leaping onto a wide rock at the highest point, he let out a long wolf howl. Rafael caught up to him and looked out over the surrounding peaks.

"Beautiful day." Skipp exhaled.

"You can say that again." Rafael grinned. "How you feeling?"

"Middle-aged," said Skipp, catching his breath with his hands on his knees. After a minute, he took off his hiking boots and hung his feet off the edge of a boulder. "My dogs are barking."

"That doesn't look good, man," said Rafael, noting the blisters on Skipp's heels. He pulled a joint out of the small pocket in his backpack and lit it.

Skipp looked down at his feet, as if just noticing his wounds for the first time. "That's not a big deal." He waved his hand.

"Want some tape?" asked Rafael, handing Skipp the joint.

Skipp inhaled, thought for a moment, and then exhaled. "Yes, please."

Rafael pawed around in his pack and pulled out a Snickers, which he handed to Skipp. Then he handed him the athletic tape. Though Skipp had traversed every continent of the world, he always managed to be unprepared for what awaited him. Rafael didn't mind picking up his friend's slack—it made him feel useful. These mountains were his home, and unlike Skipp, he was always prepared.

Feet freshly wrapped, Snickers freshly devoured, the two friends sat side by side, gazing over the verdant valleys and craggy crests of the White Mountains. Skipp lay back against the rocks and promptly fell asleep, so Rafael rummaged around his backpack for the book he was reading, which was a selection of rubais—four-line poems—by the Sufi poet Rumi.

Most of them were about love. Or about the self—or rather, the non-self—as a vessel for love. He read through a dozen of them quickly, and then arrived at:

> *If I want to mention anybody, it must be You.*
> *If I open my mouth, it's just to talk about You.*
> *If I am happy, it's because of You.*

*If I am up to no good, I can't help it. I learned it from
You.*

He felt a hollowness in his throat. He closed the book, put it in
his backpack, and after a few minutes, he nudged Skipp awake. "We
should get moving."

As they navigated the rocky trail down, Skipp asked, "Hey, did
you get your money back from The Arc yet?"

"No," said Rafael. "That's not an option. Remember? We declined
to be reimbursed when we opted not to do the Emotional Detachment Procedure the first time."

"But then you did it anyway," said Skipp.

"Yes," said Rafael. "But the refund was off the table at that point.
And I don't think it even worked. Ursula takes up just as much space
in my brain as she did when we were dating. Maybe more."

"That's messed up," said Skipp. "I mean, not that you're thinking
about her, but that they bungled it. Maybe you should talk to her."

"I want to. I miss her, all the time. But they advised us not to
reconnect," said Rafael. "The Arc people, that is."

"But do you even trust them at this point?"

"I don't know," said Rafael. "I feel unmoored. Adrift."

"I'm sorry, man," said Skipp. "You still love her?" He had a talent
for asking the only question that mattered.

"Of course," said Rafael. "She's my favorite person. My best
friend."

Skipp was only a tiny bit miffed by the demotion. "Call her.
What's the point in suffering? Who's benefiting from it?"

"I just don't know if it would do any good," said Rafael. "We just
kind of unraveled, and I still don't know why. It's like she was scared
of being boxed into some specific identity; and I guess I was scared
that she would never be satisfied with anything I could offer. And
instead of wrestling with all of that, we broke up."

"Maybe you just need more time to wrestle," said Skipp, his feet
crunching over the rocks. "You know, Callie said something to me
once. Before we got divorced. You know how she was really into

sailing? Well, she kept repeating this metaphor about how a relationship is like a knot. You don't really know if it will hold until you put pressure on it. You have to test it, and then, if it's a well-tied knot, it will get stronger under that tension. Otherwise, it will snap."

Rafael nodded. It made sense.

"I sort of ignored her at the time, and you know how things turned out there," said Skipp. "A mess. But I still think about the knot concept. The further I get from it, the more it makes sense. Maybe you and Ursula need more time to test the knot. Live with the tension. See if it holds."

Rafael was quiet.

"But what do I know?" said Skipp.

"You know a lot," said Rafael. "You're kind of deep sometimes, Skipp."

"Deep, but dumb," said Skipp. "I really am quite dumb."

"Well, I think the smartest people are the ones who realize just how dumb they are."

"That logic works for me," said Skipp.

Just then, a man and woman emerged from around a corner, and Rafael and Skipp moved to the side of the trail to let them pass.

"Gorgeous day up here," said the man cheerfully.

"Can't complain!" responded Rafael, stepping back onto the trail.

"You nailed it," confirmed Skipp. "Nice choice. Perfect delivery."

"Thanks, man," said Rafael.

They didn't pass anyone else on their way down to the hut, and they stayed mostly quiet, lost in their own thoughts, but content to be in each other's company.

The next day, they woke up in their bunks, hiked out, and began the six-hour drive back to Manhattan. They listened to the requisite Tom Petty and Neil Young for a few hours, and then, somewhere in northern Connecticut, they switched to the radio. Skipp began scanning the stations, which were all playing the same three Top 40 pop songs.

"Everything is so overproduced these days." Skipp started on a tirade from the passenger seat. "What would Hendrix think? What would Prince say? No one can *wail* anymore. Or if they can, they don't. It'll be a sad day when . . ."

"Wait," Rafael interrupted him. "Go back to that. Go back to NPR."

A familiar voice filled the car. "It's meant to be a surprising process, and that's why it's such a secretive process. We configure our couples with incredible care and precision, and we tailor our plan accordingly. Each couple has their own unique relationship arc." He recognized the voice: it was Dr. Vidal, being interviewed by Terry Gross on *Fresh Air*.

"No fucking way," said Rafael.

The interviewer said, "Hence the name 'The Arc.' And does it always work?"

"Four years since opening our New York headquarters, and we've never failed," said Dr. Vidal.

"Fuckin' liar!" yelled Rafael, surprised by his own outburst. Then, more quietly: "Such a liar."

Dr. Vidal's voice went on: "We can take two people who are perfectly suited, but who have a history of being intimacy-averse or abandonment-fearing, and we can create a course of action that will bond them together forever. It's not always linear; sometimes it's counterintuitive. But that's what relationship architecting is all about. We know how to defy the odds."

Rafael flipped the radio off and drove in silence, heading south toward the pink horizon.

Chapter 46

It was the day of his required one-year check-in at The Arc, which seemed moot at this point—there was nothing to report—but Rafael was contractually obligated to show up. It was relatively painless: He spent about fifteen minutes in a room, answering benign questions. Then he was done. There was no sign of Ursula, which was both a relief and a disappointment.

He said goodbye to Sasha, knowing that this was the last time he would see her, the last time he would walk these dim halls, the last time he would be subjected to the machinations of The Arc. He rode the elevator down, and the door opened into the foyer.

"Oh, hey," said Ursula, caught off guard. They hadn't seen or spoken to each other for over six months.

"Oh, hey. Are you . . ." he said. The door started to close and he hit the button to hold it open.

"Yeah, I'm on my way . . ." Ursula pointed upstairs.

"I was just . . ." Rafael also pointed upstairs.

"Did it take long?" Ursula asked.

"Fifteen minutes," Rafael said. "Mostly painless. A little weird, as usual."

"Okay, good," said Ursula. "I guess I should head . . ."

They switched positions cautiously, giving each other a wide berth as Ursula entered the elevator and Rafael exited.

"Are you wearing my cologne?" he asked.

"Um, yes," said Ursula. "Yes, I am. I wear it sometimes."

Rafael suppressed a smile, but inside he was elated by the fact

that she had been musking herself with his scent during their separation—a sign that she missed him as much as he missed her.

The door started to slide shut, and he stuck his arm out to stop it.
Ursula felt a jolt of pleasure at the fact that he had prolonged their
interaction. She would take every second he offered her. He had that
handsome summer sheen he'd had when they first met a year ago,
although his hair was a little shorter now.

"I wondered if I would run into you," said Rafael, "when I realized
I had to come in for this."

"And here I am," said Ursula, trying to play it cool, despite feeling
overwhelmed by his presence. He had lived only in her imagination
since that awful day in February, but now he was real again.

"And there you are," he said. They stared at each other, and then
he looked at his watch. 5:09 P.M. on a mid-August Sunday. Nothing
on his agenda that evening. "Would you want to talk? Get a drink?"

"Sure," said Ursula without hesitation. "But I need to . . ."

"I can head over to Vanelli's and wait for you there," said Rafael.
Their go-to Midtown dive bar was just four blocks away. "I'm not in
a rush."

"Okay," said Ursula, suddenly high at the thought that she would
get to spend more time with him. "I'll meet you there. Anything I
should know about what's about to happen up there?"

Rafael removed his hand so the elevator door could close. "Nothing to worry about. You'll do great."

Once Ursula was ascendant, Rafael crossed the lobby, stopping in
front of a mirror to smooth his hair, check his teeth. He was a little
sweaty, but it couldn't be helped in this heat.

Upstairs, Ursula entered the hallway of The Arc, and Sasha was
there to meet her. She led her into a small, wood-paneled room appointed with nothing but a chair and a desk.

"You'll have fifteen minutes to take the survey, and then I'll be
back to get you. Oh, and please wear this." Sasha held out the ring
that Ursula had chosen to wear during her intake week over a year
ago. She exited the room and sealed the door shut, enclosing Ursula
in the small space. She slipped the ring onto her finger and tapped

the tablet, whose screen read: "Ursula Byrne: One-Year Progress Check-in."

Some of the questions were specific: *Are you still together with your Arc match?* (No.) *If not, why not?* (Because you assholes screwed up our compatibility and then told us we were doomed, and you were right.) *Describe the circumstances of the dissolution of your relationship.* (I don't remember. We started fighting. Rafael thought I was having an affair with Mike Rutherford, which I wasn't. It all felt very dire. None of it makes sense to me anymore.) *Are you currently in love with anyone?* (Yes.) *Whom?* (Rafael.) *Are you currently loved by anyone?* (I don't know.) *Whom?* (I don't know.)

Some were more abstract: *Do you believe in love?* (Yes.) *More so or less so than when you started your process at The Arc?* (More so.) *Why?* (Because of Rafael.) *Do you believe love is a mystery?* (Yes. And a curse.) *Describe love in twelve words or fewer.* (Painful. Excruciating. Masochistic. Necessary. Elusive. Exultant. The only thing that matters.) *What is your greatest wish in life at this time?* (To be as happy and secure as I was with Rafael, before everything imploded.)

Ursula worked her way through the questionnaire and then hit Complete. Fifteen seconds later, the door slid open and Sasha walked in, a pleasant smile on her face. "That's all we'll need from you today, Ursula. Thanks so much for coming in, and best of luck with everything."

Ursula left her ring on the desk and took the elevator down. She paused in the lobby to look in the mirror, feeling something akin to first-date excitement. She tipped her head upside down and then flipped it back, arranging her hair and then tucking a few strands behind her ear. She took a lip stain out of her bag and slicked it over her lips, darkening them just a tad. She was a tiny bit sweaty, but it couldn't be helped in this heat.

During her walk to Vanelli's, she felt jittery, the way she had a year ago, when she'd first met Rafael outside the lobster shack. Only now, they were meeting in the wreckage of their relationship, rather than on the runway.

When she entered the bar, his back was to her. A ray of evening sunlight shone diagonally from the window, revealing dust particles dancing lazily through the air, and illuminating the empty stool beside Rafael. Ursula slid onto it, stealthily.

"Hey there, deer tick," she said.

"Hi, shark bite," he said.

They stopped there and adjusted to the shock of being together—both the familiarity and the electricity of it. The bartender approached and looked to Ursula for her order.

"What are you having?" Ursula looked at Rafael's half-drunk beer.

"Brooklyn Lager."

"I'll have that, too," Ursula told the bartender. She wanted to do whatever Rafael did, experience whatever he experienced. She wanted to stay next to him as long as possible. She wanted to retain as much as she could from this encounter, which she suspected would be fleeting but which she hoped would last. The excruciating pain of missing him resurfaced, although he was right beside her.

Rafael smiled at her gently. "So, how have you been? How's work?"

"I got fired." Ursula laughed, leaning her chin onto her hand, her elbow resting on the sticky wooden bar.

"What?!"

"And I fell into the Gowanus."

He almost spit out his beer. "Excuse me?"

The bartender set Ursula's drink down as she began to tell Rafael everything: her spectacular meltdown at the Brandys, followed by her unceremonious dismissal from Anonymous & Co., followed by the art she'd been making since, and her grand plunge into New York City's filthiest waterway.

"Well, damn," said Rafael. "You've had a big few months."

"I know," said Ursula. "But it has been good to have this time to just do nothing. It turns out I like not working. Who knew?!"

Rafael raised his eyebrows and smiled victoriously.

"I've had time to reflect about us, but also about everything else: my work, my life, my patterns. Oh, I'm not consulting for Mike anymore, either. At least, not right now."

"Why not?" asked Rafael.

"I needed a break. Actually, more of a breakdown. You were

right—I was overextended. And I figured if I was going to take the time off professionally, I should clear the slate completely, use the safety net I've been scared to use," said Ursula. "I'm living on savings right now and giving myself six months to sit still and reflect."

"That's amazing," he said, impressed. "You're not going too crazy without a job?"

"I was at first, but now it's exciting to think through what I could do next: consult, start my own design studio, go work for The Arc!"

"Ha," said Rafael.

"I've been drawing a lot—but that's just for fun—and ruminating on what I really want," said Ursula. "The great irony of my Brandys meltdown is that a few people in the industry have reached out to me since, because they want to hire me. They think I'm 'authentic' and 'raw.'"

"You are nothing if not authentic and raw," said Rafael.

Ursula laughed. "But for now, I'm putting myself in a professional time-out. No more jumping at opportunities just because they present themselves. No more chasing affirmation just because it feels good in the moment. I want to find something more meaningful to pour my energy into, but I'm not in a rush. Right now, I'm just Ursula on the subway."

"The version of you that gets to swim in her own ideas? Connect with her true essence, uninterrupted?" he asked, remembering the conversation Ursula had had with Sabrina long ago.

"Exactly," she said, suddenly feeling euphoric. This was the best beer she'd ever tasted. This was her favorite bar. This was her favorite moment. Rafael was her favorite person.

The music cut out, and then Johnny Cash came on, singing:

After all this time
You're still a friend of mine
So I believe in someone
After all

They smiled parallel smiles as they watched the bartender move glasses around behind the bar, and then Ursula shifted toward

Rafael, and their eyes met. Leaning over, he pulled her into his chest for a hug and inhaled her hair. If he ignored the faint scent of his own cologne that she apparently now wore, she still smelled like scones and honeysuckle and kittens. A spike of longing rose in him.

"I still have conversations with you all the time, in my head," Ursula said.

"Yeah? About what?"

"Everything. Movies we should watch, stupid premises for podcasts we could start together, ridiculous inventions like salmon-flavored bubbles you can blow at your cat," she said.

"That one's a winner."

"Talking to you in my head is the best part of my day." She looked into her beer. She didn't know if that was sad or beautiful or both.

"I wish I were there for it," he said.

"I wish you were, too," said Ursula. "I'm not sure I want to do life without you."

"I'm not sure, either."

Their eyes met briefly, but they both looked forward when the bartender approached.

"Another round?"

"Yes please," said Rafael, then he realized he hadn't checked to see if Ursula wanted the same thing. He pointed at her glass, his finger a question mark.

She nodded yes, and the bartender turned toward the tap.

Ursula closed her eyes, enjoying this space between disbelief and delight. Could the thing she'd been craving but suppressing for the last six months actually happen?

The bartender plunked their glasses down, and Ursula wrapped her hand around hers, but then turned to Rafael. "I'm just going to say this," she said, summoning all her courage. "Because I don't know if I'll ever see you again, and I have no idea what you think about me or us by now. But I love and appreciate you even more than I did when we were dating. And I wonder, if we tried again, with a mostly clean slate . . . well, an informed but clean slate . . . a tidy slate . . . a scarred but mostly . . ."

"I get it," said Rafael.

"What would happen? We know so much about each other. And I've learned a lot about myself—more than I ever wanted to know, actually. We've been through one of the most bizarre processes of all time. Certainly the weirdest experience of my life. Also the best. Also the worst." She took a breath. "Is it really over?"

"I've been wondering the same thing."

"I mean, the past six months have been hard," said Ursula. "I can't imagine how much harder they would have been if we hadn't done the Emotional Detachment Procedure."

"I've been thinking about that," said Rafael. "Do you think it even worked? Because it felt like a breakup to me."

"Yeah, a real-deal breakup," said Ursula. "Me too. Maybe that's because it's not over. I mean, what if we started from here, as free agents? We never have to mention *that entity* ever again. We can pretend it never existed. We just met outside of a lobster shack one day last August."

"This very day last August."

"Yes." Ursula nodded. Exactly one year ago.

"Honestly, sometimes I don't remember why we broke up," said Rafael. "I mean, I remember feeling mad and scared and frustrated. I remember losing hope. But I wonder if Dr. Vidal's prediction and the whole process with The Arc—sorry, *that entity* that we no longer talk about—was just too much in my head."

"Exactly. But maybe it doesn't matter—because it helped us grow. It helped *me* grow, anyway, and I looked at patterns in my life that I needed to address, parts of myself that I was scared to confront."

"I'm sorry about how I reacted. About Mike," said Rafael. "I believe you that nothing happened. And I'm ashamed of how jealous I got. I think it was linked to past betrayals that had nothing to do with you."

"It's okay," said Ursula, appreciative that he had admitted it. "Love is terrifying."

Rafael smiled. "It is. It's scary to think about opening it up again—our relationship."

Ursula's heart sank.

"But of course, I want to," he said.

Her heart rebounded, and she summoned her courage again.

"I don't want to be without you," she said with conviction. She wanted him to fight for her, but in the meantime, she would fight for him.

He took her face in his hands and kissed her softly, then pulled back and asked, "Is this safe?"

Ursula hesitated, afraid he wasn't feeling the same conviction she was.

"Not the emotional part. But now that you're a Gowanus mutant," clarified Rafael, "are you going to turn me radioactive as well?"

She grabbed his face and kissed him, and he pulled her onto his lap, clumsily. She felt the force of the universe coursing through her veins. He was her home. They made out ferociously for one minute and thirty-seven seconds and then pulled away from each other as the bartender hesitantly approached.

"Another round, guys?"

URSULA AND RAFAEL

Chapter 47

September 3, 7:49 P.M.

"I think we timed this perfectly . . . wrong," said Ursula, as they slowed to a complete halt on the highway. An endless stream of taillights lay ahead of them. "Perfectly wrong."

"Well, luckily I'm your biggest fan, and I like being trapped in small spaces with you," said Rafael. "And now that I've met your mom, all your neuroses make sense."

They had spent Labor Day in Ancramdale visiting Orla, who had loved Rafael and embraced him warmly, "even though he was a lawyer." (Her words.)

"I don't know why I was so nervous for you to get to know her," said Ursula. "I guess for all the same reasons I was nervous for you to really get to know *me*."

"Fear of rejection," said Rafael.

"I just thought you saw me as this slick, cool person," said Ursula. "And that was the woman you fell in love with. And I didn't want to disappoint you."

"You were never that slick or that cool," said Rafael. "And you could never disappoint me. You're the exact one I've always wanted, and I will always be here." Once they had reunited, he had told Ursula about his mother's assurances, and asked her if that was the kind of thing she wanted to hear more of. The answer had been a resounding yes, so he now reassured her every day that he wasn't going anywhere, and on days when she seemed distant, he said it even more.

On her side, Ursula had begun to air her self-doubt. Even more terrifying, she had started to actually name and articulate her dreams:

the things she had been too scared to try for fear of failure; the things she really wanted.

"Like what?" Rafael had pushed her.

"Like starting my own design company. And having a baby." Even saying that aloud was a lot for her. But rather than recoil or discourage her, Rafael absorbed her hopes and integrated them into his own.

"We're aligned," he said. "We've always been aligned. Our challenge is to remember that, even when things go askew. Our challenge is to keep fighting *for* each other—not *with* each other—every day."

They had agreed that their tendency to fight-spiral was destructive, so Rafael had proposed a structure: every Wednesday night, they had dinner and aired any simmering grievances before they became too big or too scary. Ursula had branded this night "WTF Wednesday," but they joked that The Arc would have called it something like an "Outburst Prevention Tactic" or a "De-Escalation Mechanism." Rafael referred to it as the night when they "let a little air out of Ursula's tires" before she got too riled up about things that hadn't even happened yet—and would probably never happen.

Rafael had accurately pinpointed that most of Ursula's fights were not with him, but were simply the residue of past hurts. She was equally scared of things that had already happened and things that might happen—and he gently helped her to stay in the present. Conflict was okay, but in resolving it, she needed to focus on the issues at hand, on the things he could do to ease her fears. With these ground rules in place, they realized they didn't actually have that much to fight about, and WTF Wednesdays usually ended up being quite fun.

They realized that The Arc's worst error was not in its miscalculation of their compatibility, but in its initial assurance that they should get along perfectly. They had hit it off so terrifically that they assumed they'd be aligned on everything to come, and had therefore avoided talking about consequential things—marriage, children, death—in a substantive way.

Now that they were together again with no Arc interference, they had agreed to start over with their communication. If the premise of their relationship was no longer the idea that they were ideally matched, they had to learn how to navigate the moments when they were not fully in agreement.

"So, you just want us to be a normal couple?" said Ursula. *"Us?"*

"Yes," said Rafael earnestly. "Let's aspire to mediocrity."

Ursula paused. "I think I can do that," she finally said.

"How's this," Rafael amended. "You can aspire to be the *best* at being mediocre."

"Now you're speaking my language," said Ursula.

Over the past few weeks, they'd both fallen back into the comfortable rhythms of the past, but had committed to each other in a way that felt new. In a way that felt their own.

"You know, this is when a normal couple would get into a huge blowout," Rafael said, nodding toward the horrendous traffic that lay before them.

"I'm too busy to fight right now," said Ursula, looking up from her sketchpad at his profile. She had made dozens of portraits over the past few months without knowing what she would ultimately do with them. To her surprise, she didn't mind the feeling of not knowing. She had even begun to thrive on it.

Chapter 48

Mallory let out a mournful wail: the sound of hunger.

"I just gave you a snack," said Ursula, looking down into the cat's mossy eyes. "Remember?"

Mallory looked up and then chirped, hard and short.

"I'm sure you remember, because it was five minutes ago, and we were both involved," explained Ursula. "I did the snack-giving, and you did the snack-eating. You got nine Greenies."

Mallory was silent.

"So you do remember," said Ursula.

Mallory yowled even louder and longer.

"Just give the poor animal a snack," Rafael said from the couch, where he was reading the *Wall Street Journal*, shirtless. "She's still adjusting to her new home. She needs comfort."

Ursula opened Rafael's cabinet (now their cabinet), grabbed the cat treats, and threw one into the living room, where Mallory galloped after it with gusto.

The decision to move into Rafael's apartment had been swift and smooth. After six years in Carroll Gardens, Ursula thought she would miss the neighborhood, her little yard, her fireplace. But so far, she didn't. Much to her surprise, the Upper East Side suited her. The people here were more straightforward. The nice ones were nice. The assholes were assholes. Whereas in Carroll Gardens, the lines had been blurred: there were an astonishing number of assholes masquerading as nice, docile people.

"The Upper East Side is the new Carroll Gardens," she explained to all who would listen, "which is the new Upper East Side. A role reversal, both in terms of identity and cost of living."

Her point was simply that the Upper East Side didn't get enough credit, especially among her Brooklyn-dwelling friends who avoided Manhattan at all costs during weekends, because they associated it with work and tourists. But Ursula was now bullish on Manhattan, specifically her new uptown neighborhood. "It reminds me of Cobble Hill before Cobble Hill became obnoxiously smug," she insisted.

"You know, I've been here for almost twenty years," said Rafael whenever Ursula tried to take credit for rediscovering the Upper East Side. "But I appreciate your pioneering spirit."

The move-in had been seamless, and the only major logistical challenge had been finding space for Ursula's books, which almost outnumbered Rafael's. They installed a new set of shelves in the living room and another in the bedroom. The walls of the apartment were now mostly covered by literature, just as they liked it, but they left a small shelf empty so that Mallory could use it as a nap cave. There was something about that sight—a cat nestled among books—that assured Ursula she was exactly where she should be. They all were.

"Have you seen this?" Rafael asked, looking up from his newspaper.

"Seen what?" Ursula asked as she sat down beside him on the couch, coffee in hand.

Rafael pointed to the headline: *MIKE RUTHERFORD'S NEXT BIG BET: WOMEN.*

It was a story on how Mike was leading a new trend in investments focused on funding formerly disenfranchised female entrepreneurs. And how his strategy was proving highly profitable. Partnering on the objective was none other than Shilpa Thakur.

Ursula's jaw dropped, and she felt a mix of pride and FOMO.

"Have you talked to him lately?" asked Rafael.

"Not for a few months."

"You should call him! Maybe you should get in on this, lead this new initiative."

Ursula was thinking the exact same thing. "It wouldn't make you feel weird? Me working with him again?"

Rafael shook his head definitively, embarrassed that he'd ever been jealous of Mike. Now that he and Ursula had reestablished a secure connection, he felt ridiculous about the suspicions he had cultivated before their breakup. He wanted Ursula to know he was over it, and that she had his full support. "I assume you somehow inspired this new investment strategy?" he asked, pointing to the headline.

Ursula smiled, thrilled that Rafael knew her well enough to read between the lines.

"I thought so," he said. "This has your little paw prints all over it."

Chapter 49

That autumn, Rafael and Ursula were happier than they'd ever been as individuals or as a couple the first time around. Something had lifted. The expectation, the pressure, the fear, the obligation. They were just together—voluntarily, joyfully, a bit bruised, but triumphant. Like warriors who had made it through the wrenching trials of battle, they were home now, at ease. Any prior nervousness or resentment had melted into pride: They had fought for and earned this bliss. It was theirs alone.

In early November, Ursula arranged a trip for Rafael's birthday. She rented the most ridiculous car she could find—a yellow Mustang convertible—and they drove out to Sag Harbor. Ursula generally avoided the Hamptons, but this charming village was the exception, and unbeknownst to Rafael, they had business to take care of.

They arrived in the evening and stopped at the restaurant in the American Legion building for lobster rolls.

"Now this," said Rafael, pointing to his plate, "is a lobster roll. This might be the best lobster roll in New York."

Ursula took a bite, chewed, pondered, and then nodded in agreement. "The best."

After dinner, they wandered up the street to Murf's for a nightcap.

"I'm still trying to name you," said Rafael as he sat at the bar, looking into Ursula's eyes. "I'll spend the rest of my life trying to name you. But for tonight, your name is skink. And I love you, skink."

"I love you, conch shell," said Ursula. They clinked glasses, sipped, put their glasses down, and kissed with adolescent ferocity. Others at the bar noticed but paid no mind.

"Shall we?" Rafael gestured to the ring game that was installed in the middle of the bar. A metal ring hung on a long string, and you had to swing it at a particular angle to get it to land perfectly on a hook installed on a nearby post. It was more difficult than it looked.

Ursula hopped up and grabbed the ring, rubbing it between her hands for luck.

"To our happiness!" She swung the string wildly and completely missed the post.

"Easy there," said Rafael.

She tried again. "To our firstborn!" She swung it again and hit a man who was passing by on his way to the bar.

"Nice and easy does it, my skink," said Rafael.

"To our crooked but enduring love, which cannot be suppressed," shouted Ursula. This time she hit the hook with a sharp *ding*, but the ring bounced off.

Rafael took the string out of her hand, considered his angle, and wound up. "To our arc," he said, releasing the ring smoothly so that it swung by its own momentum toward the post, where it glided onto the hook and stayed.

The next morning, Rafael woke in the big bed of their rented cottage. He noticed the dirt-rich smell of coffee in the air, and he could hear Ursula clanking things in the kitchen. He could even feel her energy. He could tell she was very, very awake.

"Ursula!" he called. He heard her begin to bound up the stairs, but then stop and retreat. A few moments later, she walked up them more slowly, and then entered the room with a little tray holding two mugs—coffee for her, green tea for him—and chocolate croissants.

"Happy birthday!" she squealed.

Rafael smiled and pulled himself up so that he was sitting with his back against the headboard. He leaned over to inspect the contents of the tray, took the mug filled with tea, and took a sip. Then he put it on the side table and reached out for Ursula.

"This is so nice," he said. "But there's something I have to do to you."

He pulled her onto the bed, flipped her onto her back, and kissed the long line that reached from her mouth to her belly button, and then kept descending. Ursula loved Rafael's birthday. It was her favorite holiday. But then she remembered. "Wait, we have to get up! We have an appointment."

"This is our appointment," said Rafael, his face muffled by Ursula's body.

She didn't argue. How could she argue? But as soon as they finished, she leapt out of bed. "Get dressed!"

Twenty minutes later, they were in the convertible, Ursula at the wheel.

"Where are we going?" asked Rafael, buckling his seat belt.

Ursula wouldn't answer, but she was shivering with excitement. They drove up Main Street and past the historic wooden houses of Sag Harbor. One road led to another, and the village gave way to more rural environs. After twenty-five minutes, Ursula turned onto a long dirt drive and then pulled up next to a modest house with peeling gray paint.

A smiling woman came out. "Ursula? Rafael?" she asked.

"Yes, we made it!" Ursula bounded up to her and then whispered, "So, Rafael doesn't know what's going on yet."

"Follow me," said the woman, leading them around the house to the backyard.

There, in a large wooden pen, was a beautiful chestnut-brown dog. Beside her were four fuzzy little lumps.

Rafael's eyes widened. "That's a Ridgeback."

"I know!" said Ursula. "A rescued Ridgeback!"

"We rescued her two months ago from a bad situation in Georgia," explained the woman. "And on her way here, we learned she was pregnant."

"I got you a pup!" Ursula shouted at Rafael, as if it weren't obvious.

"If you want one," clarified the woman.

"Of course we want one," said Rafael, feeling a childlike rush of excitement.

"That's good news," said the woman. "Feel free to pick them up, play with them. See which one feels like yours."

Rafael leaned over and reached into the pen, picking up a squirmy little brown ball.

"That's the little girl," said the woman. "Such a sweet one."

Rafael looked at her, then looked toward Ursula. "But what about Mallory?"

"What about her?"

"Will she be able to handle a dog sibling?"

"Mallory can handle anything. She grew up on the streets."

It was true. When they returned six weeks later, just before Christmas, and brought the puppy home, Mallory adjusted quickly. She dedicated one full day to hissing, puffing, arching, and stomping in defiance. But on the second day, Ursula found the cat licking the puppy from nose to tail, slicking her in saliva as if she were bathing her own baby.

Chapter 50

"It's one of those weird global warming days," said Ursula, standing out on the terrace and holding her hands up to detect the air temperature. Though it was late January, she didn't feel cold without a coat.

Inside the apartment, Rafael was pulling on his sneakers. He grabbed the turquoise dog harness from a coat hook.

"Brenda!" he called. After much debate, they'd named the dog after Shannen Doherty's character from *Beverly Hills 90210*.

The puppy looked up from her spot under Ursula's desk, but didn't come.

"Brenda!" he said again, more emphatically. He walked over to fit the harness around Brenda's sleek body, and he paused to look at the in-progress work on Ursula's desk: commissioned pet portraits she had begun selling through her new Etsy shop. For a brief period, she had hoped this might become a full-time occupation, but after drawing five French bulldogs in a row, she realized she would need something else to feed the other parts of her brain. In search of balance, she had met with Mike and Shilpa in December, and they had come up with an arrangement: Ursula would be paid a finder's fee for bringing them investment opportunities focused on women's empowerment, and she would do occasional brand-strategy consulting for startups that were particularly compelling. This flexibility both suited and motivated her. Now, she could ramp her workload up or down at her own volition—while still carving out time for her side business. This was the balance she hadn't known she was seeking, and though she suspected it wouldn't last, she appreciated it for now. Setting these boundaries around her work also led to a welcome by-product within her relationship: Now that she had more autonomy in her career, she was less fixated on guarding her autonomy in regard to Rafael. They were closer than ever before, and rather than making her feel vulnerable—as past relationships had—their increasing trust in one another made her feel strong, steady, serene.

"Ready?" asked Ursula, shutting the terrace door behind her. They rode down in the elevator, the puppy scuffling about their feet, and greeted Dalmat on their way out. It was just a few long blocks to Central Park, but it took them a while, because Brenda had to stop and sniff everything: other dogs, trees, pieces of garbage. She was transfixed by all of it.

When they got to the entrance of the park, Issa and Eric were waiting for them on a stone bench, eating muffins and dropping crumbs all over the fronts of their coats.

"Brenda! My baby!" Issa ignored Ursula and Rafael as she zeroed in on the puppy. Eric greeted them on behalf of his wife, and the five of them made their way into the park.

It was the weekend of Issa and Eric's anniversary. They'd now been married for seven years.

"But it's really been twelve years," said Ursula.

"Yep," said Issa.

"Twelve years with this hissing cobra?" Rafael asked Eric, squeezing Issa's shoulder.

Issa giggled, enjoying the idea of herself as a hostile reptile.

"I know. Can you believe I've endured it?" asked Eric, wrapping his arm around Issa's waist.

They could all believe it. Issa was one of the most joyful people any of them had ever met, which made her a perfect antidote to the more tempestuous Ursula.

"Wait, but how long have *you* guys been together now?" asked Eric, pointing to Ursula and furrowing his brow. "I lost track."

"Depends on your definition of together," said Ursula.

"You met, what? A year and a half ago?" Issa tried to do the math.

"Yeah, about that. So a year and a half if you don't include the blip. About a year if you do," said Ursula.

"That's interesting, actually," said Rafael. "I forgot about this, but in our original contract, The Arc guaranteed we'd be together eighteen months after our first date."

"Right," said Issa. "But you weren't. I mean you are now, but you weren't necessarily . . ."

"The contract didn't specify we'd *stay* together for eighteen consecutive months," said Rafael.

"Did it not?" asked Ursula, trying to remember the exact terms. "That was my understanding."

"They just said we would be together eighteen months *after* our initial meeting," said Rafael. "I'm pretty sure of it. But I can check the contract when we get home."

"You still have it?" asked Ursula. She'd shredded hers months ago, during their hiatus.

"Of course," said Rafael. He was a lawyer, after all.

"That's so sneaky of them," said Issa.

"They're nothing if not sneaky," said Rafael. "I think they know no one reads that kind of fine print. Except me. And all lawyers."

"Either way, we're not together because of some contractual loophole," said Ursula. "We're together because we fought to be together. Because in the end, we out-Arced The Arc."

"Oh, that reminds me!" said Issa, lightly slapping the top of Eric's thigh. "Remember? We just got the latest mailer from the 92nd Street Y with their upcoming events. There's a panel about 'The Art of the Modern Relationship'—wait, was that it?"

"I think it was 'Architecting Relationships and Chemistry . . .'" Eric tried to recall.

"Yeah, that was it. Architecting Relationships and Chemistry in the Twenty-first Century. Something like that. And guess who is on the panel?" said Issa with rising excitement.

Ursula stopped walking, although Brenda continued to pull on her leash with determination. "No way . . ."

"The doctor from The Arc!" continued Issa.

"Dr. Vidal?"

"Yeah." Issa turned to Eric for confirmation. He nodded.

"That's absurd," said Ursula. "I can't believe they'd give her that platform."

"And it's on Valentine's Day, no less. Should we go and protest?" asked Issa.

"Definitely. Dr. Vidal would be thrilled to see us," said Rafael, joking. But then he thought about it more seriously. "Maybe we *should* go."

"Are you serious?" asked Ursula. "Why would we put ourselves through that? Just to watch her perpetuate her scam?"

"We could confront her!" proposed Issa, getting excited.

"It irks me that she's still peddling her fraudulent ideas," said Rafael, turning to Ursula. "Don't you think we have a duty to report her?"

Ursula pondered. "I guess it could be a good way to achieve some justice. Close the loop. Wrap this whole thing up."

"You know what would be the *best* way to wrap this whole thing up?" said Issa. "You guys go to City Hall, and then send The Arc your marriage certificate, and tell them to screw themselves."

Ursula smirked, and Brenda jerked her forward.

Later, when the couples had parted ways and Ursula and Rafael were nearing their apartment, he grabbed her hand and stopped her.

"It wasn't the worst idea, you know," he said.

"What? Going to the 92nd Street Y thing?" asked Ursula.

"No." He smiled. "Issa's idea. About us going to City Hall."

Ursula was hit by a surge of warmth and then something explosive near her heart. She smiled, slipping her hands under his coat and around his back, squeezing herself into him.

"It's not the worst idea at all," Ursula said, tilting her head up to kiss him as Brenda tugged gently in the direction of home.

Chapter 51

Eric, Issa, Ursula, and Rafael settled into their seats in the auditorium of the 92nd Street Y, ready to gather intel. They were far enough from the stage that Dr. Vidal wouldn't be able to spot them, but they had a clear view of the chairs where the panelists would sit.

Issa pulled a box of fancy chocolates out of her purse and handed them out. "Happy Valentine's Day, my loves. Someone gave these to me at work."

Ursula unwrapped one, put it between her front teeth, and then dropped it into Rafael's mouth, like a mother bird feeding its young.

"Weirdoes," said Issa. But then, inspired, she did the same thing to Eric.

"Did you see this?" Rafael leaned over to Ursula, pointing to something on his phone. It was his credit card statement, with a charge of $10,000 from The Arc. "That's the final 20 percent of our fee. Eighteen months to the day. They don't mess around."

"Yes, I got a fraud alert this morning!" said Ursula. "I *wish* it were fraud. It was painful having to tell American Express that I willingly signed up for this crap." Ursula pulled out her phone to show him, but the lights began to dim over the packed auditorium. The crowd quieted, and the panelists filed onto the stage. The interviewer was a sociologist at Columbia, and in addition to Dr. Vidal, the panel included a well-known couples-therapist-slash-author and the founder of one of the major dating apps.

"She's super chic," whispered Issa, referring to Dr. Vidal, who was wearing a white tailored pantsuit.

Dr. Vidal was introduced as "a groundbreaking researcher" and "the most ambitious relationship architect of our time."

Ursula and Rafael exchanged their first eye roll of the night and squeezed each other's hands.

The panel started out predictably enough: an acknowledgement of how complicated it had become to find a partner in the modern dating landscape. There was talk of how, as a society, we are both more promiscuous and more uncompromising than past generations. Technology has accelerated the breadth of people we can meet and the rate at which we can assess and cycle through them. We expect more from our partners than ever before. The institution of marriage is under a microscope—does it even serve us anymore? And yet, and yet . . . We still seek love, or partnership, or "an aspiration to foreverness," as Dr. Vidal put it. The audience murmured affirmatively. Damn, she was good.

"Now, I have to ask," said the interviewer, addressing Dr. Vidal, "because we're all dying to know. How *does* your process work? And I know, I know: 'it's proprietary.' But we're all here on Valentine's Day, searching for love." (Knowing laughter from the audience.) "And there are so many success stories coming out of The Arc these days. So give us something. Let us in."

Dr. Vidal smiled, sphinx-like. "We have a process, of course. But—and I'm not just saying this—the path is different for every couple. For some, this may be their first real relationship, their first real experience of love; and therefore, they need to be educated, guided. For others, this may be the final relationship after a long series of disappointments; therefore, they need to be reassured, reinvigorated. Others may need a wake-up call, or they may need to be humbled. We assess every couple and attend to their needs in a bespoke manner."

"She's so creepy," Ursula whispered to Rafael.

"No two couples take the same journey," continued Dr. Vidal. "For some, we remove obstacles. For others, we create them."

"Hm," Rafael grunted softly, trying to figure out what that meant.

"It all comes back to emotional programming. How did they grow up? What was their family model? Do they run from stress, or do they thrive on it? Do they know how to resolve conflict, or do they avoid it altogether?" said Dr. Vidal. "Some couples need a nudge, whether they know it or not. Ultimately, they enjoy a bit of adversity. They grow from it. They want to fight for their relationship—they want to feel they have agency."

Rafael looked at Ursula, but her eyes were fixed on the stage.

"Love can be scary, especially for people of a certain age who have been burned. Some clients need the guarantee of a safety net to fully throw themselves in. We provide that safety net, but of course, there is no *real* safety net in love. So we also provide a structure where couples can then establish the relationship on their own terms—weave their own safety net, as it were."

Fascinated, Issa leaned in, her fists supporting her chin.

"Every client comes to us for help, but in the end, they want to claim their own story, overcome their own obstacles," continued Dr. Vidal. "For instance, one of the more interesting and complex arcs we've ever created was between two notably strong and unique individuals. The chemistry between them was electric and undeniable. We debated how to handle it, since strong initial chemistry can sometimes turn against itself. I can't say more, because of our confidentiality standards, but theirs wasn't a straightforward path. It never is, is it? Like Yeats wrote: *Love is the crooked thing.*"

Ursula looked at Rafael, her brow furrowed.

"Ultimately, it's important for us to empower our clients, to help them grow, to make them the heroes of their own stories." Dr. Vidal paused. "And sometimes we have to go to extreme measures to do so."

The interviewer pressed. "Extreme measures like . . . ?"

Dr. Vidal lowered her chin in a slow, confessional nod. "We might create or accelerate what we call 'requisite conflict.' That feeling of overcoming a setback is even more powerful when it's mutual—when two people have stumbled, wrestled with difficult questions, and then emerged from that fog with even more conviction. Being decisive, and seeing your partner be decisive, can create an incredibly powerful connection. Because in the end, we all want to be chosen—not merely matched, but actively *chosen*. So occasionally, we might go so far as to facilitate a breakup and a reconciliation—carefully controlled, of course—in order to give our clients a sense that they are charting their own course."

Ursula's stomach flipped.

The interviewer probed, "A breakup? And yet you're in the business of matchmaking."

"Not matchmaking," Dr. Vidal corrected her. "*Relationship architecture.* My job is not to facilitate a perfect relationship for my clients. My job is to show them that real love exists, and then to give them a path to cultivate it in their own way."

Ursula and Rafael felt heat surge through their clenched hands.

The audience was enthralled. "I wish we could talk to one of these couples! Are any of them here tonight?" the interviewer joked, shielding her eyes and peering out into the crowd.

Dr. Vidal smiled. "Anything is possible."

Acknowledgments

I am so grateful to the many people who rallied (at a safe social distance, of course) to bring this book into being.

To my indefatigable agent, Erin Malone: Thank you for opening this door for me, for believing in this story, and for patiently guiding me as I learn the ropes of the publishing world. I am so incredibly lucky to work with you. And thank you to my whole team at WME—Hilary Zaitz Michael, Laura Bonner, Matilda Forbes Watson, Camille Morgan, Gwen Beal, and Anna Dixon—for instantly "getting it" and helping this book find its audience.

To my brilliant editor, Sarah Cantin: What a joy it is to work with someone so smart, intuitive, and kind. This story has so much more heart and depth thanks to your thoughtful feedback. I couldn't have asked for a better collaborator. Thank you also to the broader team at St. Martin's Press—Sallie Lotz, Carla Benton, Jennifer Enderlin, Lisa Senz, Sally Richardson, Jonathan Bush, Katy Robitzski, Elizabeth Catalano, Erica Martirano, and Jessica Zimmerman—for bringing this book to life.

To Sarah Hodgson at Corvus: Thank you for giving *The Arc* a home in the UK.

To my mother, Caroline: You made me! Thank you for pouring all your love, wisdom, sass, and support into me and my many endeavors. Everything I do is possible because of you.

To my family—the Hoens (Nick, Oliver, Annie, Alice, Eli) and the Henwoods (Jamie, Susan, Robbie, Piers, Blake, Elena, India): Thank you for the encouragement, advice, feedback, and love.

Thank you to my adored friends—Darin Kingston, Ethan Feirstein, Izzy Tang, Ari Heckman, Dan Kurtz-Phelan, Amy Boyle— without whose thoughtful feedback and steady encouragement I would never have had the audacity to write this book.

To my courageous readers Jennifer Braunschweiger, Renee Casertano, Lucy and Ray Park, Dana Drori, Frances Denny, Melissa Roy, José Luis Martinez, and Ursula Burke: Thank you for your sharp insights—and for convincing me that I could actually pull this off.

Thank you to the many mentors, champions, and advisers who have inspired me and encouraged my writing over the years: Maria Grasso, Marti Noxon, Ashlea Halpern, Lauren DeCarlo, Lesley M. M. Blume, Amy Thomas, Erica Berman, Simone Blaser, Jim and Jessie Kingston, Chris Schonberger, Charlotte Cowles, Emily Murphy, Alex Tilney, Grant Ginder, Sarah LaFleur, Annie Thorp, Callie Kant, and my whole M.M.LaFleur crew.

Thank you to my favorite Brooklyn restaurant, Al Di La, whose café served as my unofficial office while I wrote Ursula and Rafael's love story.

And finally, to my favorite collaborator and muse, Ben Lavely: Thank you for your endless support, your generosity, your creativity, your hilarious insights. Thank you for informing me that you don't "bounce" a basketball—you dribble it. Thank you for believing in me from the very beginning. For so many reasons, this book wouldn't exist without you.